J. J. Connington and The Murder Room

>>> This title is part of The Murder Room, our series dedicated to making available out-of-print or hard-to-find titles by classic crime writers.

Crime fiction has always held up a mirror to society. The Victorians were fascinated by sensational murder and the emerging science of detection; now we are obsessed with the forensic detail of violent death. And no other genre has so captivated and enthralled readers.

Vast troves of classic crime writing have for a long time been unavailable to all but the most dedicated frequenters of second-hand bookshops. The advent of digital publishing means that we are now able to bring you the backlists of a huge range of titles by classic and contemporary crime writers, some of which have been out of print for decades.

From the genteel amateur private eyes of the Golden Age and the femmes fatales of pulp fiction, to the morally ambiguous hard-boiled detectives of mid twentieth-century America and their descendants who walk our twenty-first century streets, The Murder Room has it all. >>>

The Murder Room
Where Criminal Minds Meet

themurderroom.com

T0351829

J. J. Connington (1880–1947)

Alfred Walter Stewart, who wrote under the pen name J. J. Connington, was born in Glasgow, the youngest of three sons of Reverend Dr Stewart. He graduated from Glasgow University and pursued an academic career as a chemistry professor, working for the Admiralty during the First World War. Known for his ingenious and carefully worked-out puzzles and in-depth character development, he was admired by a host of his better-known contemporaries, including Dorothy L. Sayers and John Dickson Carr, who both paid tribute to his influence on their work. He married Jessie Lily Courts in 1916 and they had one daughter.

By J. J. Connington

Sir Clinton Driffield Mysteries
Murder in the Maze (1927)
Tragedy at Ravensthorpe (1927)
The Case with Nine Solutions (1928)
Mystery at Lynden Sands (1928)
Nemesis at Raynham Parva (1929)
 (a.k.a. Grim Vengenace)
The Boathouse Riddle (1931)
The Sweepstake Murders (1931)
The Castleford Conundrum (1932)
The Ha-Ha Case (1934)
 (a.k.a. The Brandon Case)
In Whose Dim Shadow (1935)
 (a.k.a. The Tau Cross Mystery)
A Minor Operation (1937)
Murder Will Speak (1938)
Truth Comes Limping (1938)
The Twenty-One Clues (1941)
No Past is Dead (1942)
Jack-in-the-Box (1944)
Common Sense Is All You Need (1947)

Supt Ross Mysteries
The Eye in the Museum (1929)
The Two Tickets Puzzle (1930)

Novels
Death at Swaythling Court (1926)
The Dangerfield Talisman (1926)
Tom Tiddler's Island (1933)
 (a.k.a. Gold Brick Island)
The Counsellor (1939)
The Four Defences (1940)

Jack-in-the-Box

J. J. Connington

An Orion book

Copyright © The Professor A. W. Stewart Deceased Trust 1947, 2013

The right of J. J. Connington to be identified as the author of this work has been asserted in accordance with the Copyright, Designs and Patents Act 1988.

This edition published by
The Orion Publishing Group Ltd
Orion House
5 Upper St Martin's Lane
London WC2H 9EA

An Hachette UK company
A CIP catalogue record for this book is available from the British Library

ISBN 978 1 4719 0623 7

www.orionbooks.co.uk

Contents

Introduction
by
Curtis Evans

During the Golden Age of the detective novel, in the 1920s and 1930s, J. J. Connington stood with fellow crime writers R. Austin Freeman, Cecil John Charles Street and Freeman Wills Crofts as the foremost practitioner in British mystery fiction of the science of pure detection. I use the word 'science' advisedly, for the man behind J. J. Connington, Alfred Walter Stewart, was an esteemed Scottish-born scientist. A 'small, unassuming, moustached polymath', Stewart was 'a strikingly effective lecturer with an excellent sense of humor, fertile imagination and fantastically retentive memory', qualities that also served him well in his fiction. He held the Chair of Chemistry at Queens University, Belfast for twenty-five years, from 1919 until his retirement in 1944.

During roughly this period, the busy Professor Stewart found time to author a remarkable apocalyptic science fiction tale, *Nordenholt's Million* (1923), a mainstream novel, *Almighty Gold* (1924), a collection of essays, *Alias J. J. Connington* (1947), and, between 1926 and 1947, twenty-four mysteries (all but one tales of detection), many of them sterling examples of the Golden Age puzzle-oriented detective novel at its considerable best. 'For those who ask first of all in a detective story for exact and mathematical accuracy in the construction of the plot', avowed a contemporary *London Daily Mail* reviewer, 'there is no author to equal the distinguished scientist who writes under the name of J. J. Connington.'[1]

Alfred Stewart's background as a man of science is reflected in his fiction, not only in the impressive puzzle plot mechanics he devised for his mysteries but in his choices of themes and depictions of characters. Along with Stanley Nordenholt of *Nordenholt's Million*, a novel about a plutocrat's pitiless efforts to preserve a ruthlessly remolded remnant of human life after a global environmental calamity, Stewart's most notable character is Chief Constable Sir Clinton Driffield, the detective in seventeen of the twenty-four Connington crime novels. Driffield is one of crime fiction's most highhanded investigators, occasionally taking on the functions of judge and jury as well as chief of police.

Absent from Stewart's fiction is the hail-fellow-well-met quality found in John Street's works or the religious ethos suffusing those of Freeman Wills Crofts, not to mention the effervescent novel-of-manners style of the British Golden Age Crime Queens Dorothy L. Sayers, Margery Allingham and Ngaio Marsh. Instead we see an often disdainful cynicism about the human animal and a marked admiration for detached supermen with superior intellects. For this reason, reading a Connington novel can be a challenging experience for modern readers inculcated in gentler social beliefs. Yet Alfred Stewart produced a classic apocalyptic science fiction tale in *Nordenholt's Million* (justly dubbed 'exciting and terrifying reading' by the *Spectator*) as well as superb detective novels boasting well-wrought puzzles, bracing characterization and an occasional leavening of dry humor. Not long after Stewart's death in 1947, the Connington novels fell entirely out of print. The recent embrace of Stewart's fiction by Orion's Murder Room imprint is a welcome event indeed, correcting as it does over sixty years of underserved neglect of an accomplished genre writer.

Born in Glasgow on 5 September 1880, Alfred Stewart had significant exposure to religion in his earlier life. His father was William Stewart, longtime Professor of Divinity and Biblical Criticism at Glasgow University, and he married Lily Coats, a daughter of the Reverend Jervis Coats and member of one of

Scotland's preeminent Baptist families. Religious sensibility is entirely absent from the Connington corpus, however. A confirmed secularist, Stewart once referred to one of his wife's brothers, the Reverend William Holms Coats (1881–1954), principal of the Scottish Baptist College, as his 'mental and spiritual antithesis', bemusedly adding: 'It's quite an education to see what one would look like if one were turned into one's mirror-image.'

Stewart's J. J. Connington pseudonym was derived from a nineteenth-century Oxford Professor of Latin and translator of Horace, indicating that Stewart's literary interests lay not in pietistic writing but rather in the pre-Christian classics ('I prefer the *Odyssey* to *Paradise Lost*,' the author once avowed). Possessing an inquisitive and expansive mind, Stewart was in fact an uncommonly well-read individual, freely ranging over a variety of literary genres. His deep immersion in French literature and supernatural horror fiction, for example, is documented in his lively correspondence with the noted horologist Rupert Thomas Gould.[2]

It thus is not surprising that in the 1920s the intellectually restless Stewart, having achieved a distinguished middle age as a highly regarded man of science, decided to apply his creative energy to a new endeavor, the writing of fiction. After several years he settled, like other gifted men and women of his generation, on the wildly popular mystery genre. Stewart was modest about his accomplishments in this particular field of light fiction, telling Rupert Gould later in life that 'I write these things [what Stewart called tec yarns] because they amuse me in parts when I am putting them together and because they are the only writings of mine that the public will look at. Also, in a minor degree, because I like to think some people get pleasure out of them.' No doubt Stewart's single most impressive literary accomplishment is *Nordenholt's Million*, yet in their time the two dozen J. J. Connington mysteries did indeed give readers in Great Britain, the United States and other countries much diversionary reading pleasure. Today these works constitute an estimable addition to British crime fiction.

After his 'prentice pastiche mystery, *Death at Swaythling Court* (1926), a rural English country-house tale set in the highly traditional village of Fernhurst Parva, Stewart published another, superior country-house affair, *The Dangerfield Talisman* (1926), a novel about the baffling theft of a precious family heirloom, an ancient, jewel-encrusted armlet. This clever, murderless tale, which likely is the one that the author told Rupert Gould he wrote in under six weeks, was praised in *The Bookman* as 'continuously exciting and interesting' and in the *New York Times Book Review* as 'ingeniously fitted together and, what is more, written with a deal of real literary charm'. Despite its virtues, however, *The Dangerfield Talisman* is not fully characteristic of mature Connington detective fiction. The author needed a memorable series sleuth, more representative of his own forceful personality.

It was the next year, 1927, that saw J. J. Connington make his break to the front of the murdermongerer's pack with a third country-house mystery, *Murder in the Maze*, wherein debuted as the author's great series detective the assertive and acerbic Sir Clinton Driffield, along with Sir Clinton's neighbor and 'Watson', the more genial (if much less astute) Squire Wendover. In this much-praised novel, Stewart's detective duo confronts some truly diabolical doings, including slayings by means of curare-tipped darts in the double-centered hedge maze at a country estate, Whistlefield. No less a fan of the genre than T. S. Eliot praised *Murder in the Maze* for its construction ('we are provided early in the story with all the clues which guide the detective') and its liveliness ('The very idea of murder in a box-hedge labyrinth does the author great credit, and he makes full use of its possibilities'). The delighted Eliot concluded that

Murder in the Maze was 'a really first-rate detective story'. For his part, the critic H. C. Harwood declared in *The Outlook* that with the publication of *Murder in the Maze* Connington demanded and deserved 'comparison with the masters'. 'Buy, borrow, or – anyhow – get hold of it', he amusingly advised. Two decades later, in his 1946 critical essay 'The Grandest Game in the World', the great locked-room detective novelist John Dickson Carr echoed Eliot's assessment of the novel's virtuoso setting, writing: 'These 1920s [. . .] thronged with sheer brains. What would be one of the best possible settings for violent death? J. J. Connington found the answer, with *Murder in the Maze*.' Certainly in retrospect *Murder in the Maze* stands as one of the finest English country-house mysteries of the 1920s, cleverly yet fairly clued, imaginatively detailed and often grimly suspenseful. As the great American true-crime writer Edmund Lester Pearson noted in his review of *Murder in the Maze* in *The Outlook*, this Connington novel had everything that one could desire in a detective story: 'A shrubbery maze, a hot day, and somebody potting at you with an air gun loaded with darts covered with a deadly South-American arrow-poison – *there* is a situation to wheedle two dollars out of anybody's pocket.'[3]

Staying with what had worked so well for him to date, Stewart the same year produced yet another country-house mystery, *Tragedy at Ravensthorpe*, an ingenious tale of murders and thefts at the ancestral home of the Chacewaters, old family friends of Sir Clinton Driffield. There is much clever matter in *Ravensthorpe*. Especially fascinating is the author's inspired integration of faerie folklore into his plot. Stewart, who had a lifelong – though skeptical – interest in paranormal phenomena, probably was inspired in this instance by the recent hubbub over the Cottingly Faeries photographs that in the early 1920s had famously duped, among other individuals, Arthur Conan Doyle.[4] As with *Murder in the Maze*, critics raved about this new Connington mystery. In the *Spectator*, for example, a reviewer hailed *Tragedy at Ravensthorpe* in the strongest terms, declaring of the novel: 'This is more than a good detective tale. Alike in plot, characterization, and literary style, it is a work of art.'

In 1928 there appeared two additional Sir Clinton Driffield detective novels, *Mystery at Lynden Sands* and *The Case with Nine Solutions*. Once again there was great praise for the latest Conningtons. H. C. Harwood, the critic who had so much admired *Murder in the Maze*, opined of *Mystery at Lynden Sands* that it 'may just fail of being the detective story of the century', while in the United States author and book reviewer Frederic F. Van de Water expressed nearly as high an opinion of *The Case with Nine Solutions*. 'This book is a thoroughbred of a distinguished lineage that runs back to "The Gold Bug" of [Edgar Allan] Poe,' he avowed. 'It represents the highest type of detective fiction.' In both of these Connington novels, Stewart moved away from his customary country-house milieu, setting *Lynden Sands* at a fashionable beach resort and *Nine Solutions* at a scientific research institute. *Nine Solutions* is of particular interest today, I think, for its relatively frank sexual subject matter and its modern urban setting among science professionals, which rather resembles the locales found in P. D. James' classic detective novels *A Mind to Murder* (1963) and *Shroud for a Nightingale* (1971).

By the end of the 1920s, J. J. Connington's critical reputation had achieved enviable heights indeed. At this time Stewart became one of the charter members of the Detection Club, an assemblage of the finest writers of British detective fiction that included, among other distinguished individuals, Agatha Christie, Dorothy L. Sayers and G. K. Chesterton. Certainly Victor Gollancz, the British publisher of the J. J. Connington mysteries, did not stint praise for the author, informing readers that 'J. J. Connington is now established as, in the opinion of many, the greatest living master of the story of pure detection. He is one of those who, discarding all the superfluities, has made of deductive fiction a genuine minor art, with its own laws and its own conventions.'

Such warm praise for J. J. Connington makes it all the more surprising that at this juncture the esteemed author tinkered with his successful formula by dispensing with his original series detective. In the fifth Clinton Driffield detective novel, *Nemesis at Raynham Parva* (1929), Alfred Walter Stewart, rather like Arthur Conan Doyle before him, seemed with a dramatic dénouement to have devised his popular series detective's permanent exit from the fictional stage (read it and see for yourself). The next two Connington detective novels, *The Eye in the Museum* (1929) and *The Two Tickets Puzzle* (1930), have a different series detective, Superintendent Ross, a rather dull dog of a policeman. While both these mysteries are competently done – the railway material in *The Two Tickets Puzzle* is particularly effective and should have appeal today – the presence of Sir Clinton Driffield (no superfluity he!) is missed.

Probably Stewart detected that the public minded the absence of the brilliant and biting Sir Clinton, for the Chief Constable – accompanied, naturally, by his friend Squire Wendover – triumphantly returned in 1931 in *The Boathouse Riddle*, another well-constructed criminous country-house affair. Later in the year came *The Sweepstake Murders*, which boasts the perennially popular tontine multiple-murder plot, in this case a rapid succession of puzzling suspicious deaths afflicting the members of a sweepstake syndicate that has just won nearly £250,000.[5] Adding piquancy to this plot is the fact that Wendover is one of the imperiled syndicate members. Altogether the novel is, as the late Jacques Barzun and his colleague Wendell Hertig Taylor put it in *A Catalogue of Crime* (1971, 1989), their magisterial survey of detective fiction, 'one of Connington's best conceptions'.

Stewart's productivity as a fiction writer slowed in the 1930s, so that, barring the year 1938, at most only one new Connington appeared annually. However, in 1932 Stewart produced one of the best Connington mysteries, *The Castleford Conundrum*. A classic country-house detective novel, Castleford introduces to readers Stewart's most delightfully unpleasant set of greedy relations and one of his most deserving murderees, Winifred Castleford. Stewart also fashions a wonderfully rich puzzle plot, full of meaty material clues for the reader's delectation. *Castleford* presented critics with no conundrum over its quality. 'In *The Castleford Conundrum* Mr Connington goes to work like an accomplished chess player. The moves in the games his detectives are called on to play are a delight to watch,' raved the reviewer for the *Sunday Times*, adding that 'the clues would have rejoiced Mr. Holmes' heart.' For its part, the *Spectator* concurred in the *Sunday Times*' assessment of the novel's masterfully constructed plot: 'Few detective stories show such sound reasoning as that by which the Chief Constable brings the crime home to the culprit.' Additionally, E. C. Bentley, much admired himself as the author of the landmark detective novel *Trent's Last Case*, took time to praise Connington's purely literary virtues, noting: 'Mr Connington has never written better, or drawn characters more full of life.'

With *Tom Tiddler's Island* in 1933 Stewart produced a different sort of Connington, a criminal-gang mystery in the rather more breathless style of such hugely popular English thriller writers as Sapper, Sax Rohmer, John Buchan and Edgar Wallace (in violation of the strict detective fiction rules of Ronald Knox, there is even a secret passage in the novel). Detailing the startling discoveries made by a newlywed couple honeymooning on a remote Scottish island, *Tom Tiddler's Island* is an atmospheric and entertaining tale, though it is not as mentally stimulating for armchair sleuths as Stewart's true detective novels. The title, incidentally, refers to an ancient British children's game, 'Tom Tiddler's Ground', in which one child tries to hold a height against other children.

After his fictional Scottish excursion into thrillerdom, Stewart returned the next year to his English country-house roots with *The Ha-Ha Case* (1934), his last masterwork in this classic mystery setting (for elucidation of non-British readers, a ha-ha is a sunken wall, placed so as to delineate property boundaries while not obstructing views). Although *The Ha-Ha Case* is not set in Scotland, Stewart drew inspiration for the novel from a notorious Scottish true crime, the 1893 Ardlamont murder case. From the facts of the Ardlamont affair Stewart drew several of the key characters in *The Ha-Ha Case*, as well as the circumstances of the novel's murder (a shooting 'accident' while hunting), though he added complications that take the tale in a new direction.[6]

In newspaper reviews both Dorothy L. Sayers and 'Francis Iles' (crime novelist Anthony Berkeley Cox) highly praised this latest mystery by 'The Clever Mr Connington', as he was now dubbed on book jackets by his new English publisher, Hodder & Stoughton. Sayers particularly noted the effective characterisation in *The Ha-Ha Case*: 'There is no need to say that Mr Connington has given us a sound and interesting plot, very carefully and ingeniously worked out. In addition, there are the three portraits of the three brothers, cleverly and rather subtly characterised, of the [governess], and of Inspector Hinton, whose admirable qualities are counteracted by that besetting sin of the man who has made his own way: a jealousy of delegating responsibility.' The reviewer for the *Times Literary Supplement* detected signs that the sardonic Sir Clinton Driffield had begun mellowing with age: 'Those who have never really liked Sir Clinton's perhaps excessively soldierly manner will be surprised to find that he makes his discovery not only by the pure light of intelligence, but partly as a reward for amiability and tact, qualities in which the Inspector [Hinton] was strikingly deficient.' This is true enough, although the classic Sir Clinton emerges a number of times in the novel, as in his subtly sarcastic recurrent backhanded praise of Inspector Hinton: 'He writes a first class report.'

Clinton Driffield returned the next year in the detective novel *In Whose Dim Shadow* (1935), a tale set in a recently erected English suburb, the denizens of which seem to have committed an impressive number of indiscretions, including sexual ones. The intriguing title of the British edition of the novel is drawn from a poem by the British historian Thomas Babington Macaulay: 'Those trees in whose dim shadow/The ghastly priest doth reign/The priest who slew the slayer/And shall himself be slain.' Stewart's puzzle plot in *In Whose Dim Shadow* is well clued and compelling, the kicker of a closing paragraph is a classic of its kind and, additionally, the author paints some excellent character portraits. I fully concur with the *Sunday Times'* assessment of the tale: 'Quiet domestic murder, full of the neatest detective points [. . .] These are not the detective's stock figures, but fully realised human beings.'[7]

Uncharacteristically for Stewart, nearly twenty months elapsed between the publication of *In Whose Dim Shadow* and his next book, *A Minor Operation* (1937). The reason for the author's delay in production was the onset in 1935–36 of the afflictions of cataracts and heart disease (Stewart ultimately succumbed to heart disease in 1947). Despite these grave health complications, Stewart in late 1936 was able to complete *A Minor Operation*, a first-rate Clinton Driffield story of murder and a most baffling disappearance. A *Times Literary Supplement* reviewer found that *A Minor Operation* treated the reader 'to exactly the right mixture of mystification and clue' and that, in addition to its impressive construction, the novel boasted 'character-drawing above the average' for a detective novel.

Alfred Stewart's final eight mysteries, which appeared between 1938 and 1947, the year of the author's death, are, on the whole, a somewhat weaker group of tales than the sixteen that appeared between 1926 and 1937, yet they are not without interest. In 1938 Stewart for the last time managed to publish two detective novels, *Truth Comes Limping* and *For Murder Will Speak* (also published as *Murder Will Speak*). The latter tale is much the superior of the two, having an interesting suburban setting and a bevy of female characters found to have motives when a contemptible philandering businessman meets with foul play. Sexual neurosis plays a major role in *For Murder Will Speak*, the ever-thorough Stewart obviously having made a study of the subject when writing the novel. The somewhat squeamish reviewer for *Scribner's Magazine* considered the subject matter of *For Murder Will Speak* 'rather unsavory at times', yet this individual conceded that the novel nevertheless made 'first-class reading for those who enjoy a good puzzle intricately worked out'. 'Judge Lynch' in the *Saturday Review* apparently had no such moral reservations about the latest Clinton Driffield murder case, avowing simply of the novel: 'They don't come any better'.

Over the next couple of years Stewart again sent Sir Clinton Driffield temporarily packing, replacing him with a new series detective, a brash radio personality named Mark Brand, in *The Counsellor* (1939) and *The Four Defences* (1940). The better of these two novels is *The Four Defences*, which Stewart based on another notorious British true-crime case, the Alfred Rouse blazing-car murder. (Rouse is believed to have fabricated his death by murdering an unknown man, placing the dead man's body in his car and setting the car on fire, in the hope that the murdered man's body would be taken for his.) Though admittedly a thinly characterised academic exercise in ratiocination, Stewart's *Four Defences* surely is also one of the most complexly plotted Golden Age detective novels and should delight devotees of classical detection. Taking the Rouse blazing-car affair as his theme, Stewart composes from it a stunning set of diabolically ingenious criminal variations. 'This is in the cold-blooded category which [. . .] excites a crossword puzzle kind of interest,' the reviewer for the *Times Literary Supplement* acutely noted of the novel. 'Nothing in the Rouse case would prepare you for these complications upon complications [. . .] What they prove is that Mr Connington has the power of penetrating into the puzzle-corner of the brain. He leaves it dazedly wondering whether in the records of actual crime there can be any dark deed to equal this in its planned convolutions.'

Sir Clinton Driffield returned to action in the remaining four detective novels in the Connington oeuvre, *The Twenty-One Clues* (1941), *No Past is Dead* (1942), *Jack-in-the-Box* (1944) and *Commonsense is All You Need* (1947), all of which were written as Stewart's heart disease steadily worsened and reflect to some extent his diminishing physical and mental energy. Although *The Twenty-One Clues* was inspired by the notorious Hall-Mills double murder case – probably the most publicised murder case in the United States in the 1920s – and the American critic and novelist Anthony Boucher commended *Jack-in-the-Box*, I believe the best of these later mysteries is *No Past Is Dead*, which Stewart partly based on a bizarre French true-crime affair, the 1891 Achet-Lepine murder case.[8] Besides providing an interesting background for the tale, the ailing author managed some virtuoso plot twists, of the sort most associated today with that ingenious Golden Age Queen of Crime, Agatha Christie.

What Stewart with characteristic bluntness referred to as 'my complete crack-up' forced his retirement from Queen's University in 1944. 'I am afraid,' Stewart wrote a friend, the chemist and forensic scientist F. Gerald Tryhorn, in August 1946, eleven months before his death, 'that I shall never be much use again. Very stupidly, I tried for a session to combine a full course of lecturing with angina pectoris; and ended up by establishing that the two are immiscible.' He added that since retiring in 1944, he had been physically 'limited to my house, since even a fifty-yard crawl brings on the usual cramps'. Stewart completed his essay collection and a final novel before he died at his study desk in his Belfast home on 1 July 1947, at the age of sixty-six. When death came to the author he was busy at work, writing.

More than six decades after Alfred Walter Stewart's death, his J. J. Connington fiction is again available to a wider audience of classic-mystery fans, rather than strictly limited to a select company of rare-book collectors with deep pockets. This is fitting for an individual who was one of the finest writers of British genre fiction between the two world wars. 'Heaven forfend that you should imagine I take myself for anything out of the common in the tec yarn stuff,' Stewart once self-deprecatingly declared in a letter to Rupert Gould. Yet, as contemporary critics recognised, as a writer of detective and science fiction Stewart indeed was something out of the common. Now more modern readers can find this out for themselves. They have much good sleuthing in store.

1. For more on Street, Crofts and particularly Stewart, see Curtis Evans, *Masters of the 'Humdrum' Mystery: Cecil John Charles Street, Freeman Wills Crofts, Alfred Walter Stewart and the British Detective Novel, 1920–1961* (Jefferson, NC: McFarland, 2012). On the academic career of Alfred Walter Stewart, see his entry in *Oxford Dictionary of National Biography* (London and New York: Oxford University Press, 2004), vol. 52, 627–628.
2. The Gould-Stewart correspondence is discussed in considerable detail in *Masters of the 'Humdrum' Mystery*. For more on the life of the fascinating Rupert Thomas Gould, see Jonathan Betts, *Time Restored: The Harrison Timekeepers and R. T. Gould, the*

Man Who Knew (Almost) Everything (London and New York: Oxford University Press, 2006) and *Longitude,* the 2000 British film adaptation of Dava Sobel's book *Longitude:The True Story of a Lone Genius Who Solved the Greatest Scientific Problem of His Time* (London: Harper Collins, 1995), which details Gould's restoration of the marine chronometers built by in the eighteenth century by the clockmaker John Harrison.

3. Potential purchasers of *Murder in the Maze* should keep in mind that $2 in 1927 is worth over $26 today.

4. In a 1920 article in *The Strand Magazine,* Arthur Conan Doyle endorsed as real prank photographs of purported fairies taken by two English girls in the garden of a house in the village of Cottingley. In the aftermath of the Great War Doyle had become a fervent believer in Spiritualism and other paranormal phenomena. Especially embarrassing to Doyle's admirers today, he also published *The Coming of the Faeries* (1922), wherein he argued that these mystical creatures genuinely existed. 'When the spirits came in, the common sense oozed out,' Stewart once wrote bluntly to his friend Rupert Gould of the creator of Sherlock Holmes. Like Gould, however, Stewart had an intense interest in the subject of the Loch Ness Monster, believing that he, his wife and daughter had sighted a large marine creature of some sort in Loch Ness in 1935. A year earlier Gould had authored *The Loch Ness Monster and Others,* and it was this book that led Stewart, after he made his 'Nessie' sighting, to initiate correspondence with Gould.

5. A tontine is a financial arrangement wherein shareowners in a common fund receive annuities that increase in value with the death of each participant, with the entire amount of the fund going to the last survivor. The impetus that the tontine provided to the deadly creative imaginations of Golden Age mystery writers should be sufficiently obvious.

6. At Ardlamont, a large country estate in Argyll, Cecil Hambrough died from a gunshot wound while hunting. Cecil's tutor, Alfred John Monson, and another man, both of whom were out hunting with Cecil, claimed that Cecil had accidentally shot himself, but Monson was arrested and tried for Cecil's murder. The verdict delivered was 'not proven', but Monson was then – and is today – considered almost certain to have been guilty of the murder. On the Ardlamont case, see William Roughead, *Classic Crimes* (1951; repr., New York: New York Review Books Classics, 2000), 378–464.

7. For the genesis of the title, see Macaulay's 'The Battle of the Lake

Regillus', from his narrative poem collection *Lays of Ancient Rome*. In this poem Macaulay alludes to the ancient cult of Diana Nemorensis, which elevated its priests through trial by combat. Study of the practices of the Diana Nemorensis cult influenced Sir James George Frazer's cultural interpretation of religion in his most renowned work, *The Golden Bough: A Study in Magic and Religion*. As with *Tom Tiddler's Island* and *The Ha-Ha Case* the title *In Whose Dim Shadow* proved too esoteric for Connington's American publishers, Little, Brown and Co., who altered it to the more prosaic *The Tau Cross Mystery*.

8. Stewart analysed the Achet-Lepine case in detail in 'The Mystery of Chantelle', one of the best essays in his 1947 collection *Alias J. J. Connington*.

"AMBLEDOWN EVIDENTLY HAD A BIT OF A KNOCK IN THAT raid last week," said Sir Clinton, glancing about him at the wreckage as the car ran through the streets. " Thirty-seven dead, weren't there ? "

" Forty-three by now. Six of them died in hospital of injuries," said Wendover, gruffly. " Quite enough for a simple country place. It makes a difference when you happen to have known some of the casualties before they became casualties," he added.

" Quite a lot of damage for a dozen planes," commented the Chief Constable. " They didn't get the magneto factory, did they ? "

" No," answered Wendover. " They were trying for it, but they were off the target. Their biggest bomb dropped miles out of the town. You'll see the results. It fell close to this Roman camp that Deverell and his colleagues are digging up. I wish the rest of the H.E. had landed there, too. One bomb fell right on the best bit of Elizabethan stuff in Ambledown, and blew it to rubble and splinters. Irreplaceable. I'm all for winning the war, Clinton, but I wish that damned factory had never been put up. It's the attraction."

"You never were keen on industrialism," Sir Clinton reminded him. " I can see patriotic fervour at grips with an anti-factory complex in that mind of yours, Squire, nowadays. Let's change the subject. You hustled me off after dinner in such a hurry that I'm still a bit in the dark about the object of this trip."

" The phone message came in while we were having our coffee," Wendover pointed out, " so it was easier to start first and explain afterwards. Here's the business in a nutshell. There's a little Natural History Society in Ambledown. My father was one of the founders, and I take an interest in it myself. It began as a Natural History affair, keeping tag of the local butterflies and moths, and when the cuckoo was first heard each year, and when the corncrake stops craking, and so on ; but by degrees they branched out until now almost anything's fish for their net : traditions of the district, curious countryside customs, biographies of local worthies, all that sort of thing. A few years ago they started an archæology section with Deverell as President of it. I don't know what his qualifications amount to, beyond zeal ; but he's very keen about digging up things ; and he did chance on quite a good sample of a kitchen-midden on my ground. I'll hunt out a copy of his paper, if you're interested."

"Not in the slightest," said the Chief Constable, hastily. "Pray don't put yourself to the trouble, Squire. In these days of rationing, my own food hardly interests me at all ; and I simply couldn't get excited over bones that were gnawed by my ancestors in the dawn of time. Go on with your tale. I've no doubt it will be of absorbing interest when you get started."

"Well, I like to see people taking an interest in old things," declared Wendover, "so I've helped them now and again with expenses. That's why they rang me up to-night with the first news of their find, I suppose. A while ago, Deverell got smitten with the notion of doing a bit of excavation at Cæsar's Camp, on a tract of waste land to the west of Amble-down. The place is an old Roman camp undoubtedly ; but it probably has about as much connection with Cæsar as the Menai Bridge or Buckingham Palace."

"Cæsar won't mind, I'm sure," interjected the Chief Constable. "A lot of income tax has been paid since he passed over, Squire. This is May 12th, 1942, if I may remind you. And I am still breathlessly awaiting the reason for my being dragged away from my coffee."

Wendover ignored this.

"There's a local legend about the place," he pursued relentlessly. "There's supposed to be a treasure hidden somewhere thereabouts, with a curse attached, promising death to the finder."

"If people started to dig up every spot which has a local treasure legend attached to it," said Sir Clinton, "the surface of Britain would be a good deal altered. And there's usually a curse attached. So you haven't startled me so far, Squire."

"Let me get on with my tale," retorted Wendover. "Deverell started excavating at what he took to be the site of the quæstorium, the paymaster's tent. He hoped to chance on some coins there, which might throw light on the date of the camp. But the local legionaries must have been thrifty fellows, for he didn't come upon a single stiver. He tried one or two other sites, and drew blank every time. So to-day he decided to dig at the *porta sinistra*. I suppose he thought the soldiery might have done some chaffering with the natives at the gate, buying local produce ; and a coin or two might have been dropped by accident. He started digging, anyhow. And he's come on something

2

more interesting than coins. But here we are at the camp. Deverell can tell you about it himself."

He drew up his car after crossing a little bridge, and Sir Clinton—following his indication—saw a low mound rising from the surrounding stretches of waste land. Little groups of people were gathered about it.

"You can see where they've been digging," Wendover pointed out, as he locked his car. "And if you look over yonder, away to the right, you'll see the crater made by that big bomb. It's just as well it didn't drop in Amble-down. The hole's forty feet deep, I'm told ; and you can see for yourself what the diameter of it is."

At the sight of their approaching figures, a short, stout man had detached himself from one of the groups and hastened to meet them.

"A wonderful find ! " he panted to Wendover, as he came up. "Wonderful ! I can hardly believe it ! "

"Congratulations, Mr. Deverell ! " said Wendover, warmly.

"Oh, it's all thanks to you, thanks to you," returned Deverell. "If you hadn't financed our excavation work, we'd never have hit on it. Never ! I'm afraid I'm rather excited by it still," he confessed apologetically, "but I never expected anything like this. A few coins, perhaps, or possibly a Roman grave . . ." He paused for breath.

"This is the Chief Constable," Wendover explained. "He's staying with me just now, and I brought him along. Perhaps you'll tell us the whole story of to-day's excavation. He knows about your digging at the *quæstorium*."

"I hope it won't bore you, sir," said Deverell. "Naturally to an archæologist it's been an exciting day, but I can't expect a layman to see so much in it as I do. I'll make it short. To tell you the truth, I'm rather tired. The excite-ment, you know. And it has been very exciting to me. We started our excavation this afternoon, a short distance from one of the gates of the camp. You can see the place there. Those people are standing round the pit. Of course, it isn't merely a matter of digging. The soil has to be riddled carefully and examined bit by bit as it's taken out, and notes have to be made."

"Quite so," said Wendover, anxious to get Deverell to the interesting point in his tale.

"We dug quite deep," the archæologist went on, "and we found nothing, absolutely nothing whatever. Most dis-couraging, that, when one is trying just on chance, you know. I'd begun to think of stopping and trying elsewhere,

3

when in one of the riddles we found a coin. Nothing very interesting, but Roman, though, Roman. So we went on digging, more carefully of course, after that. And then, all of a sudden—I must let you see that coin afterwards, by the by—as we dug further down, we came upon gold. And then more gold, a perfect hoard of it."

He paused, with an expression of wonder on his usually rather inexpressive face. Evidently the find had impressed him deeply.

" Ingots or bars ? " demanded Sir Clinton.

Deverell shook his head. The expression on his face showed that he had a surprise in store.

" Neither ingots nor bars," he said. " A collection of vessels and utensils, all gold, some of them with beautiful ornamentation ; and all battered and twisted out of their original shapes. It's hard to recognise what some of them were, because they've been so brutally treated. Chalices have been beaten flat ; there's something which may have been a ciborium ; a few censers ; some cruets ; the remains of a couple of monstrances that look as if an elephant had crushed them with its foot ; one or two Agnus bells hammered out of shape ; and a lot of other things. It's the most shocking piece of vandalism that one could well imagine. The only things left more or less intact were those that were flat to start with, like a pax ; and even there the handle had been smashed down. There's a great gold crucifix with the figure beaten out of shape. As for candlesticks and candelabra, they've been wrenched and twisted to make them compact. Portability was what the brutes wanted. The only thing which wasn't much disfigured is a crosier."

" Ah ! " said Sir Clinton. " Now I see what you've found. It's a second Traprain Law case, is it ? "

Deverell was obviously surprised to find the Chief Constable offering this solution.

" I don't know how you recalled that affair," he said. " I thought only archæologists bothered about it. But you've hit it, sir ; you've hit it, in my opinion. As soon as I saw the first specimens taken out of our excavation, I said to myself : ' This is the Traprain Law find over again, only bigger, much bigger.' "

" Traprain Law was a hill near the coast, though," objected Wendover.

" That is so, that is so," agreed Deverell. " But although we're not on the coast here, there's the river down yonder, only a few miles off ; and the Northmen used to come up rivers at times when they made their raids. Now here's how I interpret the facts. Look at the kind of things we've unearthed : they're all ecclesiastical affairs ; the chalices, the monstrances, and the bells—they all tell the same tale. This is the plunder of an abbey, just as the Traprain Law hoard was. What's more, the plunderers were heathen. No Christian in those days would ever have dared to destroy the vessels which had held the Host. That spells just one thing : Vikings, sea-raiders from the North, pagan pirates, neither more nor less. Where this booty came from, there's no saying. Perhaps from Normandy ; there were rich abbeys there in those days which would attract plunderers who had no fear of the Church. I think that was the explanation offered in the Traprain Law case, and it seems plausible enough, at least to me. A galley of Northmen comes down and loots an abbey, putting to sea again with the spoil. Now suppose that the pirate comes over to England and, being short of stores, runs up the river a bit, looking for some village to plunder. He finds one on the bank or near it, lands, puts the villagers to the sword. That's a reasonable hypothesis. But now assume that someone is on his track, avengers from France or perhaps another pirate with a bigger ship and a stronger force. Escape down-stream is cut off ; cut off, that is, without a fight against heavy odds, which might mean losing the treasure in case of defeat. What's the solution ? "

" Take to the land, I suppose you mean," said Wendover, " and bury the treasure where it can be recovered later."

" Exactly, exactly. So the pirate captain takes that course. Naturally he wants to keep his hiding-place to himself. He can't carry the treasure single-handed ; it's too heavy for long-distance transit. But he wants to keep the secret to himself. No doubt he got it away while his crew were sleeping off a carouse after the sack of the village. He loaded it on one of the village ponies ; and obviously he would have to batter it into easily-portable form first. Then he looks about for a hiding-place which he'll recognise without difficulty when he returns. This Roman camp is a regular land-mark, so he chooses it. He digs his pit and tumbles in the treasure. Probably in the digging he comes on that Roman coin we found, but it's of no value compared with what he has, so he pays no attention to it even if he sees it at all. The Roman coin gets shovelled in along with the loose earth which he is replacing. Then he returns to his ship. . . . "

" And gets wiped out in some affray or other, so that he

never comes back to recover his treasure ? " Wendover cut in, to end the story quickly. " It sounds likely enough, Mr. Deverell. Well, it's a valuable find in more ways than one. I congratulate you indeed."

" There's one thing which is worrying me," Deverell confessed. " This is treasure trove, and belongs to the Crown, doesn't it ? "

He glanced at Sir Clinton for confirmation, and the Chief Constable nodded.

" Of course the Crown will give you full value for it, less a certain percentage," he assured Deverell. " That should make a nest-egg to cover the cost of any other excavations your Society undertakes."

" It wasn't that that I had in mind. If the Crown takes over these things, no doubt they will be sent to the British Museum. That's quite right. But . . . Well, I *should* like some of them to be placed in our local Museum—as souvenirs, you know, just as souvenirs. After all, it's a matter of local interest ; and it would be a pity if we hadn't something to show for it, a great pity indeed, I feel. Just one or two of the pieces, you understand ? "

" I'd feel the same, were I in your shoes," Sir Clinton affirmed sympathetically. " It's outside my province, though. No doubt you can arrange w'th the Coroner about that, and get him to put a recommendation about it into his report. You've notified him ? "

" Oh, yes, of course, of course," Deverell assured him. " He was informed immediately we made the discovery, and I believe he's coming up this evening to make an inspection of the things. But there's another matter which has occurred to me. You can understand that we want to publish a full account of all this in the Transactions of our Society. It's but fair that we should be first in the field. Now that will entail very careful description of each article, which will take time, a good deal of time. And I'd like, if we can manage it, to do the thing thoroughly : reproduce photographs of the specially interesting articles. That will add to the expense, of course, and we may not be able to manage it. . . ."

" That will be all right," interrupted Wendover. " It would be a pity not to do the thing properly for want of a pound or two. The cash will be forthcoming when it's needed, Mr. Deverell. Don't worry."

Deverell was quick to see Wendover's implication.

" That's very kind of you," he said, warmly. " Very kind indeed. It takes a weight off my mind. Our Society isn't rich, as you know ; and I was hesitating about asking it to bear the cost of doing the thing properly. But of course there's another possible difficulty. A good deal depends on whether the Crown will allow us to retain those things here, until we've had time to go over them thoroughly, draw up full descriptions, and photograph them."

" If you put it nicely to the Coroner, I've no doubt he'll manage that for you, somehow," said Wendover, reassuringly. " There should be no great difficulty, provided the stuff is in safe keeping. If it were put into the strong-room of your bank, that would cover most risks ; and you could have a few pieces out at a time for examination. I think the Coroner would agree to that. Try him, anyhow. He's not a stickler for needless red-tape, I know."

" Oh, no ; no, indeed," Deverell concurred. " I know Dr. Bellenden very well, personally. I think that's an excellent suggestion of yours."

" Then you'd better lose no time in trying it," said Wendover, with a gesture towards the road, where a car had just drawn up. " That's Bellenden arriving now, I think. Tackle him immediately. We'll move on and have a look round for ourselves."

" Thanks. I shall, I shall," declared the archæologist, turning away as he spoke, and preparing to meet the Coroner as he came up.

Sir Clinton's eyes followed his retreating figure, and then passed on to the line of cars drawn up on the road.

" There'll be a good deal less of that kind of thing before long, Squire," he commented. " These disasters in the Far East are going to run us short of a lot of things : rubber, tin, coffee, tungsten perhaps, and certainly petrol. Pleasure motoring will have to stop."

" Don't let's start talking about the war," said Wendover, testily. " It's too much like holding post-mortems at bridge for my taste, as things are at present. Let's go up and have a look at this find of Deverell's."

They walked on and joined a group of people gathered around a large sheet spread out on the turf. Two or three members of the Archæological Section stood guard over the hoard and were keeping the bystanders from crowding too closely ; but Wendover was well known, and a way was made for him and the Chief Constable. They fell to examining the various articles in the display ; and at the sight of a specially bad case of vandalism, Wendover uttered an ejaculation of anger.

7

" Yes, pretty bad, isn't it ? " said a voice at his elbow.

Sir Clinton glanced round and found himself face to face with the speaker, a tall, powerfully-built man of about forty, with keen eyes, greying hair, and well-cut features which some people would have called handsome. At the moment he hardly looked his best, however, for his clothes, hands, and even his face were smutched liberally.

" Oh, it's you, Felden ? " said Wendover, as he turned and recognised the newcomer. " Yes, damnable, isn't it ? Look at that chalice ; it must have been a beautiful thing before it was battered out of shape. Only a barbarian could do a thing like that. But that breed survives even yet, worse luck. Crosby's house is in your district, isn't it ? "

" It was," corrected Felden. " Rubble and splinters, plus a hole in the ground, don't make a house."

" No," agreed Wendover, angrily. " That's what passes for progress, nowadays. Fine old mansion stands unharmed for close on four centuries. Some swine in a flying rattle-trap comes along for five minutes. Down comes a bomb, and up goes an architectural gem in splinters. If this is what's called civilisation, the dictionaries will need revision."

" Things might have been worse if that bomb had fallen in the town," Felden pointed out. " Have you looked at the crater ? I was fool enough to scramble down into the pit out of curiosity, and I've got myself into a filthy mess " —he held out his grimy hands—" with the loose soil and the dirt from the explosive. I don't advise you to follow my example. This will make a heavy inroad into my soap-ration before I can feel clean again," he added, with a gesture of humorous resignation.

" Quite true," admitted Wendover. " We might have been harder hit. After all, human life's more important than bricks and mortar."

" Is it ? " retorted Felden with more than a shade of scepticism in his tone. " I used to think so myself, but war has a way of changing one's perspective. Human life's cheap nowadays. One begins to realise that nobody's indispensable. I have to admit that the world could get along quite comfortably without me. That's a salutary reflection. Don't you think so ? "

Before Wendover could answer this, there was a stir in the little group as a flushed individual shouldered his way to the front rank. At the sight of him, Felden left Sir Clinton's side and began to move towards the newcomer. Wendover made a gesture of disgust.

8

" I'm afraid you're in for an exhibition, Clinton," he grumbled. " This is our local dipsomaniac."

" Who is he ? " asked the Chief Constable.

" Gainford's his name. He's a cousin of Felden's, and Felden looks after him, more or less. He seems to be half-seas over, as usual. Probably he started out fairly sober, but brought a flask in his pocket and has felt thirsty now and again."

" Can't Felden get him away quietly and take him home ? "

" No, I've seen him in this state before ; and if anyone tries to interfere with him he bursts into a flood of obscene language. We don't want that here. Too many girls in the party. If he's left alone, he usually keeps within bounds."

The tipsy man had now reached the inner ring about the treasure, and seemed flattered by the attention which he had attracted. He raised his hand with drunken solemnity as if to ask for silence, and began to hold forth in elaborate parody of an after-dinner speaker, with occasional stammerings, aphasic pauses, and a certain difficulty with some sibilants.

" Ladies an' gen'lemen ! The importance of thish occasion demands a word or two ; an' ash nobody else volunteers, I'll shay 'em myshelf. I've mush pleasure in pr'posin' th' health of our good frien' Bob Deverell, who made thish impor'ant discovery, which ish very impor'ant indeed, I shay. ' For he'sh a jolly goo' fellow, an' so say all of ush! ' An' so on, an' so forth, ash you've no doubt often heard before. As I shay, you've often heard that before, sho no use my saying it over again, ish there? No? Qui' righ'. But as I was about to shay, it takes more than a shpade with a fool at th' end of it to fin' a treasure such ash you see before you to-night, an' if you can't see it, then come to the front of the kirk, where it'sh all in plain sight. Now it takes, ash I said, more than a fool with a shpade at the end of it to fin' this par . . . part . . . particular find. It takesh an in . . . in in . . . an in-trep-id fellow to dig up thassort of thing. An'll tell you why, so's you'll know what a goo' f'llow Bob Deverell really is. You're all fam . . . falim . . . fam-il-i-ar (Got it !) . . . You're all, I shay, fa-mil-i-ar . . . 't least, I hope so . . . with a l'le rhyme composed by our local Nos . . . Noster . . . Nos-tra-dam-us (hard word, that !) in th' year 1563 . . . or wash it 1653 ? No matter. Long time ago, an'how. Heard it myself when I wash a boy an' no doubt you did, too. Can't recall the exact words, but no matter. Dogg'rel, not po'try

9

at all, really. But quite def . . . de-fin-ite bit of predica-
tion . . . No, s' you were ! . . . pre-dic-tion is the word.
Usual ghost-an'-bloody-bones thing, y'know, about a treasure-
an'-a-curse :

> " ' *I rede ye beware, an' all searching eschew,*
> *For Death lies in wait ; an' the finder will rue . . .*'

Keep off the grass ! Don't pull the goods about ! Anybody
so mush as touchin' the treasure's ash good as dead. That'sh
what Anthony Gainford wrote in 1356 or thereabouts.
Ancestor of mine, likely. Prob'bly great-great-great-and-so-
on uncle. Same name, anyhow, an' let it go at that. Local
Nos-tra-dam-us, Anthony. Made a lot o' prophecies in's
time, so he'd plenny of practice. Sho it's jussas like's not
that one of 'em'll turn out right—jussas like's not. An'
p'raps liker than not, f'r all I can tell you. Sho thatsh why
I shay it took an in . . . in . . . an in-trep-id f'llow to go
Dig, Dig, Dig like the Dwarfsh in ' Snow-White.' An' I
shay, too, an' you c'n mark my wor's, I shay ash clear ash
I can, now and at thish moment, in fac' I shay : ' Keep
y'r eye on Bob Deverell an' you'll shee shomething.' I put
my shirt on the local Nos-tra-dam-us every time. You
watch Bob Deverell an' you'll shee shomethin' funny'll turn
up. Shomething v-e-r-y funny, thash what I shay. Give
you all a goo' laugh an' not cost you a penny. Can't fly
in face of local Nos-tra-dam-us without catchin' trouble ;
no, can't be done. Bogey man'll get'm, you'll shee. Shorry
f't Bob. ' Jolly goo' f'llow, an' sho shay all of us,' ash I
shaid before. But you wait'n see, an' you'll see shomethin'
funny. Standsh to reason, after local Nos . . . Noster . . .
Well, y'know who I mean . . . after he shaid what he did
shay, then all *I* can shay is that only a dam' half-wit'd go
Dig, Dig, Dig, after bein' well warned, and thstsh what
Bob Deverell did, 'f you see what I mean, gen'lemen. An'
wha's more, I've got good authority on m' side. Here's
m'good frien' Mr. Jehudi Ashmun . . ." He pointed vaguely
towards a dark-skinned man standing in the inner circle
of the group. " Mr. Jehudi Ashmun.s well-known to ev'ry-
body as great authority on Mumbo-Jumbo, Hocus-Pocus,
Few-Faw-Fum, an' all the rest of 'em. An' 'f anyone dou'ts
my wor', there's ad . . . advertisements in th' papers to
tell'm. Ash I shaid, Mr. Ashmun agrees with me, an' he's
fr'en' o' mine an' a stout f'llow too. Knows what's talking
about . . . Prin . . . Prin . . . Prin-ci-pal-i-ties an'

Powers, an' all thassort of thing . . . Keep paws off
treasure, or else—— Well, wish y'hadn't, thassall ... . Not
that I care a damn f'r Powers of Darkness m'self. Touch
treasure as soon's look at it. See here ! "

He stooped unsteadily and picked up the battered crosier
which lay on the sheet in front of him.

"All rot, 'f you ask me. Still, there't is ! An' now,
gen'lemen, I've great pleasure in drinkin' health of our goo'
fr'en' Bob Deverell, an' hope you'll do same an' no heel-taps."

He concluded by pulling a flask from his pocket, uncorking
it, and taking a long drink. Felden, who had been waiting
his opportunity, took him persuasively by the arm and led
him away from the group toward the line of waiting cars.

Sir Clinton was on the verge of making a caustic comment
on the episode when a warning glance from Wendover
restrained him. A man with a strong facial resemblance
to the drunkard had joined them.

"I'm afraid that brother of mine has been making a
nuisance of himself," said the newcomer apologetically,
addressing himself to Wendover who was apparently an old
acquaintance. "He's difficult to manage, you know."

Wendover muttered something non-committal, whilst the
Chief Constable examined the speaker. Though some ten
years younger than Anthony, Derek Gainford was so worn
that he looked much the same age as his brother. He had
the stigma of the chronic invalid, stooping shoulders, a lack of
spring in his movements, and something anxious in the expression of his eyes. The high whistling sound of his breathing
told a plain tale of bronchial trouble in an advanced stage.

"Kenneth and I wanted to see this find that Bob's made,"
Derek Gainford continued, "and we had to bring Tony
along with us. He's been difficult lately, and one never
knows what he might be up to if one left him to his own
devices too long. Break into the wine-cellar, most likely.
How he got hold of that flask, I can't imagine. We've been
keeping him on short allowance, and evidently he made up
for it this evening."

He spoke of his brother's condition in a detached, rather
cynical tone. Sir Clinton had no difficulty in inferring that
Anthony Gainford's failings were public property, and that
his relations had abandoned any pretence in the matter,
even before a stranger.

"Can't your doctor do something ? " asked Wendover,
breaking what promised to be an awkward silence.

"Young Allardyce ? No, he's tried this, that, and the

11

other, but nothing comes of it. Just the same as this asthma of mine. Some things you can't cure, and it's no good expecting a doctor to work miracles, is it? Allardyce is up to date, I admit, and willing to try anything fresh that comes out. But we don't bother him much. We'd just be wasting his time. Besides, he's more interested in his maternity cases. Girls swear by him, with all this twilight sleep stunt of his, and I believe he really does know his way about, there. But as for me or for Tony, one may as well face the plain fact that nothing's likely to cure either of us."

"There's always the chance of something quite fresh turning up," Wendover pointed out encouragingly. "Look at insulin."

"Oh, I suppose so," admitted Derek Gainford, though his tone was one of complete scepticism. "In any case, it's nothing to worry . . ."

He broke off abruptly and began to cough, long and painfully, with gasps for breath between the paroxysms. His face took on a bluish tinge, and beads of sweat broke out on it. Catching hold of Wendover's shoulder to support himself, he groped hurriedly in one of his pockets and extracted a tiny cloth-covered packet. Another effort secured his pocket-handkerchief which he applied to his face after dropping the packet into it. There was a snapping sound, and he buried his face in the handkerchief, inhaling noisily the while. Gradually the symptoms of the attack died away, whilst an odour of pear-drops spread itself in the still air.

"Ah-h-h-h! That's better!" the sufferer gasped at length, taking away the handkerchief and revealing a deeply-flushed face. "I hate to use this stuff except in the last resort. It gives you the devil's own headache; but it's worth it, to get rid of that suffocation. I'll be all right in a moment or two . . . until the next time."

"Amyl nitrite, I suppose?" queried Sir Clinton.

"That's it," said Derek Gainford, drawing a long breath with evident relief. "Makes the blood rush to one's head, though; or feels like that, anyhow. I'd better be getting down to our car, I think, while the effect lasts. Sorry to have made such an exhibition of myself. Our family really should not appear in public at all."

He turned away with a gesture of farewell, and walked rather unsteadily in the direction of the road.

"Poor devil!" said Wendover, gazing after the retreating figure. "He's been like that since he was a child, never had a month of what one might call normal health for the last twenty-five years . . . Now suppose we go over and take a look at that crater, since we *are* here."

"Just as you please," agreed Sir Clinton, "though I confess I'm rather *blasé* of air raid damage nowadays. We had enough of it, that time the *Luftwaffe* mistook us for Trendon and unloaded everything they had in stock, thinking they were knocking out the railway junction and repair shops."

Wendover let his eyes range over the gorse-strewn tract around them.

"Luckily they couldn't kill much out here, except a rabbit or two," he said thankfully. "The only human being in the neighbourhood is a ne'er-do-well who lives alone in that tumble-down cottage you see over yonder, under that rise with the trees on it."

"Why hasn't this district been developed?" demanded Sir Clinton. "It's west of Ambledown, and most towns spread west. And it's just a convenient distance by car. I'd have expected it to be built up in that boom after the last war. One could turn it into quite a decent suburb with fair-sized houses and good gardens, if one set about it."

"There's some sort of building restriction on it," said Wendover carelessly. "The only inhabitant is this fellow Pirbright. His family have lived in that cottage for three or four generations, and I don't suppose it's worth while to turn him out. He gets some sort of screw from the owners for seeing that picnic parties don't leave fires burning, or cause damage any other way. No doubt he blackmails the picnic parties as well. Certainly he does nothing honest for a living, so far as I ever heard."

"He'll be able to live on rabbits most of his time," suggested the Chief Constable. "There are scores of them about."

He clapped his hands lightly, and a dozen white scuts showed up in the dusk as their owners fled in panic.

"There's the fellow I've been talking about," said Wendover, who has been looking round. "That ragged-looking object over yonder, I mean. The fellow with the beard. Too lazy even to shave," he added, in a tone of disgust.

"He must have a lot of unused clothes coupons in stock, by the look of him," commented Sir Clinton. "It's a pity he has no family to take over his surplus. But come along, Squire, and let's see this crater you're so proud of before it grows too dark."

WENDOVER AND THE CHIEF CONSTABLE PICKED THEIR WAY across the broken ground and approached the crater. As they drew near it, a head appeared on its lip, followed by the rest of a small boy with a very dirty face and a generally dishevelled appearance. Wendover recognised him, and hailed him as they came to close quarters.

" Hello, Noel ! A nice state you've got yourself into ! "

" Yes, haven't I ? " replied the ten-year-old, cheerfully. " I expect I'm in for a row when I get home. But it's worth it, Mr. Wendover. Look ! I've found a bit of the bomb."

He held up a ragged piece of metal. Wendover took it from his hand and examined it with some interest.

" I'm afraid you'll have to give this up, Noel," he said, as he passed it to Sir Clinton. The authorities may want to have it analysed, to see how the Germans are getting on in the metal line."

Noel East's face fell when he heard this dictum.

" Do you think so, Mr. Wendover ? I did want to keep it as a souvenir. In my collection, you know."

" A present from Germany, eh ? " said Wendover, with a smile. " Well, Noel, here's the Chief Constable. You'd better apply to him and hear what he's got to say about it."

" *Must* I give it up, sir ? " asked the younger, turning to Sir Clinton with slightly revived hopes.

The Chief Constable examined the sliver of metal ; then, taking advantage of a weak spot in it, he succeeded after a little trouble in breaking off a portion.

" I think one bit will be enough for the authorities," he decided, passing both pieces back to the young finder. "But be sure you hand that over as soon as you can. One never can tell what's important in that line, and you might be giving them a most important tip. Did you find anything else ? "

" Nothing that came from the bomb, sir. But I found something amongst the earth that got splashed about."

He delved in his pocket and produced a coin.

" I found that over there, sir. It's Roman, isn't it ? The bit of inscription that's left on it looks like Latin. I'd like to keep it. May I keep it, sir ? It doesn't belong to anyone, does it ? "

" Let's have a look at it," said Wendover, taking it from the boy and examining it. " It is Roman. Where did you say you'd found it, Noel ? . . . Oh, then it doesn't belong to Mr. Deverell's find. I suppose you want to put it into your own little museum ? Well, I see no harm in that. But perhaps you'd rather present it to the Town Museum ? Get it exhibited with a ticket saying it was found by you and presented to their collection ? It would be fame for you, in a small way. Think it over and do what you like about it. Anything else you found ? "

Noel dived again into his pocket and produced some rounded pebbles.

" I got these black things at the bottom of the crater, sir. Can you tell me what they are ? I don't suppose they're anything much, really. I just picked them up, in case. Do you think they're rare, sir ? I looked about for more of them, but these were all I could see, so they might be rare, mightn't they ? "

" I'm afraid my geology does no further than hitting a rock with a hammer and knowing that if it says ' Puff ! ' then it's probably tuff," said Wendover. " You had better show these things to the Curator of the Museum and see what he says about them. Anything else in that pocket of yours ? "

" Just this, sir : a flint arrow-head. I found it amongst the earth that the bomb threw up. It's all blackened with the flash, but I think it'll clean ; don't you, sir ? "

" You'd better keep it for your own collection, Noel. These Germans have fairly stirred England up with that bomb, when you've found this flint arrow-head and a Roman coin amongst the mess. But look here ! Do you see how the water's beginning to trickle into the crater from that streamlet ? Don't go scrambling down into that pit again. The water will start to flood it in no time, now, and you might be caught and drowned before you could struggle out. See how it's coming down : a regular little cascade. There'll be twenty feet of water there in next to no time. Keep out of it."

" Very well, sir," said Noel obediently, glancing down at the bottom of the pit which was already changing into a slough as the water poured down the side. .' It's lucky I got down there soon."

" Oh, by the way," added Wendover, " you'd better show that coin to Mr. Deverell. He's anxious to find out the date when this camp was occupied, and the coin may throw some light on that. Tell him I said you might keep the thing, if he suggests impounding it. Any other curiosities been added to your private collection lately ? "

" Oh, yes, sir. I've got a dud incendiary bomb, absolutely perfect."

" The deuce you have ! " ejaculated Wendover.

" It's one of those fish-shaped ones," explained Noel, taking Wendover's exclamation as a tribute to his good luck. " You know the kind I mean, sir, like a little silver torpedo with its nose sawn off flat, and fins at the tail-end to make it fall head-first."

" Is the firing-pin there ? You know, the spike sticking out from the middle of the flat head ? "

" Yes, it is," confirmed Noel. " It's absolutely perfect, just as I said."

" Sorry, young man, but you'll have to give it up to the authorities immediately. They want everything of that sort. You'd be fined if they found you'd stuck to it and said nothing about it. But I can't understand why it didn't go off when it fell. It may have glanced off something, of course, and fallen on its side instead of on its nose."

" Or it may have landed in soft ground which wouldn't drive in the firing-pin," suggested Sir Clinton. " Where did you come across it, Noel ? "

" It fell into one of the flower-beds in our garden, and I dug it out, sir."

" Ah ! That might account for it not going off. But Mr. Wendover's right, Noel. You must give it up at once. It's probably alive, and if you dropped it, it might go off and set your house ablaze. Besides, it may be a new pattern, and our people might get a tip or two by pulling it to bits. So please take it round to the nearest police-station as soon as you get home. You'll do that ? "

" If you say I must, sir," agreed Noel, though his disappointment was plain enough in his tone.

" And you'd better tell them at the station that I know about it, and I said it would be all right," added Sir Clinton. " Otherwise they might make trouble over your having kept it, you know."

" Thanks, sir. By the way, Mr. Wendover, I found a couple of dead rabbits over yonder, and three more alongside that clump of gorse, just outside their burrow. There doesn't seem to be anything wrong with them. I mean they haven't been torn or anything like that. They're just dead, without a mark on them. Do you think it was the blast of the explosion that killed them, sir ? That's what I thought."

" Quite likely," Wendover agreed. " They may have

been out feeding when the bomb detonated, and the shock would kill them."

Noel seemed curiously relieved by this dictum.

"You see, sir," he explained, "Mr. Ashmun saw me with them, and came over and talked to me about the explosion. *He* said that when old strata got exposed to daylight, there might be evil spirits in them that got loose and began hunting for things to kill. I forget what he called them—elementals, I think was the word. I didn't like what he said. He makes it all sound so likely, somehow ; and father says spirits are all rot."

"I agree with your father," said Wendover, comfortingly. "The only dangerous spirits are the ones you drink, and they're dangerous only if you drink too much of them. Whisky, and so on, you know. Don't worry over anything Mr. Ashmun says, Noel. He's got a bee in his bonnet about that kind of thing, from all I've been told. Anyhow, you needn't be afraid of elementals tickling your toes as you get into bed. And that reminds me, isn't it getting on towards your bed-time? I'll give you a lift back in my car, if you like?"

But it seemed that Noel had already made his own transport arrangements, and required no help from Wendover. They left him scrabbling hopefully among the débris around the crater in search of fresh discoveries. As they made their way back to their car, they came upon a young man and a pretty girl, to whom Wendover raised his cap.

"That's a nice-looking pair," Sir Clinton commented when they were out of earshot. "Who are they, Squire ? "

"That's the doctor whom Gainford was speaking about—Frank Allardyce. The girl's Daphne Stanway. I can't make head or tail of this young generation," said Wendover, in a faintly fretful tone. "In the old days, those two would have been officially engaged, all open and above-board, and one would have known just where one was. Nowadays, they go about together as if they meant to get married ; but if I were to take it for granted, no doubt they'd glare at me and give me a plain hint to mind my own business. I've no use for this casual way of treating serious things. If they know their own minds, why not say so ? It's not as if they were inexperienced. Allardyce must be nearly thirty, and Daphne's twenty-four. What's more, she was engaged once before, to Kenneth Felden ; but it was broken off."

"Why ? " asked Sir Clinton, lazily.

"Oh, she was only nineteen at the time. I suppose it

was her first proposal, and perhaps she was flattered by finding herself run after by a man fifteen years older than herself. Far too old for her, in my view ; and evidently she thought so herself, once the excitement was over, for she broke off the engagement."

Sir Clinton smiled. He had heard Wendover's opinion on such points more than once in the past.

" If that be so," he said,' " I can see a sound reason why the girl should choose to keep out of a second engagement until she's quite certain of her own feelings. That's a sign of common sense in her, surely. Besides, it's a matter for nobody but themselves."

" Oh, I suppose it is," conceded Wendover. " Still, I was sorry for Felden at the time. It hit him pretty hard, I think. And he's a good fellow. A bit sceptical for my taste, sometimes, but sound stuff. He's Chief Warden for his district, and in that last raid he did a bit of rescue work which came near costing him his life. A woman and child got pinned under some wreckage ; and he burrowed his way in and got them out safely. But it was touch and go. He'd just struggled out with the child when the whole affair collapsed like a house of cards. Twenty seconds more, and he'd have had his back broken. Some of us wanted to have him recommended for a George Medal ; but he got wind of that and stopped us, pretty bluntly, too."

" And what about his successor, the doctor ? "

" Young Allardyce ? He's a pleasnt young fellow. I knew his father before him, a medical also. I'll say this for Allardyce, he's kind enough to regard me as a human being and not as a fossil, which is something to be thankful for, in these days. He comes to dinner, now and again, and he doesn't seem actively bored. If he gets Daphne, he'll do very well for himself. She's a girl worth having."

" She's very good-looking, certainly," said Sir Clinton, slyly. " Still the same, Squire ! Taking an avuncular interest in all the pretty girls in the neighbourhood."

" Do you want me to ignore them, merely because they're pretty ? I take a friendly interest in most of my neighbours."

They had reached the line of cars, and as they walked along it they found Felden pacing up and down.

" Not gone yet ? " inquired Wendover needlessly. " Derek went off to join you a while ago. Hasn't he turned up ? "

" Yes, he and Tony are in my car, but I'm waiting for somebody else."

" No bombers' moon to-night," said Wendover, glancing

reflectively at the clear sky in which the stars were beginning to appear. " Perhaps they'll leave us alone for the present."

" I hope so," said Felden. " I want to get some work done to-night, if I can. These raids play old Harry with my affairs. I can only work after dark, and often I've got to go on warden's duty."

" How is that work of yours getting on ? " asked Wendover, evidently more from politeness than from real interest.

" Oh, so, so. These things are always slow, especially when one works single-handed. By the way, one can't float a company nowadays, can one ? "

" Have you got as far as that ? " asked Wendover. " No, the Government has put its foot on company flotation for the duration. If you want to start anything, you'll need to borrow or else get the Government to finance you. They probably would, if your affair is useful for war purposes."

" Think so ? Unfortunately, I haven't got the thing anywhere near complete yet. Remember the joke about the Irish farmer who was coining money in the last war ? The one about him meeting the parish priest on the road and asking him anxiously : ' D'ye think the war'll *hould*, yer Riverence ? ' I'm in much the same state. Is the war going to ' hould ' until it suits my purpose ? "

" How should I know ? " asked Wendover, obviously disgusted by this callous way of looking at the subject.

" How, indeed ? " retorted Felden, evidently noticing Wendover's tone. " But it'll be a bore if I've spent all this time for nothing. My stunt is of no use for any peace-time purpose that I can see. Naturally I want to be of some service, and that depends on the war ' houlding ' for a bit."

" I'd rather see the war finished," said Wendover, shortly. " I see your point, though, now you put it in this way."

" No offence," Felden assured him, with something bordering on a grin. " Even the best of us is misunderstood at times."

" Well, we must be moving on," said Wendover, with a nod of farewell.

He and Sir Clinton walked along the line until they reached their own car.

" I'm sorry I rasped Felden's feelings," confessed Wendover penitently, as he settled himself at the wheel and drove off. " But what he said at first sounded as if he wanted the war to go on merely that he might make some filthy lucre out of it. And he has the name of being a bit close in the matter of cash, which is a pity, I think. But I see his point, now."

"He didn't seem much annoyed," Sir Clinton reassured him. "By the way, what is this stunt of his?"

"Nobody knows," answered Wendover. "I've heard a rumour that it has to do with infra-red rays. It might be some radio-location business, for all I know: getting on to planes by the heat-waves from their exhausts, or something of that sort. But that's the merest surmise. Felden's got enough brains to know that if you want a secret kept, you'd better begin by keeping your own mouth shut. All I know is that he runs about the country-side by night, at times driving a ramshackle old motor-van stuffed with apparatus and stopping here, there, and everywhere to make his experiments. As he said, he hasn't much time for his research: he's a Warden, you know; and when that magneto factory started, he took over some job in it, so he's got his hands full."

"What was he doing before that?" inquired the Chief Constable, idly.

"He's a technical chemist, by trade," explained Wendover. "At one time he had a post in a nickel-extraction company, I remember. Then, five or six years ago, his father died and he came into a little money. The father was Felden of Rodway, Deverell & Felden, that speculative builder crew who did so much to destroy the looks of this district, confound 'em! They went to smash finally, which was perhaps the best thing they ever did, to my mind; but Felden senior retired with a modest capital just before the crash came. Lucky for him! So his son has two or three hundred a year, which keeps him going and lets him fiddle about with this scientific stuff which is doing humanity such a lot of good in these times."

"A magneto factory doesn't offer much scope for a chemist, beyond analysing raw materials and seeing that they're up to scratch," Sir Clinton pointed out.

"Oh, I gather that Felden's a bit of a physicist as well," Wendover averred. "You might guess so from this research stunt of his."

"You mentioned a firm of builders," said Sir Clinton, switching to a fresh subject. "Is your architectural friend Deverell a partner?"

"Oh, no," Wendover replied. "The firm went smash, completely. Bob Deverell's an accountant in Ambledown."

"Not much scope in a place of that size," Sir Clinton commented.

" No. But that doesn't matter to Deverell. His wants are modest. He's a bachelor, something of an old jenny, as you've seen for yourself, and he lives alone, except for a deaf old servant who looks after him."

" Ah ! And these two brothers . . . Gainford, is that their name ? Who are they ? "

" Felden's cousins. Tony Gainford's no better than a dipsomaniac. His brother's no use in controlling him, as you could guess from that asthmatic attack you saw ; so he persuaded Felden to share a house with the two of them, which means that there's one sound man on the premises to keep Tony in hand. Quite a good idea ; and Felden seems to have some influence over that drunkard. Not enough to cure him, but sufficient to moderate his transports except for an occasional outbreak now and again. And, luckily, his house is an isolated one, so no one's disturbed if Tony grows noisy in his cups."

" Neither of the Gainfords seem fit to make a living," commented the Chief Constable. " How do they scrape along ? "

" Very comfortably," said Wendover. " Their father left them enough money to keep them afloat with ease. Neither of them has ever had to earn a living."

" In fact, everything is for the best in this best of all possible worlds, as Pangloss believed," said Sir Clinton sardonically. " And now, Squire, since we seem to be turn-ing the pages of your local *Who's Who ?*, you might say a word or two about the dark-skinned gentleman with the smile like an open domino-box. That drunk fellow called him Judy Ashman, or something like that, and declared that he was an authority on Mumbo-Jumbo. That sounds interesting."

" His name's Jehudi Ashmun," corrected Wendover. " I'm told that he's a Monrovian mulatto, but in that case I'd expect him to be called John Smith or something like that, after a white father. It seems more likely that he's got only a quarter of white blood, and that his mulatto mother married a black Monrovian called Ashmun."

" He might have had a black father and a white mother," suggested Sir Clinton, captiously.

" Not very likely in Monrovia," countered Wendover.

" No ? I've never been there, so have it your own way, Squire. But what about his expertise in Mumbo-Jumbo ? That rather tickles my fancy."

Wendover obviously did not take the Chief Constable's

light-hearted view of the matter, as the tone of his voice betrayed when he replied :

" I've nothing that I could actually prove, against the fellow ; but he's a bad influence in times like these. We've seen a lapse into barbarism in Europe, a regular landslide under German influence. So far, we and America haven't been touched by it ; but it doesn't take more than an incautious step in the snow to start an avalanche, you know. Nowadays, anything may be a danger if it tends towards atavism and a revival of savagery, even though it seems trivial at the first glance. Well, that's my case against this fellow Ashmun. He's made himself the centre of a group of people about here. Some of them are quite innocent of ill intention, I'm sure ; but I'm not so certain about some of the rest. You know as well as I do, Clinton, that superstition flourishes during big wars. You remember how that crop of fraudulent mediums battened on the bereaved in the last affair."

" I seem to recall it," said the Chief Constable, ironically. " I helped to gaol a few of them. So this fellow sets up as a Spiritualist, does he ? Is he making money out of it ? "

" I've a strong suspicion that he does, but I think you'd find it difficult to prove," said Wendover, doubtfully. " He's not the sort of fellow who would fall into the trap of a police-woman offering him five bob to tell her fortune. He's out for much bigger game than that, and he's dealing with people who wouldn't offer evidence against him if it came to the pinch."

" The Witchcraft Act of 1735 throws a pretty wide net," said the Chief Constable, ominously. " What's his particular line, Squire, if you have any idea of it ? "

" I've no real evidence," Wendover confessed frankly. " I hear only the vaguest rumours. There's some talk about love-philtres . . ."

" H'm ! " interrupted Sir Clinton, in a ruminative tone. " He comes from West Africa, you say. So do one or two queer drugs. One of them used to be called yohimbine ; they've got a fresh name for it now, I'm told. It might fill the bill."

" My vet used it once," Wendover confirmed.

" Well, what are his other lines ? " demanded the Chief Constable, dismissing this side of the subject.

" I'm not tying myself down to anything definite," Wendover pointed out. " But I get the impression that he has his clients divided up into groups. He has a lot of women hangers-on, and they're favoured with physical manifestations of some sort or other : poltergeist stuff, with some crystal-gazing and so forth thrown in. That's for the sillier section, and he couples it with some of the old Black Art stunts. Then with cleverer people he talks a different lingo : new Forces, latent Powers, and that sort of stuff. In fact, he seems to be pretty well provided with goods to suit every likely taste. But I've no real information about him. One gets a scrap here and a scrap there, that's all. He seems to have his flock well in hand."

"Even that's suggestive," Sir Clinton opined. "I like this kind of thing no more than you do, Squire. We don't want the notions of the God of the Congo planted on us at this particular juncture ; they can't do us much good, and I agree with what you say about possible harm. But I gather that he doesn't charge a subscription for his shows or take up a retiring collection, or anything of that sort ? "

"I've never heard anything of the sort," admitted Wendover frankly.

"Then, if he *is* making money out of it he must be bleeding some of his clients, either in payment for his displays or in blackmail, once he's got them into his clutches."

"I don't see your blackmail idea," objected Wendover.

"No ? Well, suppose somebody has been buying his love-philtres and using them illicitly. That brings the user within reach of the law, and Ashmun could blackmail him on the strength of it . . . H'm ! . . . Do you know any people in that circle of his ? "

"One or two," admitted Wendover, rather reluctantly. "But they're not the sort of people who'd do anything illegal. I expect they're in it out of pure curiosity."

"All the better ? Who are they ? "

"You can try those two you saw to-night : Allardyce and Miss Stanway," said Wendover, with even more reluctance. "I believe they're both in Ashmun's set. I can introduce them to you if you like. After that, you must fend for yourself, Clinton. I take no responsibility."

Suddenly, above the quiet hum of the car engine, a new sound arose : the modulated clamour of the Ambledown sirens, running up and down the scale.

"Another raid ! " said Sir Clinton, disgustedly. "Our fighters can't be here for ten minutes at least. Push ahead, Squire ! We must get into town and make ourselves useful. . . . Ah ! . . . There goes their first flare ! Evidently they're determined to get that magneto factory, since they're coming twice in a week."

"THAT'S THE THIRD RAID THIS WEEK," GRUMBLED WEN-dover, some days later as he took his seat at the breakfast table after a night spent on A.R.P. duty. "They were here on the 12th. Then again on the 15th. And now last night. Talk about the Merry Month of May!"

"And since they didn't get the magneto factory after all, you may expect another visit from them soon," commented Sir Clinton. "They seem very persevering fellows, Squire. Even the loss of two bombers out of nine, last time, hasn't diminished their zeal. Ambledown must be marked with a star in the *Luftwaffe* Baedeker, evidently."

"I hope the casualties have been light," said Wendover. "Pass the toast, please."

"Incongruous ideas," said the Chief Cosntable, "but here's your toast. It's queer how intensely boring these affairs are, unless a bomb falls close at hand. Nobody fore-saw that psychological curiosity in pre-war days."

"It seems to be the general feeling, though," Wendover confirmed. "One's inclined to copy the rough-diamond host at the end of a long, dragging party, and say to our German guests : 'Ain't you folks got no homes to go back to?' I can't say that my nerves worry me in these raids, but I do welcome the 'All Clear' as a relief from that *ennui* which creeps over one."

"Well, let's change the subject," suggested Sir Clinton briskly. "The only kinds of post-mortems that attract me are the ones I meet professionally. Raids are like bridge hands ; once they've been played, they cease to interest me. And the war news is too depressing for the breakfast table."

"It is," agreed Wendover, tersely. "Try pictures, taste, Shakespeare, and the musical glasses, if you like. Anything for a change."

"Very well. Anything to please you, Squire. And now, I've got some news on an entirely fresh topic. You intro-duced me to Miss Stanway and young Allardyce, you remember?"

Wendover nodded without comment.

"I inquired about Ashmun's Magic Circle," Sir Clinton went on. "He's not quite such a bright spark as I expected. Evidently he failed to appreciate the impressiveness of oaths

24

and all that kind of thing on the nitwits whom he's striving to recruit."

"I wouldn't call Daphne Stanway or young Allardyce nitwitted," objected Wendover, crossly.

"Nor would I," agreed Sir Clinton immediately. "But I don't think either of them is the type that Ashmun sets most store by. They're only supers, brought in to make up the mob scene, I believe. The real nitwits by themselves would be too few to make it look like a real live Circle ; hence some people of normal intelligence have to be enrolled as well. But that's not the point. It seems that Ashmun forgot to swear his Circle to secrecy. Or else he wished to leave them free to spread the news and recruit more members. Anyhow, there was nothing to hinder these two youngsters from telling me anything I wanted to know. I hadn't time, just then, to get the tale out of them ; but I said I'd see them again when I'd more leisure and hear the whole business."

"I'll ask the pair of them to dinner any time you want their story," Wendover suggested.

"So that you'll hear it too ? " said Sir Clinton, slyly. "I know your methods, Squire. You're burning to hear all about it, but you don't want any responsibility. All right, then. I'll tell you when to issue your invitation."

Wendover was saved from the need of an answer by the entrance of a maid who gave him a message.

"Inspector Camlet ? He wants you, Clinton. Dr. Allardyce is with him. There's no need to interrupt your breakfast, is there ? Let's have them both in here."

"Your methods again ? I've no objection," agreed the Chief Constable.

Wendover gave some directions to the maid, who withdrew and almost immediately ushered the two visitors into the room. Allardyce was a good-looking man of about thirty, cool, collected, and with a manner which had stood him in good stead in many a sick-room. Inspector Camlet's stocky figure and glum expression were familiar to Wendover.

"You're just off duty, like ourselves, I suppose," said their involuntary host hospitably. "Sit down, if you haven't had any breakfast. I've ordered something for you. It'll be here in a moment."

"Thanks," said Allardyce, without ado. "I'm too hungry to do anything but accept your offer, even if it means trenching on your rations."

He seated himself at the table, and Camlet, after a glance

of inquiry at the Chief Constable, took a chair also with a word of thanks.

"You'll know more than we do about the damage last night," said Wendover. "I hope it hasn't been severe?"

"Fairly light, this time, sir," said the inspector. "So far, only twenty-three casualties reported, five of them fatal : two men, two women and a child. There may be more to come, of course ; but I don't think they'll be many. It was an incendiary raid in the main. Only a few bombs came down."

"What about the material damage?" asked Wendover, relieved to hear that few lives had been lost.

"Some incendiaries landed on Stroud's factory. Looked at one time as if damage might be serious. Fire Service fixed them, double-quick. Good work. Factory's reported O.K. so far as working capacity goes. About twenty shops on fire. One of them might have been a nasty affair : Shipman, the druggist's in Arthur Street. Three women and two children living in flat above the shop. Might have been roasted alive. Luckily they were got out. The shop's gone. The flat, too. You may remember Mr. Felden, sir."

Wendover nodded in answer to the implied question.

"He got into the shop while it was blazing. Wouldn't allow anyone else to risk it. Managed to keep the fire under while the gang upstairs were being rescued. Very plucky. Came out a bit singed. Carried on through the rest of the show. Very cool."

"These incendiaries are nasty things," commented Wendover.

"Think so, sir?" queried Camlet sceptically. "Not if you catch 'em immediately they come down. Before they spark out properly. Catch 'em by the fins on the tail, then, and no harm done. Fling 'em into a safe corner without so much as a blister. Once they get going, of course, it's a different matter. Nasty things, once they're well ablaze."

"Is Shipman's stock damaged?" asked Allardyce. "I get most of my dispensary stuffs from him, and I'm pretty short of some things just now."

"Damaged?" echoed Camlet. "There's nothing left of the place. The roof had fallen in when I saw it, doctor. You'll get no drugs from Shipman for a bit."

"What other damage was there?" inquired Wendover.

"Some at the railway station, sir. Nothing much. Half a dozen villas smashed completely. Bombs, that was. A nasty affair. Other houses damaged or gutted. About two hundred to two-fifty people at the Rest Centres. Very light raid, over all. I saw one bomber blow up. Rumour says that two more were crippled. Honours about easy, on that basis, reckoning five to the bomber crew. No panic amongst our people. Took it very well. Getting used to it, I suppose."

Having made his terse report, Camlet turned to his breakfast, and Wendover forebore to question him further at the moment.

" And what about you, Allardyce ? " he asked.

The doctor glanced up from his plate.

" I ? Oh, just the usual thing : Casualty Service. I've nothing to report except this business of Inspector Camlet's. It's his affair, really, so I'll leave him to tell his tale for himself. Oh, yes. There was one funny thing happened. I chanced on a street shelter in John Street, crammed with local children from the artisans' houses round there. They seemed all right, as noisy as a nest of daws, but I thought I'd have a look inside to see how they were faring. They were all very bright. These kids have no imagination, apparently. Just as I got inside, a bomb came down, about a quarter of a mile off. Silence for a second or two, then one brat squeaked out : ' Oh, I *do* hope that was on our school !' Loud applause from his friends. That seems to throw a sinister light on our modern educational system, doesn't it ? "

" I never liked school myself," said Camlet, without looking up. " Main thing is, they weren't in a funk."

Sir Clinton waited until the inspector had taken the edge off his appetite before putting any questions to him.

" And now, what about it, Inspector ? "

" This is it, sir. A man Deverell—Robert Deverell—was killed in the raid last night . . ."

" Is this your archæological friend, by any chance ? " asked Sir Clinton, turning to Wendover. " Where does he live ? "

" In a small villa standing by itself at the end of Braden Drive," Wendover explained. " ' Polehurst,' I think it's called.

" That's the man, sir," said Camlet.

" I'm sorry," said Wendover. " He wasn't a friend of mine, but I knew him slightly. Yes, go on."

" A queer affair," continued the inspector. " Most unlikely thing to happen. But I'll come to that in due course. When the sirens started, all the A.R.P. people got to their posts as usual. Rather short of fire-watchers, they are, in Braden Drive. Had to enrol a school-girl, it seems, and give her a tin hat like the rest. Betty Brown's her name.

About sixteen, but very cool and efficient and keen on her job. She was patrolling the Drive when a clump of incendiaries came down. Molotov bread-basket, perhaps. One of them landed on a roof, and some others looked dangerous. She scurried off, brought the stirrup-pump squad to fix these things. Then she set off down the Drive to look for more trouble. More incendiaries started, and she had to run back and report another fire on the go. After that, she went further along. By that time, Deverell's villa seems to have been well alight."

"She seems to be a useful youngster," interjected the Chief Constable.

"Quite, sir. She rushed up to the front door. Found it unlocked and burst in. You know what it's like in a burning house, sir. Smoke so thick that you can't see your hand at arm's length. It was like that. All she could see was the red glow of the fire through the smoke. She got into the hall. Cool as a cucumber. Very plucky. The first thing she met in the smoke was Deverell's body lying on the floor. A shock, that, for a child. Blood about, too. Very nasty. Didn't make her lose her nerve, though. She knew Deverell's old housekeeper slept in the back premises, alongside the kitchen. Deaf as a post. Betty Brown tried the wrong door, first. Landed in Deverell's sitting-room. Practically intact at that time. Then she found her way through the smoke to the old woman's room. Sleeping like a dormouse through it all. Heard nothing evidently. Sirens. Incendiary bomb. Never waked her. Smoke hadn't got through her door, luckily. Betty Brown roused her. The old woman was troublesome, I gather. Maidenly modesty. Didn't want men to see her in her nightie. Wanted to dress before she'd shift. Old fool ! Betty Brown hustled her out by the back door into the garden and went off herself to summoh the hose gang. No stirrup pump would touch the fire by then. It had got a firm hold. Betty Brown forgot to shut the front door, and the draught from it fanned the fire. Even the hoses had a job getting it under, when they did arrive."

"How did she know she entered Deverell's sitting-room ? " asked Sir Clinton.

"The electric lights were on, sir, she says. And there wasn't so much smoke in the room as in the hall. She could see fairly well. That's O.K. She was able to describe the room, more or less."

"Was the electric light still burning in the hall ? "

"That I can't say, sir."

" The place is gutted, I suppose ? But are the walls of the hall still intact ? "

" They are, sir. I was at the house myself, later on."

" Go on, Inspector. I hardly see where I come into the story yet."

" The hall's lit by a skylight window in the roof, sir. In peace-time, I mean ; it's been painted over since war started. Deverell's body was alongside the stairs, right under the skylight. The incendiary must have come through the skylight and hit him on the head as he stood there. Couldn't happen once in a million times. That's where the blood came from. Dr. Allardyce can tell you all about that. He examined the body."

Sir Clinton nodded without comment, and turned to the doctor. Allardyce took the unspoken hint.

" Curiously enough, I must have been the last person to see him, before his death," he began. " He was a patient of mine, and for a while back he's been anxious about his blood-pressure. It was too high for his age—a good deal too high—so he used to ask me to come round now and again and test it for him. He phoned me last night, after dinner ; so I promised to take my car round about ten o'clock and see what was what. When I got there, he opened the front door to me himself. His old housekeeper's too deaf to hear the bell ring, I think. We went into his sitting-room. On the table he had some of the gold things that were dug up at Cæsar's Camp the other day ; not the whole bunch, just the big gold crosier and three or four other affairs. His brother, Henry, was there too, having a look at them. Deverell had been busy, taking measurements and jotting down notes for the paper he was drawing up. Henry Deverell didn't wait long. When he'd gone away, I tested Robert's blood-pressure, which wasn't too good. I had a word to say about the risk of over-exertion, and the sight of the gold reminded me of the digging. He swore he'd left all that to his assistants, and kept strictly to note-taking and sieving the soil. We chatted for a while, and then I got up to go. He let me out. That was the last I saw of him alive."

" What time did you leave the house ? " asked Sir Clinton.

" I really don't know. Between eleven and half-past, probably."

" Then you were called in again later, and you saw the body?"

" Yes. I got news of the affair at our post, and I thought it well to go up before the body was moved. I'd time on my hands. There were very few casualties coming in. It was a small raid, just a few planes, and the bombs fell outside my district. What we got at our station were mostly A.F.S. people who'd got burns during the fire-fighting. So I went up to Braden Drive. When I reached there, they'd got the fire under control—practically out. I examined the body. The skull was smashed by a heavy blow. You don't want technical details? No? You'll see them in my evidence at the inquest, if you need them. It looked to me as if he'd been stooping down to pick up a fire-bucket or his stirrup-pump. The remains of them were lying in the angle of the stairway, I noticed. At that moment, down came the bomb and hit him on the right side of the head. Then it must have glanced off and gone ablaze. I found the steel tail-fins of it on the floor, close to the body. All the rest of it had flamed away, of course. And I noticed glass from the skylight there, too—a lot of it."

"The flames of the fire would surge up the staircase, of course," interjected Sir Clinton, "and that would bring down most of the glass that was left in the skylight, quite apart from what the bomb itself knocked out in its passage. What clothes was he wearing when he was killed?"

"The same as the ones I saw him in, earlier on. Of course they were all burned and soaked with water from the hoses ; but it was the same suit. You're thinking that he went to bed after I left him and got up again when the raid started? No. When I said good night, he mentioned that he had an hour or two's work to do. He was always a late bird, hardly ever went to bed before one or two in the morning."

"Had he a wrist-watch on?" asked the Chief Constable.

"He had, sir," said the inspector. "The heat had cracked the glass of it and stopped the hands at 1.45. The works were all right, for I wound it up one or two clicks just to see if the spring was intact, and it wasn't run down by the feel of it. He must have been killed round about that time."

"That's very satisfactory," commended Sir Clinton. "But I don't see, as yet, where I come in. All this is coroner's business, surely."

"I'm giving you the facts in chronological order," Allardyce pointed out. "I thought you'd prefer it so. We haven't come to the crux of the thing yet. The body was rather badly burned, of course, since it was just alongside the incendiary bomb ; but after examining it, I came to the conclusion that the burns were post-mortem ones, as I expected. At least, any blisters that I tested were air-filled and had no serum in them. We'll get more definite evidence when we examine the lungs ; but I'll be surprised if we find any smoke-particles in them. He was dead before the bomb went off and never breathed any smoke, I'm sure. Inspector Camlet turned up just as I was finishing my examination. Somebody else summoned him. I'd nothing to do with that. I left him to make his own search. I wanted to make a note or two while I had the facts fresh in my mind, so I went into the sitting-room. The smoke was less unbreathable there, and the electric light was still on. After jotting down my notes, I glanced about me ; and then it suddenly occurred to me that something was wrong. As I told you, when I left Deverell earlier in the evening, he was busy with these gold ornaments which were lying on the table ; and he mentioned to me, in parting, that he still had an hour or two's work to finish up. Now when I glanced round, I found only one of the articles left, something that looked like a crushed-up chalice, and it was lying on the floor under the table. The big gold crosier had gone, and so had several other things. I hadn't noted them carefully when I saw them on my first visit ; but I'm sure about the crosier."

"Never mind," interjected Sir Clinton. "The bank can give us the list. They'll have his receipt for them. Go on."

"I called Inspector Camlet into the room and explained the state of affairs," Allardyce went on. "We hunted all over the place. The fire was completely out by this time, and we were able to search the premises. We didn't find a trace of the crosier or any of the other articles."

He glanced at Camlet for corroboration.

"That's correct, sir," said the inspector. "Except for the hall and stair the house is structurally undamaged. We were able to get into all the rooms. Everything in a filthy mess, of course. Smoke and water all over the place. But not a trace of the stuff anywhere. And they must have been there when the alert sounded. In the sitting-room, I picked up a sheet of paper. He'd been interrupted while he was putting down the measurements of that crosier. His writing breaks off in the middle of a sentence. And I found a steel tape-measure on the floor. It's a plain case of looting."

"We've never yet had any looting in this district," Wendover interrupted in a tone which showed that he was jealous of the good name of his neighbours. "The people hereabouts are a decent lot, Inspector, as you know quite well. How do you suppose a looter did his work ? "

"My theory, sir, is that he got in while Betty Brown was away summoning assistance," explained Camlet. "We know the front door was open. She left it so, as I found out by asking the firemen. The housekeeper was in the back garden, well out of the way. Besides, if she'd seen a man about, she'd be more interested in her modesty than in anything else, I judge. A man could easily have walked in, grabbed the stuff, and walked out again before the A.F.S. turned up. If Deverell himself put the things away for safety when the raid started, he'd have taken the lot. A thief, in a hurry, might quite well miss the one we found on the floor."

"Is there a safe or anything of that sort on the premises?" asked Sir Clinton.

"No, sir. There's no place where the missing things could have been put for safety. I've been over the whole villa, every corner of it. Took me a good while, because I wanted to be sure. Then Dr. Allardyce gave me a lift in his car to his house, and we got a clean-up before coming on to you. It being a case of looting, I wanted to report it to you as soon as possible, in case you'd care to examine the place yourself before anything's shifted."

"Looting seems the only probable explanation," admitted the Chief Constable, "since the stuff has been removed from the premises. But your hypothesis doesn't cover all possibilities, Inspector. You know the regulations about leaving one's front door unlocked during a raid, so that anyone can take refuge in the house if need be. Your looter may have got in much earlier than you postulated. Deverell may have admitted him voluntarily at the start of the raid. Then the man may have seen the gold on the table." He turned to Allardyce. "Would you take your oath, Doctor, that it was the incendiary bomb which killed Deverell? Or would you stop short of that and simply say that he died from a blow on the head caused by something or other?"

Allardyce made the gesture of a pinked fencer.

"You have me there," he admitted, frankly. "I couldn't swear that it *was* the bomb, if you put me up against it in the witness-box."

"Could you swear to the exact time of the death?" demanded Sir Clinton with a smile.

"No, I couldn't," said Allardyce without hesitation. "Nobody could, in the circumstances. With that fire blazing and with the state of the body, any estimate would be pure guess-work."

" Where are the gas and electric meters in Deverell's house ? " asked Sir Clinton, turning to the inspector.

" Under the stair, sir," said Camlet, readily. " I noticed them when we were hunting for the gold. I thought he might have put it in the cupboard under the stair—for safety—and looked in there."

" We're warned to turn off gas at the meter when a raid starts," Sir Clinton reminded them. " Deverell was a rather fussy person, judging from the little I saw of him once. He'd go at once to turn off the gas as soon as the raid started. That would take him to the cupboard in the hall, and it was alongside the cupboard door that his body was found, wasn't it ? "

" That's so, sir," admitted the inspector, in a grudging tone. " You think a stranger came into the house when the raid started. Deverell took him into the sitting-room. He saw the gold there. It tempted him. When Deverell went out to the meter, this fellow followed him and hit him on the head. Then the stranger grabbed up the missing stuff and decamped before Betty Brown appeared at all. That's your idea of what happened ? "

" It's an alternative hypothesis," corrected Sir Clinton.

" And the incendiary came down by coincidence just about that time, sir ? Seems straining things a bit, surely. Dashed lucky for the murderer, that, if I may say so."

" Say what you like," said the Chief Constable, cheerfully. " But if *I* may say so, Inspector, you seem to be thrusting on to me quite a number of hypotheses which I certainly never put into words myself. I didn't assert that the newcomer was a stranger, for one thing. He may have been an acquaintance or even a relation of Deverell, for all I can tell."

" You have me there," admitted Camlet. " But you must admit, sir, the fall of that incendiary's a bit of a coincidence to ask for. It must have come down very pat, just when it was wanted."

" I never mentioned the incendiary at all," Sir Clinton pointed out dryly. " In any case, coincidences can sometimes be arranged, if it's worth somebody's while to do so."

" But you don't mean that the Germans arranged to hit that particular house at that particular time, sir ? Surely that would be going a bit far."

" I don't remember that I mentioned Germans," said the Chief Constable, with a twinkle in his eye. " You're putting too many things into my mouth, Inspector, especially as I've barely finished breakfast. Now let me say a few words of my own. Will you go into the box and swear that the incendiary actually did come through the skylight? All the proof I've heard, hitherto, is that there's broken glass down on the hall floor. But the heat of the fire on the stair brought down glass from the skylight. Where's the proof that it wasn't all brought down in this way?"

The inspector made a gesture as if he was going to reply on the spur of the moment; but second thoughts evidently prevailed, and he remained silent, thinking hard, for several seconds.

"I'll admit you've pulled my leg, sir," he said at last. "But one thing you *can't* get round. That incendiary bomb was inside the house. The skylight was the only way in for it."

"Was it?" queried Sir Clinton. "I can think of other ways."

The inspector shrugged his shoulders incredulously, and then looked rather guilty.

"I don't see how you make that out, sir," he declared.

"Don't you? Well, here's one suggestion. Somebody may have brought it in and set it going at the place where its steel fins were found by Dr. Allardyce. I don't assert that this happened. All I say is that it may have happened, and you haven't excluded the possibility by anything you've produced."

"Maybe, sir. But how would anyone get hold of it?"

"Oh, come, come!" retorted the Chief Constable. "You know quite well that some incendiaries don't go off. Some of them come down in soft soil and the striker-pin doesn't act. Why, I heard of one only the other day, found by a young friend of mine, completely intact and ready for action, if anyone chose to give its head a good hard knock on the floor."

The inspector looked at Sir Clinton with more than a little suspicion.

"Is all this what you really think, sir? Or just a bit of leg-pulling for my benefit? You make it sound plausible enough. I'll admit that. But still . . ."

"All I want is to make sure that you don't jump at one explanation of the facts and stick to it without looking for anything else."

"I never thought of murder, I'll admit that," confessed Camlet.

"I don't say it *was* murder," Sir Clinton warned him. "All I've tried to do is to show you that you can't call it accident until you've proved that. The matter's an open one. But there's one thing which might help towards a choice between the alternatives."

" If you could discover the missing gold ? " interjected Allardyce. " That might be a help."

" Yes," confirmed the Chief Constable. " Somebody removed that gold. And if we could put our hands on him, we might have a fair chance of learning something further. That's obvious. The problem is to pick out the right man —or woman—from a local population running into a few thousand. The solution to *that* isn't quite so plain. Now, if you people have finished your breakfasts, I'd like to go along and look at things myself. Can you spare the time to come with us, Doctor ? "

Allardyce glanced at his watch.

" Yes, certainly, if you need me," he agreed.

" Then if you'll take the inspector in your car, Wendover and I can follow you immediately."

When his two guests had gone, Wendover turned to Sir Clinton.

" These medicals are very callous," he said, with faint displeasure. " Allardyce was an acquaintance of poor Deverell's, but he showed less sympathy than I'd spare over the death of one of my dogs. I suppose it's their training that makes them so, or else death loses the unexpectedness it always has for a layman like myself. It's just business with them."

" Just as a casual murder is in my case," agreed the Chief Constable. " Matter of business, as you say, Squire. Well, suppose we go about my business, now, instead of standing talking about it."

CHAPTER IV   *The Death Zone*

SOME DAYS PASSED BEFORE WENDOVER FULFILLED HIS promise to invite Daphne Stanway and Allardyce to dinner. During the meal, while the servants were present, the topic of Jehudi Ashmun was ignored ; and even when the party had left the table and gone into another room, there was a delay in broaching the subject. Wendover busied himself with offering cigarettes to the girl.

" I'm sorry for people who have rubber shares just now," he said, by way of making conversation until they had all settled down comfortably. " It must be awkward to see a steady income cut off abruptly."

" You can be sorry for me, then," retorted the doctor,

with a curt and uncomfortable laugh. " I'm one of them. Keep off a sore subject, Wendover. Most of my capital was in rubber."

Wendover made a sympathetic noise, but Allardyce cut it short, being apparently ashamed of his grumble as soon as it was made.

" What's money, after all ? Nothing, when you think of what's happened to our people in Malaya. Besides . . ."

He halted, leaving his phrase unfinished.

Daphne glanced at him amusedly.

" Poor man ! He's too shy to break good news. He leaves it to the brazen female. The fact is, Mr. Wendover, Frank and I are going to get married, shortly. I haven't got a ring to show as a guarantee of good faith, for we only fixed things up as were coming here to-night. So unromantic, being proposed to in a car with a dinner engagement looming ahead. Girls have a lot to put up with, nowadays. You're the first to hear about it, if that's any satisfaction."

" It doubles the pleasure," said Wendover. " I've been hoping for something of the sort . . ."

" I suspected as much," Daphne rejoined, dryly. " Those puzzled looks at the pair of us, and all that sort of thing. Well, it's all open and above-board now, so your mind's relieved, I hope. Wish us happiness, prosperity, long life, and many happy returns, and the thing's done."

" Mind-reader ! " retorted Wendover. " That's just what I do wish you both. I'm too old-fashioned to think of anything else, you see."

Sir Clinton added his own congratulations, which Daphne accepted prettily.

" There, that's over ! " she added. " Now let's get to business, shall we ? Where do we begin ? "

" I'll break the ice," Wendover volunteered. " I've kept one or two newspaper cuttings as curiosities. They'll be new to you, Clinton, and they'll start you off at the beginning. Just a moment."

He took an envelope from his pocket, extracted some cuttings, and began to read them out in turn.

" Here's the first one :

" ' *To All True Seekers. In the name of the* 6, 9, 22, 5— 23, 15, 18, 12, 4, 19. *The time for the building of the New Temple of* 21, 18, 9, 26, 5, 14. *is at hand. This is to invite all True Seekers in the name of the* 6, 15, 21, 18—26, 15, 1, 19, *to meet on the* 7th *prox. and join in laying the first stone in this visible world of the material representative of the* 20, 18, 21, 5—

36

2, 1, 19, 9, 12, 9, 3, 1, *of the spiritual* 11, 9, 14, 7, 4, 15, 13, *of* 21, 18, 9, 26, 5, 14. *Given under the hand and Seal of the Magus,* 10, 5, 8, 21, 4, 9—1, 19, 8, 13, 21, 14, *and by Authority. For further particulars, apply Box* 7235.'

"Too many genitives, altogether," Wendover ended, "four of them one after another."

"Read it over again, slower, please," directed Sir Clinton, who had pulled out a pencil and a notebook.

Wendover obeyed, reading at dictation speed while the Chief Constable jotted down a note or two, smiling to himself as he did so.

"And now, the next one, please," he demanded.

Wendover took up the next cutting and read out :

"' *To All True Seekers. In the name of the* 6, 9, 22, 5—23, 15, 18, 12, 4, 19. *A Conclave of the* 14, 15, 22, 9, 3, 5, 19, *of the* 5, 1, 18, 20, 8, *will be held on* 19*th inst. to advance certain* 9, 14, 9, 20, 9, 1, 20, 5, 19, *to be* 6, 12, 1, 13, 5, 14, 19, *of the* 1, 9, 18, *by authority.* 10, 5, 8, 21, 4, 9—1, 19, 8, 13, 21, 14, *Magus.*'

"I see you've deciphered it, Clinton. I managed it myself, and I'm no cipher expert. Just read out what you make of it, will you ? Though I don't see how I can have gone wrong in so simple a thing."

Sir Clinton picked up his jottings and read the advertisement *en clair*.

"' *To All True Seekers. In the name of the Four Worlds. The time for the building of the New Temple of Urizen is at hand. This is to invite all True Seekers in the name of the Four Zoas to meet on the* 7*th prox. and join in laying the first stone in this visible world of the material representative of the True Basilica of the spiritual Kingdom of Urizen. Given under the hand and Seal of the Magus Jehudi Ashmun and by Authority. For further particulars, apply Box* 7235.'

"Evidently Mr. Ashmun appeals to feeble intellects who can't be trusted to use complicated ciphers. All he's done is to replace *A* by 1, *B* by 2, and so on."

"Thanks for your 'feeble intellects '," said Daphne, ironically. "So nice to know just where one stands, isn't it, Frank ? "

"I won't bother to apologise," retorted the Chief Constable. "I didn't refer to all the members. Some may be quite intelligent for all I can tell. But don't let's waste time. The second advertisement runs in English : ' A Conslave of the Novices will be held on 19th inst. to advance certain Initiates to be Flamens of Air by Authority. JEHUDI

Ashmun, Magus.' Is it worth while going further, Squire? Just give us your own results and save time."

"There isn't much in it," answered Wendover, shuffling his cuttings as he spoke. "There seems to be three grades in the show : Novices of the Earth ; then above them, Flamens of the Air ; and finally Primates of the Fire. The advertisements got simpler as time went on. This sort of thing : ' Primates, 9 p.m., 15th inst.,' which is obviously a call to a meeting at some fixed place. What do you make of it, Clinton ? "

"I give Mr. Ashmun credit for an excellent flat-catching device, though I suspect he borrowed it from Cagliostro," said the Chief Constable. "Unless I'm far wrong, friend Ashmun aimed first at collecting a gang of inquisitive nit-wits. Put yourself in the position of such a person and imagine yourself faced with that first advertisement. It would catch you, straight off. It's plain enough to attract attention, and yet sufficiently mysterious to arouse curiosity. All it's going to cost you is the postage on a letter to Box 7235. The kind of flat that Mr. Ashmun was after would not be deterred by that expense. Then, when the letters came in, Mr. Ashmun could guess from their contents, and better still from the addresses, whether the writers were worth bothering about further. Meanwhile, nobody could come and worry him personally, since he hadn't given his address. So he could pick out his first batch of dupes at his leisure. A good many of his applicants wouldn't have even the sense to substitute letters for the figures in the advertisements, but that wouldn't hinder them from writing to ask what it was all about."

"And once he picked out his first batch, they'd bring in others of their own kidney when he wanted them, I suppose," said Wendover. "It's certainly ingenious."

"He's no fool," declared the Chief Constable. "Here's another proof of that. If you start a new religion or anything like that, you need some sort of gospel to go on with. Swedenborg's been worked to death, and so have most other possibles. But no one has touched William Blake yet ; and his prophetic books are obscure enough for anyone's taste. Hence the reference to the Four Zoas and Urizen, I presume. Am I right ? " he asked, turning to Daphne.

"You are. At least, I was advised to study Blake if I wanted to become a real Adept, and all that."

"So was I," confirmed Allardyce. "I'd never looked at Blake before, but I took a glance at him then. Weird stuff about dining with Isaiah and Ezekiel, and black and white spiders, and a printing-house in Hell, and an angel going blue in the face. I rather liked it. Quite demented, of course, but interesting to read."

" Another thing," said Sir Clinton. " I suppose there are pass-words amongst the initiates. It's the kind of thing which pleases some people."

" I'm breaking no oath that I care twopence about," answered Allardyce, " but if you went to Mr. Ashmun and said : ' Did you ever see Tyger spelt with a " y " ? ' he'd probably say : ' Yes, Blake spelt it so,' or words to that effect."

" And I suppose all the initiates are instructed about the cipher, so that they can read any advertisements he chooses to put abroad ? "

" That's so," said Allardyce, contemptuously. " And if you saw some of the initiates, you'd guess at once why it had to be a cipher that a six-year-old would understand. Anything complex would be beyond them completely."

" How do they manage about passing up from lower to higher grades in the hierarchy ? " asked the Chief Constable.

" It's done by drawing cards. An ace gets you one step up. If no one draws an ace, there's nothing doing. That avoids jealousy and leaves promotion in the hands of Providence."

" Or in the hands of the fellow who can force a card ? " commented Sir Clinton. " Any amateur conjurer can do that. Now what about these grades ? "

" Some people never seem to climb higher than being Novices," Allardyce explained. " The ruck with no money and few brains are left in that group, so far as I can make out. They're kept amused with planchette and a few odd Black Art ceremonies. I was promoted clean up to being a Primate first go off, so I don't know what the Flamens of the Air do. You can ask Daphne. She got stuck in that class."

Sir Clinton turned to the girl.

" Can you give us some idea of it ? "

" Well," she said, thoughtfully, " one or two things *are* a bit peculiar, and I don't profess to account for them. And I certainly didn't follow Mr. Ashmun's explanations. Vague, they seemed to me, and full of a lot of ideas I'd never heard of before. Almost as bad as Blake ; and I simply can't read Blake, at any price. The only thing I did get hold of in a way was something about unloosing a new Force by playing notes on a violin . . ."

"Ah?" interjected Sir Clinton, but pulled himself up at once.

"I'd better tell you just what I saw," continued Daphne, finding that he did not go on. "He tried some of us sitting round a light card table, the way they do in spiritualistic séances, you know; and the table did shift about a bit—levitated, isn't that what they call it? That didn't seem to please him—something about using up too much power—so next time he had the table screwed down to the floor so that it couldn't shift or levitate, or do anything but stay quiet. And this time, I remember, there was no turning down the lights or anything of that sort. After we'd sat for a bit and nothing happened, he took a violin and played a phrase. Nothing musical; rather set my teeth on edge, to tell you the truth. But that did start something. The table began to talk."

"Rapping, you mean?" asked Wendover.

"Rapping I do *not* mean," retorted Daphne. "I mean talking in words. Perfectly weird, it sounded, as if something not quite human was speaking in a cathedral. If the lights hadn't been on, I'd have felt too creepy for anything."

"A loud-speaker?" suggested Wendover, sceptically.

Daphne shook her head very decidedly.

"It came from the top of the table, right in the middle of us," she said in the tone of certainty. "You can't get any loud-speaker into the top of an ordinary card-table, one of these slim-jim folding affairs with a top hardly thicker than plywood. It can't be done. I'm not quite a fool, Mr. Wendover, and I looked carefully. There were no wires or anything of that sort that I could see."

"And what did it say, when it began?" asked Sir Clinton.

"Oh, it started with moans, or something that sounded like 'em. Nothing but vowels to begin with: O-ee-i-ah! Ooh-o-o-o-ee-ah-ay! Like that, more or less. It made me feel downright uncomfortable. I persuaded myself, of course, that it was just some new trick; but it got on my nerves all the same. You know how a couple of cats outside your window can twist your nerves? You say to yourself, 'It's just cats,' but that doesn't help, somehow. These cat-sounds always affect me in the eeriest way at night. This thing was much the same, only worse, running up and down the scale just like a cat but with some extra vile in it, as if it was getting a kick out of grating on our nerves. I hated it. Then gradually consonants began to creep in, but the stuff was mere gibberish for a while. Then after a bit it settled down to talk in something like English."

"And what did it say then?" demanded Wendover.

"Not very much and very disjointed. Something about Cæsar's Camp and being disturbed and death, and . . . I think it mentioned Mr. Deverell being killed. And then it stopped talking and went back to gibberish and finally faded away into moans again. And that was the end of it. I didn't want any more. I'd had quite enough, especially when it moaned. Ugh! Horrible!"

She paused for a moment as though disturbed even by the memory. Then she continued :

"I've persuaded myself that it's some trick or other. But it made me so uncomfortable that I refused flatly to try *that* experiment again. Materialising flowers or taking corks out of pickle-jars are all in the day's work at séances, and I wouldn't mind them if I came across them. But that voice . . . Well, anyone can listen in if they like. But I won't, and I told Mr. Ashmun so, very plainly. He seemed a bit disappointed. Perhaps that's why I was never pushed up into the Primate Class."

"Anything else that struck you?" asked Sir Clinton.

"Yes, there was another thing I made neither head nor tail of. I don't mean to say that I ever saw anything that I could say outright was a trick, for I didn't. But this thing struck me specially. There was a small glass aquarium. Just the usual thing, with a few plants growing in it and a kind of little rockery in the middle, and a lot of minnows swimming about in the water. Mr. Ashmun said he'd show us a sample of his new Force and what it could do. So he put one or two big standard lamps round the aquarium, and lit it up as brightly as anything. Then he went away to the other end of the room and played a note or two on his violin, and the minnows all stopped swimming and sank down to the bottom, dead."

"Electric shock, perhaps?" queried Wendover.

"No, I don't think so," Daphne replied soberly. "I'd thought of some dodge of that sort, and I noticed that Mr. Ashmun didn't forbid us to touch the aquarium, so I put my finger on it in an accidental kind of way. And my finger was on the metal-work of it at the very moment those minnows died. That doesn't look like electric shock, does it?"

"That was clever, Miss Stanway," said Sir Clinton, with obvious sincerity. "You couldn't have bettered it. And you must have sound nerves if you made up your mind to risk it. Nobody likes electric shocks, even mild ones."

"I didn't think much of my nerves when I heard that voice, though," Daphne confessed, frankly. "If it *was* a voice. You don't think we could have been hypnotised and made to imagine it, do you? It sounded real enough at the time, but . . . Hypnotism might account for it, mightn't it?"

"I never heard of an authentic case where a dozen people were simultaneously hypnotised without their knowledge," said Sir Clinton, "but I'm not an expert on hypnotism, remember. And now, I want to ask a question or two. How are you people summoned to these meetings? By advertisement?"

"Occasionally by advertisement, I believe," Daphne explained. "But oftener, nowadays, by a letter written in the same style as the advertisements. I think the advertisements are being dropped for fear of attracting too much attention."

"Evidently he has netted the people he wants, already," commented the Chief Constable. "Has he ever tried to get any money from you?"

Daphne shook her head.

"No, so far as I'm concerned, he gets absolutely nothing out of it, not even a subscription. But the people with money aren't in my group. They go higher up. Frank may have seen something of that."

Sir Clinton turned to the doctor.

"No," Allardyce answered the unspoken question. "He hasn't asked me for a farthing, not even to cover postages. The treatment's entirely gratuitous. But, from one thing and another, I suspect that he does get cash somewhere. Old Silwood is an ass with money. I notice he gives himself airs of being more in the know than the rest of us. Special mysteries revealed to him, and so on. I've no proof that he's being bled. Pretty sure in my own mind, though. And there's your sister, Daphne . . ."

"Agatha?" queried Daphne, doubtfully. "She certainly seems to swallow anything that Mr. Ashmun says. She was always a bit inclined towards that sort of thing : palmistry, spiritualism, omens, and superstitions generally, you know. And she has plenty of money. But . . . I doubt if she would part with any of it except on very good grounds."

"Probably you're right," admitted Allardyce. "I hope so, for her own sake."

"They're talking about Mrs. Pinfold," Wendover explained aside to Sir Clinton. "She's a young widow."

Sir Clinton nodded, and then turned to Allardyce.

"Have you seen any signs and wonders yourself, up amongst these Primates?"

"Generally speaking, we get more talk than deeds," said the doctor. "He's a plausible creature, Ashmun. A great knack of talking stuff which sounds full of meaning but hasn't any, really. All about noumena, phenomena, essences, and the sixth dimension, and the unreality of real things. His long suit is a lot of gas about the fact that our senses don't confirm each other. Take a lump of sugar—if you can get one, nowadays. You can see it and touch it. Now dissolve it in water. It's there still, but you can't see it or touch it. But you know it's there because the water tastes sweet. You can't see an odour, but you can smell it. You can hear a sound, but you can't touch it, taste it, see it or smell it. You can see a tree blown down, but you don't see the wind that overturns it. Childish stuff, to my mind. But wrap it up in polysyllables, and it seems to impress dunderheads wonderfully. The less they understand, the more amazing they find it. Makes them feel learned, I suppose, and that must be a new sensation for them."

"Hardly worth paying heavily for, though," said Sir Clinton.

"You'd be surprised," retorted Allardyce. "But I think I see where the cash comes in. Ever heard of a man called Keely?"

"John Worrell Keely?" queried Sir Clinton. "The Philadelphia crank?"

"Ashmun didn't call him a crank," retorted Allardyce. "According to him, Keely discovered some new source of power which he could tap but couldn't quite control."

"I remember reading articles about the Keely motor in the *New Review* when I was a youngster," Sir Clinton said. "He played a note on a violin, didn't he? And then things happened : a cannon-ball rising into the air and other quaint affairs. If he had any secret, it died with him."

"Not according to Ashmun," contradicted Allardyce. "He claims that some of Keely's papers came into his hands, and that he's worked along similar lines—successfully."

"And he needs cash in quantities to pursue his researches ? Now I begin to see daylight," commented Sir Clinton. "'Give me the dibs now, and when my invention's perfected the cash will roll in.' That's the idea, is it?"

"I can't swear to it," said Allardyce, "but I think it's something of the sort."

" And has he ever given demonstrations of the New Force, à la Keely ? " asked Sir Clinton, with open scepticism.

" Yes, he has," rejoined Allardyce, unexpectedly. " And, what's more, I can make neither head nor tail of it."

" That sounds interesting," said the Chief Constable. " Is it anything on the same lines as those affairs that Miss Stanway's been telling us about ? "

" It's even weirder, in its way," declared the doctor. " Part of it seemed to me just clotted superstition, and no use to any sensible man. But the results can't be denied. I tested the thing as fully as possible. Here's what happened. One night, Ashmun detained me after the rest of them had gone. Then he started to lay off a long tale about Unknown Forces. You could almost hear the capital letters. I spare you all the frills he put on his yarn, just wind and no more, mere bosh wrapped up in a lot of vague phrases that would sound plausible to people with no brains. So it sounded to me, anyhow. He dragged in Keely at one stage, that cannon-ball business and some more of the same kind. Then he hitched that on to the old witch-craft yarns, riding through the air on broom-sticks, and elfin bolts that killed people without leaving any marks on them. And he coupled that with a yarn about some well-known medium who floated out of one third-floor window and in at another."

" D. D. Home ? " interjected Wendover.

" That was the name," Allardyce confirmed. " The point is that Ashmun made out that these Unknown Forces are discovered at intervals by various people : Keely, Home, and the fellows who personated the Devil in the old witch-cult. Then the secret's lost for a while, until somebody else gets on the track. He dragged in Poltergeist phenomena, too. Somebody hits on a way of generating a Force, but can't control it. To cut it short, he laid off a lot of cases which he said were earlier samples of this affair of his. Then he declared that in certain circumstances this New Force of his could extend its operations over quite consider-able distances. There was something about newly-opened-up strata acting as reflectors, or resonators, or amplifiers. Bosh, I thought it. But just to pull his leg, I asked if he meant that a quarry-face or a bomb-crater would fill the bill. He said these were just the sort of things he did mean. Naturally I asked if he had any evidence, and not just talk. He surprised me, more than a bit, by saying he had evidence. What's more, he undertook to satisfy me, there and then, that he wasn't talking through his hat. But he'd have to be careful, he explained. It meant tampering with dangerous Forces, and one was apt to get more than one bargained for if one wasn't careful. Still, he thought he could throttle down the thing and do as little damage as possible."

" Did he seem serious in all this ? " demanded Sir Clinton.

" Oh, quite serious," returned the doctor. " Eyes like saucers and a grin with the whole domino-box open. Not exactly a humorous grin, though. More like a fellow who's scored a point and yet feels that perhaps he's gone too far. However, I pinned him down ; and finally he gave in with quite a good grace, grinning away in a most accommodating style. He warned me that the whole thing might be a flam. His Force sometimes didn't come up to scratch. He hoped to get over that eventually, but at present things were rather uncertain. And so on. Quite in the style of the nervous scientific lecturer when he isn't too sure whether his experiment will go off click, or just turn out a fiasco."

" And I suppose it did turn out a fiasco," commented Wendover sceptically.

" You'll hear," Allardyce promised. " At last he decided to do his stuff. He didn't say beforehand what he meant to do. He excused himself for a minute with some talk about arranging the conditions, and went out of the room. Then he came back, leaving the door open, with a fiddle in his hand. He fell to tuning his fiddle, but barring that he tuned his E string a shade flat and his A string a trifle sharp, I saw nothing amazing. Then, when he was ready, he asked me to look at my watch and note the time."

" Why did he do that ? " demanded Wendover.

" You'll see, later," the doctor assured him. " I'm telling you just what happened. Naturally, I took particular notice of details. I looked at my watch. Then Ashmun gave a super-special grin in my direction, put his fiddle up, and played three long chords on the open strings . . . and nothing happened. Absolutely nix. I thought I'd got him cold. Not a bit of it. He put down his fiddle, grinned, and said we'd have to go a good distance to hunt for the results. Explanations must stand over. So we got into my car and he directed me to drive up to Cæsar's Camp. When we got there, he stayed in the car, to make sure that I didn't suspect him of having anything to do with the results. I was to get out and look around myself. I asked him what I was expected to find. ' Something dead.' It was pretty dark, and a dimmed torch doesn't give much help. Still, after a bit, I stumbled on a dead rabbit. Nothing much in that, but it seemed to have died rather painfully, judging by its attitude. Then I found another rabbit, and another . . . five in all, and all dead as door-nails."

" Were they on the road ? " asked Sir Clinton.

" Meaning that a car might have come along and knocked them out ? " said Allardyce. " No, the first one was in the middle of the road, but two more were on the grass border, another one was lying beside a burrow twenty yards away from the highway and the last one I found was at the roadside, about a hundred yards farther on. Quite likely there were more than I found. They weren't in a clump. They were scattered pretty far apart and took some finding."

" You say they'd died painfully," said Sir Clinton. " Do you mean they were torn or mutilated ? "

" Not a bit. No blood or anything. Just dead. I carried them back to the car. He laughed. You know that African laugh. Frightfully pleased with himself, it seemed. ' Now take the time,' he said. So I glanced at my watch again. ' And now take their temperatures,' he ordered. ' You've got a thermometer, haven't you, being a doctor ? ' I saw what he was after, then. So I took the temperatures of all the bodies and noted the times."

" I see," interjected Sir Clinton. " He wanted you to work out from the temperature how long the creatures had been dead. But you need a control, don't you ? Or do you happen to know the rate of cooling in a dead rabbit ? "

" I'll come to that later," Allardyce assured him. " I'm telling you things just as they happened. Ashmun asked me to take every precaution I thought necessary. He wanted me to be completely satisfied, he said. And he asked if I'd have any objection to describing the affair from my point of view, to his nitwits. I didn't object. Truth's truth. and I saw no harm in telling what I'd seen. After all, no doubt they had put up some money to finance these experiments ; I hadn't parted with a stiver, so my tale would help to even things up."

" That's why he enlisted you so readily," suggested Sir Clinton. " Your rôle in the affair was that of the scientific man confounded for the joy of the true believers."

" Likely enough. And I don't mind confessing that I *was* confounded. Ashmun played perfectly fair. I admit that. He refused to touch the dead rabbits. I can swear he never came near them. I laid them in proper order in a row on the back seat of my car, so that I could examine them at leisure and see what they'd died of. Then I drove Ashmun to his house. I thanked him for an interesting evening. I owed him that. He grinned as usual. At my expense, I suspect. Then I said adieu and drove home. I wasn't going to run any risk of an exchange of rabbits while my back was turned."

"That seems all above-board," commented Wendover. "And what did you find, when you examined the rabbits?"

"All in good time," rejoined Allardyce. "I'm telling this tale just as it happened, so don't put me off till I've finished. I was dead puzzled by the whole affair. When I got home, I sat down and smoked a pipe and jotted down some notes of what I'd seen, while it was all fresh in my mind. Hence the fluency and accuracy of this my tale. Then I started to think over the whole business. And the more I thought about it, the less I seemed to make of it. I'm not a fool, I'm quite prepared to admit that we don't know everything yet. No one before Becquerel ever dreamed of radioactivity, and yet it had been going on all the time in thorium and uranium. It's possible that Ashmun has hit on something quite fresh. And it's also possible that if he has done so, he's putting abroad a lot of rubbish just to mislead people and prevent them getting on the track of the thing themselves. He's not like us medicals, bound by etiquette. A four-flusher, I'd say. But even four-flushers at poker may be honest at draughts, if you get my meaning."

Allardyce paused while he lighted a fresh cigarette. Then he continued:

"The first thing to do was to get a live rabbit or two and check the rate at which a rabbit's body cools after it's killed. As it happens, I know a fellow Pirbright who lives on the ground near Cæsar's Camp. A shiftless devil. The only good thing I know about him is that he plays the fiddle rather well. I once looked after him when he fell ill, and he's as grateful as that sort of fellow has it in him to be, which isn't much. He keeps ferrets, and I remembered seeing nets in his shack, so he seemed likely to be able to put his hand on a live rabbit or two. They swarm on the ground where he lives. So next morning I paid Pirbright a visit, and by the evening he had half a dozen live bunnies ready for me. Rabbits are out of season just now, and in any case I don't care for rabbit myself. But I've got some poor patients who welcome them, so it wasn't a useless waste of life to kill 'em. I killed the lot and worked out the cooling-scale by laying them out in my garden at the right time of night. There isn't a bit of doubt about it. Those rabbits up at Cæsar's camp must have died just about the time

47

when Ashmun was doing his bit of violin practice in front of me. I'd swear to that in the box, making allowance for the difficulty of estimating these temperature affairs exactly."

"Obviously Ashmun had a confederate who killed the rabbits at the right moment and left them for you to find," said Wendover, with the air of a man scoring a point. "Perhaps your fellow Pirbright was the man."

"Great minds fall into the same trap alike," retorted Allardyce. "That's just what I thought myself, to start with. Question was, how had they been killed? So I did a P.M. examination of the carcases of the Ashmun samples. The spinal column was intact, so they hadn't been killed in the usual way. Then I remembered that they didn't seem to have died comfortably. Strychnine might fit the case. So I tried for strychnine in the stomach contents. There's a test with bi-chromate and sulphuric which detects even one ten-thousandth of a grain of strychnine; you simply can't miss it. Not a sign could I see. I tried for other alkaloids as well. Nothing doing. I won't swear to it; but in my own mind I'm absolutely certain that the poor brutes weren't poisoned. I shaved the hair off a couple of them and looked for the marks of a hypodermic injection. No trace of any needle-prick. So there you have it. I'm not infallible; but those rabbits died in a way I've never come across yet, either in hospital or in practice. There wasn't a mark on them, either internally or externally, to show why they petered out. Every organ present and correct. Animals in the pink of health, so far as I could see. But dead as mutton. And if you want to make comments, now's the time."

"Do you think the minnow business and the rabbit-killing were due to the same agency?" queried Wendover. "The technique seems to have been the same, so far as the violin chords go."

"I didn't see the minnows die. Nor did I examine their corpses. Therefore, so far as I'm concerned, the cases aren't parallel," retorted Allardyce. "I stick to what I saw with my own eyes. That puzzles me enough, without hunting for extras."

Sir Clinton nodded without comment, and then turned to Daphne.

"You didn't tell me who introduced you into Ashmun's circle."

"Ione Herongate persuaded my sister and me to join. I wasn't a bit keen, but Agatha made such a fuss that it was easier to give in and join. When Frank heard about it, he insisted on joining too. He thought I needed someone to look after me, I suppose. Mr. Ashmun seemed quite keen to enrol him."

"What grades have Miss Herongate and your sister reached, do you know?" asked Sir Clinton.

"They're both Primates," Allardyce volunteered. "Miss Herongate's one of Ashmun's strongest supporters. Something of a recruiting-agent for the cause, I gather, and useful in spreading his gospel abroad. Ashmun may be stricken with her looks, which are much above the average. But he needn't expect encouragement from her in that line. Her mind's firmly fixed elsewhere. Not even one of his love philtres, extra strong, would shift it."

"I wish you wouldn't talk like that, Frank," said Daphne, reprovingly. "Ione may have made an exhibition of herself over Kenneth Felden; but that was a while ago, and you might forget about it instead of dragging it out afresh."

"She doesn't give one a chance to forget it," said Allardyce. Then, catching sight of Daphne's expression, he hastily added, "Oh, very well. I'll say no more."

He turned to Sir Clinton and changed the subject.

"Anything fresh about the Deverell business? I thought the coroner slid over the thin ice rather gracefully. I suppose you gave him a tip?"

Sir Clinton evaded a direct reply.

"We haven't found the missing gold yet," he admitted.

"Then you're not likely to find it at all," said Allardyce confidently. "With all those dealers crying for gold and no questions asked, the ordinary fence must be having a thin time of it, these days. Easy to melt the stuff down and sell a bit here and a bit there. And that collection must have been worth a fair sum. Between two and three thousand, perhaps. The crosier alone was a heavy item."

"We live in hope," said Sir Clinton, with a wry smile. "But before I forget it, can you give me the exact date of this rabbit affair?"

Allardyce consulted his engagement-book.

"January 9th," he said. "I made a note of it at the time."

Wendover decided that the Ashmun question had now been sufficiently thrashed out.

"What about some bridge?" he asked.

They played for the rest of the evening, and finally Allardyce and Daphne took their leave. When they had gone, Sir Clinton turned to Wendover with a question.

"What sort of person is this Mrs. Pinfold, Squire?"

"Not a bit like her sister," said Wendover. "No brains to speak of, selfish to the bone, and ready to take up any new craze that comes along. Quite good-looking, in her way, and married a rich man old enough to be her father. He's dead, but the cash remains. I can't say I've much use for her."

"And what about this Miss Herongate?"

Wendover's face betrayed that Ione was no favourite of his.

"She's the daughter of old John Herongate of Heron Hill. You remember the place? Ione owns it, now that her father and mother have gone. A handsome girl," Wendover conceded grudgingly, "but not quite my style in looks. Dark and rather sphinx-like, so far as features go. You'd look at her twice because she's uncommon. Brooding eyes, if you know what I mean."

"I don't," Sir Clinton admitted frankly.

"Well, when I'm talking to her, I get the impression from the look in her eyes, half the time, that she's thinking of something more important than myself. Dreamy isn't the word. Smouldering, perhaps, is better. I'm no hand at describing these things."

"That's obvious," said Sir Clinton, more frank than polite. "But never mind. I'm not specially interested in her eyes. It was that little bit of by-play between your two young guests that caught my attention when her name was mentioned to-night. Where does Felden come into the picture?"

Wendover considered for a moment or two before replying.

"You remember I told you that Daphne and Felden were engaged at one time? I've an impression that Ione Herongate was rather cut up when that engagement was announced. Certainly when it was broken off she did her best to console Felden. Sometimes a girl can catch a man she's keen on, in that way, if she's prepared to put up with shop-soiled affections. But it didn't come off in Felden's case. Ione's done her best for the last year or two, but the results have been negligible. Some men are flattered if a girl throws herself at them; but Felden isn't that type. Personally, I think she's wasting her time and making herself cheap into the bargain. Felden, on the surface, seems to have taken his jilting very well. He's very friendly with Daphne and Allardyce; shows not a trace of jealousy or ill-feeling. In fact, Allardyce is the doctor he calls in when that dipsomaniac Tony Gainford gets too near the verge of D.T. Still, I'm not sure that he's forgotten. I've caught him glancing at Daphne now and again in a way he wouldn't do if he thought anyone was watching him. He was rather hard hit, you know."

" You never can tell how a man will take it," said Sir Clinton, ruminatively. " Sometimes he drops the whole affair and gets cured. Or else the romantic part and the chivalry of the original business decay away while a purely physical longing remains and grows, especially if a second man has replaced him. I suppose wounded pride lies at the root of that. It's a queer affair, very interesting for an onlooker, but painful for the patient, no doubt. And, of course, there's always the case where the man simply goes on hoping that things will come all right in the end. Care for a game of chess, Squire ? Or shall we go to bed ? "

CHAPTER V   *Exit Pirbright*

" EVERYBODY'S JABBERING ABOUT A GRAND NEW WORLD, nowadays," grumbled Inspector Camlet to Sergeant Robson. " They can have it ! All I want, myself, is to get back to the old world again, like before the war. Good enough for me. A sight better than what we're living in now."

The sergeant had heard all this before, many times. Whenever the inspector broached the subject of the future, Robson listened to the sounds and thought about something else of more practical interest ; so now he merely nodded and hoped that the gramophone would run down if he let it alone. He was not to escape, however.

" What's *your* idea of a better world ? " demanded the inspector.

" Heaven, you mean ? " said the sergeant, coming out of his trance at this direct attack. " Tell you the truth, I never bother my head about it. All in good time ; I'm not dead yet."

" Nobody's talking about Heaven," explained Camlet, wrathfully. " I mean this stuff that's all the go, in speeches, nowadays. See it in the papers. What's *your* idea of a better world, down here ? "

The sergeant was a man of simple and limited needs. He produced his recipe for the Earthly Paradise in spurts, pausing for reflection between his phrase :

" Well, if they'd take the tax off baccy . . . and give us enough matches to light our pipes with . . . and free beer, perhaps . . . and let the pubs stay open longer . . . and abolish this new-fangled Income Tax; it's cruel . . . and . . . Well, I think that would do pretty well for a start, until we'd got time to turn round and think up something more."

He examined Camlet's face with some concern. There was no pleasing that man, in these days. Perhaps he was worried about the war; though why this particular war should be specially annoying, the sergeant could not fathom. To him, it seemed just like all our wars : a lot of bad news at the start—as usual ; then just one dam' thing after another ; and everybody saying it looked pretty bad—as usual ; and then one day we'd wake up and find that we'd won, hands down—also as usual.

Actually, the cause of the inspector's irritation was simple, though the head constable failed to guess it. He had not made the slightest progress in his search for the gold which had gone amissing on the night of Deverell's death. Camlet prided himself on his acumen, and his ill-success had been a severe shock to his self-esteem. Unable to make a public admission of failure, he vented his ill-feeling in criticism of " these new-fangled notions " which disturbed his complacently conservative nature ; and this activity had made him a burden to his subordinates. Even the sergeant, armoured in unimaginativeness, was beginning to feel that he had had enough.

But on this occasion, relief was at hand. A telephone bell rang and a constable summoned Camlet to the instrument. A short, staccato conversation followed ; then the inspector put down the receiver and dealt out questions and orders to his subordinates.

" Is there a car outside ? . . . Right ! The police surgeon's on leave, isn't he ? Who's his locum ? . . . Allardyce ? He'll do. Ring him up, you. If he's out, follow him up. Tell him to be at Cæsar's Camp as quick as he can manage . . . After that, send an ambulance up there. I want Sergeant Robson and Constable Carter to come with me in the car. Lucky we've had our breakfasts."

Then, in response to a question by the sergeant, he explained matters briefly :

" A man Pirbright's been found dead near Cæsar's Camp. Driver of a Colverdown Dairy van noticed the body as he passed along. Phoned up from the nearest box. That's all I know about it. Carry on. You two, come along with me now."

The morning air was sharp ; and as he drove along,

Camlet began to wonder if it was merely a case of death from exposure. But an objection to this hypothesis presented itself immediately. The inspector knew his district well, and he remembered the man Pirbright well enough. The fellow had a cottage up yonder, where he could find shelter easily. He wasn't a stray tramp who might have lain down by the roadside and died from the cold. Unless, of course, Pirbright had been down at a pub, got drunk, and fell asleep on the way home.

It did not take the car very long to reach Cæsar's Camp, and, as the inspector slowed down, he came in sight of the body, lying on a patch of grass some twenty yards off the unfenced road. Camlet pulled up, ordered his men out, meticulously locked the car, and then the three men moved over to the body. Camlet took out his notebook and made a jotting or two, commenting aloud as he did so, to impress the points on the minds of his subordinates.

" A bit blue in the face," he began, since this was the first sympton he noticed. " Been sick, too. Body's twisted a bit. Cramp, or something like that."

" Mightn't it be strychnine poisoning, sir ? " put in the constable. " I call to mind that once on a time, about six years ago, we had a case of suicide where strychnine was used, out of some vermin-killer, if I remember right, and the body was twisted about a bit, same as this one here."

Camlet shook his head decisively.

" Strychnine makes 'em arch their backs. No sign of that here. Just a general twist-up. The way you go when you get an electric shock."

" Him being sick looks like poison of some sort," opined the sergeant.

" Leave that to the doctor," said Camlet, brusquely. " What we want now is facts. Not guesses. He's fully dressed. Got his boots on. Collar quite loose. Note that in case it's apoplexy. Not likely, with his build, but you never know. Go through his pockets, sergeant. Don't shift him."

Pirbright lay on his back, so Sergeant Robson was able to search the pockets without disturbing the body to any extent.

" Nothing much here," he reported. " A new ten-bob note, two half-crowns, a couple of bob, three of these brass threepenny bits with the corners on, and five pennies. An old pipe and a rubber baccy-pouch, and a half-empty box of lights. Clasp-knife. Stub of a pencil. No nose-rag. No papers except his identity-card. His wrist-watch is going ; hands at 8.57."

" That's two minutes slow," noted the inspector, checking the time by his own watch and making a jotting in his notebook. Then he stood for a moment or two looking down thoughtfully at the body.

" Didn't die peacefully, anyhow," he concluded. " See that tuft of grass in his right hand ? Torn up in his death-throe, obviously. See where it came from—there. Might have been poison. Might have been a fit of some sort. Sudden business, anyhow. Never have wandered this distance from his hut if he'd been in violent pain. Carter, just cast around and see if you can find a trail. He may have been sick on the way here."

The constable obeyed ; but after making a search of the ground, he reported that he could find nothing of the sort.

" Turned sick all of a sudden, then," inferred Camlet. " Well, that side of it's for the doctor. We've no responsibility there. He gives the medical evidence at the inquest."

Camlet knew that he was out of his depth in toxicology and had no intention of touching that side of the matter. It was with some relief that he saw Dr. Allardyce's car appear. The doctor listened without comment to the inspector's account of the case up to date. Then he went over to the body and made a careful examination. When he rose to his feet again, his first words surprised the inspector.

" The Chief Constable will probably want to see that body before it's touched. Can you get hold of him as quick as possible ? "

" He's staying with Mr. Wendover at the Grange, just now," Camlet pointed out. "I'll send Carter here down in the car to get him on the phone, if you like, Doctor. But what's he to say ? "

" Say it's important, of course," retorted Allardyce sharply. " And say I want him to come. Tell him it's a case of the rabbits, over again."

To the inspector, this sounded like some mysterious password, but he had no desire to betray his bewilderment before his subordinates.

" Very good, sir. Heard that, Carter ? Take the car. Here's the key. Phone that message to Sir Clinton at Talgarth Grange. Get back here as quick as you can."

When the constable had gone, Camlet expected some enlightenment from the doctor ; but at his first question, Allardyce cut him short with a certain lack of courtesy.

" I'll wait for Sir Clinton," he said, abruptly. " There's no point in telling the same story twice, is there ? "

" Suppose there isn't," admitted Camlet, glumly.

It was evident that the doctor and the Chief Constable shared some information about this case ; and Camlet disliked the feeling of being left out in the cold. He assumed an air of dignified aloofness ; but it obviously failed to impress Allardyce, who filled in the time of waiting by casting about the ground, apparently in search of something. The inspector was glad when Sir Clinton's car appeared. Wendover accompanied the Chief Constable. Camlet hastened to meet them and got in his oar first by making a concise report of the case, so far as he knew about it. He had hardly finished before Allardyce came up to them.

" This is a rum business," said the doctor, without wasting words on preliminaries. " You remember those rabbits I told you about ? This man's case seems on all fours with that affair."

" What rabbits ? " demanded the inspector, breaking in.

" Some rabbits I found lying about here, dead, a while ago," said Allardyce, curtly.

" By the way," Wendover interjected in his turn, " it crossed my mind that we found other rabbits dead up here. You remember, Clinton, that evening when I brought you up to look at the archæologist's find ? Young Noel East told us he'd found some rabbits killed by the blast of that bomb."

" It doesn't seem a healthy spot for rabbits," said Sir Clinton, dryly. " But now we've something more important to worry us than a bunny or two. What do you make of it ? " he demanded, turning to the doctor.

Allardyce shrugged his shoulders as though giving up the problem.

" Too soon to say," he declared. " It might, of course, be poison. His pupils are dilated a bit. We can't be sure until after a P.M. If it is poison, then it must have been a heavy dose, I think. But, judging from the rabbits, I'm quite prepared to find no poison."

" You've examined him ? " asked the Chief Constable. " Can you make a guess at the time of death ? "

" The temperature of the body's about 60 deg. Fahrenheit," answered Allardyce. " That would put the death back ten or twelve hours, roughly. It can't have been earlier than that."

" Why not ? " demanded the inspector, anxious to assert himself.

" Because I saw him alive at about half-past nine last night," retorted the doctor.

" Oh, indeed ? " said Camlet. ". You didn't tell me tha t."

" I said I preferred to tell the story once and for all," rejoined Allardyce, rather impatiently.

" And how did you come to see him ? " persisted the inspector.

" I went up to his hut to pay him for some rabbits he'd supplied to me."

" Rabbits are out of season . . ." began the inspector.

" I didn't eat them, if that's what's worrying you. I needed them for some experiments," explained Allardyce, acidly.

" Experiments ? " echoed Camlet, suspiciously. " You need a vivisection licence for experiments on animals. Have you got one ? "

Allardyce was obviously growing impatient under this examination.

" The experiment I made was to hold them up by the ears and hit them on the back of the neck," he said, tartly. " Does one need a licence for that ? "

" Oh, killing 'em ? " said Camlet, crestfallen. " No, that isn't vivisection."

But he studiously avoided any form of apology.

" Sir Clinton knows all about it," said Allardyce.

The inspector nodded an acknowledgment of this ; but evidently he was far from satisfied.

" You were paying this man Pirbright for these rabbits ? " he went on. " How did you pay him ? I mean, how much did they cost and what money did you give him ? "

Allardyce considered for a moment, as though consulting his memory.

" I paid him half a crown apiece. Six rabbits. Fifteen shillings. I was at the bank this morning, drawing some money, pound and ten shilling notes and some silver. I gave Pirbright a ten-shilling note and two half-crowns. One of the half-crowns was a split new one, 1942 date. The ten-shilling note came from this batch "—he pulled out his note-case and extracted a small wad of notes which he examined—" and as they're new notes and are numbered consecutively, it ought to be possible to tell the number of the note I gave Pirbright. Look over the bundle for yourself."

He handed the notes to the inspector who, after examining them, took from his pocket the envelope in which he had stowed the money found in Pirbright's possession.

" That seems to tally," he admitted, handing back Allardyce's notes. " The ten-bob note that Pirbright had in his pocket belongs to your series. And one of the half-crowns is a 1942 one. You saw Pirbright alive at half-past nine last night, Doctor. Was he all right, then?"

"In perfect health and spirits, so far as I can judge," said Allardyce. "When I dropped in, he was playing his fiddle. He played not badly," he explained, turning to the Chief Constable, "mainly by ear, though he could read music if he was put to it."

The inspector had no musical leanings.

"When did you get to Pirbright's hut?" he demanded.

"About a quarter past nine last night. There, or thereabouts. I didn't look at my watch. And I must have left him again about a quarter to ten at the latest."

"Did he go with you to your car?" asked Wendover.

Allardyce shook his head.

"No, I left him at his door. I heard him start on his fiddling again as I was moving away."

"And he was quite well then, and now he's dead," remarked Camlet, irrelevantly. "There wasn't anyone in the hut with him when you were there?"

"No, nobody. And he wasn't expecting anyone. He happened to mention that, because he pressed me to stay a bit longer."

"Ah! And you met nobody about? Nobody passed you as you went down the path to your car?"

"No, nobody," Allardyce assured him, with an amused smile.

"A rum affair," said the inspector, discontentedly.

It exasperated him to find a second mystery on his hands before he had even made a fair start in clearing up the Deverell affair. And his annoyance was deepened by a feeling that he had been left out of something which the other three shared between them. This last grievance, however, was removed by the Chief Constable who had noted his subordinate's vexation.

"I think you'd better tell Inspector Camlet about these dead rabbits, Doctor," he suggested. "He must be rather in the dark about them."

"Very well," said Allardyce, equably. "Not that it helps much, so far as I can see. This man Ashmun, Inspector, claims to have discovered something fresh. One night, when I was at his house, he played some peculiar chords on a violin and talked a lot of stuff. Then he brought me up here, and I found some rabbits lying about, dead. I took them home and examined them. I could find no reason for their deaths, which must have coincided, more or less, with Ashmun's experiment. Pirbright seems to have died in much the same way as the rabbits, so far as I can see. That's all I know about the matter. Quite likely the whole thing's just coincidence. You can take the Mumbo-Jumbo explanation if you like and suppose that Ashmun's able to cast spells. I won't agree with you if you do."

Inspector Camlet snorted contemptuously at the mere suggestion of occult affairs.

" I've no use for that kind of rubbish," he declared.

Sir Clinton had been gazing down the road.

" Here's the ambulance coming," he interrupted. " Probably the photographer's inside with his kit. You can get the body removed to the mortuary, Inspector, once the pictures have been taken. And preserve things for analysis, of course. He's evidently been very sick, and it may be a poisoning case for all one knows. Our pathologist will do the P.M. I'll ring him up about it, later on. Meanwhile, I've seen all I want to see here. Let's go over to Pirbright's hut and have a look round."

CHAPTER VI   *The Crosier*

PIRBRIGHT'S ABODE WAS A DECREPIT, TWO-ROOMED ERECTION which had been allowed to fall into disrepair through shiftlessness. One of the window panes was broken and had been mended by pasting a sheet of brown paper over the remaining glass. Adjoining the building was a netted hen-run in which a few scrawny fowls clucked and scratched disconsolately, and beyond was an untidy potato-patch, where a rusty fork stood planted in the ground as the owner had left it. Sir Clinton pushed open the door of the hut, and his companions followed him inside.

" A nice pig-sty," commented Camlet disgustedly, as he glanced about him.

Everything bespoke the slovenliness of the owner. Unwashed cups, plates, and pans lay about awaiting attention. A dish-tub full of soapy water stood in one corner. In another was a bag of feeding-stuff for the fowls, the contents of which had leaked over the floor. Higgledy-piggledy on the shelves were tins, coils of twine, ferret muzzles, cardboard boxes, dirty knives and forks, nets, and potatoes. A milk-bottle with some dregs of sour milk stood beside a half-finished loaf, and the remnants of some butter on a piece of paper. In a home-made ferret-hutch, the occupants wandered restlessly, their pink eyes following the movements of the new-comers with a hostile scrutiny. From nails on the wall depended a well-worn violin and its bow. The table in the centre of the room was cleared, except for a whisky bottle and one cup.

Sir Clinton stepped into the adjoining bedroom, glanced at the untidy, unmade bed, and then returned to the living-room. The whisky bottle caught his eye, and he examined it carefully without touching it. Bending down, he recovered from the floor under the table a rusty cork-screw, bearing the cork of the bottle ; and this he inspected attentively before laying it down on the table.

" Pirbright did himself fairly well," he said. " He didn't look affluent, and yet he could afford whisky at something over a pound a bottle. Was he much of a drinker ? " he asked, turning to Allardyce.

The doctor shook his head.

" Not that I ever noticed, when I had him through my hands," he replied, after a slight hesitation. " I wouldn't call him a steady drinker, if that's what you mean. Beer would be his line, not spirits. I never saw a whisky bottle in this place before. Too dear, nowadays, for one thing. And this is ' Black Swan,' too. I keep that myself, but only for special occasions."

Sir Clinton glanced again at the bottle and cork on the table.

" It's a good brand," he agreed. " But here's a queer point. Nowadays, ' Black Swan ' bottles are closed with a screw cap and not with a cork. You don't need a cork-screw. One of the minor changes brought in by the war. On the face of it, this bottle wasn't bought lately. And yet Pirbright was hardly the man to lay down a cellar. He lived from hand-to-mouth, by the look of the premises. Let's have a look about and see if we can find any more liquor."

They all joined in searching the hut, but they found nothing. Sir Clinton returned to the table and examined the level of the whisky in the bottle, taking care not to touch the glass as he did so.

" He's got away with at least four double whiskies since he opened the bottle—rather more than that, if anything," he pointed out. " And he opened it to-night ; there's the metal foil that he tore off it, lying on the floor beside his chair."

" Poor devil ! " said Wendover, sympathetically. " He wasn't a millionaire. The cost of four double whiskies amounts to something like riotous living, by his standards."

" A short life and a gay one ? " interjected Camlet, who had his sinister moments. " Sure it wasn't suicide, doctor ? But no ! He'd have finished the bottle, if that was his game."

" You'll try the bottle and the cork-screw for finger-prints," said Sir Clinton to the inspector. " And that cup, also. I don't expect you'll find anything but his own prints on them, but one may as well be thorough. And you'd better keep the dregs in the cup and the whisky in the bottle, in case we want to have them analysed. By the way," he added, turning to the doctor, " had he started on this bottle at the time you came to pay him for your rabbits ? "

" No. I didn't see either bottle or cup then. He was playing his fiddle to pass the time."

Sir Clinton glanced at the violin and then, walking across to it, plucked the strings in turn.

" The E string's flat," he pointed out, but without seeming to attach much importance to the point. " Now suppose we look around and see if anything suggests itself."

Allardyce glanced at his watch.

" About time I was going," he said, half apologetically. " I've got a patient I ought to look up. You don't need me any longer ? I'll let you have a written report later in the day."

The Chief Constable raised no objection, and the doctor took himself off. When he had gone, Sir Clinton turned to the inspector with further instructions.

" You'll need to arrange to have these fowls looked after, and the ferrets, also. You might throw out some food to the birds now, just to keep them going."

He set an example by taking a couple of handfuls from the bag of feeding-stuff and going out to the chicken-run. When he had scattered the grain, his eye was caught by a spade which stood propped against the end of the enclosure, and he paused to examine it.

" Look here, Inspector ! Would you say that this earth on the blade is fairly fresh ? " he asked.

Camlet examined the tool in his turn and tried the soil with his finger.

" It's moist, sir, certainly. Might be the dew, though. Likely he was digging up some potatoes last night."

Sir Clinton gave a nod towards the potato-patch.

" He used a potato-fork for that," he pointed out. " This

spade must have been used for something else, I think. Let's have a look round and see what he's been digging up."

Camlet obviously regarded this as a pure waste of time, but he made no overt objection, and they began to search the vicinity for signs of disturbance. In a very few minutes, they discovered some freshly-turned earth, an area about a yard square in one corner of the vegetable patch.

"Just see if there's anything fit to dig with," Sir Clinton directed. "No, not that spade. We may want to try its handle for finger-prints. See if you can get something else."

Camlet, after a short hunt, discovered a worn-out spade stowed away in a lean-to shed.

"That'll do," said the Chief Constable. "Now suppose you dig up this place, gently. Likely enough we shall find nothing, but it's well to make sure."

The inspector's face showed that he regarded this task as futile, and he began to dig very gingerly. But before he had lifted a dozen spadefuls of earth, his tool struck something solid.

"There's something here, sir!"

"Go gently, then . . . Ah! This is interesting."

There was a gleam of gold amongst the loose earth. Camlet knelt down and began to grub with his hands, getting a grip on the object. Then with a good tug, he lifted it from the cavity.

"The crosier!" exclaimed Wendover, as the object came in view.

"That's it, right enough!" confirmed Camlet, shaking it free from adherent earth. "Never expected to see *that* again. Thought it was melted down, long ago. Takes a load off my mind, sir, that does."

"Put it down and try again," directed Sir Clinton.

Camlet laid down the crosier and resumed his excavation. One by one, the various objects appeared which had vanished from Deverell's house on the night of the incendiary bomb.

"That's the lot, sir. All that's missing," the inspector reported as he brought up the last article. "Did you guess they were here?"

"Not I," admitted the Chief Constable, frankly. "I was merely curious to know why the spade had been used."

Camlet stuck his spade into the soil and stood back.

"Well, I'm glad to see the end of that business, sir," he declared. "I began to think we'd never get to the bottom of it. Very worrying. Now we know where we are."

"Do we?" queried Sir Clinton, artlessly. "And where are we?"

"Plain as a pikestaff, sir," declared Camlet in obvious surprise at the Chief Constable's obtuseness. "This fellow Pirbright was loafing around when that archæological lot were digging at Cæsar's Camp. He saw all the stuff laid out. Anyone could, that evening. I came up myself out of curiosity. Saw Pirbright staring at it, with all the rest. Everybody was talking about what was to be done with it. Into the bank strong-room, first of all. Then Deverell was to get it on loan, bit by bit. I heard all that. Pirbright would hear it, too. Couldn't miss it."

"That's quite probable," admitted Sir Clinton. "And then?"

"Gold's the easiest thing to sell, sir, nowadays. No questions asked. Pirbright would know that as well as the next man. Obviously he saw his chance. Do a bit of looting under cover of the next raid whenever it came. Bit of luck for him that Jerry came over on a night when Deverell had the biggest article of the lot out of the bank. Anyhow, he got away with the stuff. Brought it up here and cached it. Safe as houses. No one would suspect him, specially. Never thought of him, myself. And I've thought enough about it, lately, I can tell you. All he had to do was to wait a bit till the hunt cooled off. Then melt it up and sell it. An ounce or two at a time. By post, to different dealers in other towns, most likely. That would be his idea."

"I don't say you're wrong, Inspector," conceded Sir Clinton, blandly. "But that doesn't mean that you're right, of course. And your explanation doesn't go far enough, unless you're assuming that Pirbright died suddenly of a sharp attack of conscience. It's not a fatal disease, so far as I know, unless it leads to suicide. You're not going to suggest that he died of alcoholic poisoning after four double whiskies, are you?"

"No, sir," protested the inspector. "I never suggested that."

"No more you did," admitted the Chief Constable. "But you covered the case at a hand-gallop, and perhaps I got a bit confused in trying to take it in, in such a hurry. Let's go slower; and take it step by step. We needn't quarrel over the likelihood that Pirbright knew about Deverell having some of the gold out for examination. I admit all that part. Let's take your assumptions up at that point. You say that Pirbright made up his mind to steal the gold. That's not impossible; though you haven't proved it."

"What more proof do you want, sir?" rejoined Camlet.

" Here's the gold in front of us. Dug up in Pirbright's ground. How did it get here, if he didn't steal it ? "

" We haven't got that length, yet," objected Sir Clinton. " I may have a word or two to say about it when we do reach it. Stick to the theft for the present. How do you picture it ? "

" This way, sir. Pirbright knew his best chance was during a raid. Everything a bit in confusion, then. People have plenty to think about without bothering about what other people are doing. So I expect he hung about Deverell's house, night after night. Waiting for Jerry to pay us another visit. When the planes came over, I guess he hammered on Deverell's front door. Asked for shelter. Deverell would let him in. He'd know him. He'd seen him up here, when they were digging. You said yourself that the thief was someone Deverell knew."

" I said he *might* have been," corrected Sir Clinton.

" Well, it fits, anyhow, sir. Deverell let him in. Down came the incendiary and killed Deverell. Pirbright had nothing to do but pick up the gold and get off the premises. He certainly got away before Betty Brown turned up. That's my notion of how it happened. Or are you suggesting that Pirbright knocked Deverell on the head himself ? "

" I shouldn't care to say that," said Sir Clinton, " until we know more about it. Now let's take the next stage. What did Pirbright do—according to you—once he'd got the gold ? "

" Brought it up here, of course," declared the inspector. " And buried it where we found it ourselves. Plain as a pike-staff, that is."

" Ah ! " said the Chief Constable, in a reflective tone. " We've had a good spell of dry weather lately. And yesterday afternoon a very heavy shower came down and lasted for a while. I'm a great believer in practical demon-strations, Inspector, especially when someone else supplies the energy. Would you mind taking that spade again and digging another hole . . . over here, so as not to mix it up with the old one ? Thank you. Now I want you to dig vertically, so as to show how deep the wetting has gone. . . . That'll do, thanks. Now if you glance at that exposed face you'll see that the rain didn't penetrate far into the ground. Below about six inches depth the soil is bone dry. Now take a look at the soil adhering to the crosier. A bit moist, in parts, isn't it ? Obviously, when the crosier was buried, some of the top-dressing of wet soil get shovelled in to the hole and mixed up with the lower bone-dry stratum. Whence I infer that the burying was done not earlier than yesterday evening, after the rain stopped. Simple, yet correct, I believe. Now, how do you fit *that* into your hypothesis ? "

." It doesn't seem to fit," admittedly Camlet, rather crest-fallen. " But how did you come to think of it, sir ? "

" I looked at the soil on the crosier when you dug it up. Some of it seemed stickier than it had any reason to be, if the burying dated back for a week or more."

" Seems a bit funny, sir. This crosier disappeared from Deverell's house quite a while ago. You say it was buried here last night. Where's it been between-times ? "

" Somewhere else, obviously," said Sir Clinton. " That's all I can tell you. Now it's my turn to ask questions, Inspector. Let's turn to what happened in this hut last night. What's your explanation of Pirbright's sudden plunge into the joys of alcohol ? "

" I really can't say, sir. I suppose he felt so inclined."

" And he was so fortunate as to have a good brand of highly-taxed whisky ready to hand for his carouse, was he ? "

" Obviously he was, sir. The bottle's there to prove it."

" The cork and the foil prove that it's the kind of bottle one can't buy nowadays. He must have been keeping it in reserve for quite a while then ? Extraordinary restraint for a man of his type. Can you suggest why he selected last night, specially, for a spree ? "

" No, sir, I can't," said the inspector in a tone of slight exasperation.

" Neither can I," confessed the Chief Constable, un-expectedly. " But one can always make a guess, for what it's worth. Suppose we add another fact, first. Come back into the hut."

He led them into the living-room, went over to a shelf, and gently lifted an inverted cup which stood there. On the wood of the shelf was a ring of moisture left by the rim of the cup.

" I noticed that when we were hunting through the place before," Sir Clinton explained. " I noticed also that Pir-bright hadn't a glass in his stock. He did all his drinking out of cups. Probably he'd smashed any tumblers he had, and never troubled to replace them. He was a slovenly character at the best, you know."

The inspector had been thinking swiftly.

" I see what you're after, sir," he declared. " You say

there were two men in this drinking last night. Pirbright's cup's on the table. This one's been washed and put back on the shelf."

" To be strictly accurate, Inspector, I said nothing of the sort. All I *am* prepared to say is that this cup seems to suggest something."

" Quite so, sir. One thing it suggests to me, then, is that two men could easily tackle four double whiskies in a short time. And it *was* a short time. Dr. Allardyce left here at a quarter to ten. He told us Pirbright might have been dead by eleven o'clock, if not earlier. Pirbright walked to Cæsar's Camp before he died. Quarter of an hour for that. Say he started from here at a quarter to eleven. That means, at the outside, an hour for the whisky-drinking, supposing it started immediately after Dr. Allardyce left here. But it didn't. The doctor saw nobody about. So he said. And he saw no whisky while he was here. So he said. Now I see why this wet cup was suggestive, sir. It is suggestive. Very."

" Then perhaps the bottle of whisky may suggest something else," prompted the Chief Constable.

" It does, sir, now you mention it. It suggests to me that this visitor brought it with him."

" That's not impossible," admitted Sir Clinton.

" And that suggests the kind of visitor he was," went on Camlet. " Somebody of a different sort from Pirbright. Somebody who can afford a good brand of whisky. And somebody who keeps plenty of whisky in stock. Not a man who buys it a bottle at a time. The cork and the foil point to that, don't they ? In fact, sir, somebody like Dr. Allardyce, who told us he drinks this very brand of whisky."

" Dr. Allardyce would have told us if he'd made a present of whisky to Pirbright," interrupted Wendover, sharply. " You're not suggesting that he had anything to do with Pirbright's death, are you ? "

Camlet's face took on a rather mulish expression.

" I'm like Sir Clinton, here," he retorted. "I'm not suggesting anything. I only said the man who was here last night was better-class, with a taste in whisky like the doctor's. That's merely descriptive. Not suggestive."

" It sounded like an innuendo," said Wendover, bluntly. " I'd be more careful of what you say, if I were you, Inspector."

" I'll bear it in mind," said Camlet.

His tone conveyed another meaning, for it implied : " Thank you for nothing," very plainly indeed. Wendover ignored this. Defending an absent man was one thing; entering into a squabble with the inspector on a personal matter was something quite different, and was outside the Squire's code. After all, he reflected, it was Camlet's trade to suspect anyone, without fear or favour. With a little effort, Wendover recovered control of his temper.

"What do you make of it all, seriously?" he asked, turning to the Chief Constable.

"Not much," admitted Sir Clinton, frankly.

He took his case from his pocket, lit a cigarette, sat down on a corner of the table, after dusting it fastidiously, and then continued :

"First of all, it was common knowledge that Deverell had part of that treasure-trove at his house. There was no secret about it. It's a fact that a theft took place at the time when he had one of the most valuable items—that crosier—in his charge ; but I don't lay much stress on that, in view of what happened later. We'll come to that point shortly ; no need to elaborate it now. All I'm implying is that it's not of much use inquiring who actually knew that the crosier was in his house on that particular night. Any number of people must have known it was there. Deverell was a fussy little man, ready to talk ; and he probably bored quite a lot of people by chattering about what he was doing and how he was getting on with his examination of the stuff. That's my reading of him, based on a very brief acquaintance."

"He *was* rather full of himself and his doings," Wendover admitted. "I found him something of a bore at times, poor fellow."

"My opinion, for what it's worth, is that the air raid was what dated the theft. Everyone knows what the Germans are after : the magneto factory. They'll go on raiding until they knock it out. Anyone could forecast that fresh raids were coming. All one had to do was to wait and keep a watch on Deverell's house so as to be ready to take advantage of the next *Luftwaffe* visit. As you said, Inspector, an air raid causes enough confusion to cover up a lot of things. On the other hand, it's not an ideal occasion for burglary. Once the sirens go, most people are astir, going on duty or else taking shelter. A burglar would have a poor chance in such conditions. Especially in Deverell's house. He had no special shelter to retire into. I noticed that when I visited the villa. He wouldn't be tucked away under cover, leaving the coast clear for burglars. He'd be wandering about the house, looking for incendiaries, or else he'd be sitting under the stairs."

" His body was actually beside the stairs when we found it, sir," the inspector reminded him. " But that doesn't prove much."

" No, it doesn't," admitted Sir Clinton. " But now let's turn to Deverell's death and take it along with the theft. The affair was either accidental or else planned. If it was accidental, you have to assume that some bad hat chanced to be passing when the bomb fell and killed Deverell, and that then this bad hat discovered the gold and made off with it. It's possible, but it lands you in all sorts of complications before you can work the tale up to the present moment, with the gold in the garden outside."

" The bad hat may have been Pirbright, sir," suggested Camlet. " That would account for the gold being buried on his ground."

" But then you've got to explain Pirbright's death. And you've also got to account for the gold being buried outside only last night," countered the Chief Constable. " I just don't see it so. It's much easier to assume that the whole thing was planned in advance. Somebody meant to steal the gold and waited for the opportunity furnished by a raid. This person got into the villa as a refugee, knocked Deverell on the head, ignited an incendiary to cover up the murder, if possible, and then got away with the crosier and the other things. If the refugee was someone whom Deverell knew by sight, then the murder would be essential to the intruder's safety. Now that's one set of possibilities. We've based them on the idea that the theft was the keystone of the affair. But there's always the chance that the thing was a murder first of all, and that the theft was merely thrown in to obscure the trail."

" But then you'd need some motive for a murder, sir," the inspector objected. " Where's your motive? Deverell wasn't known to have enemies. Not one. We went through his papers. Not a sign of anything of the sort. He was just a fussy little man. No fortune. No expectations from any quarter that would make murder worth while. The coroner's jury returned a verdict in accordance with the medical evidence. I'd have done the same if I'd been one of them. Put theft as the object, and you've got a motive straight away. If you're giving me the choice, then I say the gold was the thing."

" Very well," said the Chief Constable. " I'm quite

content to leave Deverell's death alone, until we know more about it. I merely wanted to clear my own mind. Now let's turn to the gold, and see what evidence we have about it. First of all, the bank officials tell us that they handed it over to Deverell, and they produce his receipt. Next, Dr. Allardyce called at Deverell's house on the night of that raid, and he testifies that he saw the crosier and other things on Deverell's table when he was leaving the villa. When he was recalled to the house, he tells us, he noticed that the whole lot was gone. And you searched the premises shortly afterwards, Inspector, and found no trace of the gold. There seems no doubt that it disappeared during the raid. Deverell didn't remove it. Therefore somebody else collared it and took it away."

"Q.E.D.," said Wendover, with a smile. "Almost Euclidian, that effort of yours. But how did the thief get it away unnoticed? Even in a raid, people would notice a man wandering about with a gold crosier under his arm and his pockets bulging with gold ornaments."

"What are suit-cases for?" retorted Sir Clinton. "A good many people keep suit-cases handy, ready-packed with a change of clothes, food-cards, valuable papers, and such like things, just in case of losing their house in a raid. A man with a suit-case walking towards a street-shelter wouldn't be likely to rouse suspicion. People would say he was a fool for not dumping his suit-case with a neighbour before the raid started; but that would be all. And if you don't like the suit-case notion, I'll give you another. The stuff might have been removed in a car. In a raid, there are plenty of cars about: doctors, Casualty Service, W.V.S., and what not. No one would notice a car specially. There's no difficulty in suggesting ways of getting the stuff shifted inconspicuously. The real problem is, where it went to."

With a muttered word of apology, the inspector slipped into Pirbright's bedroom for a moment. When he returned, there was unmistakable satisfaction on his face.

"No suit-case here, sir," he reported. "Nor anything like one. And Pirbright had no car."

"Don't stop short, just when your story gets interesting," said the Chief Constable in mock reproach. "Finish up in Euclid's style. 'Therefore, Pirbright did not bring the gold here in either a suit-case or a car. Q.E.D.' I never supposed that he did. As a matter of plain fact, now, can you give me a scrap of proof that Pirbright was the man who got into Deverell's house that night? If so, fork it out and put me out of suspense. I'd very much like to know the name of the thief—and possibly murderer."

"Well, sir," rejoined the inspector, "if Pirbright didn't steal the gold, how came it to be buried in his back-yard?"

"That's another thing I'd like to be sure about," retorted the Chief Constable. "It's not beyond conjecture, however, if you look at the facts. But I won't spoil the pleasure you'll get by exercising your acumen on it. Let's pass on to the next bit of the problem. Who was this visitor who seems to have called on Pirbright last night?"

"We don't know his name," said Wendover, "but we do know some things about him."

"Such as?" queried Sir Clinton, with an air of interest.

Wendover ticked off the points on his fingers as he replied.

"I've no doubt he brought that bottle of 'Black Swan' with him; therefore he probably was—as the inspector said—a better-class person than his host. He drank with Pirbright; the cup shows that. Pirbright died very soon afterwards; which suggests that he was poisoned. If it was a case of poisoning, I see only one motive: to shut Pirbright's mouth about something. Now the gold was buried here only yesterday evening, and Pirbright died last night. Is it possible that, after the Deverell affair, the gold was cached somewhere and lay hidden for a while. Then Pirbright discovered it somehow, dug it up, and re-buried it outside here, last night. Something in the original cache may have put him on the track of the man who buried the stuff there, and he may have tried to blackmail him straight off. Hence the need for shutting Pirbright's mouth as soon as possible."

"Excellent," declared Sir Clinton, cheerfully. "In fact, we know all about it, barring about six details. *Exempli gratia*, the name of the original thief; the place where the gold was first cached; how Pirbright came across it; the clue which put him on the track of the thief; the agency which brought about Pirbright's death; and, finally, the reason why the thief didn't dig up the gold again and bury it somewhere else for safety, after disposing of Pirbright. It seems quite a lot. But don't let's get discouraged. Suppose we start with Pirbright's death, and put it alongside that story of Dr. Allardyce about the rabbits. The symptoms in both cases seem to be similar, and Allardyce found no poison in the rabbits."

"Dr. Allardyce is hardly an expert, sir," pointed out Camlet. "I wouldn't put too much weight on that."

"Admitted," agreed Sir Clinton at once. "We'd better

wait to hear what our pathologist makes of Pirbright's case. But something else might be important. In the rabbit case, Mr. Jehudi Ashmun was the moving spirit—or claimed to be that. I wonder what he was doing last night between 9.30 and 10.30 p.m."

" I can tell you that, sir," said the inspector, unexpectedly. " He lost a key-ring with some keys on it, yesterday. At about a quarter to ten last night, he rang up our station. We were able to tell him the keys had been found. He had a metal tag on his ring. The Amicable Key Insurance Register people hand them out in return for a small subscription. The tag tells the finder he'll get five bob by handing in the keys to the police. The number on the tag tells us who the keys belong to. That nigger dropped his keys in Prince's Street. A youngster found them. Handed them in to us. We'd looked up the number on the tag and got the nigger's address. In fact, a constable had gone off with them to restore them to the owner, just a few minutes before the nigger rang us up. He called at Ashmun's house —that would be about 10.15 p.m.—and delivered the key-ring to the nigger personally. He was kept waiting a few minutes, our man I mean. The maid told him the nigger was engaged with friends. A party of some sort, our man thought, by the sounds when Ashmun opened the drawing-room door and came out to see him. That pins down Ashmun to his house between 9.45 and 10.15 p.m., which was about the time when Pirbright died up here. We could find out more, easy enough. The maid could tell us the names of people who were at the spree. They'd tell us if Ashmun had any chance of getting here. He could hardly leave guests for half an hour or more."

" He didn't need to leave his house when the rabbits died," Wendover pointed out.

" You're evidently hankering after Mumbo-Jumbo," said Sir Clinton, with a smile. " But if Ashmun killed Pirbright by loosing some mysterious Force on him, why wasn't the visitor extinguished simultaneously? That seems to demand an explanation. But perhaps the visitor had a cantrip or a mascot to ward off the effects of this Force. One never knows. Still, one's entitled to one's own opinion about mysterious Forces and all that sort of business. Have it your own way, if you wish. In the meanwhile, Inspector, you might look into the sordid matter of finger-prints on that spade-handle and checking up Mr. Ashmun's alibi. I don't suppose you'll catch much ; but one may as well have certainty."

INSPECTOR CAMLET SAT DOWN BEFORE THE OFFICE TYPE-
writer with a sigh. He had never mastered touch-typing,
but worked the machine on what he termed the " peek and
peck " system. For letter-writing, this method served his
turn well enough. When his work involved the copying of
documents, however, he found " peek and peck " a weari-
some operation, with its continual shifting of his eyes from
the keyboard to the paper from which he was transcribing.
And this morning he saw himself faced by a considerable
amount of copying.

He sighed again, inserted paper and carbons into his
machine, and then, to put off the evil moment a little longer,
filled and lit his pipe. He always thought more clearly
when he was smoking. After filling in the usual filing refer-
ences at the head of the paper, he typed a heading : " *For
the Attention of the Coroner. Re Death of Anthony Gainford.*"
Then he sat back in his chair, pulled at his pipe, and pondered over his opening sentence ; for, like many other authors,
he found that the initial sentence cost him more trouble than
a dozen others. At last he forced himself to begin.

" At 11 a.m. on June 30th, I was rung up by Dr. F.
Allardyce, who informed me that Anthony Gainford, residing
at ' Longcroft,' Maybury Gardens, had died during the
previous night, apparently through gas poisoning. Dr.
Allardyce was not prepared to give a certificate, but thought
it was a matter for the coroner. I went to the house at
once. The household consisted of the householder, Kenneth
Felden, the deceased Anthony Gainford, his brother Derek
Gainford, and a housekeeper, Mrs. Miriam Doggett. I
examined the body of Anthony Gainford and summoned
Dr. Berkeley Greenholme to inspect it. I then took the
following statements."

Statement made by Kenneth Felden.

" I am an analytical chemist, and also an Air Raid
Warden. I reside at ' Longcroft,' Maybury Gardens. On
June 29th, the other inmates of my house were Anthony
Gainford, Derek Gainford, and my housekeeper, Mrs.
Miriam Doggett. The two Gainfords are my cousins. The
reason for their sharing my house was that Anthony Gainford

was addicted to alcohol and his brother Derek, suffering severely from asthma, was unable to supervise him properly. Derek Gainford proposed that, as I had some influence with Anthony, the two of them should live with me ; and to this I agreed. They have resided at ' Longcroft ' for some years now.

" On June 29th I gave a small dinner-party to celebrate the engagement of my cousin, Miss Daphne Stanway, to Dr. Frank Allardyce. The people present at this dinner were : myself, the Gainford brothers, Dr. Allardyce, Miss Stanway, Miss Ione Herongate, Miss Olive Belmont, and Mrs. Jenner.

" Anthony Gainford was in ordinary health that day, except for a cold in the head. He had taken a fair amount of alcohol during the day but was not drunk, otherwise I should not have allowed him to be there. He promised me to be careful while guests were present. He drank a fair amount of alcohol during dinner, but he could stand a good deal without showing its effect. He was in good spirits, but not unduly excited.

" During dinner, Derek Gainford had a severe asthmatic attack. Dr. Allardyce went upstairs and brought down some amyl nitrite capsules from Derek's bedroom, which relieved the spasms, so that Gainford became normal again. Dr. Allardyce knew where to find the capsules, as he is the doctor employed by the Gainfords, and knows his way about the premises.

" After dinner, we went into the drawing-room and began to play bridge. About 10.45 p.m. my telephone rang, and I was warned of an impending raid. I went back to the drawing-room and informed my guests. Dr. Allardyce is in the Casualty Service, and he set off at once in his car to get to his post. The other guests, after consultation, decided to get home if possible before the raid began. We have no special shelter accommodation in my house. I said good night to my guests, and went upstairs to change into uniform. While I was dressing, I heard Anthony Gainford going into his bedroom and slamming the door behind him.

" He usually went to bed fairly early and, after undressing, he invariably took a night-cap : a hot whisky which he believed helped him to sleep better. Originally, we let him have a decanter in his room, but that tempted him to take too much. Nowadays, we arrange that a half-tumbler of whisky is left on his bed-table, along with a thermos flask of hot water. The housekeeper leaves this at the time she makes down the beds. At times, when he was unable to sleep, he used to get up during the night, put on a dressing-gown, and sit by the gas fire until he felt drowsier.

" Shortly after hearing him slam his bedroom door, I went downstairs again to go on duty. Our visitors had gone by that time. Derek Gainford and the housekeeper were sitting in the safest corner of the hall. Derek Gainford was reading a novel and Mrs. Doggett was knitting. I said good night to them and went out.

" As I reached the garden gate, a bomb fell and exploded not far away. This, I think, was the bomb which dropped in Hansler Road. It was out of my district, so it was no affair of mine. I spent the rest of the raid on patrol, reporting at intervals at the post at the end of Maybury Gardens. When the All Clear sounded, I went round the gardens in my area, to see if any time-bombs had fallen unnoticed. Finding nothing, I returned home and went to bed. Derek Gainford and Mrs. Doggett had gone to their rooms before I got in.

" Next morning, on coming down to breakfast, at 8 a.m., I rang up the three ladies and ascertained that they had got home safely. While I was doing this, my housekeeper came to tell me that she had taken up Anthony Gainford's breakfast tray. He invariably breakfasted in bed. She had knocked several times at his door, and had done her best to attract his attention, without getting any response. I went up to his room and found him in bed. I examined him and found him dead. The room smelt of gas, and I found the tap of the gas fire full on. I turned it off and opened the windows which he always kept shut, and for-bade anyone to enter the room. Then I went downstairs and rang up Dr. Allardyce, who came along immediately. He diagnosed gas poisoning and advised me to ring up the police, which I then did.

" (*Signed*) KENNETH FELDEN."

Inspector Camlet adjusted fresh paper in his machine, opened a fresh section of his notebook, sighed involuntarily, and fell again to his " peek and peck " process.

Statement made by Derek Gainford.

" I am of independent means and have no occupation. The deceased man was my brother." (Here follow some particulars about the dinner-party and the guests, which merely confirm the corresponding section of Kenneth Felden's statement.) "When dressing for dinner, I forgot to transfer the capsules of amyl nitrite which I use in acute attacks of asthma. At dinner, I had a very severe attack of my trouble. Dr. Allardyce, finding that I had no capsule at hand, ran upstairs to my bedroom and brought down a couple which served to relieve me. I was very sorry to disturb the dinner-party by my unfortunate fit, which must have been very distressing to witnesses, since it was an extremely severe one. Dr. Allardyce spoke to me about my carelessness in forgetting my capsules, and warned me that such neglect might have dangerous consequences.

"During the evening, my brother behaved well. He was in a good frame of mind and made a number of jokes, though some of them were not quite suitable for the company, I thought. He was far from intoxicated, even after dinner, as we had taken pains to see that he was kept within limits in his drinking. He was quite able to play a moderate game of bridge afterwards. I have never heard him, at any time, say anything which might indicate suicidal tendencies. He was not inclined to be nervous during an air raid, and he preferred to go to bed and stay there. That had been his habit during previous raids. He refused to get up and come down to shelter with me in the hall. I cannot say why he felt safer in bed, but evidently he did so. When my cousin, Kenneth Felden, gave us the news (which he received over the telephone) that an air raid was imminent, he went upstairs to put on his uniform. My brother, almost immediately, said good night to our guests and went upstairs ; and I heard him slam the door of his bedroom. Meanwhile I had seen our guests off the premises, as they had decided to go home, except Dr. Allardyce, who had to go to his post. I then took shelter, along with Mrs. Doggett, the housekeeper, in the hall. My cousin came downstairs, having dressed very quickly, and, after saying good night to us, went out on duty. Shortly after that, I heard a big bomb explode not far away. I do not stand raids very well. There is a heavy A.A. gun in Lower Lorne Gardens which shakes our premises from roof to basement every time it fires ; and it produces in me a peculiar susceptibility to my asthma trouble. The attack at dinner-time gave me a serious shock, and when the raid started I forgot to turn off the gas at the meter, as I ought to have done. Very shortly after the bomb fell near our house, the electric light went out, and Mrs. Doggett and

I had to spend some time in darkness as I had forgotten to provide myself with a torch. Later in the night, I had another bad bout of my asthma trouble, but I was able to alleviate it by means of amyl nitrite. I had a terrible headache, due to the effects of the drug. Mrs. Doggett behaved very well during the raid.

" When the All Clear sounded, I went upstairs, undressed, and went to bed. My cousin had not returned by the time we went upstairs. I slept very well, probably because the two attacks in succession had worn me out.

" I slept later than usual, and it was not until I came downstairs that I heard about my brother's death. By that time, Dr. Allardyce had arrived. I took no part in the investigations. They did not seem to need me, and I was not feeling up to the mark.

" My brother and I have always had perfect confidence in Dr. Allardyce, and he understood my brother's case perfectly, as well as my own. My brother had a considerable admiration for the doctor, and I believe that Dr. Allardyce stands to gain £500 under my brother's will. I wish to say that I entirely agree with my brother's decision in this matter, and I have made a similar provision in my own will. I say this lest anyone should think that my brother's legacy to the doctor was the result of undue influence. He discussed the matter frequently with me, and I entirely agreed with his views. We were both glad to hear of the engagement between Dr. Allardyce and our cousin, Miss Stanway. It seemed to both of us a very suitable match, and we had decided to give them wedding-presents which would testify to our feelings towards them both. " (Signed) DEREK GAINFORD."

The inspector removed the sheet from his machine ; but before laying it aside, he studied the final paragraph once more, as though it suggested something of more importance than the rest. Then he laid the sheet with its predecessors and continued his task.

Statement made by Dr. Frank Allardyce.

" I have acted as physician to the deceased Anthony Gainford during the last five years. He was addicted to alcohol, but refused to subject himself to any curative treatment. As a general rule, he drank steadily, but only occasionally did he carry the process to an excess which produced advanced intoxication. When I took over his case, he had lost all desire to conquer the habit. His liver was affected by cirrhosis, and his heart had become enlarged. It would not have surprised me had he died suddenly from the mere effects of his alcoholic habits. He used to share a house with his brother, Derek Gainford, but some years ago the two brothers decided to give up their house and to live with Kenneth Felden, their cousin. This was an advantage, as Kenneth Felden appeared to have sufficient authority to keep Anthony Gainford's drinking within limits and prevent all but occasional excesses."

' (Dr. Allardyce then confirms the evidence of the other witnesses with regard to the events at the dinner-party.)

"When the Alert sounded on the evening of June 29th, I left the house at once, to take up my post. I was busy there until the All Clear went, and was detained after that for a short time. I then went home. About 8.30 a.m. I was rung up by Kenneth Felden, who informed me that his cousin had been found dead in bed. I supposed that he had died from the effects of his alcoholism ; but on arriving at Maybury Gardens I found that gas poisoning was the cause. When I got there, the room had been aired by opening the windows, and as there was a fair wind blowing, all traces of gas had disappeared. Kenneth Felden informed me that he had found the tap of the gas fire full on, and had turned it off. I then recalled that on the previous evening the deceased had suffered from a severe cold in the head which might have interfered with his sense of smell and prevented him from detecting gas in his bedroom. The appearance of the body suggested gas-poisoning. I estimated the time of death to be ten or eleven hours earlier than when I saw the body—i.e. about midnight or earlier. I informed Kenneth Felden that, in the circumstances, I was not prepared to sign the usual death certificate, and that it was a case for the Coroner. He agreed. I then suggested that the police should be notified. He agreed to this also, and telephoned to them.

"I have never noticed any suicidal tendency in the deceased. On the previous evening, he was apparently in good spirits in spite of a streaming cold. He was not drunk, or anywhere near it when I saw him alive last ; but after that, I understand, he took more whisky when he went to bed, so I cannot say what his final state may have been.

"(*Signed*) FRANK ALLARDYCE."

" Short, anyway," commented the inspector, pausing to relight his pipe. " Now for the housekeeper."

Statement made by Mrs. Miriam Doggett.

" I am a widow and have acted as housekeeper to Mr. Kenneth Felden for the last five years. Three years ago, about, the two Mr. Gainfords came to live with Mr. Felden, and I got higher wages on account of the extra work. Mr. Derek Gainford was my favourite. He was so good-tempered in spite of that dreadful asthma he had, and he gave very little trouble, being so thoughtful. Mr. Anthony Gainford drank a good deal, and that wasn't very pleasant at times. Sometimes he was real troublesome ; but Mr. Felden had a way with him, and usually managed to keep him in order, though he did break out and get intoxicated now and again. He kept very irregular hours, and used to get up in the night and wander about the house, looking for drink, but that was always kept under lock and key by Mr. Felden, and Mr. Gainford only got too much by going down to the ' Green Man ' during the day-time or else when Mr. Felden was away from home and Mr. Anthony could wheedle extra drink out of his brother, who kept the keys then. Since the war began, I've always been worried about Mr. Anthony wandering about in the night, for fear he might pull the black-out curtains aside, not being in a state to remember how important it was to keep them drawn.

" A week ago, Mr. Felden told me he had invited five people to dinner last night, and that I was to get a nice dinner and not mind the expense if I had to buy unrationed things. I thought that very nice of him, for it seems he meant the dinner to be for Dr. Allardyce and Miss Stanway and everybody knows that Mr. Felden was once engaged to Miss Stanway himself, only she threw him over, and now she's engaged to Dr. Allardyce. Not that I say any-thing against Dr. Allardyce, for he cured me of rheumatism one winter and was very kind about it.

" Last night there was Miss Stanway, Miss Herongate, Miss Belmont, Mrs. Jenner, and Dr. Allardyce that came to dinner. I knew I'd be kept pretty busy, bringing the courses in, so while they were eating their soup, I took Mr. Anthony's whisky—what he calls his night-cap—up to his bedroom. Just a tray with a thermos of hot water and a tumbler half full of whisky. He always liked one special brand of whisky in his night-cap, ' Black Swan ' it's called,

77

and he says it's the only kind he can trust to make him sleep well, though often it didn't help him much, as I knew from hearing him wandering about the house if I happened to be wakeful myself. When he came here first, I used to leave a decanter of whisky on his tray, but Mr. Felden stopped that and told me to fill a glass half-full instead, so that he shouldn't take too much in his night-cap. There were some words about that, I remember, but Mr. Felden put his foot down, and when he puts his foot down, that's an end of it. And I used to put a half lemon on a plate on the tray, but you can't get lemons now, so that's stopped. I shut the windows of Mr. Anthony's room, too, when I was up. He hated open windows.

" I showed the ladies up to the spare bedroom to take off their things before dinner. Dr. Allardyce just hung up his hat and coat in the cloak-room.

" All I remember about the dinner is that Mr. Anthony behaved very well, for I'd been a bit afraid of what he might do. But he was in good spirits, very cheery and chatty, and one would hardly have known what his trouble was. And I remember that between two courses, I forget which, Mr. Derek had an attack of his asthma, a fearful turn it was, and he'd forgotten to bring down these little things he uses, these little things he breaks in his handkerchief and snuffs up. Dr. Allardyce ran upstairs, three at a time, to Mr. Derek's room and fetched some down, and they put him right again, after a while ; but he didn't enjoy his dinner on account of it, I could see. But I really didn't notice much of what went on at table, being so worried with bringing in the dishes and clearing them away, not to say thinking of what a lot of washing-up I was going to have on my hands afterwards.

" When dinner was finished, the ladies went into the drawing-room, and Miss Stanway turned back at the door and said to me : ' I've left my bag upstairs.' I offered to go and get it for her, but she went up herself, and I saw her with it in her hand as she came down again.

" I was busy washing-up the dinner dishes when the sirens went. The ladies all went off, and Dr. Allardyce, too. Mr. Felden went upstairs to put on his uniform, and then he went out on duty. Mr. Anthony went up to bed. He never would sit up through a raid. Mr. Derek and I sat up. Raids don't really bother me, though that's not to say I like them. I just sit and get on with my knitting. Mr. Derek read a book until the electric light went out.

Then I groped about and got a couple of candles, and we sat with them till the All Clear went. After that Mr. Derek went to bed. He had another of these asthma turns of his in the night, and he was looking pretty bad. Then I got to bed myself.

"Next morning I lit the kitchen fire and took up Mr. Anthony's breakfast tray as usual, but could get no answer from him. I thought I smelt gas, so I got worried and told Mr. Felden, and he came up and went into the room where Mr. Anthony was lying in bed, dead. Then the doctor came. And then the police.

"I don't remember noticing any smell of gas in the room when I took up Mr. Anthony's tray of whisky last night. I haven't been in that room since then.

"About the 'Black Swan' whisky, there's a very big lot of it in stock in the house. When the war came, Mr. Anthony insisted on ordering it. He said the price would go up, and it was cheaper to buy it in quantity. I don't know how much there is, forty or fifty dozen likely. And he was quite right to lay it in, for the price has gone up a lot since then. He drank other brands too, brought in from time to time, but lately it's been hard to get enough, and he's been drinking 'Black Swan' from the house stock mostly for a while. He would have nothing else for his night-cap as he called it. "(*Signed*) MIRIAM DOGGETT."

"Just as well I took all that stuff down in shorthand," commented the inspector to himself. "There's a point or two in it. Swamped by a lot of chatter, of course. My questions at the tail-end show up a bit. Not that it matters. Now for the ladies."

Statement made by Daphne Stanway.

"I am at present employed by Messrs. Astley & Spelman, Ltd., taking the place of one of their male employés now on military service. Kenneth Felden, Anthony Gainford and Derek Gainford are cousins of mine. Recently I became engaged to Dr. Frank Allardyce. It is true that I was at one time engaged to Kenneth Felden, but this was broken off years ago and left no ill-feeling on either side. The dinner-party on June 29th was, I believe, given to celebrate the engagement of Dr. Allardyce and myself."

(She then confirms the foregoing evidence about what happened at the dinner-party and afterwards.)

79

" I was absent from the company for a few minutes immediately after dinner, when I went upstairs to fetch my bag, which I had forgotten.

" Anthony Gainford was in good spirits that evening. He proposed the toast of Dr. Allardyce and myself. There was no formal speech or anything of that sort. I never noticed anything in Anthony Gainford which might have suggested a tendency to suicide. On that night he was not intoxicated so far as I observed him. I think I'd have noticed if he had been drinking more than usual. I talked to him during dinner. We discussed a Mr. Jehudi Ashmun, for whom my cousin had a liking. I really do not know how friendly they were. My cousin had a fair income derived from investments, but I have no idea of what it actually amounted to in figures. I understand that he has left a legacy to Dr. Allardyce. He mentioned this to me at dinner, in connection with our engagement, but he gave no figures, and I paid little attention to it. He was very grateful to Dr. Allardyce on purely professional grounds, he told me. I am acquainted with Mr. Ashmun, but am not an intimate friend of his. Dr. Allardyce is also acquainted with him.

" After dinner, we played bridge. Dr. Allardyce and I were playing against Mrs. Jenner and my cousin Anthony. They lost a good deal, but that was due to the way the cards ran, and not to my cousin having drunk too much. He played quite a sound game and took his losses very well. This, and other things, convince me that he was not suffering from too much alcohol up to that time, though he had helped himself freely during dinner.

" The party broke up when my cousin Kenneth Felden was called away to the telephone, and came back with the news that enemy planes were in the vicinity. He wished us good night and good luck, and went up to put on his uniform. None of us was much perturbed, except Miss Ione Herongate, who seemed rather anxious. My cousin, Anthony Gainford, also said good night, and I think he went upstairs. His brother saw us off at the door and lent me his torch, as I found that the battery of my own torch was exhausted. We all had our own cars and got home without mishap.

" *(Signed)* DAPHNE STANWAY."

Inspector Camlet picked up his notes, read them over carefully, and then continued his typing.

" There are further statements by Ione Herongate, Olive Belmont, and Mrs. Jenner, but they merely confirm the evidence given above and add nothing to it."

He paused here for a while, collecting his ideas, and then went on with his report.

" I examined the bedroom in which the deceased died. It has one large window and one small one. The three casements of the large window and the casement of the small window were all wide open. Kenneth Felden informed me that he had opened them immediately he entered the room that morning, as the place was full of gas. I examined the tap of the gas fire and found it closed. I turned it on, and found the gas flowing normally. I noticed a very faint smell of gas in the room, but it was hardly detectable. The wind was strong enough to blow the curtains about when the casements were open. There was an electric clock on the mantelpiece which had stopped at 10.57. I tested the clock and found it in working order.

" On the bed-table, I found a thermos flask, still containing some warm water, and a tumbler with a heel-tap of whisky in it. These I took away, and have had them examined for finger-prints. On the casing of the thermos flask a large number of prints were found which corresponded with the finger-prints of the deceased and Mrs. Doggett. On the tumbler, the only prints detected had been made by the deceased and Mrs. Doggett. The liquid in the thermos flask and the heel-tap of whisky in the tumbler have been handed over to an analyst for examination and report.

" I asked Kenneth Felden for his keys and examined the stock of whisky which Miriam Doggett mentioned in her statement. It is a large one, evidently bought pre-war or in the early stages of this war, as the bottles have corks covered with metal foil, and not the screw stoppers which are used for ' Black Swan ' whisky nowadays. On making inquiries from Aitken & Hunt, Ltd., who supplied the deceased with wine and spirits, my inference was confirmed. They state that the deceased ordered large supplies at the outbreak of the war, and further large consignments at later dates. Thereafter, week by week, he had ordered more. But these later supplies were in screw-top bottles. Frequently, Aitken & Hunt had been unable to give the deceased any ' Black Swan ' brand, and in that event he took anything they chanced to have in hand. Sometimes they were completely out of stock and could not fill his orders, though they had done their best, as he was a valued customer."

Inspector Camlet removed the papers and carbons from his machine, grouped the sheets into their sets, and signed them.

" One for the Coroner, one for Driffield, one for our file, and one for myself," he said, counting them over. " And that's a job done, anyhow."

CHAPTER VIII   *The Suspicions of an Inspector*

SIR CLINTON AND WENDOVER WERE OLD FRIENDS WITH many tastes in common, such as chess, fishing, and criminology ; and when the Chief Constable's official duties brought him into the Ambledown district, he invariably stayed with Wendover at Talgarth Grange, even though it were only for the night.

Inspector Camlet knew that the Chief Constable was at the Grange ; and when, just after he had finished typing his report, he received the results of the post-mortem examination of Anthony Gainford's body, he decided to make them an excuse for taking all the documents to his superior without delay. Though he hated to admit it, even to himself, he knew very well that he had made no real progress toward satisfactory solutions of the deaths of Deverell, Pirbright, and Gainford. He had a strong suspicion that the three events were in some way linked together, but it was no more than suspicion. Try as he might, he could find no definite thread to connect them, and suspicion, *per se*, amounted to nothing. As a last resort, he decided to lay the whole affair before Sir Clinton in the hope that the Chief Constable might, in the course of informal talk, let fall something which would be helpful. It was a forlorn hope, for Camlet knew from experience that Sir Clinton preferred to keep his own counsel until he had come near a solution of any case presented to him. Still, the inspector hoped that he might pick up a hint without having to admit that he himself was completely in a fog. With this in his mind, he rang up the Grange and asked permission to present himself after dinner with his documents.

When he reached the Grange, he found Wendover and

Sir Clinton in the smoking-room. Wendover, always hospitable, busied himself unostentatiously with supplying his visitor's needs. Camlet offered his sheaf of reports, and Sir Clinton read them through without comment. Then he laid the papers on his knee and looked at the inspector.

" Quite a lot of facts here," he said with a faint smile. " But what about inferences ? "

" I'd rather take the facts first, sir. The inferences can follow, after we've put the facts in order."

" Certainly, if you wish," agreed the Chief Constable. " Suppose you put them in order for us."

" Take the Deverell case," began the inspector. " No smoke particles in Deverell's lungs. The P.M. proved that. Heaps of smoke about when Betty Brown appeared on the scene. If Deverell had breathed at all, after the incendiary started, he'd have inhaled some smoke. It would have left traces in his lungs and his bronchi. It's plain he was dead before the bomb started a fire."

Sir Clinton made a slight gesture of caution.

" That sounds more like an inference than a fact," he objected. " I thought you were going to keep them apart."

" Well, sir, it's a bit difficult . . ."

" I expected it would be," commented the Chief Constable. " Never mind. Give us it in any way you think best. All I want is to prevent an inference masquerading as a fact."

" Very good, sir. I'm convinced that Deverell died before any smoke arose. And *that's* a fact . . ."

" I grant you it's fact," agreed Sir Clinton. " But it isn't evidence. It's merely an opinion, and opinions depend very much on the man who holds them, you know. I'm not being merely captious, Inspector, though I see that you think I am. This is an intricate affair, and we must keep things straight as we go along. That's really my point."

" I see, sir," admitted Camlet. " Now my point is, that on the face of things, Deverell was dead before the fire got going."

" I share your opinion entirely," said the Chief Constable carefully. " And what next ? "

" My *opinion*," said Camlet meticulously, " is that somebody killed him. I can't prove that. What *can* be proved, sir, is this. The gold crosier and some other things were in Deverell's house before the raid. After the raid, they weren't there any longer. That's a fact. And my inference is that somebody removed them."

" Now we're getting along famously," said Sir Clinton, unimpressed. " Proceed."

" The gold disappeared from Deverell's house, sir. It turned up on Pirbright's ground later on. That connects the two cases."

He paused, as if expecting criticism, but Sir Clinton merely nodded.

" Now turn to Pirbright's death, sir. Some fresh evidence is on hand since I talked it over with you. Dr. Greenholme did a P.M. on Pirbright. The rigor mortis was quite normal. So Pirbright didn't die from strychnine, in spite of the convulsions he'd suffered. Dr. Greenholme looked for strychnine in the stomach. Not a trace of it. But he found something else. Some stuff was there in too small a quantity to isolate. An extract of it was dropped into a cat's eye. The pupil dilated. Mydriatic alkaloids act that way. Things like atropine, hyoscine, hyoscyamine and their derivatives. Pirbright's eyes had dilated pupils. These are the facts. Inference is : he'd swallowed one of these alkaloids."

" And as these alkaloids can't be procured for the mere asking," Sir Clinton added, " there's a further inference we can draw : that someone administered the poison to Pirbright, someone who *had* an easy means of obtaining a supply."

" I was just going to say that, sir," rejoined Camlet. " Now, another point. There's no evidence to prove that the poison was given in that whisky we found on Pirbright's table. Dr. Greenholme examined both the heel-tap of whisky in the cup and the whisky left in the bottle. Neither had anything in it that affected a cat's eye. And the finger-prints on the bottle and the cup are Pirbright's. Nobody else's prints were found on either of them."

" One can easily account for that," Sir Clinton pointed out. " This, Inspector, is neither a fact nor an inference. It's mere hypothesis, and it stands or falls on its likelihood. Let's assume that the cup we found on the table was not the one from which Pirbright drank. The unknown visitor used it, I think. Pirbright took it down from the shelf and so left his finger-prints on it. The stranger wore gloves, and probably was careful to hold the cup by the handle only, thus leaving Pirbright's prints unsmudged. After Pirbright had drawn the cork and poured whisky into both cups— leaving his prints on the bottle in the process—the visitor could easily distract his attention for a moment and tip the drug into the proper cup. Take hyoscine as an example.

What's the fatal dose? You've got some forensic medicine books in that library of yours, Wendover. See if you can dig out anything about it. I know that it's very small."

Wendover consulted several technical works.

"It dilates the patient's pupils," he reported. "Were Pirbright's pupils dilated?"

"They were," said Camlet. "And that's in Dr. Green-holme's report too."

"Hyoscine seems to vary a lot in its action," Wendover pursued. "Some people stand it better than others. Soll-mann says that for ordinary patients it's unsafe to give more than the hundred-and-twentieth part of a grain; Cushmy says that quantity is 'generally enough to induce quiet'; Sydney Smith mentions that half-a-grain has proved fatal; Glaister puts the medicinal dose anywhere between one-fiftieth and one two-hundredth part of a grain."

"Not much difficulty in dropping that quantity into a man's glass if his back's turned for a moment," Sir Clinton pointed out. "But there's another point, while you've got these books handy. How long does it take a man to die, after he's swallowed a fatal dose of hyoscine?"

Wendover consulted his literature.

"Smith gives some examples," he reported. "One man died after six hours; another died after ten hours; another lived for twenty-four hours."

"Dr. Allardyce left Pirbright at 9.45 p.m. Add six hours and you get 4 a.m. roughly, since the unknown visitor came after Allardyce left. If he died from hyoscine poison-ing, Pirbright could hardly have expired before 4 a.m. But the temperature of the body pointed to his having died about 11 p.m. at latest. The inference is that he didn't die from the effects of the hyoscine," Sir Clinton pointed out.

"Then why use hyoscine at all, sir?" demanded Camlet.

"To stupefy him, perhaps; but that's merely a guess. The point I wish to make is that by the time the visitor had washed out the cup and put it back on the shelf, all traces of the hyoscine would have vanished. Thus, although hyoscine was used, no sign of it was to be found in either the bottle or the cup left on the table. However, this is a mere interlude. Please go on, Inspector."

"Well, sir, we dug up the crosier and some other things in Pirbright's ground. That's a fact. It's also a fact that things don't fly away and bury themselves. Not in my experience, anyhow. Inference is, that some gold objects were buried by somebody. Either by Pirbright himself or by somebody else. Further inference—drawn by yourself, sir—is that the gold was buried not earlier than the evening before Pirbright's death. My *opinion*"—Camlet faintly parodied Sir Clinton's manner—"is that the gold wasn't buried by Pirbright himself. The last thing he'd want to do, if he'd stolen it, was to cache it on his own premises. He had all that waste land to hide it in."

"Quite true," said the Chief Constable. "But at the time we dug it up, I told you that the reason for burying the gold there was not beyond conjecture. My conjecture, for what it's worth, is simply that the cache was meant for the police to find. If you remember, it took us next to no time to discover it. A perfect gift, in fact. No one who really meant the stuff to remain hidden would ever have chosen such a site. If you want my opinion about it, I don't mind saying that I believe it was buried by someone mixed up in the Deverell affair and the idea was to throw suspicion on Pirbright. Then, to complete the job, Pirbright's mouth was shut, once and for all, so that he could not clear himself even if he wanted. That's mere guesswork, I admit. It's not provable by the evidence we've got so far. All I say in its favour is that it seems to square with the facts. The next question is : who had an interest in doing these things ? "

"I'd rather leave that, sir. For the moment, at least. Until you've considered Gainford's case."

"You're linking it up with the other two, are you ? " asked the Chief Constable.

"I think there's a connection between them all, sir."

"Anthony Gainford would have been interested by that," said Sir Clinton. "I heard him prophesying Deverell's death, and quoting what he called a ' local Nostradamus ' to the effect that anyone who touched that treasure-trove would come by a bad end. He touched it himself out of bravado, I remember. Curious coincidence ; but it needn't detain us. Please go on."

"Very good, sir. On the face of it, Gainford died of gas-poisoning. You saw the medical report ? He'd been sick. Symptoms of cyanosis, too. Blood spectrum showed the carboxyhæmoglobin bands. Positive results with Hoppe-Seyler's test and Kunkuel's test for carbon monoxide in the blood. Minute hæmorrhages in the brain. All according to Cocker. The only abnormal thing was a trace of nickel in the stomach. Dr. Greenholme mentioned that in his report, as you've seen. But nickel isn't a poison he says."

Sir Clinton picked up one of Wendover's books and consulted it.

" ' Nickel and cobalt,' " he read out. " ' These metals are only absorbed when given in the strongest solutions. The local action is that of metals in general, with nothing particularly characteristic. Nickel salts have been used as emetics, but are not to be recommended. Nickel cooking vessels give up a harmless trace of the metal to the food.' Obviously Gainford wasn't poisoned by nickel."

" No, sir. That's quite certain. It was the gas that did for him. Question is : how did he get gassed ? Felden found the tap of the gas fire open next morning, and the room full of gas. Obvious explanation is that Gainford was drunk when he went up to bed. He turned the tap on, failed to light the gas, and forgot to turn off the tap. But there's doubt about that. First, he wasn't drunk when he went to bed. All the witnesses are firm about that."

" The witnesses only saw him after what he drank at dinner," objected Wendover. " He drank another half-tumbler of whisky after he got upstairs. That might well have tipped the scale."

" Not in the case of Gainford, sir," declared the inspector with the air of an expert. " Confirmed soaker, he was. His type gets drunk by growing muzzy by degrees. You or I might drink enough to bring us to the point where an extra half-tumbler would put us clean over at one go. But Gainford was different. Quite different."

" There's something in what you say," admitted Wendover, handsomely.

" Certain about it, sir. Had a lot of experience of drunks, one way and another. He drank his whisky right enough. Finger-prints on the tumbler prove it. But it wouldn't make him drunk—really drunk, I mean—before he had time to fiddle with the fire. Again, that fire was an oldish one. No electric lighter-gadget on it. If he wanted to light up, he'd have to use a petrol lighter or else matches. No petrol lighter in his pockets. Box of matches instead. But I looked everywhere for a spent match. Not one in the whole room. So he didn't even try to light the fire. And if he turned on the tap, when it's full on it makes quite a roar. He'd have heard that. It'd have reminded him to turn off the tap again when he didn't light the fire."

" Grant all that for the sake of argument," conceded the Chief Constable. " I gather that you've got some alternative notion in your mind ? "

" Suppose the tap was only *half* on, sir. I tried it that way. It doesn't make a noticeable sound. He wouldn't notice it, by ear. He had a cold in his head. He wouldn't spot the smell of gas. Not like a normal person, anyway. Now my view is this, sir. Someone else turned the tap on slightly before Gainford went upstairs. During the night, the gas gradually leaked into the room and poisoned him finally."

Wendover made a gesture of disbelief.

" When did he die, according to the medical evidence ? " he asked. " I haven't seen these reports you brought with you."

Sir Clinton picked up the papers on his knee and ran through them.

" Allardyce put the time of death at midnight, or earlier," he said.

" And when did Gainford go upstairs ? " persisted Wendover.

" The Alert went at about 10.45 p.m." said Sir Clinton. " Gainford went up to bed shortly after that, within a few minutes, apparently."

" Then he undressed and got into bed and had his night-cap," said Wendover. " The gas concentration can't have been anywhere near lethal then, or he'd never have survived to go all through that procedure. And yet, in about an hour or less, he was dead. Even granting a windy night and some blow-down in the chimney, it implies a very quick rise in gas concentration in the room."

" That's just what I think myself," said Camlet, unexpectedly.

" Were Gainford's clothes neatly arranged, or were they simply flung down anyhow ? " Sir Clinton inquired.

" They were quite tidy, sir, when I saw them," Camlet explained. " You mean that he can't have been really drunk when he undressed? Else he'd have chucked his duds down anywhere ? "

" Something more than that," suggested the Chief Constable. " The electric clock stopped at 10.57, remember. The current failed, so the electric light must have gone off at the same moment. Do you think Gainford could undress in the dark and stack his clothes tidily, not to speak of drinking his night-cap neatly, without spilling it ? "

" I doubt it, sir."

" Then obviously he must have got between the sheets at 10.56 at the latest. Further, he wasn't affected by gas to any extent before that, or he'd hardly have been so spry in his movements."

" That's covered by my explanation, sir. A slow leak from

the gas fire. The gas would take a while to accumulate, even if the windows were shut. The housekeeper mentions that she shut them when she took up the whisky."

"Very ingenious," admitted Sir Clinton. "It seems to cover the facts you've given me. The question is : does it cover *all* the facts ? But don't bother about that just now. Give us your inferences next."

But this the inspector seemed reluctant to do. He shot an uneasy glance at Wendover, which Sir Clinton noticed.

"You can speak quite freely before Mr. Wendover. He's a magistrate, you know."

This left Camlet no option, but obviously he felt himself in an awkward position.

"Well, sir," he began, dragging out his words reluctantly. "I'll just put some of the facts together by themselves. This is how I see it. Take the Deverell affair, first of all. Dr. Allardyce was the last person to see Deverell before he died. That's his own statement. We all heard it. He took his car round to Polehurst at 10 p.m. Deverell was busy writing up his notes on the treasure. The crosier and other things were on the table. Deverell went to the front door himself to let Allardyce in. Likely enough, he just laid down his pen the moment the bell rang. His notes would break off in the middle of a sentence. Dr. Allardyce told us he stayed in the house till 11 p.m. or 11.30 p.m. and then left. There's no corroboration. For all we can say, he may have waited till the raid started. The next independent witness is Betty Brown. She found Deverell's body. Then I came in and found the gold gone."

Wendover evidently intended to say something at this point, but a look from Sir Clinton restrained him. The inspector continued.

"The next thing is the story he told about those rabbits. I haven't confirmed it. It didn't seem worth while."

"I'm not sure I agree with you there, Inspector," said the Chief Constable. "These rabbits interest me. But go on."

"Take the Pirbright business next," continued Camlet. "We have Allardyce's own statement that he visited Pirbright that evening. Same as the Deverell case. . . . Ah ! I see what you mean about the rabbits, sir ! His excuse for calling on Pirbright was that he had to pay for them. Yes, might be worth checking up those rabbits, after all."

"It's a point, certainly," agreed Sir Clinton. "But don't let it detain us now."

"Allardyce went up to see Pirbright," continued the

inspector. "He went in his car. He could carry heavy stuff in his car without attracting notice. We found that bottle of 'Black Swan' whisky at Pirbright's. Allardyce volunteered that he drinks 'Black Swan' himself. It was Allardyce who examined Pirbright's body and fixed the time of death. We've no corroboration of that time. Apart from Allardyce's evidence there's nothing to say when Pirbright actually died. Pirbright's body contained some hyoscine or some drug like it. Hyoscine's not common. I can't trace any suspicious purchases of it, locally. *But Allardyce has hyoscine in his possession.* He uses it constantly in that twilight sleep business."

The inspector paused and glanced at Wendover with something like unconcealed triumph in his expression. Sir Clinton intervened before Wendover could speak.

"Very interesting. I congratulate you, Inspector. But we've still the Gainford affair to examine before starting to discuss your case."

"I'm coming to that, sir. The question is : who turned on the gas tap."

"I think there's a question before that, Inspector," said the Chief Constable. "But take it as you please."

"Allardyce was at that dinner-party" Camlet went on. "The gas tap wasn't turned on until after they'd sat down. That's proved by the housekeeper's evidence, sir. She went upstairs with Gainford's whisky while the soup was on the table. She smelt no gas in the bedroom then. So the tap was turned on after that. During the dinner, Allardyce went up to fetch the amyl nitrite capsule from Derek Gainford's bedroom. No one else went upstairs with him. He knows the lie of the land in that house, being the family doctor. It doesn't take two ticks to go into a room and turn on a gas tap. As for the exact time of Gainford's death, the only estimate of it was made by Allardyce himself. He may quite well have given me a wrong one. Deliberately. For all we know, Gainford may have died at any time during the night."

"I'd like to see some sign of a motive," Sir Clinton confessed.

"Motive, sir ? No need to look far for that. Allardyce had all his money in rubber. I hadn't any bother of learning that. Lot of folk in this town got their fingers nipped over this Malayan smash-up. Go about squealing and comparing notes. Allardyce is one of them. Makes no bones about it. Lost a lot of steady income and says so. Now doctors carry heavy insurances. Have to. Provision against old age. No one wants a doctor when he gets old. Premiums have to be paid on the nail. Where's cash to come from? Now Gainford's dead, Allardyce comes into a legacy. £500. Not a fortune. But enough to pay an insurance premium. And if he doesn't get the cash instanter, he can borrow on the strength of the will. There's your motive, if you want one."

Wendover listened to the inspector's recital with growing dismay. He scouted the notion that Allardyce had any hand in the deaths of these three men. To him, that seemed merely fantastic. None the less, when all the evidence was marshalled, the thing had an ugly look, and nothing was to be gained by denying it. If Camlet bruited his suspicions abroad, plenty of people would believe that " after all, there's something in it, even if they can't prove it." A doctor's livelihood depends on his being above suspicion, and the mere circulation of such imputations would ruin Allardyce's practice, once and for all. That was where the danger lay.

" That sounds very convincing, as you put it, Inspector," said the Chief Constable after a few moments' consideration. " But I'd like to test it at one or two points before making up my mind. Do you mind if I use your phone, Wendover? I see it's over there."

He got up, consulted the telephone directory, dialled a number, and then began to speak. Wendover, noting the form of the conversation, inferred that Sir Clinton deliberately echoed his interlocutor's statements for the benefit of the inspector.

" This is Sir Clinton Driffield. I should like to speak to Miss Stanway, if it is convenient. . . . Thanks. . . . Is that you, Miss Stanway? I'd like to ask a question or two, if I may. . . . You remember that on the night of Mr. Anthony Gainford's death, Dr. Allardyce went upstairs during dinner to fetch an amyl nitrite capsule for Mr. Derek Gainford? . . . . And immediately after dinner you went upstairs yourself to get a bag that you had forgotten to bring down with you? . . . Your visit upstairs was a good deal later than Dr. Allardyce's, I think. Can you give me an idea of how long? . . . . twenty minutes or half an hour? . . . . You can't give it more exactly? . . . No, of course one doesn't notice these things. Call it twenty minutes at least? . . . . Yes, that's near enough, I think. Now another point. You know the house, I believe. Do you remember if any of the bedroom doors were open when you went up to get your bag? . . . . Mr. Felden's door was wide open and Mr. Anthony Gainford's was ajar? And the rest were shut ? . . . . Thanks. Now, did you notice any-thing, anything at all abnormal while you were upstairs ? . . . . Nothing ? No smell of cooking, for instance ? Or something burning ? Or gas ? . . . . Nothing whatever ? Thanks. That's very satisfactory. . . . No, there's nothing else I need trouble you about. It's not important. We're merely anxious to have all the facts, in case some people ask questions at the inquest. . . . Yes, thank you."

Sir Clinton laid down the receiver and turned back towards the inspector.

"You heard that ? Miss Stanway noticed no smell of gas. Gainford's door was open, and she went up half-an-hour or so after Allardyce. In that time, if Allardyce opened the tap, quite a smellable amount of gas would have been in Gainford's room and some of it would have diffused out into the corridor. That doesn't help your hypothesis, Inspector, I'm afraid. But let's try again. The electric current failed at 10.57 when the electric clock stopped in Gainford's bed-room. That was about the time when a bomb fell in Hansler Road. Gas mains and electric mains often run close to each other. We'll try the Gas Office now. With these raids going on, there's bound to be somebody on duty in the break-down department."

He went back to the telephone and dialled another number.

"This is the Chief Constable. Will you put me through to the breakdown department, please ? Thank you. . . . Are you the breakdown department ? I'm the Chief Con-stable. Can you tell me if you had any trouble in Hansler Road on June 29th. A bomb fell there. . . . Ah ! You had the gas main damaged ? . . . How long was the gas off, can you tell me ? . . . From 11 p.m. to 8.15 a.m. ? Thanks. You keep a log of these affairs, I suppose ? . . . Yes, thanks very much."

Again he laid down the receiver and turned to the inspector.

"I'm afraid it won't do," he said, sympathetically. "You see, Inspector, Miss Stanway noticed no gas escape, though on your hypothesis there must have been a flow for almost half an hour before she went upstairs. One must infer that the tap was not turned on during that dinner. If it was turned on at any time after eleven o'clock, there was no gas in the pipe, for the bomb smashed the main in Hansler Road and cut off supplies. By the way, were you in the kitchen of the house ? I take it that they've no gas stove, but do their cooking on a range for the sake of hot water ? "

"That's so, sir," the inspector confirmed. "You mean

that accounts for Mrs. Doggett not noticing that the gas was off when she got up in the morning ? "

" Exactly."

The inspector was puzzled and betrayed it.

" Well, I don't understand it, sir," he confessed candidly. " Here's a man dead of gas poisoning, and the gas supply's cut off. That's a rum start ! "

" It's more to the point," said Wendover, " that you practically accused Dr. Allardyce of murder, and now it turns out that he had nothing whatever to do with the case. I don't think much of that piece of work, Inspector. And if you've been wrong in the Gainford affair, there's no guarantee that you were nearer the mark in the other two cases."

But Wendover's intervention had an effect opposite to the one he desired. Instead of browbeating the inspector, all he succeeded in doing was to make him obstinate.

" I'll admit I was wrong in the Gainford case," he conceded in a grumbling tone. " But that leaves all the evidence untouched in the other cases. This isn't a case of a chain of evidence, sir. In a chain, if one link's weak, all the rest goes by the board. But here it's a lot of facts fitting together like a jig-saw. Even if a few of them don't fall into place, the rest make a pattern. The Deverell and Pirbright evidence stands."

" Where's your motive ? " demanded Wendover, abruptly. " I know you don't need to prove in court that there was a sound one ; but, short of homicidal mania, people don't go about killing, just for the fun of it. What has Dr. Allardyce got out of the deaths of Deverell and Pirbright ? "

" That will transpire later, sir," declared Camlet, with an air of wisdom.

" Yes, I know. Judgment Day will bring a lot of things to light," retorted Wendover, tartly. " It's a long time to wait, though."

" Well, sir, the same thing applies here as in the Gainford case . . ."

" Not a very lucky precedent for you," interjected Wendover.

" No, sir," admitted the inspector, gravely. " Fact remains. Allardyce is in immediate need of a few hundreds. That gold was easily convertible into cash. There's your motive for the Deverell business. And if Pirbright knew anything about that and blackmailed Allardyce, then there's your motive for the Pirbright affair. And by that time the gold would be a risky thing to hang on to. If Pirbright spotted something, other people might. So Allardyce cut his losses. Buried the gold where it would throw suspicion on Pirbright in connection with the Deverell business. Oh, a motive won't be hard to find, once we get the thing cleared up."

"Which we haven't done yet," Sir Clinton pointed out. "You talked about a jig-saw puzzle, Inspector. One of the pieces is called Jehudi Ashmun. Where do he and his rabbits fit into your scheme ? "

"Judy Ashmun, sir ? All I know about him is that he's a wrong 'un. Or so I believe. Nobody publishes flat-catching ads. like his if they're on the square. I got a friend to answer one of them, just out of curiosity. Nothing doing. His address wasn't classy enough, likely. But I know who goes to Judy's meetings. Dibs and no brains, mostly. That's enough for me. Where did he get that name of his ? Sounds a bit unlikely."

"I believe he comes from Liberia," explained Wendover, glad to have the inspector at a disadvantage. "Liberia was founded by a man called Jehudi Ashmun. Probably your friend was called after him."

"Liberia ? " echoed the inspector. "Never heard of it."

"It's a black Republic in Africa, alongside Sierra Leone," said Wendover, instructively. "It was founded as a dump for freed slaves from America ; and the official language is English. It isn't completely civilised even yet, though. Some of the forest tribes are still cannibals, I'm told."

"Very interesting," said the inspector, in a tone which belied his words. "But why do you drag in Judy Ashmun, sir ? " he asked, turning to Sir Clinton. "He doesn't seem to me to mean much."

"Haven't you forgotten the resemblance between the Pirbright case and the matter of those dead rabbits which Dr. Allardyce found ? "

"Oh, that ! " said Camlet, contemptuously. "I don't take much stock in that rabbit yarn."

"You and I differ, then," rejoined Sir Clinton. "I'm inclined to lay some stress on it. We must wait and see which of us is right."

When the inspector had gone, the Chief Constable turned to Wendover.

"I suppose you've noticed, Squire, that the Ambledown Golf Club is running a bridge drive in aid of the Russian Red Cross. I've booked three tables in your name at my own expense. I like to do good by stealth and, anyway, I'm not a member of the Club. Now I want you to produce guests to fill the seats. I don't know enough local people myself."

" Any preferences ? " asked Wendover, carelessly.

" Oh, just some people I know, for a start. I don't want to be planted down with a gang of total strangers. Felden, say, to begin with. I like the look of him. Then Allardyce and Miss Stanway ; I know them already. And what about Miss Stanway's sister, this Mrs. Pinfold who's so keen on friend Ashmun ? I'd like to meet her. And perhaps friend Ashmun . . ."

" No friend of mine," said Wendover, decidedly. " I draw the line at having him as my guest, even nominally."

" Oh, leave him out, then," agreed Sir Clinton. " It was just a suggestion. Let's see. Are there any more in the Stanway family ? "

" A brother, Max Stanway," said Wendover. " He comes in between the sisters."

" Put him down too, then. What about Derek Gainford ? '

" You can score him off," said Wendover. " He hates appearing in public, with that asthma of his."

" Understandable enough," admitted Sir Clinton, sympathetically. " It would be awkward if he had one of his attacks. This list seems a bit short of women, so far. Put that Miss Herongate down also, Squire. Sphinxes are always interesting until you find there's nothing behind the smile. H'm ! Is there anyone else ? Oh, yes. That archæologist man had a brother, hadn't he ? I remember seeing him at the inquest."

" Henry Deverell ? I come across him occasionally at the Natural History Society meetings. I dare say I could rake him in if you want him. No one goes into mourning nowadays, and it's a charitable show, anyhow."

" Just one further point," said Sir Clinton. " Will you see that all these people are in one batch at the refreshment interval ? You can easily fix that with the Club secretary."

" I suppose it can be managed," said Wendover. " But why ? "

" No mystery there," explained Sir Clinton. " I hope to hear both sides of the Ashmun problem. You're too prejudiced, Squire, to be any use as a witness. But with a little tact I hope to get up an argument about him with Felden for the prosecution, and Mrs. Pinfold and Miss Herongate for the defence. Probably others will join in, and I shall learn a thing or two."

" I had a fair notion that you weren't doing this merely to help the Russians," said Wendover, shrewdly. " But as for Ashmun, you can have him for all I care. I'm not interested in quacks of that sort.

"THAT FINISHES THE RUBBER," SAID FELDEN, PUTTING DOWN his scoring card. "Hardly worth while starting afresh, is it?"

"No," agreed Ione Herongate, glancing at her watch. "They'll be ringing the refreshment bell in a minute or two for the first section, and we're in it. By the way, Kenneth, what's the war doing? I missed the six o'clock news."

"Oh, don't start talking about the war!" interrupted Mrs. Pinfold, pettishly. "It's trouble enough, without dragging it into every conversation. What with this ten shilling income tax, and the rationing, and the miserable allowance of petrol they give us, and all the bother with the Government taking over foreign investments, and one's maids threatening to leave because they can get more money in munitions, the war is a downright nuisance."

"I suppose you find the air raids trying," said Sir Clinton.

"Oh, no. I'm too far out of town to be hit," Mrs. Pinfold explained. "They don't worry me a bit. But the whole thing's so *boring*, you know. The best thing to do is just to ignore it."

"Excellent notion," said Felden, sardonically. "If we ignore it long enough, it'll get tired of showing off, eh? Stop for lack of public interest, maybe. Something in that, perhaps."

Mrs. Pinfold stared at him with a suspicious eye.

"I suppose that's sarcastic, or ironical, or something, Kenneth. You're always making fun of serious things, I know. Now Mr. Ashmun agrees with me entirely."

"That finishes it, of course," said Felden, with a faint grimace.

"I'd much rather be guided by him than by you," retorted Mrs. Pinfold, with an air of finality.

In her 'teens she had been very pretty in the pink and white style; but instead of developing she seemed to have remained in her nonage both in looks and mentality. The expression in her big eyes was childish rather than childlike; and at the slightest contradiction her lower lip drooped a little, like that of a child on the verge of tears. Her obstinacy was the case-hardened stubbornness of a weak character, arising partly from conceit and partly from stupidity.

"You're not likely to be guided by both of us," said Felden. "We pull different ways, usually. Any more wonders, lately?"

"Oh, of course you sneer, Kenneth," rejoined Mrs.

Pinfold, waspishly. " It's your nature, and you can't help it, I suppose. You always were cynical and sceptical and suspicious and ready to disparage everybody you don't like. It's just your way, as we all know. But you're quite wrong about Mr. Ashmun, entirely wrong. Perhaps it's just jealousy because he's cleverer than you are."

" He's cleverer, certainly, in some ways," said Felden darkly.

" I'm surprised you admit even that," declared Mrs. Pinfold, failing to take his meaning. " You couldn't do a tenth of what he does, for all your scientific smartness, Kenneth. It's not your fault, altogether of course. You live entirely in three dimensions . . ."

" Oh, dear no ! " protested Felden. " Time's the fourth dimension, and I live in it like everybody else."

" That's what *he* says," interrupted Mrs. Pinfold, in triumph. " But he goes further than you can. He knows all about the Fifth Dimension."

" Is that where his spooks come from ? " queried Felden. " He can have the lot of them and not bother to share with me. I'm not greedy when it comes to spooks, my dear cousin."

" Oh, of course you scientific people think you can dispose of everything by saying : ' Spooks ! Pshaw ! '," retorted Mrs. Pinfold crossly. " You don't even take the trouble to learn anything about the things you jeer at. Have you ever seen any of Mr. Ashmun's manifestations ? "

Felden shook his head contemptuously.

" Heaven forfend ! " he said.

" Well, you might learn something by going to one or two. I don't just jeer at these things. *I* go and investigate and learn a lot. I've heard things, strange things, voices . . ."

" Anyone can hear voices. I hear 'em every day myself. Nothing in that," rejoined Felden. " Most people have tongues in their heads."

" I don't mean that kind of voice ; I mean Voices that tell me all sorts of strange things."

" Fish stories ? " suggested Felden, irritatingly.

" Oh, that's just the silly sort of thing you *would* say ! " exclaimed Mrs. Pinfold angrily. " Do any of your voices speak from the top of a card-table when it's got nothing on it or under it—just an ordinary card-table ? And it can tell you all sorts of strange things about yourself, too. If you've seen things of that sort, then you may know something. If you haven't, then I have ; so I know more about it than you do, for all your cleverness, Kenneth."

" Sounds a good conjuring trick," said Felden, sceptically. " I'd like to examine that table."

" I've examined it, *most* carefully," declared Mrs. Pinfold. " It's just an ordinary card-table, one of the kind you can fold up flat ; and if you think you can hide a gramophone or a loud-speaker in the top of an ordinary card-table, you must be . . . Daphne ! " she turned to the next table where the party had finished their play, " Daphne ! Kenneth won't believe me about that Voice we heard at Mr. Ashmun's. Tell him you heard it, too. Perhaps he'll believe you, since he won't listen to me."

" I certainly heard it," Daphne confirmed.

" And so did I, Kenneth," added Ione. " That story's quite true. Honestly, it is."

" Oh, then, to save argument, I'll admit that you all heard something talking. Question is : Did it say anything worth while, when it started to chatter ? "

" It did indeed ! " declared Mrs. Pinfold, coldly. " It told me a lot of things that Mr. Ashmun couldn't have known. About my own affairs, and Stephen's last illness, and things like that."

" Ah ! " said Felden, obviously unconvinced.

" Oh, it's no good talking to you, Kenneth ! You're so shut up in this silly scientific way of thinking that you can't see anything beyond your nose if it doesn't fit in with your own little ideas. But you'll see ! Mr. Ashmun's going to make a lot of money for us with this New Force that he's discovered. If you could discover a New Force yourself you might talk."

" I might, certainly," admitted Felden. " But not till I'd taken out a patent or two."

" Patents ! " said Mrs. Pinfold, scornfully. " One doesn't need any patents to protect a discovery like this New Force. It can be worked by a secret process, and nobody could find out anything about it. That's better than patents. It's absolutely secure, Mr. Ashmun told me so."

A bell announced the refreshment interval, and half the gathering began to filter into the adjoining room where the buffet had been installed. Mrs. Pinfold examined the victuals with a critical eye.

" Couldn't they do better than this ? " she asked, turning to Daphne, who had followed her. " It's most uninteresting."

" It's all contributed by the members," Daphne pointed out. " We did our best, but people can't be expected to give up all their rations for a thing of this sort, you know. Sugar's rather short."

" Well, they ought to have done as I did," said Mrs. Pinfold. " When war broke out, I bought in . . ."

She stopped, threw a suspicious glance at the Chief Constable who joined the group at this moment, and hastened to change the subject abruptly.

" Frank ! " she addressed Allardyce. " You saw Mr. Ashmun kill rabbits at a long distance, didn't you, with his New Force ? Can you explain how that was done ? "

" I saw some dead rabbits, certainly," Allardyce admitted in a cautious tone.

" And you didn't find out how they were killed, did you ? " Mrs. Pinfold challenged.

" No, I didn't," the doctor confessed candidly.

" Then, there you are, Kenneth ! What more do you want ? " Mrs. Pinfold demanded in triumph. " That was the New Force."

" I'd rather see these things with my own eyes," said Felden, unimpressed. " No offence to you, Allardyce, of course. Still, seeing's better than second-hand evidence."

" Honestly, Kenneth, it is rather rum," interjected Ione in a persuasive tone. " I've seen some minnows killed, and Mr. Ashmun was nowhere near the tank at the time."

" I dare say," conceded Felden. " But to me that's only second-hand evidence, no better than Dr. Allardyce's. I'll believe when I see these things myself."

" I suppose you don't believe in ill-luck or the evil eye, Kenneth ? " demanded Mrs. Pinfold, with the air of one humouring a child.

" No, I don't."

" I never expected you would. You're so limited in your ideas. Scientific men *are* like that, as Mr. Ashmun always says. Still, doesn't it strike you as strange that three people have died lately and all of them have been mixed up with the Viking's hoard, the gold that was dug up at Cæsar's Camp ? "

" I was on the spot myself," retorted Felden, " and I'm still alive. I saw you there too, and you don't seem to be dead yet, Agatha."

" Oh, I'm quite safe, Kenneth. You see, I have a very powerful mascot which protects me from harm. Mr. Ashmun gave it to me, and he tells me it will ward off any evil."

" He should be an authority, of course."

A young, slightly-built man joined the group in time to catch Felden's comment. From his facial likeness to Mrs. Pinfold, Sir Clinton inferred that he was her brother, Max Stanway.

" Authority on what ? " he asked.

" On Mumbo-Jumbo," explained Felden, with an obvious sneer. " Are you another believer in Ashmun, Max ? "

" Me ? Good Lord, no ! All tommy-rot, I say. If you're talking about these manifestations, that is. What's the good of it, anyhow ? All I ask is a sound tip, convertible into hard cash. Nothing very stiff in that, surely, if the game's square. But it's all bogus, in my opinion."

" That's where you're wrong, Max," retorted Mrs. Pinfold. " Mr. Ashmun is going to make us a lot of money with his New Force."

" Is he, by Jove ? That just shows the silliness of the thing. You don't need more money, Agatha. You're rolling in it already. Now if your Bogey Man would put me in the way of making a modest million or more, then I'd believe anything he asked, and glad to do it. No such luck, though."

" You're very sordid," rejoined Mrs. Pinfold in a superior tone. " That's not the way to approach such matters."

" No ? Well, then, I shan't approach 'em at all. The loss is mine. I'll bear up under it somehow, so don't worry on my account, Agatha. Perhaps I'm not missing so much, after all."

" You're just like Kenneth," said Mrs. Pinfold crossly. " You won't even investigate the phenomena, but think it a sign of superiority to turn it all into derision."

" My ! What long words Ashmun uses ! " said Max, laughing. " You learned that up by heart, I bet. But enough of this foolery. What I came across for, was this. Our table has decided to leave its winnings for the Red Cross. A sort of bonus, you know. And I've been asked to pass round the suggestion, so that other people can follow suit. What about it ? "

" I don't see why we should do that," objected Mrs. Pinfold, pouting like a pettish child. " They'll get quite enough from the money for the tables."

" But just for once, in the cause of charity ? What do you say, Daphne ? "

" I think it's a good idea. And you'll do the same, Frank ? "

" If I have any winnings," agreed Allardyce.

" It's all the same to me," said Felden in answer to a nod from Max. " What about you, Sir Clinton ? "

" Certainly, if you wish."

" And you, Ione ? "

" Of course."

Max turned to a rather sullen-looking man who had played at Daphne's table :

" You too, Deverell ? "

" I don't mind."

" Good scout ! By the way, have a drink, will you ? You're not a member here, I know, but I'm a divot-digger in good standing, myself, with Ganymede privileges. What's it to be ? "

Deverell shook his head.

" Not now, thanks. Later on, perhaps."

" Well, if you won't, you won't," said Max. " Let's change the subject. How did Christine's wedding go, Ione ? Funny notion, getting spliced at a register office. Not even a gramophone to illustrate the proceedings with a wedding march. About as romantic as buying a pound of tea."

" It went off rather well," Ione explained. " It was more impressive than I expected, somehow, and not a bit like a visit to the grocer's, Max. In fact, with a different Registrar, it might be quite a good Ersatz for a church affair."

" What's wrong with the Registrar ? " inquired Max.

" Well, he was more than half blind to begin with, and peered about like a tortoise. Cataract, somebody told me. At the tail-end of the proceedings he mistook me for the bride and offered his congratulations. Embarrassing, in a way, but I took it like a lamb and didn't disabuse the poor man."

" Ah, well, better early than never," said Max, cheerfully. " I hope he got the lovers' knot tied O.K. That's the main thing."

" He's not very bright," said Ione. " He seemed to have got Christine mixed up with someone else, and wanted her to sign as a witness or something. Not exactly dotty, but absent-minded, perhaps. However, he spoke his piece quite well, really. I suppose he says the same thing hundreds of times a year and knows it by heart backwards, so he could hardly go wrong there."

" Many at the house, afterwards ? " asked Max.

" No, only half a dozen or so. It was very quiet."

" Dangerous affairs," commented Max. " All the girls asking themselves : ' Whose turn next ? ' and looking you up and down : ' Will he do ? '

" Oh, rubbish ! " said Ione, crossly. " You're not such a catch as all that, Max. You'll get a surprise, the first time you propose to a girl, my lad. It'll do you good. Take some of the conceit out of you, I shouldn't wonder."

" I shall bear up under it," Max assured her. " But

to hark back. About this winnings biz. Care to change your mind, Agatha ? "

" No, I shan't," said Mrs. Pinfold, mulishly.

" Right ! Nothing like sticking to one's views on such sordid matters. Now I must pass the good tidings further along."

And with a nod of farewell, he moved away to tackle some of the other players.

Felden turned to Henry Deverell.

" Don't forget you promised to give me a hand to-night," he reminded him.

" I hadn't forgotten," said Deverell, as though nettled by the assumption that he had overlooked an engagement. " It'll be a chilly business, hanging about in the open in the small hours. I wish I hadn't been so quick in refusing that drink Max offered me. You won't need me for long, will you ? I hate to lose the best part of a night's sleep."

" I shan't keep you long," Felden assured him.

" Are you still going on with those silly little experiments of yours, Kenneth ? " asked Mrs. Pinfold, disdainfully. " Nothing ever seems to come out of them, so far as I can see."

" Pleasant to be encouraged," retorted Felden, unruffled. " They're going along nicely, thanks. You'll hear the results when I get my patents."

" Oh, they don't interest me," rejoined Mrs. Pinfold with undisguised contempt. " Do *you* understand what he's doing ? " she asked, turning to Deverell.

" Not in the slightest," Deverell confessed. " All I do is to stand over a recording instrument and see it doesn't get knocked over by a sheep or a cow or a nightbird, while Kenneth is doing his stunts along the road. I know nothing about the machine's innards."

" And where are you going to-night ? " Mrs. Pinfold inquired, turning to Felden.

" My experiments don't interest you," Felden pointed out placidly. " But since you ask, we're going up Cæsar's Camp way, to try something out. We pass your friend Ashmun's house. Any kind messages for him that we could leave ? "

Mrs. Pinfold ignored the irony.

" Oh, are you ? That reminds me. Mr. Ashmun was showing me some documents this afternoon, and he dropped a paper without noticing it at the time. I found it on the floor, after he'd gone. And then he rang me up and asked me to return it to him at once. I was going to drive round on my way home to-night and give it to him. But I do hate driving. much in the black-out, and it would be out of my way altogether, and we get so little petrol nowadays that I can't waste any . . ."

" So you want me to hand it in ? " interrupted Felden. " Well, pass it over. But if I forget about it, don't blame me. I'm not in practice as an errand-boy."

" I'll see it gets there," said Deverell, tersely.

" Ah ! Thanks *so* much."

She fumbled in her bag, pulling out her handkerchief and a small slip of paper. Some coins came out along with the rest, and in her attempt to retrieve them she let the slip of paper fall to the floor along with the money. Sir Clinton swiftly retrieved the various objects and handed them back to her. As he did so, his eye caught the document, which seemed to be merely a rough sketch-map.

In a flustered fashion, Mrs. Pinfold restored the coins to her bag, and then passed the paper to Deverell.

" You didn't think of putting it into an envelope ? " said Felden with an acid smile, as Deverell pocketed the paper.

" Oh, no ! " explained Mrs. Pinfold, frankly. " I meant to hand it in myself at his house, you see. And besides, paper and envelopes are getting very dear and scarce nowadays. I never like to waste them. And now, isn't it time we went back to our table again ? I hate to miss any bridge, and really these refreshments aren't very tempting."

For the rest of the evening, she devoted herself to her game, and was obviously vexed when, in the end, she failed to secure a prize. As the party broke up, Sir Clinton recalled that he wished to see one of the superintendents on duty, and Wendover drove him to the station. It was late when they returned to the Grange, but Wendover was curious to hear the impressions which the Chief Constable had formed.

" Well, did you see anything to interest you ? " he demanded.

" It's always interesting to see whether people match the descriptions you've had of them beforehand," said Sir Clinton non-committally. " Some folk think it's easy to describe a familiar thing accurately. I sometimes wonder how they'd describe the scent of violets to a foreigner who'd never seen the flowers ; and yet most of us know the scent of violets well enough."

" Meaning, I suppose, that my descriptions of these people were nowhere near the mark ? "

" Oh, no. Some points can't be missed by even the most imperfect observer," Sir Clinton conceded, ironically. " Take

103

Allardyce and Miss Stanway. That's a case of love's young dream, or, at any rate, love's dream in the twenties. Terrible affair, this love-business, Squire. It throws even the most normal person off his balance, and you never can tell what he may be capable of, under its stimulus. Then there's Felden. He hides his feelings pretty well, but I don't think he feels over-friendly towards Allardyce. And, curiously enough, I doubt if he loves Miss Stanway either, now. He still hankers after her; anyone can see that. But if she swung back to him again, I shouldn't bet much on her chance of happiness with him, judging by a look or two that I noticed."

"Disappointment and jealousy often work that way," admitted Wendover, with an air of wisdom. "But you needn't worry. She's not likely to change her mind a second time."

"Perhaps not," said Sir Clinton with a caution which was meant to annoy Wendover. "Then there's her sister, Mrs. Pinfold. You didn't do her justice, Squire. I've seldom seen a finer example of egocentrism. The whole war means nothing to that good lady, except that it's a bit of a bore. Intellectually, I should put her down at about zero. She's affluent, I gathered."

"She's quite comfortably off."

"But wants to be richer. Well, if she's depending on Ashmun to make her a millionairess, she must be more hopeful than I am. He must be a plausible fellow. You remember the dictum of the Tichborne Claimant, Squire? ' Some people has money and no brains. Some people has brains and no money. Them as has money and no brains was made for them as has brains and no money.' That seems to me to fit the Pinfold-Ashmun combination neatly. The only problem is : what scheme is friend Ashmun using to transfer the money from the brainless to the brainy side ? It'll be something hinging on her natural rapacity, I've no doubt. People of her type will fight like wild-cats to save a penny, but they're easy money for a sharp rogue with big ideas."

"What did you make of Ione Herongate ? " inquired Wendover, with rather more concern than he had shown in the case of Mrs. Pinfold.

"You described her as a bit of a Sphinx, Squire. If she's that, then my name's Œdipus, for her riddle's child's play to me. She'll net Felden, if she can, whether he likes it or not. A clear case of ' *Venus toute entière à sa proie attachée.*' If it comes to the pinch, that girl will have few scruples. Or so I judge. But Felden seems quite competent to look

after himself. A lot of cold common sense about him.
A good bridge-player, too. As for the rest of the party,
Deverell didn't impress me. Sulky-looking devil and none
too obliging. Young Max Stanway means nothing to me.
Decent young creature, no doubt ; but when you've said
that, you've told the whole story. Your young friend, Miss
Stanway, is the most attractive of the family, by a long
chalk."

The discontinuous trill of the telephone broke in before
Wendover could reply. He picked up the instrument and
then passed it to Sir Clinton.

" One of your constables."

Sir Clinton took the instrument and listened to the
message.

" Very well. I'll go up myself, now."

He turned to Wendover with a frown.

" Deverell's dead, up at Cæsar's Camp. They got the
news at the station a few minutes ago. Camlet's on his
way. I'll need to go myself. Care to come ? "

" But . . . Deverell was all right when we saw him an
hour ago."

" How you do notice things, Squire. Nothing escapes
you," said the Chief Constable, roughly. " What's that
got to do with it ? The man's dead now, whatever he was
like an hour ago. I've only got a few details, but it sounds
like the Pirbright business over again."

Wendover was staggered by the news. Deverell was no
more than an acquaintance of his ; but it was a shock to
hear that a man whom he had seen only an hour earlier,
sound in wind and limb, had been swept out of existence.
" The Pirbright business over again." Without being superstitious, Wendover felt that something uncanny was creeping
into the air. That gaunt and ugly tract of waste land by
the old Roman camp seemed to hold something lethal,
something which struck at random out of the void, time
after time, leaving a living creature cold in death at each
of the strokes.

' An eerie affair," Wendover reflected uneasily. A recollection of Gainford and the ' local Nostradamus ' intruded
into his thoughts, but he put it resolutely aside. That sort
of thing was mere coincidence which no sensible man need
take into account. A fresher memory supervened : Mrs.
Pinfold's chatter that evening about Jehudi Ashmun and
his New Force. Rubbish, of course. All nonsense from
start to finish. Just a farrago of flapdoodle devised to net

a gull and take her money. And yet . . . Frank Allardyce was an acute medical man, the last kind of witness likely to be bamboozled ; but he had confessed that those dead rabbits had mystified him completely. Pirbright's body, Wendover had seen with his own eyes, twisted in its final agony. And now, once again, Death had come to Cæsar's Camp and struck down another victim with this occult power. Like them or like them not, one had to face plain facts.

"Moonstruck, Squire ? " demanded Sir Clinton, impatiently. "I've no time to waste. Come along, if you mean to. If not, I'll wish you good night."

Wendover put his reveries aside and followed the Chief Constable to the garage.

CHAPTER X   *Cæsar's Camp*

As the car, with its dimmed headlight, crept up the road at Cæsar's Camp, an electric torch flickered in the darkness, and a dim figure signalled them to halt. The light flashed again for a moment as its holder came up and inspected the motorists.

"Oh, it's you, sir ? We're stopping all cars. Inspector Camlet's orders, sir. He's about fifty yards on, just where you see that van's head-lamp."

The constable stepped aside, and Sir Clinton drove slowly forward, pulling up a little before reaching the van, so as not to block the narrow road. Camlet, torch in hand, came up and recognised his superior.

"Glad you've come, sir. I told them at the station to phone you. It's another Pirbright case, by the look of it. There seems to be a curse on this place," he ended, unconsciously echoing Wendover's reflections.

Sir Clinton stepped out of the car.

"Who's here ? " he inquired.

"Mr. Felden—that's his van, sir—myself, Sergeant Robson, Constables Carter and Barnby. I've called up our surgeon, but he hasn't turned up yet."

"Who's acting as surgeon ? Dr. Allardyce ? " demanded Sir Clinton.

"No, sir. Dr. Greenholme's back again, so I called him."

"Very good," approved the Chief Constable formally. "Now I want to start at the beginning. I'll see Mr. Felden first."

"Very good, sir. I'll bring him over," said Camlet.

He moved into the darkness and returned in a few seconds, followed by Felden.

"Bad business, this," said the chemist, as he encountered Sir Clinton and Wendover.

"Most of my work is a bad business," said the Chief Constable, testily. "We needn't waste words on that. What I want is your account of it. Inspector Camlet writes shorthand. He'll take down what you say. You can initial it and sign a long-hand transcription later on. You can manage, Inspector, if one of the constables throws his torch on your paper?"

"Oh, yes, sir."

"The less light we show, the better," pointed out Felden. "One never knows, in these days. Suppose Inspector Camlet sits inside my van. There's a lamp in the roof, so he'll have plenty of light; and I can stand outside the door and talk. If he leaves the door just ajar, he'll hear all I say, and no light will come out. There's a box you can sit on," he added, turning to Camlet.

"That's sensible," approved Sir Clinton. "Not that it matters much. We'll hear the planes long before they arrive, if they *are* coming to-night."

Felden led the way to the van, threw open the door, and shone his torch into the interior.

"There's the battery-box," he explained, turning his beam on to a coffin-like chest which occupied one side of the van's floor. "But keep your feet away from my apparatus. It's valuable stuff."

He swung his light quickly over an array of dials, lamps, and switches which were screwed on to the van's wall, opposite the box.

"Now get inside and close the door," he directed. "Then you can turn on the roof-light. Here's the switch."

The inspector obeyed. Sir Clinton and Wendover grouped themselves round Felden, who stood with his mouth near the crevice of the door.

"You'd better start at the point where we left that bridge-party," suggested Sir Clinton.

"Right!" agreed Felden. "I think you heard me arranging with poor Deverell about helping me to-night? And you'd hear also how Mrs. Pinfold asked him to hand in some document at Ashmun's house?"

"I heard all that," said the Chief Constable, rather impatiently. "You needn't go over it."

"Well, then, Deverell and I left the club-house just about the same time as you did. I drove him to my place first of all, put up my car, and took out this van, which I use for experiments."

"You're not sending out any wireless waves, are you?" interrupted Sir Clinton. "That sort of thing's barred nowadays. But you know that, of course."

"Of course," said Felden. "No, I'm not working on wireless lines at all. Something quite different. But that's got nothing to do with this business. I'll go on. Deverell sat beside me in front of the van. He reminded me that we had to call at Ashmun's house. I drove there, first of all."

"When did you reach his place?" interjected Sir Clinton.

"Let's see," said Felden, glancing at the luminous dial of his wrist-watch. "It's about twenty-five past one now. . . . No, it's easier to work it the other way round. I must have left my house about twenty past eleven. That would bring me to Ashmun's place about eleven-thirty, more or less. I can't put it closer."

"It may be important," Sir Clinton warned him.

"I'm not going to swear to the exact time when I don't know it," said Felden, without pique. "I'm giving you the best estimate I can."

"Call it half-past eleven, then," agreed Sir Clinton. "I'm glad to meet a witness who knows his limitations. I was afraid you'd start refining when I gave you the chance."

"No, not my line. The truth, the whole truth, and nothing but the truth. That's your motto, isn't it? In Court? I wish one could say the same for some of our scientific blokes, especially the commercially-minded ones who take out patents. But that's off the line. When we got to Ashmun's, I stayed in my seat. I'm not on visiting terms with Mr. Ashmun, and don't want to be. Deverell got down. Of course, in the black-out, one can't tell whether anyone's afoot in a house or not. However, he found his way to the front door with his torch and rang the bell. I heard the door open. Of course I saw nothing; they'd switched off the hall light before they opened the door. I heard the door shutting again, but Deverell didn't come back. I took it that he'd stepped inside to explain his errand. It was about ten minutes before he came out again and sat down beside me."

"That's a long time to take in handing over a paper," commented Sir Clinton.

"So I thought, myself, sitting out there waiting for him," said Felden. "But it was none of my business."

" You're sure it was Deverell who came out ? Not some-body else ? "

" Good Lord, yes ! I don't know what you're driving at, but it was Deverell, right enough. I've got a sensitive nose, and he smokes the heaviest brand of cigar that I've met hereabouts. I winded him at once as he sat down beside me. That kind of smoke hangs about one's clothes."

" And then ? "

" I drove on up here. That would make a matter of twenty minutes or so. We probably landed here at mid-night or thereabouts. That's only an estimate, of course. Then it took me about ten minutes to get out my recording-machine and set it up on the grass on that little knoll there. You can't see it just now, but you'll recognise it in daylight. It commands the whole strip of road for a mile and a half beyond here. That's why I use it. Once I'd got the instru-ment fixed up and ready, Deverell took charge of it. It needs no expert to watch it. All I want is to make sure it isn't disturbed by any animal that happens to be afoot in the night. It's a delicate beastie, and a spill would cause a lot of trouble. Then I left him and began running my car along the road, stopping here and there."

" That means you left Deverell here about ten past twelve ? "

" About that. I can't give you exact times. Anyhow, I ran right on with my van until I came to the second cross-roads . . ."

" How far is that ? " asked Sir Clinton.

" Well over a mile," interjected Wendover, who knew the ground.

" Then I turned, and came back again to the first cross-roads, about two hundred yards from here. I was just crawling along, then, for I know that one of your constables —Barnby's his name—comes along here on patrol just about this time, and I didn't want to risk running him down in the dark. He and I are by way of being old acquaintances. I often meet him at nights when I'm up in this zone, and we sometimes have a chat."

" I'll hear what he has to say, later," said Sir Clinton. " Just finish your story, please."

" I was standing talking with your man," Felden con-tinued, " when something caught my attention : a moaning sound coming from this direction. My ears are pretty sharp, and I heard it before Barnsby did. He thought I imagined it. However, I got him up beside me and drove towards here, perhaps a hundred yards or so, and then I stopped and told him to listen again. He heard the noise clearly enough then. I drove up here, where I'd left Deverell, and we called to him, but all the answer we got was this moaning. We got down with our torches. Barnsby found Deverell before I came up. He had moved away from my recording-machine and was lying amongst the heather, all twisted up, writhing in agony. He died under our eyes, almost as soon as we came upon him."

"About this sound," said Sir Clinton ; "you didn't hear it before you met the constable, I gather."

"No. At that distance it was faint, as I've told you ; and my engine covered it. It was only after I'd switched off to talk to Barnsby that it caught my ear."

"So you can't say for certain when it began ? "

"No. All I can tell you is when it first caught my attention. It may have started earlier, for all I know."

Sir Clinton reflected for a moment or two.

"You're a chemist," he said at last. "Did what you saw give you the idea that Deverell died of poison ? "

In his turn, Felden pondered for some seconds before speaking.

"He was frightfully sick before he died," he said, thoughtfully. "Arsenic or antimony would have that effect, certainly. Other stuffs, too, probably ; but I'm no toxicologist, so you needn't take my word for it. This is a job for an expert. It might be ptomaine poisoning. Or it might just be the pain he was in, you know. Acute pain does bring on vomiting at times, I believe. Better leave that side of it to experts. I'm not a competent witness, and in any case you'll need to have a P.M. done."

Sir Clinton reflected again.

"When Deverell joined you after visiting Ashmun, did he seem quite normal ? I mean, did you notice anything about him that struck you."

"You can't see much in the black-out," Felden pointed out, reasonably. "He might have been white as a sheet, for all I know. I'd never have seen it in the dark."

"I was thinking of his voice," Sir Clinton explained, "or any signs of physical uneasiness when he was sitting beside you."

"He didn't speak to me," Felden said. "He was always a taciturn man, you know. I didn't question him about what he'd been doing with Ashmun. None of my business. Besides, the less I hear about Ashmun, the better I'm pleased. Not my sort, that fellow. As to physical uneasiness, I suppose you're thinking that Deverell might have been in pain and wriggled in his seat, or something of that sort. I noticed nothing in that way. He seemed normal enough. It never occurred to me that he was anything else."

"Didn't you speak to him when you were fixing up your recording machine ? "

"No, he'd helped me once or twice before so he knew the ropes. I didn't need to explain anything to him. I just set up the gadget and left him to watch it."

"Was he smoking after he left Ashmun's house ? "

Felden evidently had not noticed this point particularly.

"I really don't remember clearly. My impression is that he wasn't. I think I'd have recalled the reek of those cigars of his if he'd had one in his mouth. No, I'm almost certain he wasn't smoking."

He paused for a moment and then added :

"You're thinking of a doctored cigar, perhaps ? "

"I'm not thinking of anything," said Sir Clinton, incorrectly. "I'm merely collecting the facts, relevant or not."

"Well, that seems to be all I can give you," said Felden, "unless you can think of anything else you'd like to ask."

"I may think of something else later on. Just now, I've no more questions. You can think of nothing yourself ? "

"Nothing whatever. The whole affair beats me completely."

"Then I needn't bother you further at present, Mr. Felden. You'd better get along home, now. The Coroner is sure to want you as a witness at the inquest, but you'll hear from him in due course. By the way, who are Deverell's relations, do you know ? We'll have to inform them."

"His brother was the only near relation he had," said Felden, "but he's dead now—killed in one of the raids lately. There may be cousins, but I never heard of them. Certainly there's nobody hereabouts that needs to be informed, except his housekeeper."

"Thanks," said Sir Clinton, with an air of dismissal.

Felden wished them good night, getting into his driving-seat, took his van away. When he had gone, Sir Clinton turned to the inspector.

"You remember that Dr. Allardyce examined Pirbright's body for us ? It might be not a bad idea to get him up here to see what he makes of Deverell. Dr. Greenholme will do the P.M., of course ; but Allardyce knows about the Pirbright affair and he might spot something on that account. Will you send Constable Carter down to ring up from the nearest phone box, please ? He can take my car."

"Very good, sir," answered Camlet. "And now you'll want to hear Barnsby? He's here."

The constable, hearing his name, stepped forward with a smart salute which was entirely wasted in the darkness, and then pulled out his notebook which he illuminated with his torch.

"Sir," he began, "I was on patrol to-night, coming up Stockman's Lane. At 12.35 a.m., I reached Young's Corner, just over there, along this road. Just then, a motor-van came slowly along, coming this way. It stopped and I put my torch on it and recognised the driver, Mr. Felden. I often see him up here at night, for he's doing some sort of scientific experiments and he has a lot of scientific apparatus in his van. He generally stops, when he comes across me, and has a little chat, just a few minutes. To-night he stopped when he recognised me, and we talked about the weather and the raids and whether there's likely to be any more of them soon. Just passing the time of day, as you might say."

"Has he ever allowed you to look inside his van?" asked the Chief Constable.

"Once he did, sir. I think he thought I might be interested, but I wasn't, really. I don't understand much about these scientific affairs, and all I saw was a lot of dials, and switches, and coils, and a big box like a coffin on the floor with a lot of batteries in it. The lid was open, just then; that's how I know about the batteries inside. He told me he was doing some stunt or other. . . . I mean he said he was carrying out some research, so he called it, which might help with the war, but it was all hush-hush, as we used to say in the last war, sir. It was all over my head, of course, but I noticed something that looked like a wireless valve so I just asked him if he was working a wireless set—a transmitter, I mean, sir—because that wasn't allowed. But he said it was nothing of the sort. I made a note in my book about it and reported it at the time, sir."

"We looked into it, sir," Camlet intervened. "It's not a wireless transmitter."

"Go on," said Sir Clinton to Barnsby.

The constable referred again to his note-book by the help of his torch.

"At 12.37 a.m. Mr. Felden broke off in what he was saying and asked me if I didn't hear something funny. I said I heard nothing out of the common. Then he said he'd heard a sort of moaning sound. He asked me to get into the seat beside him and then he drove along till we got within about a hundred yards of here, so far as I could see in the dark.

Then he stopped his engine and asked me to listen again, and sure enough I did hear a sort of groaning, coming from this direction. So he drove on again, and stopped where you saw the van standing, sir. And when he switched off, I heard the moaning very loud, like somebody in terrible pain and gasping between whiles. So I jumped down, and he jumped down, too, and we began to hunt about and I came upon a man lying in the heather, all twisted up and writhing and groaning, and just as I got my torch on him, he gave a last sort of squirm and the sounds stopped. He must ha' died, right under my eyes, sir. So I took a good look at him, seeing there was nothing else we could do for him; and I recognised him straight off for Mr. Henry Deverell, because I'd seen him when he was giving evidence to the Coroner about the death of his brother, when I was on duty, taking the place of Constable Dickenson who was ill that day. So I waited there, sir, and sent Mr. Felden off in his motor-van to ring up the station and give them at the office about what had happened, and then when he came back, we just stood by until Inspector Camlet came along."

" That was at ten past one, sir," volunteered Camlet.

" Did you notice anything specially about Deverell when you first came upon him ? " Sir Clinton asked the constable.

" He'd been frightful sick, sir. And he had a fearful squint, too. I just happened to notice that, because one could hardly help seeing it, it was so strong. I smelt his face, thinking it might be a D.T. case, sir. But he'd been sick and that covered anything there might have been in the way of smells. It looked to me like a poisoning case, with bad gripes, sir, the way he was going on before he died. I said as much to Mr. Felden, him being a chemist and likely to know about such matters ; but he said he knew nothing about poisons and seemed a bit put out when he thought I didn't believe him, for I always thought chemistry was poisons and such like."

" You saw nobody else about ? "

" No, sir."

" Let's have a look at the body, now," said Sir Clinton to Camlet.

The inspector led him aside from the road a dozen yards or so and then turned his torch downward to illuminate the corpse of Deverell, lying in the dreadful disorder of an agonising death. Sir Clinton knelt down and made a careful examination of the face by the help of his own torch.

" Just the same as Pirbright," he commented as he rose

to his feet again and dusted the knees of his trousers mechanically. "His pupils are expanded and obviously he must have suffered a lot before he passed out. By the way, where's that recording instrument that Felden mentioned? He didn't take it away, did he?"

"No, sir. I expect he must have forgotten about it, with all this happening. It's further on, if you'll come this way."

Sir Clinton followed the inspector another twenty yards or so and turned his torch on the instrument, which stood on a low tripod amongst the grass at the top of a low mound. The Chief Constable examined it and noticed that a black funnel on the top was moving slowly from right to left and back again, evidently actuated by some mechanism inside a box.

"It looks like a bolometer," he hazarded.

"Bolometer, sir? Never heard of it," confessed Camlet.

"A machine for measuring the strength and wave-length of radiations," explained Sir Clinton. "It's used for examining the infra-red spectra. I've seen it in a scientific friend's laboratory. That oscillating funnel seems to be arranged to 'scan' the strip of road down there and pick up any heat-rays from motor-car exhausts and things of that sort. But that's only a guess of mine; I don't know for certain."

"Shall I shift the thing, sir?"

"No, you'd better leave it alone till we get our photographs taken by daylight. After that, Felden can take it away himself. It's a delicate gadget and we might put it out of order in handling it."

"Very good, sir. I think that must be Dr. Greenholme's car coming up now."

"You might bring him here, then, please."

"Very good, sir."

Sir Clinton knew Dr. Greenholme well enough to expect little information in the preliminary phases of an investigation. The doctor was a taciturn man who seldom ventured a definite assertion until he could support it by conclusive proof. He greeted the Chief Constable curtly, made a careful examination of the body, and then rose to his feet again without proffering the slightest comment.

"Well?" queried Sir Clinton.

"Well!" retorted Greenholme and relapsed into unstudied silence.

"Do you make anything of him?" inquired Sir Clinton.

"He's dead. Died about an hour ago, perhaps. Or less."

"Natural death?" asked Sir Clinton ironically.

"I don't think so. Considerable pain before the end,

apparently. That may have made him sick. Not heart-block, or he'd be blue in the face. Pupils dilated markedly. Might be some mydriatic drug like atropine or hyoscine."

" You found a mydriatic drug in the Pirbright case. Does this suggest the same state of affairs ? "

" Superficially, yes."

" Suppose it were hyoscine, what would the fatal dose be ? "

" It varies from case to case. Not safe, usually, to give more than about one-hundredth of a grain."

" And for atropine ? "

" Round about one and a half grains, it's supposed to be."

" Hyoscine's more powerful, then ? "

" It is, much. Here's a case I remember. One grain of hyoscine hydrobromide was made into a one per cent. solution with water. Two drops of this were put into each eye of a patient. Within five minutes she grew giddy and had to be helped into bed. She lost her speech and was soon unconscious. Four hours later, she woke up in a delirium which lasted for a couple of hours. Four drops of a one per cent. solution sounds harmless enough ; but that was the effect. I'm not an expert, though. Allardyce could tell you better about it. He's had practical experience of the stuff in this twilight sleep stunt."

" Is it easily procurable ? " asked Sir Clinton.

" Not by the general public. Since Crippen used hyoscine, a druggist would think twice and oftener before he sold any to a layman."

" We may want to know exactly how much was administered to Deverell, if he was dosed with it at all."

" Get one of the Home Office experts on to it, then," Greenholme advised. " That's no job for me ; I know my limitations. I'll tell you if a mydriatic drug's present, but after that get the best man you can on to the business. You'll need him."

Steps sounded, and Constable Carter appeared in the light of Sir Clinton's torch.

" I'm sorry, sir," he reported. " Dr. Allardyce's phone's out of order. I can't get on to him."

" Well, never mind," said the Chief Constable. " By the way, did you meet anyone on the road ? "

" No one walking, sir," said Carter. " But a car did drive out of a side lane as I was going down. I noted the number, just on chance. It was GZ.7777."

Sir Clinton noted Wendover's slight change of expression as he heard the figures.

" You know that car ? " he asked.

Wendover nodded and drew the Chief Constable aside.

" It's Ione Herongate's car," he explained in a low tone. " I remember the number because of the four seven's. But there's no need to drag her name into the business. That's why I didn't want to speak about it before that crowd."

Sir Clinton refused to commit himself, but he turned back to the other officials and changed the subject.

" There's nothing more that we can do here, is there ? We'll leave two constables at Dr. Greenholme's disposal. Our next business is to see this fellow Ashmun and find out what happened when Deverell paid him that call to-night. Come in my car and leave your own here for emergencies. I'll see you get home all right."

CHAPTER XI   *Jehudi Ashmun*

WENDOVER GOT INTO THE FRONT SEAT BESIDE SIR CLINTON, whilst the inspector took his place in the back of the car. For a time no one spoke. Then Sir Clinton surprised Wendover by beginning to hum an air from *The Sorcerer :*

> " *O ! my name is John Wellington Wells.*
> *I'm a dealer in magic and spells,*
> *In blessings and curses*
> *And ever-filled purses,*
> *In prophecies, witches, and knells.*"

" Very light-hearted, you seem to be," said Wendover, acidly.

" Am I ? " rejoined the Chief Constable. " That verse crossed my mind, and I was running it over to see just how much of it fits the case of your local Bogey Man. He seems to be a dealer in magic, and perhaps in spells, too, for all I know. I'm not sure about blessings ; but—*teste* the late Anthony Gainford—he certainly posed as an authority on curses and prophecies. ' Ever-filled purses ? ' He's doing his best to fill his own, anyhow, as a start, from all one can gather. As for knells, both Gainford and Henry Deverell came to grief, whether knells were rung for them or not. Take it over all, it concords fairly well, I think. I burn to make the acquaintance of this Ashmun."

" Well, I don't," declared Wendover, after a brief mental struggle between his curiosity and his distaste for Ashmun and all he represented. " I shall wait outside in the car while you visit his Den of Mystery. I've no use for the man."

" You don't care for parlour magic ? " queried Sir Clinton. " I rather enjoy it, myself. It's all right in the parlour. When it strays out of its province into the highways and byways and causes unfortunate incidents, then, of course, it becomes a matter of professional interest as well ; and I can combine business and pleasure with a clear conscience. As at this moment."

He swung the car into the little drive leading up to the door of Ashmun's house and pulled up at the front steps.

" Last words," he said, with mock-seriousness. " If you hear an owl screech or a dog howling, you'll know it's not worth waiting for us to come back. A corpse-candle in the night is also a sure sign of death. If you sneeze twice, it comes to much the same thing—or else you've caught cold. And, by the way, if friend Ashmun is really in the John Wellington Wells line, is there any little thing I can buy for you ? ' Our penny curse—one of the cheapest things in the trade—is considered infallible.' Not want one ? You could send it home to roost, you know, since you don't like our necromatic friend. Well, we shan't keep you waiting long, I hope. Come along, Inspector."

He went up the steps, located the bell-push with his torch, and rang. After a short pause, the door swung open, but the hall within remained dark. Sir Clinton, with no regard for courtesy, turned his light on the figure which stood on the threshold : a tall, powerful, swarthy man in a dark lounge suit.

" I'm the Chief Constable. I want to see Mr. Ashmun," said Sir Clinton, tersely.

" I am he," said the swarthy man, in a deep musical voice.

He made no gesture of invitation, but Sir Clinton had no intention of conducting the interview on the doorstep. He wanted to watch the man's face as he questioned him.

" We'll go inside, if you don't mind."

The mulatto's brilliant teeth showed in a broad smile.

" Ah ! Forgive my seeming discourtesy. At this hour of night—or morning, rather—one is naturally suspicious of unknown callers."

He stood aside to allow Sir Clinton and the inspector to enter. Then, closing the door, he switched on the light and ushered them into one of the public rooms of the house.

" Is my black-out defective ? " he inquired, politely. " I have taken special pains with it since these raids, but of course there may be some chink which has escaped my notice."

"I haven't called about your black-out," Sir Clinton explained. " merely to make an inquiry or two on another matter. You had a visitor earlier in the evening, I think ? "

Inspector Camlet noticed that Sir Clinton put the question in the bored tone of a man carrying out a formality which had little to interest him.

"A visitor ? " echoed Ashmun. "I had a number of visitors here this evening : Mr. Silwood, Mr. Dibdin, Miss Avarn, Mr. Bulstrode, Mrs. Stanbury, Mrs. Hammet, Miss Roding and . . . let me see . . . Mr. Speldhurst. I think that is all."

"A meeting of your . . . er . . . associates ? "

"I'm afraid I don't quite take your meaning," said Ashmun, still with the utmost courtesy, though with a faint suspicion of irony in his tone. "My . . . er . . . associates ? They are friends of mine, certainly."

"When did they leave the house ? "

Ashmun seemed inclined to jib at this point, but he covered his hesitation with one of his ingratiating smiles.

"Some of them left early. Others stayed longer. In fact, it is only twenty minutes or so since Mr. Silwood went home. He and Mr. Dibdin were the last to go. But I do not see why their visit should interest you."

"I'll be quite frank with you, Mr. Ashmun," said Sir Clinton, still in the tone of one pursuing an inquiry without any real interest in the results. "Certain rumours have come to my ears about your doings. Exaggerated, no doubt. But when tales of that kind reach the constabulary, we have to act, whether we like it or not. Probably you're not acquainted with the terms of the Witchcraft Act, 1735. ' If any person shall pretend to exercise or use any kind of witchcraft, sorcery, enchantment, or conjuration, or undertake to tell fortunes, or pretend from his or her skill or knowledge in any occult or crafty science to discover where or in what manner any goods or chattels supposed to be stolen or lost may be found . . . .' that's an offence, punishable by imprisonment. Nice old-fashioned wording, isn't it ? Now I put it to you : Have you been pretending to use any kind of witchcraft, sorcery, enchantment, or conjuration? If you have, I wish you'd favour me with a demonstration ; for personally I don't believe in witchcraft, except for official purposes."

Ashmun listened intently to the recital of the law, and then broke into a deep melodious laugh of the most unaffected kind.

"No," he declared at last, when he had got over his merriment. "I don't practice witchcraft or any of the other

things you've mentioned. I'm an investigator of odd phenomena, which is quite a different matter. If I'm doing wrong,
then you'll have to put under arrest the whole membership
of the Society for Psychical Research, for their case is the
same as mine."

" Quite so," agreed Sir Clinton. " I thought that a few
minutes conversation with you would clear the matter up and
save a lot of gossip. Psychical research, of course. That's
an interesting subject. I remember reading the Society's
Journal a while ago and coming on a contribution by Sir
William Ramsay on the psychical effects of ether narcosis. A
curious affair. Guy de Maupassant describes exactly the
same effects in his *Sur l'Eau*. Ether seems to make you think
in a sort of geometrical progression—by leaps and bounds—
instead of plodding along in arithmetical progression as we
do in our normal state. Have you ever tried experiments of
that sort, Mr. Ashmun ? Ether, atropine, hashish, hyoscine,
morphine ? They all seem to set the mental faculties askew
in a peculiar fashion."

Now that he had apparently turned aside from official
matters, Sir Clinton's voice lost the suggestion of boredom
and betrayed real interest. But Ashmun's experiments had
apparently not led him into the field of drugs. He shook his
great head with an ingratiating smile which showed his
gleaming teeth between red lips.

" That is very interesting indeed," he commented. " But
it lies outside my field, I am afraid. Drugs do not attract
me ; though we have many curious simples in my native
country, things which are as yet unstudied in Europe, poisons
and counter-poisons. I have seen some of them employed
by our native physicians—witch-doctors, if you like. Very
curious. But not in my line of inquiry."

Sir Clinton seemed disappointed by this lack of interest.
Camlet expected him to inquire what Ashmun's real field of
investigation was, but instead of doing this he switched back
to an earlier topic.

" You mentioned the names of a number of people who
were with you to-night. Mr. Silwood, Miss Avarn, and some
others. Eight in all, if my recollection is right. Would you
mind giving me their addresses ? I wish to settle this idle
chatter, you understand, once and for all. Inspector Camlet
will take down the particulars."

Ashmun seemed quite ready to supply the required information, and the inspector jotted down the list in his note-book.

" And these are all the people who came here to-night ? "

inquired Sir Clinton casually, as Ashmun reached the end of his catalogue.

"These are all the guests whom I invited," the mulatto rectified with his usual smile. "Another person came, but he stayed only for a few minutes and he has nothing to do with my psychical investigations. I hardly know him, in fact. He merely called with a message from a lady of my acquaintance, Mrs. Pinfold."

"Who was he?" asked Sir Clinton, carelessly.

"A Mr. Deverell—Henry Deverell, I think is his name. He is a brother of the Deverell who was killed in an air raid lately."

"Not one of your circle, then?"

"No, I've spoken to him only once or twice in my life. He was merely a messenger."

"What sort of a message did he bring?"

"Nothing of any importance," said Ashmun, easily. "A paper which I had mislaid and which Mrs. Pinfold kindly returned to me."

"May I see it?" demanded Sir Clinton, fussily.

"I am afraid not. It was of no permanent importance. I burned it when I'd finished with it."

The Chief Constable's eye went to the empty grate.

"In the fire?"

Ashmun nodded, as though he had not noticed the glance.

"You keep fires in your house in May?" persisted Sir Clinton.

"Oh, yes," Ashmun explained. "I was brought up in a hot climate, you see. Liberia, where I come from, is almost on the Equator. Naturally, I find even your English May rather chilly, and I keep a fire going in my study, even on what you would regard as warm days. You would like to see it? Then please come this way."

He led them into a smaller room where, sure enough, a fire was burning. Sir Clinton gave it no more than a glance.

"Mr. Deverell brought you this paper from Mrs. Pinfold. Did he simply hand it in at the door?"

"Oh, no. I asked him to come in for a moment. But he did not stay more than a minute or two. He realised that he'd called me away from a meeting, and he took himself off after he'd handed over the paper."

"Did you offer him a drink?"

Ashmun's expressive face puckered in a queer grimace of vexation.

"You remind me of my inhospitality," he said, with an air of apology. "I ought to have offered you something.

What will you have? Whisky and soda? It's here. No trouble at all."

" No, thanks," said Sir Clinton, politely. " I make it a rule not to drink when I'm on duty, as I am now."

Ashmun glanced invitingly at the inspector, who shook his head.

" You are sure you won't join me? I'm going to have a drink myself anyhow. Mr. Deverell had one with me."

He opened a cupboard, extracted a decanter, siphon, and tumbler, and mixed himself a liberal portion. Sir Clinton waited patiently until his involuntary host had taken a long drink from his glass.

" Did you notice anything strange in Deverell's behaviour when he left your house? "

" Anything strange? Remember, I hardly know the man. If you mean that he was drunk, or excited, or sleepy, I can only say that I noticed nothing of the kind. He seemed to me a rather surly person, not too well pleased at having been asked to bring me this paper. He had someone waiting for him outside, in a car. Apart from that, I can't say I observed anything worth mentioning about him. But I was anxious to get back to my guests, as you can understand."

Ashmun finished the rest of his whisky at a gulp, and then evidently suppressed a yawn.

" I see that we're keeping you from bed," said Sir Clinton apologetically. " We mustn't detain you any longer. Thanks for the information you've given us. But it's best to get these things cleared up and put a stop to gossip. Certainly I'll have no hesitation in saying to anyone that I don't suspect you of witchcraft, Mr. Ashmun."

The whisky seemed to have loosened Ashmun's tongue, for instead of allowing his visitors to go at once, he exerted himself to detain them.

" Witchcraft? " he echoed. " No, we do not believe in that nowadays, do we? Not in England, at any rate. In Africa it is different, of course."

" I only know South Africa," said Sir Clinton. " Have you been in the back country of Liberia, Mr. Ashmun? "

" Oh, yes, I spent some years in it, at one time. It is not a very pleasant district. These blacks "—his expressive face betrayed intense contempt and disgust—' they are degraded specimens. Some of them are still cannibals, you know. A loathsome lot, really. You remember Joseph Conrad's Kurtz? ' Exterminate all the brutes ! ' That was on the Congo, of course ; but sometimes I used to feel just as Kurtz did, when I was in the back lands, living in close contact with these creatures. I hated them, and I hate them still. And yet they know some things. They have a curious knowledge of drugs which is only beginning to filter out nowadays. I have seen some very funny things amongst them."

A rather unpleasant smile of reminiscence crossed his face for a moment and vanished.

"Human life is very cheap down there," he added thoughtfully. "Not so cheap as you Europeans have made it, of course, in the last thirty years or so ; but comparatively inexpensive. You remember the story of Stanley's Rear Column, perhaps, with the incident of a black girl bought for a bale of cloth and eaten on the spot? I've seen something not so very different myself. It gives one a definite idea of the comparative cheapness of human life, despite all the fuss you white men pretend to make about it."

He seemed suddenly to realise that he was letting his tongue run away with him.

"I must not detain you with these recollections of mine."

"Very instructive," said Sir Clinton, with a smile, "and I can't deny your thesis about the cheapness of human life nowadays. Our friends the enemy have certainly managed to lower the standard a good deal in that field. Well, Mr. Ashmun, good night."

"That's a nasty piece of work, sir," said the inspector, as they rejoined Wendover in the car. "He doesn't like us whites, and he despises his own black lot."

"Well, what can you expect?" chimed in Wendover, as the car moved off. "When a man grows up to despise his mother and hate his father, there's not likely to be much good in him, is there? I'm glad I didn't cross his threshold. Did he tell you anything?"

"Only indirectly," said Sir Clinton, evasively. "Now, we'll go and break into Allardyce's slumbers, and then home."

When they reached the doctor's house, they had little difficulty in rousing him. The night-bell brought him downstairs almost immediately, heavy-eyed, with rumpled hair, in his pyjamas.

"What's all the stir about?" he demanded, not too good temperedly, when he identified his visitors by the light of a torch. "Do you know that I was up all last night over a case, and now you've waked me up at this ungodly hour just when I wanted to make up some sleep?"

"Henry Deverell's dead," said Sir Clinton, curtly. "We've

just come down from Cæsar's Camp. Greenholme has the thing in charge, but I want you to see the body. The symptoms seem much the same as Pirbright's."

Allardyce seemed staggered by the news.

"Deverell? Why he was as right as rain only an hour or two ago. And what was he doing up at Cæsar's Camp, anyway? At this time of night?"

Sir Clinton gave him a succinct account of the affair.

"The body will be up there until daylight," he added. "We want some photographs; and we can't go blazing off magnesium flashlights in the black-out, of course. But I wish you'd go and have a look round before they shift him. The situation might suggest something to you, for all one can tell; otherwise I'd have waited till they got him down to the mortuary and saved knocking you up at this hour. By the way, would you mind if I used your phone?"

"Not a bit," said the doctor. Then he added hastily: "No, you can't. It's burst. I was talking over the line to-night, and wanted to look up a case-sheet during the conversation. I forgot I'd the ear-piece in my hand, and when I walked across the room I brought the whole damn thing over with a crash on to the floor. It's gone phut. I had to go to a neighbour's house to finish my conversation."

"Oh, well, it can't be helped," said Sir Clinton, philosophically. "By the way, was this case you spoke about a maternity one?"

"Yes."

"One of your twilight sleep affairs? By the way, do you ever find these patients showing signs of excitement when you give the injection? Take this last one as an example."

"Oh, no," explained Allardyce. "One gauges the dope carefully."

"On a pair of apothecaries' scales?" demanded Sir Clinton, sceptically.

"No, I've got a decent balance, of course, for use in that kind of work. Turns with less than a milligramme, and the rider makes it even more delicate."

"Well, I'm sorry we've had to bother you. You weren't too bored with that bridge-party, I hope?"

"Not a bit," said Allardyce. "Though at times I felt inclined to yawn. Sleepiness, you know, after an all-night job. But it ended at a reasonable time, and I came straight home and got to bed."

"You didn't drive Miss Stanway back, then?"

"Oh, no. She had her own car."

" Well, that finishes me for the present," said Sir Clinton,
suppressing a yawn. " You'll see Deverell before they shift
him ? Thanks. And now, I think I'll get to bed myself.
I'm not so young as you are, and I don't stand the loss of
sleep as well as you have to do, whether you like it or not.
Good night."

CHAPTER XII   *An Eligible Building Site*

AFTER DROPPING THE INSPECTOR AT HIS HOME, WENDOVER
and Sir Clinton drove back to Talgarth Grange. Despite
his earlier protestations, the Chief Constable showed no
great eagerness to go to bed.

" I see a decanter and glasses on that tray," he said,
dropping into an easy-chair. " Two fingers will be enough,
Squire. And most of the soda, I think. My throat's dry
after talking so much. Thanks. And now, the night's no
more than middle-aged ; in its prime, in fact. So unless
you're sleepy, I'd like one or two bits of information."

Wendover charged his own glass and took his accustomed
chair.

" I'm not too sleepy. Ask what you want."

" Perhaps you may remember something which happened
while we broke off for refreshments, to-night. Mrs. Pinfold
asked Deverell to call at Ashmun's house in passing and
give him a bit of paper. She happened to drop the paper
on the floor, and I picked it up for her ; and my eye caught
it as I did so. There was a scribble of some sort on one
side which I didn't read ; but on the other side there was
a kind of sketch-map. I had only a momentary glance
at it, but I've got a good visual memory, and I think I can
reproduce it very roughly."

Taking a notebook and pencil from his pockets, he reflected
for a moment or two, and then sketched a few lines on one
of the pages.

" I can't remember the scale," he explained, passing the
book to Wendover, " and of course the contouring is no
more than a wild guess. But that's roughly what it looked like."

Wendover took the sketch and examined it with a doubtful
expression on his face.

" I think you've got it upside down," suggested Sir Clinton.
" There were no compass-points in the original, but if you
turn it the other way up, I believe the North will be at the top."

124

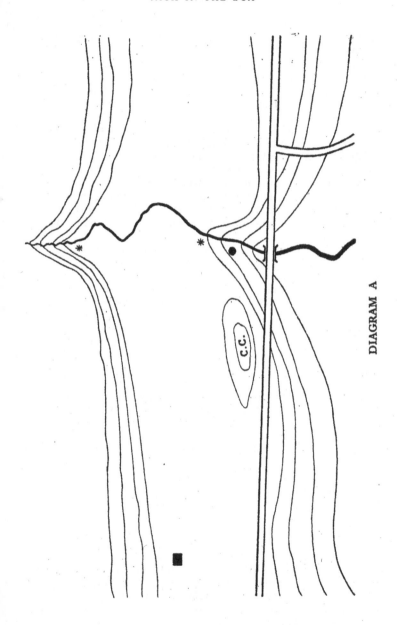

DIAGRAM A

125

Wendover reversed the map, but seemed little the wiser.

" What does ' C.C.' mean ? " he demanded.

" I'm afraid my memory of the contouring isn't all it might be," admitted the Chief Constable. " But my impression is that ' C.C.' stands for Cæsar's Camp, and the thing is a rough plan of the ground round about the place we visited to-night. That black circle represents the bomb-crater ; you see the position of the Camp ; and that little rectangle is meant for Pirbright's shack or his garden. As I told you, my scale and contours are vague ; but the general look of the thing is right enough."

Wendover re-examined the sketch.

" It's about as like the Cæsar's Camp ground as it's like anything," he admitted, rather doubtfully. " I'll get a six inches to the mile Ordnance map, if you like, and we can compare it."

" Another time, Squire," said Sir Clinton, checking him with a gesture. " The night's getting no younger, and I feel pretty sure of my guess."

" I don't see much to make a fuss about, even if you are right," confessed Wendover. " Anyone might think it worth while to trace a sketch-map of the place where there's been a mysterious crime, like Pirbright's business. I've often done it myself, so as to save the bother of unfolding a map when I wanted to study the lie of the land as evidence dribbled out in Court."

" Then I'd better tell you something further, which you missed by averting your skirts from friend Ashmun to-night. I called on him, as you probably guessed, because I knew that Deverell visited that mulatto's house before he went up to his death at Cæsar's Camp. I'd heard the talk between Mrs. Pinfold and Deverell at the golf club-house buffet, so I knew something about the paper which she wanted handed to Ashmun. Naturally I didn't bleat that abroad, but asked your dark friend a few artless questions. In reply, he up and spoke very frankly indeed. He couldn't have guessed how much I knew, yet his statements tallied well with the actual facts, so far as Deverell's concerned. This is more or less what I got out of him."

Sir Clinton gave Wendover the gist of the interview between himself and Ashmun. At the end of it, the Squire reflected for a moment or two before speaking.

" This is what strikes me, Clinton," he began. " We've got to account for three rum affairs which seem inter-connected. There's Allardyce's tale of those rabbits which

Ashmun claimed to have killed with his New Force. There's the Pirbright affair. And now there's this latest business. Every one of the victims died in cramps."

" That's so," agreed Sir Clinton.

" Both Pirbright and Deverell had dilated pupils, which points to a mydriatic alkaloid."

" But there was no mydriatic alkaloid in the rabbits, according to Allardyce's account," Sir Clinton objected.

" Rabbits are peculiar when it comes to mydriatic alkaloids," rejoined Wendover. " You know a rabbit can feed on belladonna without suffering the slightest harm, and yet it absorbs so much atropine that its flesh would be rank poison to a human being. That's plain fact."

" Admitted," said Sir Clinton. " But that seems to be arguing the wrong way round, Squire. If the rabbit case and the Pirbright and Deverell cases are on all fours, then Allardyce ought to have found the rabbits reeking with an alkaloid, according to your line of reasoning. Actually he didn't spot any mydriatic alkaloid in his rabbits."

Wendover made a gesture of impatience.

" All I argue is that rabbits react differently from human beings. It's on the cards that some mydriatic alkaloid may affect rabbits strongly and human beings much less so. Atropine the other way round, in fact. In that case, a mere trace of the stuff might kill a rabbit, and Allardyce's experiments may not have been refined enough to detect the minute quantity left in the bodies of the rabbits."

Sir Clinton shook his head doubtfully.

" It's not impossible," he conceded. " But I don't remember any mydriatic alkaloid which produces the symptoms we want."

" No more do I," said Wendover, triumphantly. " That's my very point. But a simple African native knows a thing or two in that field, more than the European has learned yet, by a long chalk. They knew all about yohimbine and things like that long ago. It's only lately that Europeans ever heard of these stuffs ; and it was the natives who put us on to them. We didn't discover them ourselves."

" Now I see what you're driving at," admitted Sir Clinton. " Friend Ashmun is an African native on one side of his family. Friend Ashmun has lived up country amongst his uncivilised but learned relations. Friend Ashmun has picked up a thing or two about alkaloids still unknown to Europeans. Therefore friend Ashmun is the fellow to watch. That's your line of argument, Squire ? Something in it, perhaps. Or, again, perhaps not. There's no charge for taking your choice."

"Oh, he's evidently fascinated you," said Wendover, tartly. "A snow-white angel, fresh from a bath of peroxide, no doubt."

"Not snow-white, exactly, I'll admit. Only lepers fit that adjective, and not all of them if you come to that. But he does interest me, Squire. All this bogey business seems to me pretty smart work for an untutored son of Ham, born and bred in Liberia. Still, mulattos are often highly intelligent, one must remember. No one could say that Dumas lacked brains, to take the first case that comes to mind. You let your prejudices run away with you, at times."

"Did you inquire about his New Force?"

"I did not. Anyone's entitled to discover fifty New Forces without infringing the law."

"But if he uses his New Force for lethal purposes?"

"Come, come, Squire! You can't have it both ways. Do you believe that he has discovered a New Force?"

"No, I don't. I think it's a damned fake, if you want my opinion."

"Then he can't have been using a New Force for lethal purposes. And where do the police come in? You can't arrest a man for using a New Force illegally, unless you can prove the reality of the New Force. Now, can you? I've no evidence to show that there's any New Force in the business at all. Officially, it's no affair of mine. If he tried to sell a method of extracting sunbeams from cucumbers, then we might have a word to say about it. But so far, I see no evidence to prove that he's done anything illegal."

"I suppose there's something in what you say," confessed Wendover, rather crestfallen. "But you can't pretend that Pirbright and Deverell died natural deaths, and it's up to you people to get to the root of such things. What do you think about it, really, Clinton?"

"The sight of that sketch-map set me thinking about something you said, a while ago," answered the Chief Constable. "Here's this tract of ground out by Cæsar's Camp. It's within easy bus reach of the magneto-factory and the other war places in Ambledown. There's been a big influx of workers since the war, and they need housing. That ground would be a very useful site for huts and so forth. Why hasn't it been developed, Squire? It would pay better to use it than to let it lie derelict as it is now. I remember you said something about a building restriction."

"There is a restriction on it," Wendover confirmed.

"But if you want the whole story, it'll take me a little time to tell."

"I don't mind sitting up for another quarter of an hour," said Sir Clinton. "It can't take longer than that, surely. Go ahead, Squire."

"Very well," Wendover acquiesced. "You've heard me grumbling at times about a firm of speculative builders who ruined part of this district by their activities? Rodway, Deverell, Felden & Co. There was no Co. The three partners held all the shares amongst them. Old Rodway, Joseph Rodway, was the brains of the concern. Just before last war—about 1913, I think—he decided to retire. He was about seventy, then, and was losing his grip. He cleared out, and by arrangement the other two partners took over his shares. I suspect that he still retained enough acuteness to drive a hard bargain. Anyhow, the firm got a bit of a shake, and after that it simply went down-hill. The collapse of the house-building trade during the last war seems to have finished them, and the firm came a complete smash. Both Felden and Deverell died during the war; but old Rodway lived on till 1918, when he died, too, aged seventy-five, and a bit senile in some ways."

"The names seem familiar," interjected Sir Clinton. "Any connection with the Felden and Deverells whom I've come across lately?"

"You'll see in a moment," Wendover assured him. "As I said, old Rodway—he was a bachelor—got a bit senile towards the end. You know the saying that if a man's his own lawyer, he's got a fool for a client. Rodway had a great idea of himself as a business man and imagined that he was competent to draw up his own will, without legal assistance. He'd no relations nearer than second cousins once removed or something equally close; but he parcelled out the main bulk of his estate amongst them. I heard at the time that there was some litigation amongst the heirs, owing to the way he drew up his will. You may cheat lawyers out of a fee for drawing up your will, but if you do, they generally seem to come out pretty well later on when it comes to settling up the estate amongst the disgruntled inheritors. But that's beside the point. These people don't come into it from our present point of view."

Sir Clinton knew that once Wendover wandered into local history he was apt to grow talkative, so he brought him back to the point.

"Cæsar's Camp, Squire,"

"I'm just coming to it," said Wendover, impatiently. "Old Rodway in his day had done a bit of land speculation. Most towns expand westward, and he had some queer notion that Ambledown would eventually become much bigger than it was. So he bought up, freehold, all that tract of land round about Cæsar's Camp, with the idea of holding it as a spec. He seems to have regarded it as sure to appreciate, if it was held long enough. I don't know that he was wrong, altogether. It would make quite a nice suburb if Ambledown ever does expand, as he expected it to do. Anyhow, he thought a lot of it.

"When he came to draw up this will of his, I think he must have had some qualms of conscience over the bargain he'd driven with his partners when he cleared out of the firm, and perhaps he took it into his head to make some sort of reparation. I don't know, of course. It's just a guess of mine. The facts are simply that he left that tract of ground in trust for the grand-children of his two partners. It was to be left undeveloped until September, 1942, and then the surviving grand-children could do what they chose with it."

"Why 1942?" demanded Sir Clinton.

"He was born in 1842," explained Wendover. "I suppose his idea was to let the thing remain undeveloped for about a quarter of a century, and he chose September, 1942, because it was the centenary of his birth, thus killing two birds with one stone. But that's only my own surmise. The point is that nobody can build or do anything else with the ground before next September. Then it belongs jointly to the grand-children of his partners, Deverell and Felden; and they can do whatever they please with it: sell it, lease it, or develop it as a building site, just as they settle among themselves."

"It may be valuable, post-war," said Sir Clinton. "There's bound to be a building boom then, just as there was after the last war. Who are the grand-children?"

"On the Deverell side, it's simple enough," answered Wendover. "Robert Deverell was old Rodway's partner. He had only one child, Wallace, who died ten or twelve years ago, leaving two sons. One of these was Robert Deverell who got killed in that air-raid lately; the archæologist fellow, I mean. The other was Henry Deverell who died to-night up at Cæsar's Camp. So that section of the inheritors is off the map completely."

"Who are the others?"

"The other partner was Paul Felden. He had two sons

and two daughters. The eldest son, Bruce Felden, was a black sheep, one of those rolling stones who never gather anything but a bad reputation. He left this neighbourhood suddenly after seducing a local girl before he'd even come of age. He wasn't a marrying sort, and cleared out rather than make a honest woman of the poor thing. She and the child died when it was born. The next I heard of him was that he was in America, living the life of a hobo, stealing rides on freight-wagons down South in the autumn, living down there through the winter and then strolling North again a mile or two behind the Spring, and railing down again after the summer was over and cold weather set in. After a bit, he got tired of that and worked his passage home, turning up here like a bad penny. His relations raised some cash for him. He came to see me with a hard-luck story and borrowed money to get out of England. He was a most plausible liar. Of course I knew I'd never get repayment, but it was worth it to get the beast out of the neighbourhood. I had an impudent letter from him, years afterwards, advising me to draw on the Lord if I wanted my cash back again : ' He that giveth to the poor, lendeth to the Lord,' you know. He quoted that to me. Evidently his idea of a good joke. I believe he went to Africa from here, then on to China, where he fell into more trouble. He was killed in New Guinea, ten or fifteen years ago, in some scrap over a native woman. A nasty creature, from start to finish."

" Well, since his offspring died at birth, he doesn't come into the scheme," said Sir Clinton. " Who remain to inherit this valuable fortune ? "

" The second son was James Felden. He's dead, too. Kenneth Felden was the only issue. You've seen him. Then there was a daughter, Anne. She married a man Gainford, who drank himself to death. She had two sons, Anthony Gainford and Derek Gainford. Anthony took after his father in the drinking line. His mother died when he was fairly young, and I doubt if the paternal environment was good for the boy. Anyhow, he's gone, too, in that gas-poisoning affair lately. You know about that. Derek Gainford you've seen—the asthmatic case. He's the only possible inheritor in that branch. Finally Paul Felden had another daughter, Edith. She married a man Stanway and had three children : Agatha—the Mrs. Pinfold you've come across—Max, and Daphne, who's engaged to young Allardyce. That's the lot."

" Have I kept track correctly ? " queried Sir Clinton. " By my reckoning the surviving grand-children are Felden,

Derek Gainford, Mrs. Pinfold, Max and Daphne Stanway—five in all."

" That's correct, five," confirmed Wendover. " But when the thing is split up amongst them, it won't mean much in hard cash. The ground isn't worth more than a few thousand at the best, so far as I can see ; and when you divide that by five, the individual share isn't a new Golconda, especially under current taxation."

" Are the Stanway parents still alive ? " asked Sir Clinton. Wendover shook his head.

" No, they're both gone. In fact, there isn't a single survivor in that generation. Only the grand-children are left."

" How do you come to have all these details so pat ? " asked the Chief Constable.

" Because old Rodway was a bit of a snob and thought it would look well if he made ' one of the local gentry '—as he used to call us—a trustee in the matter of the ground. He pitched on me for the job, and I couldn't very well decline, after he was dead. It would have looked like shirking bother, as well as being a bit ungracious."

" And why didn't you tell me this before, Squire ? "

" Well," said Wendover, in a faintly aggrieved tone, " I know I do talk a good deal about local affairs and people, and you don't make much of an effort to hide your boredom when I start on that tack. I'd meant to say something, but you've been distinctly discouraging in that field, lately, so I thought it better to wait till you actually asked some questions on the point."

" My fault, entirely, Squire," Sir Clinton admitted handsomely. " And, after all, old Rodway's will may not be the key to the puzzle, though it's queer that members of the Deverell and Felden families should be dying off, all at once. Just for the sake of argument, let's assume that the will *is* at the root of things, and see where that leads us. There were eight grand-children to start with. The two Deverells and Anthony Gainford are now dead. *Cui bono ?* Obviously the people who stand to gain directly are the five remaining inheritors : Kenneth Felden, Derek Gainford, Mrs. Pinfold, Max and Daphne Stanway."

" You needn't drag Daphne into it," objected Wendover. " She incapable of anything like that."

" I'm not dragging anybody in," retorted Sir Clinton, " I'm trying to eliminate various possible suspects, as you'd have seen if you'd shown a little more patience."

" Oh, if you put it in *that* way . . ." said Wendover.

" I do. Now let's get to doing it. I don't know whether Robert Deverell's death in that air-raid was by enemy action or by foul play. Assuming it was foul play, we could eliminate one suspect straight off. Felden was on duty that night and made himself useful by getting into a blazing shop and keeping a fire down while some women were rescued from the flat overhead. Nobody can be in two places at once, so it's clear that Felden didn't kill Robert Deverell."

" Obviously," said Wendover, with a certain satisfaction.

" The next affair is the death of Anthony Gainford," continued Sir Clinton. " The evidence isn't altogether satisfactory on the point, but we have the testimony of Mrs. Doggett that she had Derek Gainford under her eye right through the night until the ' All Clear ' went, except for a short interval when the electric light failed and she had to go and hunt out candles. Also, Derek had a severe attack of his asthma during the raid and doesn't seem to have been fit for much as a result. What's your verdict, Squire ? "

" That clears Derek, for all practical purposes," said Wendover without hesitation.

" I don't know what you mean by ' for all practical purposes,' " said Sir Clinton cautiously. " But since you're satisfied, we'll proceed. The third case is the one we've just had : the death of Henry Deverell. Felden was in the immediate neighbourhood at the time, but my man Barnsby was with him, and Barnsby is a reliable fellow. What do you think, Squire ? "

" You cleared Felden before, and Barnsby's evidence clears him in this case, too."

" Then that leaves Mrs. Pinfold next on the list," said Sir Clinton, with a smile. " What about her ? "

Wendover shrugged his shoulders as though dismissing the mere idea.

" She thinks more of her skin than most people," he declared. " I can't imagine her wandering round with murder in her heart during that air-raid when Robert Deverell was killed. The thing's ludicrous. She's got the best air-raid shelter I've heard about, round here, and she bunks into it whenever the siren sings. I've heard all about that from young Max and her sister. They look on her as a sort of family joke in that respect. You can rule her out."

" No real proof, though," Sir Clinton pointed out.

" You can get ocular evidence from her maids, if you want it," said Wendover. " She insists on them joining her in her shelter, and then she discovers she's forgotten her handkerchief, or her book, or something else, and despatches them instanter to bring her whatever's missing. Young Max spent a night in her shelter, once, and gave me all the details. As good as a drawing-room comedy, for he's not a bad mimic. Oh, you can get evidence of her whereabouts easily enough, when it's a raid night."

" Very well," said Sir Clinton. " Then what about Max Stanway himself ? I've no evidence, one way or the other."

" I don't need any," declared Wendover. " Young Max is a bit of an ass, but he's not the stuff one makes murderers from."

" Well, have it your own way, then," said Sir Clinton easily. " That leaves only Miss Stanway on the suspect list."

" Rubbish ! " ejaculated Wendover. " You've only to look at the girl ! "

" Looks are only skin-deep," retorted Sir Clinton. " You've got to dig deeper before you come to murderous intentions. But if it soothes you, Squire, I'll admit that I know nothing to connect her with the deaths of Pirbright and the Deverells. In the case of Gainford, she had a chance of visiting his bedroom and turning on the gas ; but there's nothing to prove that she did so."

" Well, your assumption about the Rodway will doesn't seem to have got you far," Wendover pointed out, with what sounded like a sigh of relief. " And, besides, it doesn't cover the whole ground. There's the Pirbright case, linked up with Robert Deverell's death and with the gold robbery. Pirbright wasn't related to either of the Deverells or the Feldens."

" Nor were Allardyce's rabbits," said Sir Clinton. " But now you've touched on another side of the business, Squire. Pirbright was caretaker at Cæsar's Camp, and he came to a bad end on that eligible building site. The rabbits also were residents, and they died, too. And to-night Deverell goes the same road on the same spot. Put Robert Deverell's death down to enemy action, and Anthony Gainford's to accidental gas-poisoning. That still leaves the deaths of the rabbits, Pirbright, and Henry Deverell. It seems a queer coincidence that all of them died near Cæsar's Camp. Something sinister about that spot. One might think the " local Nostradamus " was not so far out, after all. And there's that paper which Deverell carried to Ashmun to-night : it was a sketch-map of the Cæsar's Camp locality. But let's leave these fascinating glimpses of the occult and get back again to the main theme, which is not exhausted, as you hastily assume. We've examined various heirs to old Rodway and you won't let me find a murderer amongst them. But what about people who have no direct interest, but who might have an indirect one ? "

" I don't see your drift," Wendover confessed. " Who has an indirect interest, as you call it ? "

" Your friend Allardyce, for one," Sir Clinton pointed out. " He's engaged to one of the inheritors, isn't he ? It would suit him very well if she acquired some solid cash by next year, to make up for his losses in Malayan rubber."

" Oh, rubbish ! " said Wendover, testily.

" One should consider these things without prejudice," said Sir Clinton with a shake of his head. " Your young friend is a likeable fellow, I know ; but that has nothing to do with the case. I've met very likeable murderers before this. Now Camlet produced quite a lot of curious details which tend to link Allardyce with these affairs. Allardyce visited Robert Deverell just before that air raid. He paid a call on Pirbright on the night of the caretaker's death. He was at the party at Felden's house, the evening before Anthony Gainford passed in his checks ; and he, like Miss Stanway, went upstairs alone. Again, hyoscine or something like it, crops up in the Pirbright and Henry Deverell cases ; and Allardyce uses hyoscine regularly in his practice. Finally, we've only got Allardyce's own word for it that he went straight home after that bridge party last night. His phone was out of order, so that no one could ring up his house and ascertain if he was there or not. His tale was that he himself put the phone out of action by accident ; but for all we know, he may have disabled it intentionally, so as to leave himself free to roam over the countryside in the black-out. A lot of non-negligible details here, Squire, say what you please. I've got to keep an open mind about Allardyce, as about everyone else. That's all I'm doing."

" Are you keeping an open mind in the matter of that mulatto ? " demanded Wendover, obviously annoyed by Sir Clinton's persistence. " He's been bragging about his New Force, and the only manifestations of it, so far, have been lethal ones : those minnows and the dead rabbits Allardyce told us about. . . . "

" Allardyce again ! " interjected Sir Cliton, slyly.

" Well, what of it ? " rejoined Wendover. " It was you yourself who led him into that field by putting him on to spy. You can't deny that. What I say is simply that this damned Ashmun boasts that he can kill things with his New Force, especially on the ground near Cæsar's Camp ; so you've more reason to suspect him than all the rest put together."

" The only Force I profess to know much about is ' the Constabulary, Squire," said Sir Clinton," and it's not very new. You seem much better up in things. Now just tell me what motive friend Ashmun could have , if he's responsible for these deaths. He may be a homicidal maniac, of course, but I've no grounds for thinking that he could profit by killing the Deverells, Pirbright, and Gainford. Besides, he has a cast-iron alibi for the Pirbright affair, and he has an alibi, too, for this latest business, though we haven't checked it yet. My mind's as open as a savanna in the matter of Master Ashmun. Give me anything to incriminate him, and I'm your man. Till then, masterly inactivity is my line."

" Judging from what I saw of Henry Deverell's body, he'd been doped with some mydriatic drug before he died," said Wendover. " Now he'd called at Ashmun's house on the way up. He didn't hand the paper over and come away. Ashmun took him inside for a minute or two. When you went to Ashmun's house to-night, did he offer you a drink ? "

" Hospitality's no crime," said Sir Clinton. " He did."

" Then probably he did as much for Deverell. And you can put hyoscine into a drink."

" If you have any, you can. But even by doing so, you can't produce the symptoms that Deverell showed."

" Not with hyoscine alone, perhaps," Wendover admitted. " But you could add strychnine, or something of that sort."

" An ersatz for Angostura bitters ? " Sir Clinton shook his head. " It won't wash, Squire. Deverell's symptoms were the same as in Pirbright's case. Greenholme found none of the strychnose alkaloids in Pirbright's body. So there's no ground for assuming strychnine poisoning in Deverell's case, so far as present evidence goes."

" I suppose you're right," Wendover conceded reluctantly. " Well, I don't understand it."

" Neither do I, if that cheers you up," said the Chief Constable. " Try again, Squire."

" Did Ashmun show any surprise when he heard that Deverell was dead ? " asked Wendover.

" He did not," said Sir Clinton. " You see, I didn't mention the death to him and he didn't remark on it either. You can call that ignorance or policy, just as you please. But as you harp so much on hyoscine, I'll ask you one question : where could Ashmun get a sample of the stuff? It's not easy to come by."

" Well, I think you should watch him," said Wendover.

" Dog his footsteps ? Overhear his conversations at the

post office ? Collect his cigar-ash ? Is that what you mean ?
If I detailed a man to watch every suspect in this business,
Squire, I wouldn't have enough constables to go round.
Just remember that in the Jack the Ripper case the London
police had the streets stiff with constables for weeks on end,
and the Ripper pulled off a murder or two none the less.
I'm not much impressed by this method."

"You seem to be doing nothing," complained Wendover.
"It doesn't take many brains to do that."

"The inference being that I've no brains. Startling !
Even a bit discouraging, Squire. Let's change the subject.
Do you ever find a vague memory haunting the recesses of
your mind and refusing to come out for closer inspection ?
I'm in that irritating state just now. I read a short story
some years ago. I can't recall where I read it, or who wrote
it, or even the plot of the thing. All I know is that I've a
feeling that something in that yarn might fit on to these
affairs at Cæsar's Camp, and it exasperates me that I can't
recall anything definite about it. . . . Damn ! . . . I
know there was a murder in it, a rather ingenious affair,
but what it is all about, I simply can't bring back to mind. . . .
Perhaps if I don't worry too much about it, I may remember
it eventually."

He paused for a moment and then went on.

"Another thing of the same kind's been bothering me
lately. I can't remember the context of a couple of lines in
Milton :

> ' But that two-handed engine at the door
> Stands ready to smite once, and smite no more.'

I haven't read it for years, but I remember how it struck me
when I was a youngster. I puzzled a lot over what sort of
thing that ' two-handed engine ' could be. I finally pictured
it as a sort of mechanical figure in armour, with a battle-axe.
One chop, and you were done for. Nasty thing to have on
one's mind as a child, when one opens doors in the twilight
expecting it to be waiting on the other side. But what goes
before those two lines, Squire ? "

Wendover's textual memory was not impeccable.

"Oh . . . er. . . . Something about ' the grim wolf
with privy paw daily devours apace, and nothing said.'
And before that, there's a welter of imagery : sheep-hooks,
lean and flashy songs, scrannel pipes of wretched straw, and
so forth."

"*Lycidas*, of course ! Now I remember," said Sir Clinton,

apparently much relieved. " The ' two-handed engine ' had something to do with the civil power and the power of the church, hadn't it ? Thanks, Squire. That saves me worrying over the thing in bed to-night. I was thinking along other lines."

He finished his whisky and soda ; then, as he rose from his chair he put another question.

" Is Cæsar's Camp on Miss Herongate's road home from the golf club ? "

Wendover had been dreading some such inquiry. The last thing he wanted to see was a girl's name mixed up with the night's doings.

" Yes, it is," he hastened to explain. " I meant to tell you that."

" H'm ! Pretty late for her to be getting home, wasn't it ? "

" She must have been delayed. Perhaps she dropped in somewhere on the road back and stayed for a while."

" Likely enough," Sir Clinton admitted, as he turned towards the door.

CHAPTER XIII   *Something Fresh from Africa*

" I SEE YOU GOT A CABLE THIS MORNING," SAID WENDOVER, unable to repress his curiosity, but striving not to seem too inquisitive.

" Nothing escapes you, Squire. I did," admitted Sir Clinton.

" Anything interesting ? " persisted Wendover.

" To me, yes. It's from our Consulate in Monrovia."

" Then it's about that fellow Ashmun ? "

" It is. *Ex Africa semper aliquid novi.* Camlet and I are going to pay a call on your neighbour ; after that, we shall go for a breath of fresh air in the country. Care to join us ? "

" Why can't you let me read the cable and be done with it," Wendover grumbled. " You know I don't want to have anything to do with the fellow. But I see you're set on trampling on my prejudices, so you can have your way. I'll come with you."

" Then we'll go now," decided Sir Clinton. " Camlet's waiting for us to pick him up. He'll have a labourer and a spade with him."

" What do you want them for ? "

" Digging, perhaps, if it's needed. But we may not need to dig, for all I can tell. It's merely a notion of mine."

They drove first to the station where the inspector awaited them, and after picking up him and his companion, they went on to Ashmun's house. Sir Clinton demanded to see Ashmun and the party was ushered into the same room which Ashmun had used on the previous night. In a few moments, the mulatto presented himself, evidently not in the least perturbed by this domiciliary visit. Sir Clinton wasted no time on conventionalities but came to the point in his first words.

" You're not a British subject, Mr. Ashmun ? "

" Oh, no. I am a Liberian."

" You might let me see your papers, please : your passport and your certificate."

Ashmun produced the documents and handed them over with his usual beaming smile. Sir Clinton examined them.

" These seem to tally with the entries in my register," he said, handing them back. " I see you've entered yourself as a Clerk in Holy Orders in the section ' profession or occupation ! ' "

" That is quite correct," said Ashmun, with a slightly formal bow.

" What was your mother's name ? "

" Meta Ashmun. Like myself, she was a Liberian subject."

" And your father ? "

Ashmun's eyes flashed dangerously at this, but he maintained his pose of good humour.

" I never knew my father," he said, suavely. " He disappeared before I was old enough to know anything about him."

" Not even his name ? "

" I never took his name, and I prefer to forget it. He treated my mother badly and abandoned her very soon after I was born. He was, of course, one of you white men, a scalliwag, a scamp, and a ne'er-do-well. So I gathered, later in life."

" Were your parents married ? "

" I am afraid that I cannot produce their marriage certificate," Ashmun admitted, losing for a moment his jovial expression.

Sir Clinton made a gesture of semi-apology.

" I'm sorry. What I wish to be sure about is your Liberian citizenship. Your father was British ? Then, obviously, if he had married your mother, you would be British, and there would be no need for these formalities. If you could produce some evidence of a marriage, we could take you off our books, and you'd be free from some rather irksome restrictions."

This explanation seemed to change Ashmun's attitude.

He became again the suave and beaming personality of a few moments earlier.

"Ah! Now I understand! But I am afraid there is no help for it. I am a Liberian subject and an alien beyond doubt. I must put up with my troubles—mere trifles, after all."

"Now about this profession of yours," Sir Clinton continued. "I'd like to know how you come to be in Holy Orders."

"It is quite simple," Ashmun hastened to explain. "My mother was very poor; your compatriot, you see, had spent all the little money she had, before he left her. I suppose she was flattered by her association with one of you white men; it is quite understandable, for she was a poor, ignorant woman, very easily led and cheated. He drank some of her money, gambled away some more of it, and the rest . . ."

An expressive gesture closed the catalogue.

"My mother was a good woman according to her lights. African, of course, and naturally superstitious, but anxious to do her best for me. After her experiences with my white father, one would have thought she would hardly trust any of your people again. But, curiously enough, she fell in with some of your missionaries, decent people who were most anxious to accumulate converts. Genuine, I have no doubt, quite apart from the statistics of good work done, and all that sort of thing. They took me into a mission school and taught me when I was a child. Apparently they found me intelligent, as hybrids sometimes are. I was, in fact, their star pupil, quite clever, very biddable, and ready to accept anything I was told. I learned my catechism—man's chief end, and all that, you remember—and I suppose I must have showed a certain zeal. It is difficult to remember what one was like as a boy. At any rate, they looked on me as a credit to their training, and they conceived the idea of using me for their own purposes. You white men are so far-seeing compared with poor ignorant Africans. To cut it short, they educated me with the aim of turning me into a missionary like themselves, someone who in virtue of the tar-brush would be able to understand what they were pleased to call 'the African soul' better than they themselves could do, hampered as they were by their racial superiority which they could never quite forget. On my side, I took to it like a duck to water, for in my adolescence I was quite fervently pious. The upshot was, that I was inducted into Holy Orders before the first flush of enthusiasm wore off, and then I was sent up country to convert the heathen and justify the trouble they had spent on me. I toiled in the vineyard, as they phrased it, for quite a time, and was able to send back glowing reports to my teachers. Then I went down again to the Coast for a short rest, still most enthusiastic and all that. There was a pretty girl at the station, the daughter of one of the missionaries, out from England on a visit to her parents. I'd never seen anything so beautiful. No doubt she was really quite commonplace, but I hadn't seen many white girls of any sort. I offered her my heart and hand in a speech composed on the best models in the fiction of the station library. It was the only kind of English love-making I knew anything about, of course. She found it amusing and, looking back on it, I think she was probably right. But she wasn't particularly tactful, and I gathered without difficulty that my touch of the tar-brush put me completely out of court as a possible husband. I'm not blaming her in any way, you understand? I'd never think of marrying one of my female converts in the Hinterland. Still, the affair awakened me to certain points of view which my missionary training had not dwelt upon. I packed up and went back to my ' parish ' up country. But the grapes in that vineyard had turned sour, and after a time I retired from the business and cut my connection with my old pastors. They did not mind very much, I think. I made some sort of a living, in one way and another, for a while ; and then, having accumulated a little money, I decided to come to England and look round. I have not troubled my fellows of the cloth, over here, but when I was asked to put down a profession in that form of yours, I fell back on my clerical status, as it seemed as respectable as any of my other trades. I am afraid I have made rather a long story about a dull business, but I hope I have made it quite clear that my claim is quite a genuine one, and that I have made no mis-statements in these documents of yours."

" Thanks," said Sir Clinton, rather dryly. " That's quite correct, so far as it goes."

During his narrative, Ashmun had let a certain grimness overcloud his face, despite the light-hearted tone of his explanation ; but he now seemed to recover his customary buoyancy.

" Then there is nothing more that I can do for you ? " he asked, as though bringing the interview to an end.

" Just a question or two," said Sir Clinton, with an apologetic touch in his tone. " You were acquainted with Anthony Gainford, who died lately, weren't you ? "

" Slightly, only slightly," Ashmun replied frankly. " I met him from time to time, but he never invited me to visit him. He lived with Mr. Felden, and Mr. Felden has a very strong dislike for me, I'm told. It would have been awkward. Mr. Gainford called here now and again, possibly in search of casual drinks ; and we used to talk about matters of common interest. But I was not a friend of his, only a mere acquaintance."

" You know Mrs. Pinfold and her sister better, perhaps ? "

" I know the elder better than the younger one," Ashmun explained. " They are members of a little circle to which I belong. Charming ladies, both of them, and very intelligent. I understand that Miss Stanway is engaged to another of this circle : Dr. Allardyce. He has taken an interest, a kindly interest, in some of my little experiments."

" Experiments ? " said Sir Clinton, slightly raising his eyebrows. " Are you a scientific man, Mr. Ashmun ? I didn't know they had Universities in Liberia."

" Oh, no ! " Ashmun hastened to explain. " I have had no scientific training at all, in the current meaning of the phrase. In fact, my experiments would hardly be recognised as ' scientific ' by your pundits. I am afraid, for example, that Dr. Allardyce looks on them with some suspicion. I have not been able to convince him of the genuineness of my results. He has a very sceptical mind."

" You know him well ? "

" Only in connection with this little circle. Outside of it, I hardly come across him."

" Were you a friend of the two Deverells who died recently ? "

" Oh, no ! I saw the elder one, the archæologist, at Cæsar's Camp when he was doing those excavations, and I think I exchanged a few words with him then, congratulating him on his find. That was the limit of my acquaintance with him."

" You never met him again ? "

" Never, so far as I can recall."

" And his brother ? "

" I had only the most casual acquaintance with him, enough to nod when we happened to pass in the street. I did not find him congenial and had no desire to make a closer acquaintance with him. He had a rather surly manner, any time I happened to speak to him."

Sir Clinton harked back to an earlier topic.

" About these experiments of yours, Mr. Ashmun, I'm told that they have a commercial background. I'll give you a word of advice. Be quite sure of the genuineness of your results before you try to raise capital to exploit them. You understand? People have got themselves into awkward positions before now by being too optimistic. It doesn't do to let desire out-run performance when there's a financial side to the problem."

Ashmun's teeth showed in a broad grin of amusement.

"Ah! It is most kind of you to take an interest in my little investigations. Someone has been talking, evidently. Dr. Allardyce, perhaps? Or his so charming fiancée? You may make your mind quite easy, Mr. Chief Constable. If ever I ask my friends to share in the profits from my little researches, you may be sure that all will be on the soundest and most material basis. I shall deliver the goods, as you white men say so succinctly. You may even wish that you had a share, yourself."

"Thank you," retorted Sir Clinton, pleasantly. "I'm quite content as I am."

"And Mr. Wendover? Would you care to back my enterprise when it reaches that stage?"

Wendover shook his head abruptly He had the impression that Ashmun intended to be impudent.

"Thanks for the information you have given us," said Sir Clinton, intervening swiftly. "I'm sorry, Mr. Ashmun, that I haven't been able to release you from these rather irksome restrictions. Now I'll bid you good day."

When they got back to the car, Wendover was evidently divided in mind.

"That's a damned insolent fellow," he declared. "Now that I've met him, I think no better of him than before, for all his greasy manners. Still, one must admit that he's had some reason to dislike us whites, if his story's true."

"All that he told us was true," said the Chief Constable. "It tallied with the information in that cable I got this morning. But he didn't tell the whole story. I wanted to see what he'd leave out, and he left out what seemed to me something important."

"What?" asked Wendover.

"His father's name, for one thing. You knew the good man, Squire, if my cable's accurate. In fact, you gave me a character sketch of him which agrees pretty well with Ashmun's tale."

Wendover pondered for a moment.

"You don't mean Bruce Felden, surely!"

"That's the name in the cable, and it's hardly likely

there are two Bruce Feldens extant with such similar characters. Your friend Bruce was killed in New Guinea, you
told me, through getting mixed up with some native women.
Ashmun's father had a similar penchant : Ashmun's there
to prove that."

"Ah ! " said Wendover, reflectively. "That might explain something. If Kenneth Felden has any inkling of the
real state of affairs, it's no wonder that he hasn't a good
word for Ashmun. Nobody wants a mulatto cousin dumped
on his doorstep out of the blue."

"I've never had the experience," confessed the Chief
Constable, "but I don't suppose I'd care to have a wastrel
relation landing on me, whatever his colour was. And, judging
from my cable, Jehudi Ashmun hardly made a fortune in
Liberia, though that wasn't through a surplus of honesty."

"What about that story about his being a missionary ? "

"That seems true enough," Sir Clinton confirmed. "He
was brought up at a mission station and sent up country
to preach the Gospel. But you'll remember that he passed
lightly over his retirement from the missionary field. Judging
from my cable, it was more complicated than he led us to
believe. His story about the white girl at the station may
have been true and may have given him a twist. But the
fact is that when he went up country again, he fell into the
pit from which he was digged."

"I wish you'd speak plain English, Clinton," grumbled
Wendover.

"Oh, well, then, he took off his trousers and his civilisation, up there in the back country. Turned native. Went
fantee, in a rather disagreeable way, I gather. Naturally
the missionaries disowned him."

"If he didn't make money in Liberia, what's he living
on now ? " Wendover demanded.

"He's living pretty cheaply," said Sir Clinton. "He
keeps no maids. That house of his is a bit out-of-the-way ;
the rent's not likely to be high. Still, he must have some
cash in hand. Possibly he's extracting subsidies from that
old fellow Silwood and from his cousin, Mrs. Pinfold. Both of
them have more money than brains, apparently ; and friend
Ashmun has more brains than money, so one might expect
something of the sort. But he'd better go cautiously. I'd be
quite glad to put him behind bars if I could find the evidence."

"So Daphne's his cousin," mused Wendover. "She
doesn't know it, though, or she'd never have lent herself
to your tricks, Clinton. As for Agatha Pinfold, if she knew

about the relationship she'd have blurted it out long ago. Tony Gainford would probably have let the cat out of the bag in his cups, if he'd known the story."

"And the two Deverells are dead and can't tell," said Sir Clinton, "even if they did get let into the secret."

Wendover had no desire to discuss the topic any longer. He switched to something fresh when he spoke again.

"What are you dragging us out here for, Clinton?" he demanded.

"Fresh air. I can promise you that in any case. Also a little exploring, though I doubt if I'll find what I'm looking for. It's a bit difficult to find something when you don't know what it is, you know, Squire; and that's my present position."

"I'm sick of all this Delphic stuff," said Wendover, crossly. "Can't you talk plain English to-day, without all these frills?"

"Well, then, you remember that sketch-map I drew for you? There were two stars on it, weren't there? Making a very long shot, I'm looking for something lying somewhere between those two marks; but what the thing may be is outside my ken. I'm just going up here on chance, to look about and see if there's anything to catch my eye. Naturally until it does catch my eye, I can't describe it to you; and likely enough it won't catch my eye at all. That wouldn't surprise me in the slightest; so if this turns out a wild-goose chase, Squire, you've been fore-warned."

He drove on until they reached the little bridge below Cæsar's Camp, and then stopped his car.

"All change here!" he announced, setting an example by getting out. "We'll just stroll up-stream and look around. You take the left bank, Inspector; Mr. Wendover and I will follow the other. I can't tell you what to look out for: anything that seems unusual, like disturbed ground or dead animals or withered vegetation. If you come upon anything uncommon, just give us a hail."

The party divided, the labourer with shouldered spade following the inspector. The streamlet flowed down a little dell which led up towards some higher land in the background. At first it ran smoothly between green banks, but soon they reached a sharper pitch down which the water tinkled over a series of tiny cascades. Here they came upon the bomb crater, and Sir Clinton paused to examine it.

"Full of water," he pointed out. "I thought that burn would break bounds and flood the pit to some extent. A nuisance, that. But there's aye a way, and it really doesn't matter much."

He pulled a sheet of paper from his pocket and examined it. Wendover noticed that it was a sketch-map, more accurately drawn than the one which the Chief Constable had shown him before.

"I copied this roughly from the Ordnance map," Sir Clinton explained.

He took bearings by eye and moved on, carrying the map in his hand. Wendover noted that he did not seem to be paying much attention to details of the ground. They climbed a gentler slope and came out on a tract of level ground over which the streamlet flowed but sluggishly. Here Sir Clinton discarded his map and began to scan his surroundings with more care. The inspector had dropped behind them, but Wendover, glancing over his shoulder, could see him and the labourer plodding slowly along on the opposite bank, searching the ground minutely every ten yards or so in their advance.

"I suppose we've reached the first star on that sketch-map?" he asked, turning to the Chief Constable.

"Yes. Keep your eyes open, Squire. We may be lucky, though the chances seem the other way."

For a time, nothing of significance appeared, but at last there came a hail from the inspector.

"Somebody seems to have been digging here recently, sir," he called, pointing to the ground close beside him.

Sir Clinton, followed by Wendover, crossed the little stream and rejoined Camlet. At this point, the course of the burn bent into an arc with its convex side fringed by a strip of shingle, and on the turf above this there were plain traces of some disturbance : the grass was withered over an area of several square feet.

"This seems worth investigating," said Sir Clinton, with obvious relief in his tone. He turned to the labourer and gave directions. "You see someone's been digging here? What I want to find out is how deep he went. Can you dig a straight-sided pit on the edge of this, and let us see just how far down the soil has been disturbed under that patch?"

The labourer set to work as directed, and in a very short time he had dug a hole of some feet in depth.

"That'll do," said Sir Clinton, who had been watching the operation carefully. "If you people will look, you'll find that the old digging has stopped about three feet down. Below that, the soil's undisturbed. Now," he added, "just dig up the patch under the withered grass, please. Go cautiously, and let us have a look after each spadeful you remove."

Wendover and the inspector watched the new excavation with a mixture of eagerness and bewilderment. The digging continued, but nothing of the slightest apparent interest was unearthed, and at last the spade struck untouched soil.

" That'll do," said Sir Clinton. " Now you can fill the thing in again, and try to make the surface as neat as possible, please. We needn't leave any obvious traces of our doings."

He had evidently lost interest in the pit, for he turned away and lit a cigarette. Then he glanced up and down the course of the little stream as if noting how the curve in it had served to heap up the shingle on one side and not upon the other.

" Second thoughts are best, usually," he mused aloud. " Digging in the wrong place hasn't done much good, apparently. Still, it's always interesting to see what one gets. That seems to finish our work up here. Once this hole has been filled in, we may as well get back to town again."

" You're too apt to play the mystery-man, Clinton," said Wendover, as they walked back towards the car, leaving the inspector to see the hole properly filled up. " It's not a rôle I care much for, so I won't play it myself. I needn't have mentioned it to you, but I've been asked to attend a meeting to-night—quite informal—to discuss what's to be done about this ground, once the date fixed by old Rodway comes round."

" Indeed ? And who summoned this meeting ? "

" Derek Gainford wrote to me about it. He and his cousins seem to think we ought to have some plans ready for dealing with the ground. That's reasonable enough."

" Will friend Ashmun be among those present ? " asked Sir Clinton, with a smile.

" Why should he be ? "

" Better read old Rodway's will, Squire, before you attend this meeting. I've had it looked up. It mentions ' grand-children ' pure and simple. Nothing in it about a bar sinister. I'm no laywer. You'll need a legal shark to tell you whether Mr. Ashmun's entitled to his share of the spoil, along with the rest."

" I hadn't thought of that," admitted Wendover.

Sir Clinton waved the matter aside.

" Just to show you that I'm not playing the mystery-man, I'll tell you something that'll cheer you up, Squire, since you hate seeing a girl mixed up in unpleasant affairs. Camlet interviewed Miss Herongate about her doings on the night that Henry Deverell came to a bad end up here. You remember a constable saw her car, and I asked you if she'd pass by here on her road home. She didn't need to pass us, I understand. She turned to the right when she came out of that by-road, instead of taking the left turn and coming upon us as we stood up there."

"That's quite correct," Wendover confirmed.

"Well, it seems she told Camlet that she was badly delayed on her road that night. A broken bottle gashed one of her tyres. Hard luck, especially for a girl alone, in an evening frock. The sort of thing that doesn't happen once in a thousand times, nowadays. No one was passing at that time of night, so she had to depend on herself; and to make matters worse, the nuts of her wheel had rusted up a bit. She must have had a devil of a job getting the punctured wheel off. However, she managed it at last and got home all right on her spare. Camlet's middle name is Thomas, so he managed to get a look at her car to check her tale. Sure enough there was a gash in the rubber big enough to put your finger into."

"I guessed that something like that had happened," said Wendover. "She saw nothing of that ugly business?"

"So Camlet tells me. But she's a queer creature, Squire. I hear that her latest hobby is taking rubbings of brasses—memorial plates and that sort of thing—in the local country churches. I haven't seen much of her, I admit; but from what I *have* seen, I'd just as soon have expected her to dive into Egyptology or Hermeneutics for recreation. I wonder where she picked up this craze. You can't suggest anyone in her circle who takes an interest in brasses, can you?"

Wendover pondered for a few moments and then shook his head.

"Nobody that she's likely to know, even by sight," he said decidedly. "As you say, Clinton, it's a rummy amusement. I must ask her about it, sometime. . . . By the way, have you had the analyst's reports in the cases of Tony Gainford and Henry Deverell?"

"Yes," Sir Clinton explained. "But they don't carry us much further. In Gainford's case he found alcohol in the stomach and traces of nickel. Nothing you could say was the cause of death. The tumbler and the thermos flask got a clean bill. As for Deverell, there was alcohol in the stomach, which shows he had a drink not long before he died. But we knew that already. In addition, the analyst found traces of hyoscine—just as in the Pirbright affair—but the quantity was so minute that he rejects the notion that Deverell swallowed anything like a fatal dose. Reading between the lines, I don't believe he'd have spotted hyoscine at all if it hadn't been suggested to him beforehand. Besides, the symptoms weren't those of hyoscine. In fact, his report *per se* doesn't amount to much.".

CHAPTER XIV   *Derek Gainford*

As was his custom, Wendover arrived punctually to keep his appointment at the Stanways' house. Others were before him, however ; for as he stood in the hall, putting down his hat and driving-gloves, he heard a spasm of coughing which made him wince in sympathy. When he was ushered into the room, he found Derek Gainford lying back in an arm-chair, exhausted by his attack, and gasping painfully while he held a handkerchief to his lips. Daphne was leaning over him anxiously. Max, on the hearth-rug, was examining his cousin with the unsympathetic curiosity of a man who has never himself been ill in his life and whose imagination is insufficient to put himself mentally into the place of the patient. Mrs. Pinfold, sitting aloof, looked resentful, as she always did when anything happened to ruffle her. She had no patience with other people's woes, and her nostrils betrayed her annoyance at the fumes of the stramonium cigarette which burned in the ash-tray on the arm of Derek's chair.

" That's a dreadful cough," said Wendover sympathetically. " It must rack you badly. There's no hurry, you know. We'll wait till you feel fit to talk."

Derek Gainford made a poor effort at a smile. With an obvious effort, he gathered himself together, took a pull at his stramonium cigarette, and then lifted himself in his chair.

" Be. . . all . . . right, in a minute," he declared breathlessly. " I'm sorry . . . to make an exhibition . . . of myself."

" There's no hurry," repeated Wendover. " Mr. Felden hasn't turned up yet and we'll have to wait for him before passing to business."

" He . . . isn't coming," explained Derek Gainford, painfully. " He's on . . . duty to-night. He only told . . . me after I'd fixed . . . up with everyone else. Probably one of his . . . colleagues . . . dropped out at the . . . last moment . . . and he's had to . . . take an extra watch.

. . . He won't be coming . . . so we may as well . . . start."

Wendover looked at the lack-lustre eyes and noted the bluish skin due to the failure of oxygenation of the blood. He would have delayed a while to give the patient further time for recovery, but Derek made a petulant gesture to indicate that he resented any fuss being made about his attack.

" I've been thinking over this affair," began Wendover, obediently, raising his voice slightly to cover the rasping breathing of the invalid. " Time's growing short, and I quite agree that we should have plans cut and dried which can be put into execution as soon as the ground falls finally into your hands to do as you like with. So far as I can see, there are three courses to choose from. We can sell the ground *en bloc* as soon as it becomes available; and each of you can take your share of the proceeds. Or else we can hold on, waiting for the best moment to sell. Or, finally, we can split the ground amongst you now, and each of you can do as he or she thinks best with the share allotted. The main point is that you should come to some definite agreement amongst yourselves as to the course to be taken."

While he was speaking, Daphne left Derek Gainford's side and took a chair beside her sister.

" I think," she said, " that we should sell out immediately. I don't say I'm superstitious, for I'm not ; but it doesn't seem a very lucky sort of place, you know. Robert died up there, and no one knows how he came by his death. Pirbright, the caretaker, lost his life at almost the same place. It's a bit gruesome, no matter what you say about it. I don't like it. I'd much sooner see it off our hands. Besides, I want some money soon. . . ."

" I suppose this is Frank's notion ? " interrupted Mrs. Pinfold, with a touch of acerbity.

" Frank agrees with me," Daphne admitted.

" This is a purely family affair, to be settled amongst ourselves," said Mrs. Pinfold, frostily. " Frank is not yet a member of the family, so his views carry not the slightest weight with me, I may say. I most certainly do not agree, and I shall not agree, to any such proposal. Mr. Rodway was a far-seeing man. . . ."

" He was. No one denies that," interjected Max, with a grin. " He got out of the old firm at the right moment, and left our respected parents holding the bag. Far-seeing is the word."

" Mr. Rodway was a far-seeing man," repeated Mrs. Pinfold, ignoring the interruption completely. " He knew that this ground was going to be valuable and that it would pay well to hold on to it. It's just beginning to be valuable now, and it's simply silly to think of selling it at present, since most likely it will increase in value as time goes on. I'm quite clear in my mind that we should hold on to it."

" And you ? " asked Wendover, turning to Max.

" Me ? My notion's to divvy up the ground amongst ourselves. Then each of us can do what he likes with his share. No recriminations, then. No heart-burnings. Any bloomer is on the head of the owner."

Mrs. Pinfold gave a sniff which was intentionally audible.

" I insist that we hold on to the ground," she said, obstinately.

" You can hold on to your bit, Agatha," her brother pointed out. " No one's hindering that."

" My ' bit,' as you call it, won't be half so valuable by itself as it would be as part of a large building estate," said Mrs. Pinfold heatedly. " I don't pretend to be a business women, but I can see that, at any rate. We ought to come to some general agreement to keep the ground intact and develop it as a whole, with each of us drawing an agreed share from the annual income. That's what I propose, and it's the only sensible plan, as anyone can see."

" Something in that," admitted Max, frankly. " Where did you pick up the notion, Agatha ? Not your own, surely ? "

" It's not a question of how I ' picked it up,' as you put it, Max," retorted Mrs. Pinfold with obvious annoyance. " The point is that I'm right, and that even you can see it, after it's been explained to you. It would be pure folly to split up this ground into little patches, one to each of us. If we did that, it would ruin any general plan of developing the estate on sound lines. I insist on getting my own way about this. It's the right way, and there's no doubt about that. Don't you agree with me ? " she asked, turning to Wendover.

" I don't care for small holdings, myself," Wendover confessed. " Besides, it's not so easy to split up a piece of ground fairly. You can't do it on a mere acreage basis, because some of the tract is obviously better building land than other parts. But it's for you people to settle this amongst yourselves ; my views don't come in. What have you got to say ? " he asked, turning to Derek Gainford.

Before the invalid could begin, he was racked by another terrible fit of coughing which ended in his lying back in his chair with streaming eyes and gasping for breath. Wendover, noting the bluish tinge in his complexion, pitied him for his agony and reflected on the tenuousness of his hold upon life. "He might pass out, any minute, in one of these fits," he said to himself as he glanced at the exhausted figure in the chair. "Poor devil ! And he's been like that through most of his life. What an existence ! "

They waited until the invalid had pulled himself together, and was able to speak, though his sentences were broken by terrible gasps.

"We . . . ought to . . . sell at once," he began. "No one knows . . . how long this . . . war's going on . . . but it can't last for ever . . . thank the Lord. Now, as things are . . . Ambledown's a munitions centre . . . of sorts. And there's a cry for housing . . . accommodation for this . . . influx of workers. If we sell . . . at the earliest moment possible . . . we'll get a goodish price . . . for the ground. They can . . . put up huts on it . . . in no time . . . and they'd snatch . . . at it. . . ."

"Who's ' they ? ' interjected Max.

"Anybody who's interested . . . in housing workmen. I don't care who they are . . . in particular. . . . My point is . . . that when the war stops . . there'll be a big slump . . . in Ambledown . . . and no one will want the . . . ground for years . . . after that. No one would look . . . at it. And where should we be, then ? Completely out of it . . . with a lot of waste land . . . on our hands. I'm all for selling immediately . . to catch the market . . . while there is a market left."

The effort of putting his case had both excited and exhausted him, and he lay back again in his chair with closed eyes, his breath coming and going in deep gasps and noisy exhalations. Mrs. Pinfold opened her lips to comment, but Wendover feared the result of an altercation on Derek and he intervened swiftly, hoping to turn the talk into a fresh channel.

"Does anyone know what Mr. Felden thinks ? " he asked.

The result was not what Wendover aimed at. Derek Gainford, by a violent effort of will, pulled himself together, though his speech was even more interrupted than before.

"I know . . . all about what . . . Kenneth thinks," he said, with as much irascibility as his condition allowed. "I've . . . talked it up and down . . . with him, lately . . . and he's as pigheaded as he could be. . . . For once, you and he seem to be . . . on the same side, Agatha."

Mrs. Pinfold's face betrayed that she was not wholly

delighted to find Felden as an ally. Derek noted her expression and his mouth took on an ironical twist.

" Not pleased ? I hardly . . . expected you would be," he continued. " But it's so. Kenneth's all for hanging on to the ground on the chance of . . . a rise in value. . . . And he won't hear . . . of any piecemeal . . . arrangement. I put it . . . to him that . . . when the war stops . . . there'll be a slump . . . in Ambledown and . . . no one will want this ground. . . . No one would look . . . at it." Another paroxysm of coughing prostrated him and it was a full minute before he could continue. " Where should we be . . . then ? Out of it . . . completely out of it . . . with acres of waste land on our hands . . . fit for nothing . . . in particular. I've talked this up and down . . . with Kenneth. . . . Tried to convince him. . . . But he's simply exasperating. . . . Looks superior, as if he were . . . in the know and . . . despised everyone else's opinion. . . ."

" Oh, yes, I know," interrupted Mrs. Pinfold. " Kenneth's always like that. But, all the same, he's right for once, Derek, and I think it would be simply futile to let the ground slip through our fingers merely to get some money immediately. I won't agree even to letting it out on short leases. I'm quite determined to keep it in our control, ready for any eventuality that may turn up. No one can tell what may happen after the war."

" No," said Derek with an effort, " no one can tell. . . . And that's just why I want . . . to get rid of the thing now . . . while we know . . . where we are. I won't agree to this frantic scheme of yours and Kenneth's. There won't be any boom after this war, like last time."

Max Stanway was apparently struck by a sudden idea.

" I've got it ! " he exclaimed eagerly. " Some of us want to sell. Some of us want to hang on. Why shouldn't those who want to hang on, buy out the shares of those who want to sell ? I'm a seller, myself. What offers for my share, Agatha ? You're about the only one in the family who's got money to buy with."

" I'd need to think over that," said his sister, not too cordially, for the mere thought of parting with hard cash obviously went against the grain with her.

" Oh, no hurry," Max assured her. " Take a week. Take advice, too. Black Jack might help. Cast your horoscope or work out your nativity, or whatever it is that he does in such cases."

" I suppose you mean Mr. Ashmun," said Mrs. Pinfold,

icily. "I'd rather have his advice than yours, Max. I'll think over the matter. It would depend on the price, of course."

"You'd sell, too, Daph ? " said Max, turning to his other sister.

"Yes, I don't care who buys the ground from me. Agatha can have my share if she pays for it."

"And you, Derek ? "

"Like a . . . shot, of course," said Derek Gainford, with an effort. "At an agreed price . . . that is. Bring in a professional . . . valuer to be fair . . . all round."

Mrs. Pinfold seemed to lose her interest in the matter as these offers were made, each of them raising the total of her possible expenditure in getting her own way.

"I'll think it over," she said fretfully. "And I'll have to consult Kenneth about it, and I never like discussing things with him because he's always trying to put me in the wrong. You needn't expect too much, any of you. I may not want to buy at all, when I've had time to consider it carefully. And you needn't imagine that I'll pay anything extra because you're my relations. It's a mistake to have any business dealings with friends or relations, I find. They always take advantage of me," she ended, without the slightest regard for the feelings of the rest of the family.

"Oh, stick to facts, Agatha," said Max, lightly. "I've often tried to touch you for a fiver. Not a hope in Hades. You've never been done by me, or by any of the rest of us. But if you want to be swindled, you won't have to go far afield looking for the man to do it—and you ! "

Mrs. Pinfold ignored the obvious reference to Ashmun.

. "I'll think over the matter," she repeated. "At present, I'm not in the least inclined to do anything. We *ought* to hold on to the land, and I don't see why I should risk my money in taking over your shares. I may be easy-going, but there's a limit to that sort of thing, and this suggestion of yours, Max, seems to me over the score, quite excessive."

Derek Gainford had evidently imagined that Max's solution might be accepted, and the disappointment seemed to affect him physically. He coughed thickly and lay back, prostrated, for a few moments, struggling for breath. When he was able to speak again, he had obviously lost all patience.

"You've . . . had a . . . fair offer, Agatha. If you . . . won't take it . . . then . . . I insist that . . . we sell out . . . at once. There are three . . . of us . . . in favour of selling. . . . Kenneth can be . . . talked over or not. . . . You can keep your . . . shares of the land . . . if you like.

. . . But the three . . . of us . . . are going to see . . . our money out of it . . . now . . . and you can . . . make the . . . best of . . . that."

The effort had been too much for him. He fell back in his chair, haggard, gasping. Then he managed to croak two words:

" The capsule ! "

Daphne darted to his side and began to fumble in his jacket pocket. The sick man roused himself sufficiently to shake his head feebly.

" In your overcoat ? " she asked.

A feeble nod confirmed this, and she hurried out of the room, returning almost immediately with the cloth-covered capsule in her hand. Derek Gainford managed to pull out his handkerchief and take the tiny object from her, drawing his breath in long raucous inhalations. He buried his face in his handkerchief; there was a slight snap of breaking glass, followed by a waft of pear-drop odour as the amyl nitrite vapour spread itself.

But this time, it seemed, the remedy had come too late. Derek inhaled deeply once or twice ; then his respiratory trouble increased ; his face took on the bluish tint due to insufficient oxygenation of the blood ; and he lost consciousness.

" Get the nearest doctor—quick ! " ordered Wendover, turning to Max. " The phone. Hurry ! "

Daphne, evidently shaken by the sight of her cousin's sufferings, had dropped on her knees by his chair and took one of his hands in her own.

" He's terribly cold," she said, softly. " Derek ! "

There was no reply to the call. The sick man clenched his jaws and from time to time his breath whistled through his teeth, but the inhalations grew slower and more difficult. His eyes were fixed and staring, but evidently he saw nothing with them.

At last the hastily-summoned doctor arrived, and at the first glance Wendover augured but little good from him. " Inexperienced young cub," he reflected, " trying to hide his nervousness and not making a success of the job."

Tersely, Wendover described what had happened. The medico listened, fidgeting with his bag, picking out something and immediately discarding it in favour of a fresh choice. Then he tried Derek's pulse and looked grave.

" I can hardly feel his pulse," he said, avoiding the eyes of the onlookers. " It seems a very serious attack. Chronic case of asthma, you said ? Hum ! "

Derek's breathing seemed to have ceased.

" Can't you *do* something ? " demanded Wendover abruptly.

" I must find out what's wrong, first," retorted the doctor, defensively. " You can't treat a patient without knowing what ails him. I must find out. . . ."

" His heart's failing. Anyone can see that," rejoined Wendover. " If you don't do something, and soon, it'll stop altogether. What about strychnine ? Have you any with you ? "

" One might try it," admitted the doctor, turning to dive once more into his bag.

He produced tabloids and a sterilised hypodermic syringe with a charge of water in it. Wendover watched with increasing irritation the deliberate dissolving of a tabloid. Then the doctor seemed again to fall into doubt, and stood with the syringe in his hand, watching his patient, as though he hoped that some sudden improvement might make the injection unnecessary. Wendover turned to the two women and made a gesture, he indicated the door.

" Yes, I think we'll go," said Mrs. Pinfold coolly. " No place for us. We'll wait next door. Come, Daph ! "

Daphne, after a glance of pity through her tears, followed her sister. Wendover, turning back to the patient, found the physician still hesitating. The expression on Wendover's face galvanised him into action. He jabbed in the needle, had a last fit of irresolution, and then pressed home the piston. They watched for some reaction to the dose, but none came. The doctor laid down his syringe, put his fingers on Derek's wrist, paused for a time, and then shook his head despondently.

" His pulse has stopped. I can't feel it."

" Mean he's dead ? " asked Max, suddenly sobered.

" I think so. We must wait for a while yet to be sure."

Max was more affected than Wendover had expected.

" Poor old Derek," he muttered. " Poor old boy. He had a rotten life of it, and he stuck it marvellously. A good sort, really."

The doctor began to pack his bag. Wendover, watching him, was struck by an idea.

" Who gives the certificate in a case like this ? " he demanded.

" I don't think that's my business," said the doctor, doubtfully. " He died in an asthmatic attack, apparently. The certificate ought to be signed by the physician who's been attending him for that. Who is it ? "

" Dr. Allardyce."

" Oh, then, that's all right," said the doctor, apparently

relieved. " He'll sign the certificate for you. I'll ring him up by and by and tell him what's happened. A chronic case, evidently. Allardyce will know all about it. He's your man."

" There's no chance of Mr. Gainford reviving, I suppose ? " asked Wendover.

" You can never tell immediately in these cases," said the doctor, doubtfully. " You'd better get Allardyce to look at him to-morrow, to be sure. I'm not absolutely certain myself, but I've done all I can for him, so there's no use my staying now. I've another case waiting for me. I'll give Allardyce a ring, later on."

He was evidently anxious to get away, and Wendover saw no point in detaining him. When the doctor had gone, Max seemed to come out of a brown study.

" We can't leave him here, you know," he pointed out. " Better take him up to our spare bedroom, hadn't we ? Before my sisters come back. Matter of decency, and all that."

Evidently he was more moved than he cared to show. Wendover agreed with him, and between them they carried the dead man upstairs and laid him on the bed.

" Don't think much of that saw-bones," said Max, as they came downstairs again. " Not a quick thinker, by the look of him, and afraid to take responsibility. I wish I'd got Frank, even if it took him longer to come. Frank knows what's what. Think it would be any good ringing him up now ? He might be able to do something. One never knows."

" Anything's worth trying," confessed Wendover. " I'm afraid there's nothing to be done now ; but he's Allardyce's patient, and Allardyce ought to see him, in any case. You'd better phone."

Max went to the instrument, and Wendover returned to the room where he set himself mechanically to tidy the furniture which had got displaced. As he did so, he pondered over what he had just seen. It was " all right," of course, he assured himself. Derek Gainford was bound to die, sooner or later, in an asthmatic paroxysm. No one would think anything of that, if his death had been an isolated matter. But Wendover found that he could not isolate it from what he already knew. The Rodway heirs were dying off in succession, and in one case at least—that of Henry Deverell—the circumstances could not be called normal by any stretch of vocabulary. None the less, that death in the room here was only something which had long been foreseen. For once, the amyl nitrite had failed. Wendover sniffed the familiar peardrop odour which still hung in the air, and he began to feel a slight headache due to inhaling the diluted drug.

"Damn it!" he said to himself. "I'm getting as bad as that medico. I can't make up my mind what's the right thing to do. We don't want a scandal raised over a death which is probably all in the ordinary course. On the other hand . . ."

He was still perplexed by his problem when Max returned to the room.

"I've got hold of Frank. He says it was a thing that might have happened at any minute. Poor old Derek was in a worse way than I'd supposed. Or so Frank says, now. He'll be along later. Got a case to visit first. These body-snatchers have a gay life of it, haven't they?"

Wendover had at last solved his problem.

"Look here, Max!" he said. "We've got your sisters to think about. Send Daphne to bed. There's no need for her to come in here again, and she needn't say good night to me. And drive your other sister home. She must have had a bad shake, and I don't like the notion of her alone in a car in the black-out. See her fixed up and then come back. I'll wait here for you."

Max listened and gave a nod of assent.

"Sound idea," he admitted. "And I'll be glad to have something to keep me busy. A bit of a shake-up for all of us," he added, with a nervous titter.

"Then get started at once," suggested Wendover. "By the way, may I use your phone? I'd better ring up the Grange and let them know they needn't expect me till later. I'd told them I'd be back shortly, and my house-keeper might get nervous if I don't turn up. She's always jumpy if anyone's late in coming in now. The black-out, you know. She starts imagining accidents and that kind of thing."

"Right!" said Max. "You know where the phone is? You can ring up while I'm talking to those two."

Wendover rang up the Grange and spoke to his house-keeper. Then he asked for Sir Clinton. But the Chief Constable had gone out on some errand. Half-relieved by this news which made it impossible to call in Sir Clinton immediately, Wendover decided that he himself must do what he could. He searched the room in which Derek Gainford had died, but found nothing beyond the most obvious things to collect. Then, struck by a further idea, he paid a visit to the cloak-room and went through the pockets of Gainford's overcoat.

" Well, I've got everything of any importance, anyhow," he assured himself. "And there's nothing in it, when all's done."

CHAPTER XV   *Henry's Law*

WHEN WENDOVER RETURNED TO THE GRANGE, HE FOUND Sir Clinton there; and he at once launched into a description of that tragedy at the Stanways' house.

" Now," he wound up, " I'm sure it was the sort of thing that was bound to overtake the poor fellow, sooner or later. I happen to know the symptoms of a bad asthmatic attack, and they were all there. And there was nothing abnormal at all. If he'd died like that six months ago, I wouldn't have given the matter a thought. But . . ."

" But Gainford is one of the few remaining Rodway heirs," interjected Sir Clinton, " so you sat up and took notice, eh ? I quite understand, Squire. You've no suspicion of foul play, but you think it's a rum affair. A very proper—if confused— frame of mind. And you set yourself to hunt for material evidence. Quite right. Question is : Did you find anything ? "

" Not a rap," confessed Wendover, ruefully. " I didn't expect to find anything, and I turned out to be right. It was just one last bad paroxysm that carried the poor devil off. However, I knew you'd laugh at me if I came away absolutely empty-handed, so I brought the only things that seemed to me to have the slightest bearing on the business."

He put his hand into his pocket and drew out in turn a handkerchief, a tiny cloth packet, and a small tin case, all of which he put on the table beside Sir Clinton's chair.

Sir Clinton bent over the cloth packet and sniffed delicately at it.

" Pear-drop odour still clinging to it, and to the handkerchief as well," he remarked. " We met that once before, Squire, at Lynden Sands. It's amyl nitrite, all right. But this time it happens to be quite in place. However, we'll bottle it up in case the coroner wants to have a sniff."

He left the room for a few moments and came back with a stoppered bottle into which he dropped the little packet, replacing the stopper tightly. Then he turned to the little tin case.

" ' *Amyl Nitrite Capsules for Inhalation* '," he read from the label. " ' Take ends of packet between thumb and forefinger of each hand, crush and inhale.' The box evidently

159

holds a dozen of them when it's full, but there are only nine left now. One was used to-night, so he must have used the remaining missing pair at some other times. That's quite in order. The box would take finger-prints well ; but what use would they be to us ? It must have been handled by the packer, the druggist, Gainford himself, Miss Stanway, yourself, and finally by me, not to speak of other possible people. However, we'll let our finger-print expert do his worst on it. Nothing like being thorough."

" There can't be anything wrong with the capsules," Wendover pointed out. " As you say, he used two of them on some previous occasions, and they must have been quite all right, or he'd have noticed something amiss himself."

" As you say," echoed Sir Clinton, " he'd have noticed something amiss. He was familiar enough with these things, poor devil. Let's have a look at one of them."

He took one of the cloth packets from the tin, prised up the ends of the metal fasteners with his penknife, and gently extracted the tiny glass tube from its bed of cotton-wool. It was a little thing, about an inch long, with one end neatly rounded and the other end drawn out into a tail which had been sealed off in a blow-pipe after filling. Wendover had never seen an actual capsule before. He picked it up and examined the faintly yellow liquid in the tube.

" Not much there," he remarked. " Two or three grammes at the most. It's got a devil of a smell, considering how little of it there is. I caught the tang of it when he crushed that thing to-night, and his handkerchief still reeks of it. Headachy stuff."

Sir Clinton nodded, but he seemed to have lost interest in the exhibits, for he changed the subject abruptly.

" How did you get on with these people to-night, before Gainford's collapse ? I'd like to hear what their views were."

" Three of them were in favour of selling immediately : Daphne, young Max, and Derek Gainford. Agatha Pinfold wouldn't hear of it. Then there was some suggestion of her buying out the others, but she didn't welcome it much."

" Did they give any reasons for their views ? "

" Oh, the reasons were clear enough," said Wendover. " Daphne, of course, needs money immediately. She and Allardyce want to get married, and he's lost more than he can afford in this Malayan disaster. A sale of the ground would make marriage feasible for the two of them."

" That's understandable enough," agreed Sir Clinton.

" Young Max also wanted to sell the ground," continued

Wendover. "My impression is that he wants to get his hands on the cash and, most likely, make it fly. Derek Gainford also wanted to sell. In fact, he was the strongest advocate on that side. After all, poor devil, he couldn't look forward to a long life—to-night's affair proved *that* plain enough—and I suppose it was natural in his position to want liquid capital immediately instead of a possible steady income coming in too late to be of any use to him. Posterity wasn't a matter likely to concern him."

"I suppose Mrs. Pinfold talked in her usual vague style?"

"No, she didn't, altogether," Wendover explained. "She talked hard common sense most of the time, and that surprised me a good deal. She had all her arguments pat; and they weren't the kind of thing I'd have expected from her. It sounded to me as if she'd been well coached beforehand."

"The common sense sounds like Felden," commented Sir Clinton. "What line does he take up? He wasn't at your meeting, though."

"How did you guess that?" demanded Wendover, rather surprised.

"I'll tell you afterwards. Stick to the point, Squire."

"Felden's all for holding on to the ground. So Derek Gainford told us. He and Felden had discussed the question fully beforehand, and had got to loggerheads over it, obviously. But it wasn't Felden who coached Agatha Pinfold. She didn't even know what his ideas were, and I think she was a bit vexed when she found they were on the same side."

"H'm! Looks like Ashmun's influence, doesn't it? By the way, Ashmun wasn't amongst those present, was he?"

"Of course not. He may be an heir, if your tale's true; but I've no official knowledge of that, and he hasn't put in any claim for consideration. Naturally I let sleeping dogs lie."

"Naturally, Squire. And if it was he who did the coaching, then we can infer his views from the results. So it's three to three—or rather three to two, now that Gainford's out of it. And he was the strongest opponent of the retention of the ground, you say. Interesting point perhaps. But I'm not sure of that, yet. Your own prejudice is in favour of holding on to the ground and developing it *en bloc*? Yes, one could infer that from your character, Squire. Now just one question. You're absolutely sure that it was Miss Stanway who went out and got that capsule for Gainford?"

"Oh, positive," said Wendover. "She's the only one of them with any decent human sympathy. The rest of them just looked at him coughing and didn't stir a finger. But how did you know that Felden wasn't there with the rest?"

"Because I tried to pay him a visit this evening, and found he was taking duty for somebody else, down town. He'd left word that he was to be found at his A.R.P. Post if anyone wanted him urgently. He's got a very garrulous old housekeeper. She entertained me with endless chat about her rheumatism, and Hitler, and how difficult it was to get any variety in food when you've only two ration-books for the household, and how she was going for a holiday to-morrow for a fortnight, and . . . in fact anything else that came into her head. A talkative old dame, and very much set up by her employer's heroic deeds, in these raids. Finally, I said I'd write a note and leave it for Felden, and that turned off the eloquence-tap at last."

"What did you want to see him about?" inquired Wendover.

"Just a point about poison gas," said Sir Clinton. "Nothing of much importance, really, but I like to know just what's what, and when one has an expert chemist to hand, why not use him?"

"Just so," agreed Wendover. "What sort of establishment does he keep up? I've never been in his house."

"Comfortable, but not luxurious," said Sir Clinton. "What struck me was his library. His housekeeper showed me into his study when I said I'd write him a note; and I like to see what sort of books a man reads. He's got a better outfit than many people, and judging from it, he's got pretty wide interests. Chemistry's his main line, of course. I noticed something called Mellor's *Comprehensive Treatise on Inorganic and Theoretical Chemistry*, about twenty fat volumes of five or six hundred pages each. At three guineas a volume, it must have run him in for over £50. It made me realise that chemistry takes some learning, I can tell you. And that's only one branch. He had a lot of books on organic chemistry, too. I had the curiosity to look up hyoscine in one of them, and discovered that the formula of its hydrobromide is $C_{17}H_{21}O_4N$ HBr, which of course made me feel ever so much wiser than before. Then he's got quite a collection of popular stuff in science outside his own line. Fabre's books on insects, Jeans & Co., J. B. S. Haldane's *Science and Everyday Life*. Did you ever read that, Squire? You'd find it worth your while. And besides all this semi-technical stuff, he's got a very fair collection of things like the Mermaid Dramatists, history, poetry, modern fiction (good stuff) and so on. In fact, the sort of library where one might find something to suit any mood one happened to be in. I got quite interested, before I tore myself away."

" I suppose you must have been out at his house when I rang you up here," said Wendover, ignoring Sir Clinton's lavish description.

" There or elsewhere," admitted the Chief Constable. " As a matter of fact, I dropped in on your friend Allardyce after leaving Felden's place. I was luckier there, for I caught him at home. I wanted some tips on hyoscine and its action. He gave me all I wanted—more than that, perhaps, now I come to think over it. It seems a rummy sort of stuff, and too tricky for use by the non-expert. It doesn't prevent you from feeling pain, but you forget the pangs almost at once after they've stopped. I suppose your friend Allardyce can handle it safely. He seems to have had plenty of practice, with this twilight sleep stunt."

" I suppose so," said Wendover. " By the way, have you had any report from the Home Office expert about the results in Henry Deverell's case ? "

" I've just received it," said Sir Clinton. " There was some hyoscine in the stomach, but only a minute amount. It doesn't look as if he'd taken a fatal dose or anything like one. But there was alcohol there also."

" Then probably he had a doped drink at Ashmun's," declared Wendover. " I thought as much."

" I don't remember him taking any alcohol at that bridge party, certainly," said Sir Clinton, " and from all I hear he wasn't much of a drinker. But I can imagine even an abstemious man being glad of a tot if he was going out to hang about in the open for an hour or two in the small hours. What's more to the point, Squire, I think I know now how some of these mysterious deaths came about. I mean the cases of the rabbits—you rather sneered at the rabbits business, but you were wrong there—the rabbits, and Pirbright, and Henry Deverell. They all hang together."

" You mean they all happened up at Cæsar's Camp ? "

" That certainly does connect them," admitted Sir Clinton, " but it doesn't explain them, if I may point that out."

" You're not swallowing that stuff about a New Force, surely ? " said Wendover, with contemptuous scepticism.

" Sometimes a fresh application of an old principle looks as good as new," said Sir Clinton. " And this seems to be an exemplification of that profound reflection, in which I claim the copyright, Squire."

" Have you been taking a correspondence course from Delphi ? " demanded Wendover, irritably. " I wish you'd drop this oracular business and say what you mean in plain language, for a change. It would be an improvement."

Sir Clinton took a cigarette from his case and lit it with deliberation before answering.

" The trouble with you, Squire, is that you want the palm without the dust. I've had all the bother of digging out this business, and now you want to join the Board and reap the benefits free of charge. Not so. I'll give you all the necessary pointers, and then you can track down the solution for yourself."

Wendover's grunt showed that he was far from satisfied by this, but Sir Clinton ignored the inarticulate protest.

" You remember, Squire, that the other night I was per- plexed because I couldn't remember the details of a yarn I'd read a while ago. Now I remember all about it. It was by somebody Connington, and it appeared in the *News-Chronicle* in 1936. It came back to my mind when I noticed Haldane's book to-night. I read Haldane's book when it came out in 1939, and I remembered that one of the essays recalled the gist of the earlier short story at the time I was reading the book. Any free library will give you the back file of the *News-Chronicle* and also Haldane's book. All you have to do is to read them, and you ought then to be as wise as I am."

" Oh, very funny," said Wendover, disgustedly. " Can't you come off the tripod and tell a plain tale ? "

" You'd like it shortened ? " said Sir Clinton, agreeably. " Right ! I'll put it into two words for you. Mark them well. Henry's Law."

" Means nothing to me," said Wendover, with deepening disgust.

" Where's your general education, Squire ? *Non est inventus ?* Well, I suggest the Encyclopædia or Webster's Dictionary. Webster's probably snappier than the Encyclopædia. You have it on your shelf over there."

Wendover got up, crossed the room, and took down Webster from its place.

" ' Henry's Law '," he read aloud. " ' The generalisation that the mass of gas which a liquid will absorb is propor- tional to the pressure.' That seems about as illuminating as a flash of black light, if you ask me. Don't grin like a Cheshire cat ! Are you just pulling my leg ? "

" I wouldn't think of it," Sir Clinton assured him. " No,

Squire, I've saved you a lot of bother by putting the key into your hands. The keyhole is just opposite. But I simply refuse to save you the bother of thinking. You must worry it out for yourself. It is, as I said, merely a fresh application of an old principle."

Wendover shrugged his shoulders impatiently. Then he returned to Webster and noticed a second heading under Henry's Law.

" ' The law of partial pressures '," he read aloud. " ' See under Law.' Is that any help ? " he asked, looking up.

" You're getting hotter, perhaps," Sir Clinton assured him in the language of the old children's game.

Wendover turned over the pages of the Dictionary and gave a snort of disgust.

" There are two pages of small type about ' Law '," he protested ; but as Sir Clinton ignored his symptoms, he worked laboriously down the columns.

" Ah ! Here it is ! " he exclaimed at last. " ' Law of partial pressures, the law that in a mixture of gases each gas exerts the same pressure that it would exert if it alone occupied the space ;—called also *Dalton's Law.*' What's that got to do with rabbits ? "

He hoisted Webster's Dictionary back into its place on the shelves, and turned to find Sir Clinton regarding him quizzically.

" You seem to have got colder again, Squire. Chilly, in fact. But if you won't follow up a clue when it's put into your hands, what can I do for you ? Happy thought ! Try another line of approach. You've noted that hyoscine appears in the two Cæsar's Camp cases—Pirbright and Deverell—but Allardyce told us he found no trace of anything of the sort in the rabbits. Suggestive, perhaps. One's inclined to ask where the hyoscine came from. It's not an easily accessible stuff, as you know. And it's damnably poisonous. You'd need something better than a letter-balance to hit off the right quantity for a dose. That's suggestive, too."

" I dare say," said Wendover, refusing to be drawn. " I know what you're hinting at, Clinton, but I simply rule that out of consideration."

" Nice to be a mind-reader and know exactly what other folk are thinking," said Sir Clinton. " It must save you a lot of bother, Squire. Since you know precisely what's in my mind, I needn't expatiate further. Which saves *me* a lot of bother."

" I suppose you've been wangling the Coroner behind the scenes," said Wendover, changing the subject abruptly.

" I don't like your choice in expressions, Squire," protested the Chief Constable. " What irks you at the inquests ? "

" In Robert Deverell's case they called it death by enemy action," said Wendover, "and the theft of the gold was mentioned in the most casual way."

" The jury heard your friend Allardyce's evidence about the injuries, and the inspector's evidence about the bomb. That seems to have convinced them about the cause of death, which was all they had to consider. The Coroner kept them to the point, and didn't allow them to wander about much. Any harm in that ? If you had any evidence to prove—to *prove*, Squire—that Deverell didn't die by enemy action, then it was a public duty to bring it forward."

" Of course I've no evidence," said Wendover.

" Then what are you grousing at ? It seemed to me a verdict in accordance with the evidence submitted."

Wendover abandoned this with a shrug.

" In Pirbright's case, the inquest was adjourned."

" Why not ? Very natural, I think, since no one knows yet how he actually came by his end. The Coroner's waiting for evidence. Any fault to find with that ? "

" In Tony Gainford's case they brought in a verdict of death due to carbon monoxide poisoning. Do you believe there was nothing more in it than that ? "

" If I could answer that question, I'd have to be able to tell you exactly what happened in his house on the night of the party. I don't know. The jury came to a perfectly sound verdict on the evidence put before them."

" I dare say," said Wendover, with a faint sneer. " But you needn't think one can't see the nigger in the wood-pile or the Chief Constable in the background, advising the Coroner."

" And why not ? Anyone's entitled to give the Coroner advice if it's helpful, I suppose."

" And the inquest on Henry Deverell's adjourned," continued Wendover.

" Naturally, since it's on all-fours with the Pirbright case. I think it was the right thing to do. Now you're at the end of your stock, Squire, for there won't be an inquest on Derek Gainford. Your friend Allardyce will make no bones about signing his death certificate. Cause of death : asthmatic attack."

" What I want to know," said Wendover, irritably, " is what you're actually doing. Not much, to judge by the surface. Things can't go on this way."

" I'm watching," admitted Sir Clinton with a mask-like face. " My spies keep all suspects under observation and report to me almost incessantly. It gives them a slight change from mere routine and does no harm to anyone. Your friend Allardyce bought a large toy rabbit the other day. Paid a colossal price for it, I see. This toy ramp is really getting beyond bounds, and something should be done about it. He presented it later to his god-child, Willie Dunmore, age five. Do you suppose this had anything to do with the Cæsar's Camp rabbits? Symbolism, or anything like that? Possibly it was stuffed with hyoscine. One never knows."

" Oh, if you're in that mood, I'm going to bed," said Wendover angrily.

CHAPTER XVI *Miching Mallecho*

" CHESS ? " SUGGESTED WENDOVER, AS HE AND THE CHIEF Constable came into the smoking-room of the Grange after dinner.

Sir Clinton considered for a moment, then shook his head regretfully.

" Not to-night, Squire," he decided. " I've a notion that we'd not get far if we started, and I hate to be interrupted in a game. It's bad enough to have the phone break into one's dinner, as it did to-night; but chess is too precious for that. Try something else. What about the Game of Alibis? As old as Cain, but still full of entertainment and instruction."

He took a sheet of notepaper from his pocket and handed it to Wendover.

	RABBITS	R. DEVERELL	PIRBRIGHT	A. GAINFORD	H. DEVERELL	D. GAINFORD
Allardyce ...	A	—	—	A	—	A
Ashmun ...	A	?	A	A	A	A
Felden ...	?	A	?	A	A	A
Mrs. Pinfold ...	?	?	?	A	?	—
Miss Stanway...	?	?	?	A	?	—
Max Stanway...	?	?	?	A	?	—

A = Alibi   — = No Alibi   ? = No Information

"Here you are, Squire. I wouldn't attempt to catch you with the old race-train three-card trick. That would be too easy for you ; so here's a six-card trick instead. Puzzle : Find the Lady. Or as that's a shade ungallant in the circumstances, let's call it Spot the Murderer. You see what it means ? The names running up and down are the six cases ; the names running horizontally are those of the six persons left in the group of people interested, directly or indirectly, in the Rodway bequest. 'A' opposite a name means that we know definitely that the named person was not on the spot when the death occurred ; the dash (—) means that we have no evidence to prove an alibi. And the query sign (?) means that we've got no information at all to show where that person was when the death took place."

Wendover knitted his brows over the scheme for a short time.

"I suppose in the case of the rabbits you're assuming that Ashmun and Allardyce give each other alibis ? "

"Well, what else can one do ? " retorted Sir Clinton. "You can assume, if you like, that the whole of that story was concocted by Allardyce for our benefit. But if you take his tale as true, then he's a reliable witness, and he gives Ashmun an alibi."

Wendover nodded his assent to this.

"In the case of Anthony Gainford you give the whole six of them alibis," he pointed out. "On that basis, your murderer can't be any of the half-dozen."

"Anthony Gainford's death might have been due to accidental gas-poisoning," Sir Clinton pointed out. "Or, if the poisoning was deliberately contrived, the contriver need not have been on the premises when Gainford actually died. If you give a man arsenic, you don't need to hang about the premises until it acts and causes death."

"H'm ! So your pretty scheme doesn't help much in that case ? "

"Not if poison has been used, certainly," Sir Clinton admitted frankly. "And there's another flaw in it, which I may as well own up to at once. For all I can prove, Robert Deverell died by enemy action and not by local foul play. It all depends on how you look on that incendiary bomb. There's nothing to show that it didn't hit him as it dropped from the sky. But I wanted to have the scheme complete, for if I hadn't put in the lot you'd have accused me of picking and choosing amongst them to suit my own purposes. I haven't done that, as you see. All the cards are on the table."

The mention of Robert Deverell's death set Wendover's thoughts on a fresh track.

"Whether he died as a result of enemy action or not," he pointed out, "that gold crosier disappeared from his house on the night of his death."

"I hadn't forgotten that," said Sir Clinton, dryly.

"So in any case, a crime was committed that night," Wendover pursued. "And that theft is connected with Pirbright, since the crosier was buried in his garden."

"That hadn't escaped my attention, either," said Sir Clinton, even more dryly.

"And it had been buried in his garden for only a short time," continued Wendover, ignoring Sir Clinton's tone, "although it had been stolen some time previously to our digging it up. Therefore it must have been hidden elsewhere in the meantime. And when we went up that stream beyond Cæsar's Camp, we came on signs of fresh digging. Obviously the thief buried it there, first of all. Probably Pirbright saw him doing that and dug the gold up himself and transplanted it to his garden where we found it."

"You seem to have it all at your fingers' ends, Squire."

"Well, that furnishes a motive for the Pirbright murder, anyhow," declared Wendover, with considerable satisfaction. "Probably Pirbright recognised the man who was burying the stuff, and that made it necessary for him to be liquidated before he could talk."

"Think so?" rejoined Sir Clinton. "Suppose you catch me burying one of your tea-spoons at Cæsar's Camp. Do you suppose it would be worth my while to murder you out of hand, merely to keep my kleptomaniac tendencies dark? That seems to me to be pushing things to extremes, really. It would be much easier to plead guilty to the theft and get off with three months instead of a morning walk to the gallows. At least, that's my feeling in the matter. Your view may be quite different, and naturally you're entitled to it."

"You mean that if the theft were fastened on a man, it would lead to his conviction for Robert Deverell's murder?'

"I don't mind your thinking this, that, or the other on your own account, Squire. But when you start in to do my thinking for me, and then taxing me with the results, it's time to object, I think. I never said that the gold was buried up yonder by the stream. Nor did I say that Pirbright caught anyone burying it there. Nor yet did I assert that Robert Deverell was murdered. . . . Hello! There's the phone again. The call's for me, I think."

He went over to the instrument. The conversation was short, and the Chief Constable's contributions were monosyllabic, so Wendover gathered nothing from what he heard. Finally Sir Clinton put down the receiver and returned to his chair. Wendover sensed that his friend was faintly uneasy.

" You seem a bit worried," he commented. " What's the matter ? "

Sir Clinton lit a fresh cigarette before answering.

" That phone call while we were at dinner was from one of my men. I told you I was having all these people watched. Well, Ashmun had gone to pay a call on your friend Felden, Squire."

" But Felden loathes that mulatto," objected Wendover, taken aback.

" So we were led to suppose," said Sir Clinton stolidly. " But I didn't altogether believe it."

" What is Felden after ? Why should he entertain a brute like that ? " demanded Wendover, with a certain touch of scepticism.

" ' Marry, this is miching mallecho ; it means mischief,' " quoted Sir Clinton. " I can't say I'm surprised, Squire. It looks to me as if things were coming to a climax very soon. But I think we have the situation well in hand, barring accidents."

" What was this second call, the one you've just answered ? "

" That was from my people, giving the news that Allardyce has gone to Felden's house. It looks like a gathering of the vultures, doesn't it ? In the meantime, there's nothing to be done except wait. Let's go back to the point where the phone broke in on us. I've tapped a fresh line of information. You remember that youngster we found scrabbling in the bomb-crater when we went up that night to look at the Viking's hoard ? "

" Noel East ? Yes, I remember speaking to him."

" He had a handful of geological specimens which he'd found in the pit."

" So he had," Wendover recalled. " But he told us that he had got all the samples of the sort. There were no more."

" Quite true," agreed Sir Clinton. " And neither you nor I could tell him what the stuff was. I'm wiser now. To-day I paid Master Noel a visit and borrowed a couple of these specimens. The Curator of the Ambledown Museum gets the name of being a good enough amateur geologist so I asked him to have a look at them. Cassiterite, was his verdict. Tin-stone, in plain English. And it's the variety known as stream tin."

" Thrilling ! " said Wendover, ironically.

" Well, it thrilled me all right," declared Sir Clinton. " Stream tin is tin-stone, rolled and water-worn ; and it comes from the wearing away of tin veins or of rocks containing the ore."

Wendover shrugged his shoulders.

" It seems to me you're getting very excited over a few bits of rock, Clinton. No one's likely to make a fortune out of half-a-pound of tin-stone."

" No," agreed Sir Clinton. " But if one came across a decent-sized and easily accessible deposit of tin-stone, it might be worth a small fortune just now. We've lost the Malayan tin mines, not so long ago, and tin's an essential stuff in modern industry."

" Where's your deposit ? " demanded Wendover.

Sir Clinton took from his note-case the copy of the map which Wendover had seen him use during their exploration up the valley of the stream.*

" Look at this, Squire. Noel East found these specimens of tin-stone at the bottom of that bomb-crater, well below the present surface of the ground and alongside that streamlet. The cassiterite was water-worn, as you saw yourself. Therefore, at one time, there must have been a stream running down that valley at a lower level than the present one ; and it brought down tin-stone with its waters. Evidently at a later period, its sides caved in and filled the old bed, and after that the present stream ran forty or fifty feet above the old level. In other words, if you were to dig down fifty feet from the present bed of the stream, the chances are that you'd come upon the old bed."

" Possibly," conceded Wendover. " But that doesn't convert two or three lumps of tin-stone into a useful deposit."

" No, you've got to look for it," retorted Sir Clinton. " Suppose you draw a section along the bed of that stream, it would look something like this, wouldn't it ? There's a fairly steep drop from B to C ; then there's a long comparatively level bit of bed down to D ; and after that it drops steeply again towards F where the bomb-crater is, and G where the road crosses the stream at the bridge. Now if the stream is rolling some heavy stones down—cassiterite has a density of between six and seven—they won't tend to accumulate in the steeper parts of the bed between A and C or between D and G where the water's running fast. They'll

* See page 178.

gather somewhere in the stretch between C and D, where the current's sluggish."

"I suppose so," admitted Wendover. "Ah! now I see what you're driving at. That's the stretch between the two stars on that map of Ashmun's, isn't it? And it was on that stretch that we found traces of digging, wasn't it? Someone else had got your idea and ahead of you, Clinton."

"And now you've got it yourself, after considerable prodding," said Sir Clinton. "Better late than never,

DIAGRAM B

Squire. It's on that stretch that there'll be a tin-stone deposit if one exists on the Rodway ground at all. And it may not be anything like fifty feet down, for all I can tell. It may be quite near the surface in places."

Wendover produced an objection.

"But you dug down alongside the pit and found nothing at the bottom," he pointed out. "Whoever did the digging before you, he didn't find any tin-stone."

"True enough," confessed Sir Clinton. "But that doesn't prove that he didn't dig somewhere else, with more success."

"But we found no signs of any other digging," objected Wendover.

"True again. But I give him credit for realising what a fool he'd been to start digging in the grass when he might have dug under the shingle of the streamlet's verge. Then, when he finished his hole, and filled it in, a few spadefulls of shingle on top would conceal his work completely. I can't prove that at present; but I'm banking on it as probable. And I'm also banking on the probability that he found what he was looking for—an easily accessible biggish deposit of cassiterite."

"And Pirbright may have spotted him digging and got too inquisitive?"

"That would certainly dove-tail neatly enough into the rest of things."

"And if this is a really valuable deposit, it might be worth while shutting Pirrbight's mouth for good, before he started chattering about what he'd seen ? "

" Quite a bright effort, Squire. But why didn't you think of all this off your own bat ? "

Wendover ignored this.

" So the thing which lies behind the whole business is that somebody knew the ground was valuable, quite apart from building development, and he had to keep it dark and get as big a share as he could ? "

" So I imagine. There were nine people to share the proceeds at the start—eight of them obvious, and Ashmun as a dark horse. Now there are only five of them left. And if some of the survivors buy out the rest at building-land price, the value of the share goes up proportionately. It also goes up in the event of there being any more mysterious deaths in that group. I'm none too easy in my mind, Squire, I may as well admit it. But what can one do ? It's all surmise so far, with a certain amount of evidence in support, but not nearly enough to convince a jury. I know how two of these people were killed. Henry's Law goes that length, though I don't know the precise method. I've a notion of how two others were done in, and I'm banking on getting definite evidence shortly. If I'm not ' mistook in my judgments,' like Disko Troop, we're up against an excellent bit of criminal ingenuity, Squire. A regular ' two-handed engine,' à la Milton.' "

" What sort of evidence are you still looking for ? " queried Wendover.

" A rum assortment," returned Sir Clinton. " I want an order for ice, somebody's gas mask, a phial of hyoscine, a few nickel filings, and one of those big wire catch-'em-alive-O rabbit-traps—not the ordinary rat-trap brand. If I could lay my hands on these, I think I could fit them into the jig-saw. But one can't go taking out search-warrants broadcast, on the off-chance of finding what one's looking for. It's a case of waiting, and keeping a weather eye open in the meanwhile."

CHAPTER XVII   *Jack-in-the-Box*

WITH AN UGLY SMILE, KENNETH FELDEN GLANCED ACROSS the hearth-rug at his guest. Allardyce sprawled in his chair, his face vacant, his limbs relaxed. Beside him, on a little table, stood an empty tumbler ; and a smouldering cigarette in an ash-tray sent up a tiny spiral of smoke. For a moment or two, Felden enjoyed the sight, then he rose and going over to Allardyce, shook him roughly. There was no response except the drowsy inarticulate protest of a heavily-drugged man. Felden stooped a moment to examine the eyes, with their dilated pupils ; then, satisfied, he went to the door and called his second visitor out of the adjoining room. Jehudi Ashmun appeared ; and as his glance rested on the semi-conscious Allardyce, his teeth flashed in a grin of satisfaction much broader than Felden's thin-lipped smile.

" So you have fixed him, eh ? " he said, gloating over the stupefied figure. " This is what he and his likes call ' twilight sleep,' I suppose. Not a bad notion of yours, Kenneth, to dose him with his own medicine. There is a touch of poetic justice in the idea. By the way, I have always forgotten to ask you how you managed to procure the hyoscine."

" Luck played into my hands," explained Felden. " I knew Shipman stocked the stuff. Allardyce deals with him. I called on Shipman one evening, a while ago. Semi-official call in my capacity as Warden. His shop's in my district. I pretended to be worried about the chance of a bomb falling on his premises and blowing his assorted poisons into the street. Public danger, and so forth. He showed me where he kept his atropine and the rest of his alkaloidal poisons. Originally I'd meant to burgle the shop and take what I wanted. Easy enough job, really, when you're a Warden and above suspicion. But Fate played right into my hands when Shipman's shop went on fire in a raid. All I had to do was to walk in and help myself. Brave fellow, you know. Wouldn't let anyone else take the risk of entering the premises. I got quite high praise for that. And I came out with the bottle in my pocket. By the time the fire had done with the place, no one could tell what was missing and what wasn't, even if they'd gone over the premises with a small-toothed comb."

" That was certainly better than burglary," commented Ashmun. " It leaves no possible trail for that sleuth Clinton, who fancies himself so much. But even with the stuff to hand, I'd have been a little nervous about the dose, if it hadn't been for you. A hundredth of a grain takes careful weighing."

" Easy enough if you have an analytical balance in your private lab.," said Felden, carelessly. " You brought your official costume with you ? "

" And the book of words also," Ashmun assured him with

another broad grin. " Everything shall be done decently and in order, you may rest assured."

He glanced round the room and his eye was caught by a temporary curtain hung across one corner. It seemed to amuse him.

" The mummy-case ? " he asked, with a nod towards the screened-off portion. " Did you get the glass plate fitted ? It would be a pity to lose the chance of studying the results, step by step. Our young cousin will be much impressed, I have no doubt."

" It's all ready," said Felden, with an evil grin. " The motor-drive of the air-pump's coupled up to that power-plug. Nothing to do but switch on." He glanced at his watch. " About time we were shutting up the Jack-in-the-box, I think."

Ashmun broke into a hearty laugh.

" That is really funny," he declared when he had had his laugh out. " I wish I could coin phrases like that myself. So apt. Jack-in-the-box ! Ha ! Ha ! Ha ! "

Felden glanced at his confederate with sudden suspicion.

" Not losing your nerve, are you ? " he demanded.

" I ? " retorted Ashmun. " Lose my nerve over a trifle like this ? You've never seen a man staked out beside an ant-hill, as I've done more than once in Africa. It is most amusing. And yet you suspect me of going white at the gills over to-night's business. It means nothing to me beyond a certain titillation—what your learned white men would call a touch of sadism, I think. No, Cousin Kenneth, you can count on my nerves standing anything that yours can, and rather more."

" That's all right, then," said Felden, hastily. " I'd forgotten about your experiences." He glanced at his watch. " Now I think it's time to ring up Ione and Agatha. That'll give us plenty of time to get Jack-in-the-box ready."

" Good ! " agreed Ashmun. " While you are at the phone, I shall keep an eye upon our young friend here. Not that he looks like giving any trouble."

*   *   *   *   *

For the third time that evening the telephone rang at the Grange, and Sir Clinton got a further message.

" ' Thrice the brinded cat hath mewed '," he said as he put down the receiver. " I used to think that ' brinded ' was a misprint for ' brindled ' owing to Shakespeare's vile

175

caligraphy; but 'brinded' is the Elizabethan form after all."

Wendover was not to be deceived by this red herring.

"You've been quoting Shakespeare more than once to-night, Clinton," he said, "and that's out of your normal run. You're worried. What's gone wrong?"

"Nothing's gone wrong, that I know of," rejoined the Chief Constable. "Something's happened which I don't understand, that's all. This last ring was a message to say that Ione Herongate and Daphne Stanway have gone off in Ione Herongate's car; and from something my man picked up, it seems they're bound for Felden's house. I don't see my way through this, and I don't like it, I confess, Squire. I'd laid my plans to cope with another bit of funny business up at Cæsar's Camp, and catch the chief villain red-handed, so that there could be no doubt in the matter. That's why I wasn't worrying. But this is a fresh twist which I hadn't foreseen."

"You mean that these girls are being dragged into it?"

"Something of the sort. Now, instead of waiting comfortably for my trap to shut, we'll have to get a move on; and I'll need to trouble you for a search-warrant, Squire. Let's see . . . What are we going to look for? H'm! Call it a quantity of stolen hyoscine. That'll cover us. Perhaps we'll even find it, if we're lucky. Anyhow, with a search-warrant we can break down doors and do all sorts of interesting things if it suits us. So let's get through the formalities. You've got a Testament? Hand it over, then, and I'll swear as required."

When the warrant had been signed, Wendover handed it over. He was surprised to notice a faintly perplexed expression on Sir Clinton's face.

"What are you brooding over?" he demanded.

"I? Just something that struck me. Remember Ione Herongate's sudden craze for taking rubbings of brasses in all the churches about the country-side? Curious, this brand-new enthusiasm for such a hobby. I thought I knew all about that; but this latest news has thrown a spanner into the works. I don't see where your young friend Daphne fits in, and that worries me . . . But there's no time to waste on speculation to-night. There's something practical in hand. Come along if you like, Squire. And if you put an automatic in your pocket, I shan't grumble. Anything may happen."

*   *   *   *   *

" That's your door bell," said Ashmun. " You had better go and admit your guests, Cousin Kenneth."

Felden rose from his chair and went out into the darkened hall, pulling his torch from his pocket. When he opened the door, his light revealed Ione and Daphne on the steps.

" What's happened to Frank ? " demanded Daphne, anxiously. " Ione couldn't tell me, exactly. It isn't serious, is it, Kenneth ? "

" Not very serious, so far," he said, reassuringly. " But he'd like to see you, I think . . . Let's see . . . There's no need for you to come, Ione. Suppose you wait in the dining-room here. You don't mind ? It will only be for a minute or two."

" Oh, of course not," agreed Ione, as he ushered her into the room after switching on its lights.

Felden closed the door upon her.

" Now, if you'll come with me, Daphne . . ."

He led her along a passage to his study and paused on the threshold.

" You'll find Mr. Ashmun here," he warned her. " He knows all about the affair. Just go in."

Daphne obeyed and, entering the study, glanced round in surprise. There was no sign of her fiancé. Her eye caught the curtain which screened the corner of the room. The faint pulsation of a motor-driven pump sent its soft beat into the air, and every few seconds there came a slight hiss of escaping gas from behind the hangings. Ashmun was sitting in a chair by the fire-place, but as she came in he rose to his feet with a broad smile of welcome, and greeted her with a semblance of courtesy which made her slightly uncomfortable by its touch of affectation.

" Sit down, Daphne," said Felden, curtly. " You'll see Allardyce in a moment. But first of all, I've one or two things to explain."

Suddenly, Daphne became aware of something sinister in the atmosphere.

" What's happened to Frank ? " she demanded, with a tremor of acute disquietude in her voice. " Oh, Kenneth, is he badly hurt and you've been keeping it from me ? Tell me. Tell me at once and don't drag it out. He isn't . . . ? "

" No, he isn't . . . *yet*," answered Felden, parodying her unfinished sentence with elaborate irony. " It depends on yourself, whether . . ."

" What do you mean ? "

Kenneth Felden had thrown off his mask of suavity and

J. J. CONNINGTON

leaned forward with a dreadful avidity in his eyes. To avoid his look, she turned to Ashmun, who was lölling back in his chair with a pose of indifference ; but on his face she read only a covert interest which had stark cruelty at its base. She realised that danger threatened, but its nature eluded her. Besides, Ione was in the house ; she was not entirely alone. Kenneth Felden allowed her time to realise that she was in peril ; then, watching her intently, he began to speak slowly, as though relishing his own words.

"First and foremost," he said brutally, "it's no use your squalling. You know this house is a lonely one. No one would hear you."

"Ione ! " said Daphne, forcing the word from a dry throat.

"Ione ? " Felden laughed contemptuously. "You needn't expect much help from her ! She knows which side her bread's buttered, does Ione. Who brought you here to-night, you little fool ? Ione ! There's your answer ! You'll get no good by howling. One squeak from you and we'll gag you, understand ? That'll hurt, for a beginning."

"Where's Frank ? " asked Daphne, trying to keep her voice steady.

"You think of him first, do you ? " retorted Felden, with a scowl. "Well, Frank's quite safe . . . so far. Playing Little Jack Horner for the present, as good as gold. Don't you worry about dear Frank. That story of an accident was all my own invention."

Daphne caught at the reassurance which lay in the words, but not in the tone.

"Oh ! He's quite safe ? "

"So far, was what I said," Felden corrected her.

Daphne's nerve began to weaken.

"I don't understand a word you say," she protested, wearily. "Can't you tell me straight out what you mean, instead of talking in riddles like this ? "

"This is what's called breaking it gently," explained Felden, with a sneer. "All for your own good, really. I'm surprised at my own moderation, like Warren Hastings or somebody else. But if you want it in plain English, you can have it. We were engaged once, though you may have forgotten it. I was fool enough to fall in love with you. Adam and young Eve in the Garden, and all that sort of thing. I'd have done anything for you in those days, more fool I. And then you turned me down. That changed things for me more than a bit. It changed me, too. Now you're going to pay for that. You're keen on this fellow

178

Allardyce, are you? Well, we'll see just how keen you are, before the night's out. It's my turn now. To begin with, have a look at Jack-in-the-Box."

He rose from his chair, walked across the room, and drew back the curtain which screened the corner. Daphne saw a long box, uptilted, coffin-shaped, with a glass plate let into the lid at the upper end.

"Come and have a closer look," said Felden.

He came back, gripped her arm roughly, and led her over till she stood in front of the box. Behind the glass she saw the face of Frank Allardyce distorted by a wooden gag which had been thrust between his teeth. His eyes were dull, but through the apathy of his drugged mind something seemed to penetrate at the sight of her, and he evidently tried to speak.

"What have they been doing to you, Frank?" cried Daphne, in horror.

"Nothing much, *so far*," said Felden, with an evil smile. "But you may spare your breath. He can't hear you through that box. Besides, he's hardly fitted up for conversation, as you see. But before you sit down again, I'd like you to watch a little experiment."

He put out his hand and unscrewed an escape valve which she saw projecting from the box. Air under pressure hissed out suddenly, and then the whistling almost ceased.

"As simple as that," explained Felden. "Now, watch!"

Under Daphne's eyes, the face behind the glass plate showed first uneasiness, then pain, and finally an agony so acute that she put her hand over her eyes to shut out the sight.

"Oh, stop it! Stop it, Kenneth!" she appealed. "Don't hurt him! Please, please don't hurt him so. How can you do it? Stop it! You're killing him."

She leapt forward and tore at the lid of the box, but it was fastened down with heavy wing nuts. She began to untwist the one nearest to her hand, when Felden gripped her wrist and pulled her away.

"You evidently want to kill him," he said coolly. "I don't mind, really; but it would be a pity to waste him at this stage."

He bent over, screwed up the valve and then gave the wing-nut a twist to fasten it down again. The hissing ceased and only the rhythmical beat of the motor-driven pump broke the silence of the room.

"Now have another look," Felden ordered.

" I won't ! I can't bear it ! Oh, Kenneth, do please stop hurting him. It's dreadful. I can't bear it. I . . ."

" Feeling hurt ? " asked Felden with mock solicitude. " No physical pain, surely ? Just a mental pang or two ? Well, that gives you some slight idea of what I got when you turned me down. It's nothing, really. One gets over it in time. As you'll do, I'm sure. You see, your dear Frank is quite normal again. He's not squirming a bit now. Just see for yourself."

He stood aside, and Daphne timorously faced the glass window. As Felden had promised, Allardyce seemed to have recovered from the agonising pain, though it had left its traces behind. He looked like a man just released from cramp : sound again, but shaken by the experience.

" As simple as that," repeated Felden. " Nothing to make a fuss about, really. But I see you're trembling. Better sit down and recover for a bit. I've more to say to you."

" Let him out, Kenneth. Please let him out. You're suffocating him. Have you no pity ? "

" Just as much as you had on me, in your time," retorted Felden, with a snarl. " Suffocating him ! " he laughed. " I'm not suffocating him. He's got all the air he needs, and more. And he's still a bit drugged, so he doesn't feel the treatment too badly. Wait till the drug wears off, and then we can try again. You'll see something worth while, I can assure you."

" I shall faint," said Daphne, dully. " I can't stand it."

" Faint if you like," returned Felden, brutally. " What do I care ? We've got quite a while before us yet, and can wait until you revive again."

" I'll do anything, if you'll let him out."

" We seem to be getting down to brass tacks at last," commented Felden, with a horrid geniality. " Well, to start with, I want you to sign a paper for me. It's quite simple : merely a document to enable me to handle your share of the Cæsar's Camp ground exactly like my own. Care to do that ? You will ? That's very good of you. Of course I might have insisted on your transferring your share to me, but that would not have looked so well to outsiders, probably."

He drew a paper from his pocket, unfolded it on his desk, and offered Daphne a fountain-pen. She scrawled her signature at the foot without even reading what she was signing.

" Merely as a formality," said Felden, " I ask you to say

that you've signed this of your own free will. You needn't, if you like the alternative better. It's all the same to me, you know. The resources of civilisation are not exhausted."

" If you want me to say it, I'll say it," said Daphne, glancing piteously towards the box in the corner, " I'm signing this of my own free will, Now, please, please let him out, Kenneth."

Felden ignored her appeal and turned to Ashmun.

" Just sign as a witness, will you ? And you'll remember what she said."

" Certainly," said the mulatto with a flash of gleaming teeth. " Give me the pen, please."

He came across and affixed his signature as a witness.

" And now, Kenneth, do let him out," repeated Daphne. " I've done what you wanted. Now do what you promised."

" Promised ? " Felden lifted his eyebrows. " I promised nothing of that sort. I asked you to sign that paper ' to start with.' There's another little formality still to come. But first, have another peep."

He turned round to the box and unscrewed the valve.

" You don't seem eager," he commented, as Daphne shrank back. " Come along ! I want you to have a good look."

He stepped behind her, gripped her arms above the elbows and swung her round by brute force until her face was level with the glass window.

" She's shut her eyes," Ashmun pointed out, lazily. " You're wasting your time."

" No matter," said Felden. " The longer she keeps her eyes shut, the longer I keep Jack-in-the-Box uncomfortable. He's beginning to squirm now, but that's her affair. Open your eyes, you little fool ! Do you want him to die, merely to save your delicate feelings ? "

Under that compulsion, Daphne raised her eyelids and saw before her the agony-distorted face of Allardyce.

" Oh, stop ! " she pleaded, brokenly. " I'll do anything, anything you like, if you'll only make him well again. Quick ! Oh, how can you do it ? Haven't you any human feelings ? Look how he's suffering ! "

" I suffered a bit in my time," retorted Felden, " but I don't remember you turning a hair over it. However, that's an old story now. Get back to your chair."

He screwed up the valve once more and drew the curtain across in front of the box.

" Now, you quite understand where we are, I hope," he

said composedly, as he seated himself before the girl. " I don't want the bother of any more experiments. Besides, it's on the cards that your dear Frank might not quite get over a third experience. It wouldn't worry me. I've seen other people in that box, and they didn't live long to look back on the experience."

He paused, and for a moment or two Daphne failed to catch the meaning of his reference. Then it dawned on her, and her eyes showed her terror.

" You mean . . . You mean it was *you* who murdered Pirbright, and Harry Deverell ; and you killed them like this ? "

" Yes, Unpleasant, isn't it ? But you can add Tony and Derek Gainford to your list, though they went out by a different door. I'm more versatile than you'd think, Daphne. And your dear Frank will go the same road to-night, unless you do as you're told. Make no mistake about that."

Suddenly Daphne's heart leaped as she heard the trill of an electric bell. Someone was at the front door of the house. She opened her mouth to scream for help, but Felden leapt from his chair and gripped her throat, tightening his hold until she gasped for breath. The brutality of the act shook her courage and left her without the nerve even to struggle.

" That's Agatha," said Felden, turning to speak to Ashmun, but retaining his clasp on Daphne's throat. " Ione will open the door to her."

Daphne's short-lived hope died away at the words. Obviously her sister was the last person capable of coping with these two relentless brutes. There was nothing to be gained by further resistance. Felden saw her surrender in her face, and relaxed his grip slightly.

" Going to be a good little girl ? " he asked. " That's better. You'd gain nothing by yelping. It would take more than Agatha to throw us out of our stride, I assure you. Now before I let you free, just understand this, because there's no second deal in this game. One squeak from you after this, and dear Frank goes the long road. ' No traveller returns . . .' as Shakespeare says. Take that for sure. Now sit down again and listen to what I say. I don't want any comments. And I'm not in a sympathetic mood to-night, so you needn't waste breath in appeals. They'll cut no ice with me."

He pushed her roughly back into the chair and stood

over her. She heard the front door opened and the voices of Ione and Agatha Pinfold in the hall. Then the door of the dining-room closed behind the two women. Felden had evidently been waiting for this before speaking again.

" Now, Daphne, allow me to introduce you to a long-lost relation : Cousin Jehudi."

He nodded towards Ashmun, who rose and made an ironical formal acknowledgment, accompanied by a broad smile.

" He's the son of our estimable relation, Uncle Bruce, about whom the less said, the better, perhaps. What is more to our purpose to-night, he's an ordained clergyman."

Daphne listened without understanding the drift of his talk. What had Ashmun's clerical status got to do with her ? Marriage ? But you had to go through all sorts of formalities before a marriage : banns, registrar's certificate, residence qualification. She knew all about these things, for she had gone into them in connection with her approaching marriage with Frank.

Felden evidently guessed how her thoughts were trending.

" Of course you're like most girls," he said with obvious contempt. " You want a nice church wedding, I suppose, with guests, and a choir, and speeches, and the organ doing its bit with ' *The Voice that breathed o'er Eden*,' and all the rest of it. But it's war-time, you see. You'll have to be content with the essentials and do without the frills. And you're lucky, I may tell you, to get even the essentials."

He felt in his pocket and produced a document, which he unfolded.

" This is a Special Licence issued by the Archbishop of Canterbury through a proctor at Doctor's Commons, Knightrider Street, E.C.4. Rather expensive. It cost me £30 plus a few necessary lies which took me some time to think out. But in a case like this, one mustn't spare trouble or expense. The main point about it is that it authorises a clergyman to perform the marriage at any time and in any place that one chooses. Valid for three months. Our clerical friend had better glance over it and see that everything's correct."

He passed the paper to Ashmun, who pretended to study it meticulously and then put it down with a nod to indicate that he was satisfied.

" Now let's see what we've got," continued Felden. " The clergyman, we have him here. The licence, that's all right. The bride, also present. The bridegroom, no difficulty about him. Witnesses, Ione and Agatha are next door. Yes, we seem to be all ready. But before we actually get to business, Daphne . . ."

Daphne, after a moment of incredulity, grasped his purpose.

"Do you mean to say that I'm to marry *you*," she said, with dilated eyes. "Now that I know what you are, I'd die sooner than that."

"Nobody's suggesting that *you* should die," said Felden, with a sneer. "I'd never think of such a thing, I assure you. But you can take it from me that if you refuse to marry me, then your dear Frank will die without fail within the next half-hour—and just as uncomfortably as I can manage it. You've seen a sample of what can be done in that line. Well, it's up to you. Refuse, and you'll have his blood on your hands just as much as I shall. And you'll live on with the happy knowledge that you could have saved him at the cost of a little inconvenience to yourself. You love him, apparently. Then make a small sacrifice on his account. And hurry up about it, will you? I've had enough of your blowing hot and cold in the past. Yes or No? Don't waste any more of our time."

"Give me a few minutes to think," pleaded Daphne.

She was fighting for time, in the hope that something might happen to save Frank Allardyce at the last moment.

"Sixty seconds," said Felden, glancing at his watch.

Daphne searched her mind for some expedient to spin out matters at any cost, but she could think of nothing which promised success. If she pretended to faint, Felden would unscrew that horrible valve again and bring her to her bearings immediately. She decided to fence in the hope of luring him into an argument.

"Why do you want me to marry you?" she demanded, putting on as bold a front as she could. "You know I hate you now. What's the good of it?"

Felden smiled grimly.

"You're not the only person who can hate, my dear girl. When you jilted me, my pride got a nasty jar. Now it's your pride's turn to get a shock. And it'll *be* a shock; you may count on that, Daphne. Besides, by marrying you I'll prevent you marrying Frank, you know. That's one gain, from my point of view. Anything to give pain. But there's a much more solid reason still. You've seen a bit too much to-night for my comfort. Your good friend Driffield—oh, I know all about him and his doings—he would be very glad to put you into the witness-box against me. But he won't. A wife can't give evidence against her husband. See? That you spikes his pocket-cannon. Your minute's up. Say yes or no, and no more about it."

Daphne saw the relentlessness in his eyes and knew that the crucial moment had come. Further procrastination was impossible. She made one final effort.

" It'll be only a formality ? "

" Will it ? " retorted Felden viciously. " No, you're too pretty for that. I'm no Galahad."

" No, you're just a beast," said Daphne, her anger flaming up and conquering her fear, now that all was lost. " Well, you seem to have been very clever, Kenneth, and you've beaten me. Get what you can out of that. I give in."

" I thought you would," declared Felden with evil satisfaction. " Nothing else for you to do, so far as I can see." He turned to the mulatto. " You'd better get into your fancy dress, Jehudi."

Ashmun grinned an acknowledgment of the order. He lifted a suit-case from beside his chair, opened it, and drew out a crumpled surplice which he put on. Felden turned back to Daphne.

" When these two come in, you'll say that you're going through this business of your own free will. Make it sound genuine. And, of course, you'll go through the ceremony without a hitch. If there's the slightest trouble, your dear Frank will be much the worse for wear within thirty seconds."

He imitated the motion of unscrewing the valve.

" You quite understand ? "

" I understand," said Daphne. " Go on with your farce if you like. No marriage of this sort was ever binding. You know that as well as I do."

" Wait and see," said Felden, curtly.

He left the room and came back almost immediately, ushering in Ione and Agatha. Apparently Ione had explained some matters while the two women were in the dining-room together, for Agatha Pinfold showed no surprise at seeing Ashmun in his surplice.

" I suppose Ione has told you," Felden said as he came into the room behind them. " Daphne's discovered that Allardyce isn't all she thought him, and she's changed her mind again. Off with the new love and on with the old. She's going to marry me instead. That's so, isn't it, Daphne ? "

His eyes flickered meaningly towards the drawn curtain.

" Yes, that is so," agreed Daphne, white to the lips.

" I never thought much of you, Kenneth," said Mrs. Pinfold with her usual disregard for the feelings of her relations, " but I was never very keen on Dr. Allardyce either. So it's all the same to me, so long as Daphne's satisfied, and of course I wish you both all the happiness you're likely to get out of such a hugger-mugger kind of wedding. It seems very sudden, but if you're pleased, that's your own affair and I've no wish to object, or to offer you advice which you probably wouldn't take. The less I have to do with it, the better I'll be pleased, so I think you'd better start and get it over as quick as possible. I don't want to be kept here all night on your account."

" It won't take long," Felden assured her. Then, motioning Daphne to rise, he turned to Ashmun.

" Go ahead."

The mulatto ranged himself before the couple, drew a small volume from his pocket, opened it at a mark and began to intone:

" Dearly beloved, we are gathered together. . . ."

Daphne went through the service almost without caring what she did. She made the responses mechanically and allowed Felden to thrust a ring on her finger without resistance. Through the whole ceremony two thoughts occupied her mind : " I mustn't give him any excuse for hurting Frank " and " This means nothing ; I'm not his wife." She was so wrapped up in these twin obsessions that she hardly perceived that the rite had come to its end.

Mrs. Pinfold had other things to think about, as her first words proved when she opened her mouth at the close of the function.

" I suppose we've got to sign something now, and then I can get home again. I must say, Daphne, you might have chosen a more convenient hour. You know how I hate driving in the black-out. And I never do think it's a proper wedding unless it's in a church."

" It's quite proper," interjected Felden. " I got a special licence."

" Oh, it doesn't matter to me," retorted Mrs. Pinfold. " It's your affair and Daphne's entirely. I suppose we go into the dining-room now and drink your healths. I hope your champagne is all right, Kenneth. You've no palate, never had."

" I'm afraid it won't run to even sherry and a biscuit," said Felden, offensively. " We'll have to take your good wishes for granted, Agatha."

" Oh, as you're rude, I won't impose on you any longer,"
said Mrs. Pinfold, in an obvious huff. " But next time,
when you ask a favour of me, I shall think twice about it,
Kenneth. Come along, Ione."

Ione Herongate hesitated. She glanced at Daphne and
then, with mistrust plainly in her eyes, to Felden.

" I think I'll stay a little longer, Agatha. I have my own
car, you know."

Felden's frown showed that this proposal met with no
approval on his part.

" Sorry, Ione, but I think you'd better follow Agatha's
example. I've some things to settle with my wife, private
affairs, and you'd be a little bit in the way."

For a moment or two, Ione betrayed hesitation before
accepting the implied order. She scanned Felden's face
keenly, as though seeking some reassurance which she
expected. Then, with a faint shrug, she decided to fall in
with his wishes.

" Very well," she said, " just as you please, Kenneth.
I'll say good night. Don't bother to come to the door."

Without a glance at Daphne, she left the room ; and in a
few minutes they heard the front door close behind her. Ashmun, still in his surplice, took his seat again in his arm-chair
and seemed to fall into the rôle of spectator, not without a
certain obvious relish. Felden walked a few paces up and
down the room, evidently with the intention of keeping
Daphne on the strain as long as possible before he spoke.
At last he made up his mind.

" Well, I've. got you, now," he said at last. " Didn't
look like it at one time, did it ? And I'm not quite in the
mood I was in, in those days. Not much in love with
you, I mean. Still, it's something to be able to square the
account."

Daphne summoned all her courage, for she saw that the
crisis had come.

" Is that all you have to tell me ? " she asked, keeping her
voice level with an effort. " You don't suppose I lay the
least weight on this burlesque you've staged ? It means
nothing."

" It may mean something to you before another twelve
hours," said Felden, with cool malevolence. " I've treated
you better than I need have done."

Daphne decided to put everything to the touch.

" I see no point in waiting here any longer. I'm going
home now."

She rose from her chair, but Felden forced her back into it again with his hand on her shoulder.

"I'll show you the point, if you can't see it. You're staying here. And if you don't behave yourself and do as you're told. . . . Well, Jack-in-the-box will suffer."

He nodded towards the curtained recess.

"No doubt you're shy before Cousin Ashmun there. I quite understand. So we'll leave him down here and go off by ourselves. He'll look after Jack-in-the-box. And, remember, he'll be listening. I've only got to give him a call, and that valve comes loose again. You quite understand? Then come along."

"I won't," cried Daphne. "I hate you, I never thought I could hate anyone so much. I. . . ."

She sprang from her chair and made an effort to reach the door, but Felden pinned her before she had got to her feet and she felt his hand gripping her throat.

"Here!" he said to Ashmun. "Stuff something into her mouth, will you. She'll yell the place down, if she gets half a chance. And tie her hands while you're about it. Jack-in-the-box shall pay for this caper, my good girl. Don't you make any mistake about that."

Helpless in the hands of the two, Daphne realised that struggling could not avail. She reserved her strength and allowed herself to be gagged and bound. When this was done, Felden thrust her back into her chair.

"Now you're going to pay for that," he said furiously. "This time Jack-in-the-box will get something worth seeing."

He pulled the curtain roughly aside and felt for the valve. But at that moment a heavy knocking resounded through the house.

"Damnation!" said Ashmun, startled. "You'd better go to the door, Kenneth. It may be a policeman complaining about the black-out. Get rid of him. No use my going, and having to explain who I am. It's your house."

Felden cooled suddenly.

"Something in that," he agreed. "I'll go."

He twitched the curtain back into place and walked out into the hall.

188

S IR CLINTON PULLED UP AT SOME DISTANCE FROM FELDEN'S house.

"All change here," he said. "Out you get, Squire."

Wendover stepped out and the Chicf Constable immobilised the car. As he did so, Inspector Camlet's figure loomed up through the darkness.

"I've got half-a-dozen men round the house, sir," he reported. "Nobody can get away. A short time ago, a lady drove up and went in. That was after Miss Herongate and Miss Stanway came. I don't know who she is. Her car number's GZ 8182."

"That's Mrs. Pinfold's car," said Wendover.

"Is it?" said Sir Clinton. "I hardly expected her. But here's your search warrant, Inspector. I think it's about time we put the cat among the pigeons. Though pigeons is hardly the right word for some of them."

He switched on his torch, and by its glow they found their way to the gate of Felden's house, before which three cars were standing.

"Ashmun came on foot," explained the inspector. "These three belong to Allardyce, Miss Herongate, and Mrs. Pinfold."

Sir Clinton looked at the black bulk of the house before him.

"No use trying to see anything through the windows," he said. "This black-out business has its drawbacks. We'll just have to go in."

He moved towards the gate, but as he did so the front door of the house opened. With an out-stretched hand, Sir Clinton restrained his companions and brought them back to where the cars were standing. Two torches glowed on the door-steps and began to move towards the gate.

"I call it most inconsiderate of them to bring me out in the black-out like this," complained the voice of Mrs. Pinfold in the gloom. "Why couldn't they arrange to get married at some reasonable hour? It's just like Kenneth; he's got no thought for anyone's convenience. But I was surprised to see Mr. Ashmun in a surplice. Did you know that he was a clergyman, Ione? It seems strange. But really it's not my affair. I suppose Daphne thinks this sort of thing is romantic. Why can't she be content to do as other people do? It's all very troublesome."

"Don't ask me," Ione replied, impatiently.

The twin lamps drew near the waiting group, and as they reached the cars, Sir Clinton stepped forward. Mrs. Pinfold gave a faint cry of surprise. Ione Herongate swung her light on to the faces of the three men and Mrs. Pinfold recognised Wendover.

" What a start you gave me," she grumbled. " I thought it might be a set of roughs waiting to rob us."

" It's the police," explained Wendover, reassuringly, " so you're quite safe. You know Sir Clinton, I think. And this is Inspector Camlet here. They'd like a word with you."

" Oh, dear," said Mrs. Pinfold in a tone of mingled annoyance and resignation. " I hope they won't keep me long. I do want to get home. Really, everyone seems most inconsiderate to-night. Another time, I shall simply refuse to stir out of doors."

" I'm afraid we shall have to detain you for a short time," said Sir Clinton. " You were speaking about a marriage, I think. Who was present at this ceremony ? "

" Just ourselves, my sister, Kenneth Felden, and Mr. Ashmun. I don't understand it at all, so you needn't ask me about it."

" You didn't see Dr. Allardyce ? "

" Oh, no. What would he be doing there ? "

Sir Clinton ignored this.

" You acted as a witness at this marriage to-night, I suppose," he said, turning to Ione. " A queer affair, surely. By the way, are you still as interested as ever in church brasses ? "

Evidently something lay behind the apparently casual question, for Wendover saw the girl start slightly when it was put to her. She recovered herself at once, however, and answered languidly :

" Oh, yes. I find them positively fascinating."

" I must have a talk about them, some time," Sir Clinton rejoined with perceptible irony in his tone. " I've a lot to learn about that subject. But for the moment, I think you and Mrs. Pinfold should sit in one of these cars. I'll leave one of my men to protect you, just in case of accidents."

Mrs. Pinfold evidently wished to protest against this, but the Chief Constable turned away.

" Oh, get in, Agatha," ordered Ione. " We've got to do as we're told evidently. No use making a fuss."

Accompanied by the inspector and a constable, Sir Clinton walked up to the front door, Wendover following the group in some perplexity. The Chief Constable did not trouble to look for the bell but beat heavily on the door. There was a pause, then heavy steps came along the hall and the door opened. Sir Clinton flashed an unmasked torch and revealed Felden's grim face.

" Take him ! " said Sir Clinton curtly.

Camlet and the constable threw themselves on Felden who, taken at a disadvantage, made a furious but unavailing struggle. Sir Clinton pushed past them into the hall, with Wendover close on his heels. They were at the threshold of the study before the grapple at the door had ended. Sir Clinton burst in, and Wendover, in the light from the room, saw a heavy automatic in his hand. Ashmun had started to his feet at the sound of the fracas in the hall, and Wendover saw the fury in the face above the disordered surplice.

" Ah ! Very pretty," said Sir Clinton, coolly.

Then, as Ashmun made a dash for the curtain, the Chief Constable lifted his pistol.

" No nonsense ! "

But Ashmun was past heeding anyone. His hand went up to twitch the curtain aside, and almost immediately Sir Clinton's pistol exploded. The bullet passed through Ashmun's palm and with a yell of pain he clapped his hand under his arm-pit and bent almost double in his anguish.

" It does hurt, when you get it amongst the metacarpals," said Sir Clinton unsympathetically. " Well, my man, you've earned it. Just keep him covered, Wendover, in case of accidents, while I set Miss Stanway free."

He stooped over the girl, cut the cords and freed her from the gag.

" Don't bother about talking, just now," he advised. " Just lie back and rest for a while."

" Frank ! " gasped Daphne, pointing towards the curtain.

Sir Clinton nodded, pulled the curtain aside, and examined Allardyce's face through the glass window for a few moments. Then he went back to the girl's side.

" He's all right," he said in a reassuring tone which seemed to carry confidence. I'll see that no harm comes to him. Don't be the least afraid. It'll take a little while, but in less than an hour he'll be fit to tell us his side of this affair. I can promise that. But in the meanwhile, we must get this fellow secured."

He whistled, and Inspector Camlet came in, with a constable at his heels.

" Just take charge of this man, please," ordered Sir Clinton. " Keep him separate from Felden. I may want to speak to them later on. And when you're finished with that, you might come back here. I think you'll be interested."

When the police and their prisoner had left the room, Sir Clinton turned again to the girl. She was plainly near the end of her resources for the time being, but her eyes were still fixed on the box in the corner of the room.

" Now we must see about Dr. Allardyce," said Sir Clinton, cheerfully.

He stepped over to the box and examined it carefully. The compressor was still panting gently and a faint hiss of air came from an escape-valve. A small pressure-gauge had been screwed into the casing and Sir Clinton inspected the dial thoughtfully.

" Very ingenious," he commented in an almost admiring tone. " I've suspected the existence of this contrivance, but I hadn't expected to find it so neatly designed. All these fittings unscrew, you see, and then it's only a battery-box which wouldn't excite suspicion even on examination. Well, we can examine it later. The first thing to do is to get the prisoner out of his cell."

He put out his hand to the valve, but at the sight of his action Daphne sprang from her chair and pulled away his arm.

" You'll kill him ! " she cried in terror. " You don't know what you're doing ! That's what they did when they tortured him."

Sir Clinton put his arm round her and gently led her back to her seat.

" Drink this," he said, taking a flask from his pocket and pouring out a stiff dose into the cup. " I know just what you're afraid of, but we'll take care that it doesn't happen. I know this business through and through, Miss Stanway. You can trust me implicitly. Dr. Allardyce will come out of that box absolutely sound."

He waited till Daphne had gulped down the spirit, which brought a faint flush to her cheeks.

" You can watch, if you like," said Sir Clinton, " and I'll stop instantly if you see the slightest sign that I'm giving him pain. It will be a slow business for I'm taking no risks. Now come and look."

Daphne pulled herself together and went with him to the box.

" You'll stop as soon as I tell you ? " she asked.

" You won't even have to check me," said Sir Clinton confidently.

With his eye on the pressure-gauge, he unscrewed the valve slightly, but so little did he loosen it that there was no perceptible change in the hissing note of the escaping air. Daphne was watching Allardyce's face intently through the glass window, ready to cry out in warning at the slightest sign of discomfort. But she could see nothing untoward in the doctor's expression. Sir Clinton glanced again at the dial and then at his watch.

" That's all for the present," he said. " We must wait awhile for the next step. You'd better sit down again. You're not fit to stand."

" I'd rather be here and watch," said Daphne. " I can't bear to leave him."

Before Sir Clinton could reply, Inspector Camlet returned.

" I've fixed Ashmun up, sir," he began. Then his eye caught the box, which he had not seen before, and he broke off his report. " What's this, sir ? "

" You might call it a battery-box," said Sir Clinton. " You sat on it once, I remember ; but it hadn't a glass window in it then."

" But there's a man inside of it, sir. Aren't you going to let him out ? "

" As soon as I can, but it will take time," replied Sir Clinton.

He scrutinised the gauge and made a slight change in the escape valve. Daphne unconsciously put out her hand to hinder him but drew back again, keeping her eyes fixed on Allardyce's face.

" It's going quite satisfactorily," Sir Clinton assured her. " No need to be anxious. But we've got a while before us yet. Do you think you could tell us what has happened to you this evening ? Inspector Camlet will take down what you say."

Wendover made a movement of protest, for the girl was obviously over-wrought. Then he guessed that Sir Clinton's object was to distract her attention as far as possible from the operations, and he restrained himself. Whether Daphne herself understood the Chief Constable's motive or not, she fell in with his wishes, though she still kept her gaze fixed on the glass window.

" Ione Herongate came to my house in her car after dinner," she began. " She was excited, and she told me that Frank had met with an accident and had been taken in here. She had been passing at the time, and Kenneth Felden sent her on to fetch me. Of course I went with her immediately, and we came here."

" Your brother wasn't in your house ? " asked Sir Clinton.
" No, he'd gone out to dinner somewhere."

Sir Clinton asked no further questions, but allowed her
to tell the whole story of the night's happenings in her own
way, while Camlet took down her statement in shorthand.
When she had finished, he made a further adjustment in
the escape-valve.

" That's going very nicely," he said. " It won't be long
before we've finished. You see we're doing no harm."

Daphne nodded, evidently wholly reassured by what she
had seen of the manipulations.

" There's just one thing I'd like to be sure about now,"
she said. " This marriage isn't valid, is it ? I never thought
it was, but still I'd like to be quite certain."

" It wouldn't hold good even if you had consented
willingly," said Sir Clinton, to the surprise of Wendover.
" You needn't give it another thought."

Wendover picked up a paper from the table and scanned
it with a puzzled expression on his face. It was the special
marriage licence, and he could see no flaw in it which would
justify Sir Clinton's certainty. A glance from the Chief
Constable stifled the question which was on his lips. Evidently Sir Clinton had no desire to discuss the point at
that moment.

" I gather that Mrs. Pinfold wasn't one of the conspirators,"
he said, turning to Daphne. " She knew nothing about
the pressure that was put on you ? "

" Oh, no," declared Daphne. " I'm sure of that. I
wouldn't say as much for Ione, though."

" Then there's no need for us to keep Mrs. Pinfold here
all night," said the Chief Constable. " She seems very
anxious to get home. Will you go out, Inspector, and bring
them both into the house, please. Put Miss Herongate in
charge of one of your men and keep her apart from the
others. Then take a statement from Mrs. Pinfold, and when
you've got it, you can send her home. We shan't need her."

Inspector Camlet left the room, and Sir Clinton turned
again to Daphne.

" You'd better lie down on that settee," he suggested.
" I don't suppose you can sleep. You're all on edge, and
no wonder. But rest, anyhow. I'll wake you up as soon
as this business is finished. It will last a while yet, because
I'm not going to take the slightest risk by hurrying."

Daphne had come to the end of her physical resources,
and with a pathetic willingness she obeyed the Chief Con-

stable's instructions. Wendover would have liked to put a question or two, but Sir Clinton's warning gesture arrested him before he could open his mouth. He sat down and contented himself with watching the further operations which were mere repetitions of what had gone before. Wendover saw that Sir Clinton's object was to reduce the pressure in the box very gradually, while still keeping up a constant flow of fresh air to the prisoner ; but the reason for these precautions escaped him entirely.

At last the Chief Constable seemed satisfied. With the aid of Wendover and the inspector, he lifted the box from its corner and laid it horizontally on the floor, still keeping the pump at work. Then, very carefully he unscrewed the wing-nuts and removed the lid. Allardyce, still under the influence of the drug, made some feeble attempts to rise, but Sir Clinton, after cutting the gag loose, gently persuaded him to keep quiet.

" There ! " he said, turning to Daphne. " Now we'll leave him in your hands, Miss Stanway. Don't let him exert himself for a while yet. We'll be back shortly."

And with a gesture ordering Camlet and Wendover to follow him, he left the room. Once the door was closed, he turned to the inspector.

" You got Mrs. Pinfold's statement ? "

" Yes, sir. She seems to have no notion that there was anything in the business except some freak on Miss Stanway's part. Just a bit of romantic foolery. She's not very bright, sir."

" No, not very," agreed the Chief Constable. " You've packed her off home ? Good ! Now, I think, we'll tackle Miss Herongate. Where is she ? "

" In here, sir," explained Camlet, leading the way to another room.

Ione Herongate had not lost her coolness in the events of the night. She did not get up from her chair as the three men entered, but favoured them with an inquisitive glance without opening her mouth. The inspector, under some tacit prompting by Sir Clinton, took the initiative.

" If you wish to make a statement, Miss, it's my duty to warn you that your words will be taken down and may be given in evidence."

Ione Herongate stared at him with a slightly scornful expression.

" Indeed ? I shan't put you to the trouble. I don't propose to make any statement."

Sir Clinton intervened with a smile.

" Perhaps I had better make the matter clearer to you. You're entitled to say anything which might clear yourself ; and nothing you say can be used against Kenneth Felden."

This last phrase made Ione glance sharply at the Chief Constable.

" You seem to know more than I guessed," she admitted. " Rather clever of you, Sir Clinton. What put you on to that ? "

" Your craze for taking rubbings of church brasses," said the Chief Constable, lightly. " It was hardly in character, was it ? So I looked up the records."

" Ah ! " replied Ione, with a tinge of respect in her tone. " That *was* clever of you."

She pondered for a moment or two.

" Since you know that," she went on at last, " what are you charging me with now ? "

Sir Clinton dropped his faint levity and became purely the official.

" We are charging you in the first instance with being an accessory to Kenneth Felden in causing grievous bodily harm to Frank Allardyce. That's sufficient for the present. There will probably be further charges later, as you'll hear in due course."

Ione considered this for a few seconds.

" I think I'll consult my solicitor before making any statement at all," she decided.

" Very wise," admitted the Chief Constable. " Not that it makes much difference. We have all the evidence necessary."

" Well, I shall say nothing," declared Ione, firmly.

Sir Clinton nodded and turned to Camlet.

" You'd better send her down to Headquarters now, with one of your men," he said, curtly. " Get that fixed, and then we'll deal with the other two."

When it came to the turns of Felden and Ashmun, neither of them was more communicative than Ione had been. Sir Clinton made no attempt to press them, and they were despatched under guard to the police station. When they had been taken away, Camlet ventured to put a question :

" Are you sure you can prove a case against them, sir ? I don't quite see how you're going to manage it, except in this last affair, and all you could call *that* would be attempted murder."

" Thank heaven for George Joseph Smith, of the Brides-

196

in-the-Bath case," said Sir Clinton, piously. " I shouldn't care to bet that we could bring conclusive proof in any single one of these cases, if it were isolated from the rest. But after the Smith trial, it's possible to link together a whole series of cases on the ground that you're proving that ' a system ' runs through the lot. And that's what will hang Kenneth Felden, and probably friend Ashmun as well."

" And the girl, sir ? "

Sir Clinton shook his head doubtfully.

" Not the girl, I imagine. She's got more than one line of defence, if her lawyers know their business. But we've more work before us to-night, Inspector. Don't let's waste time talking."

" What are you looking for, sir ? "

" If Felden filed his tradesmen's receipts, I want those of his fishmonger for the last few months," explained the Chief Constable to the obvious amazement of the inspector. Then he reconsidered this hastily. " No, we can postpone that. His accounts will probably be in his study, and we may as well leave Allardyce and Miss Stanway alone for a bit yet. No use disturbing them. You've still got a man or two at hand ? Well, tell them to go through the house and find me a large-sized rabbit-trap if they can. You know the sort of thing I mean : a big wire box with a door at one end working on a spring. Like the ordinary Catch-'em-alive-O ! mouse-trap on a big scale. It may be at Ashmun's house ; but we may as well try here first of all."

" Very good, sir," said the inspector, plainly puzzled by this order. " I'll set them on to it now."

When Camlet returned, Sir Clinton was ready for more work.

" We've got to find Felden's little private laboratory."

" I can take you to it, sir," said the inspector. " I blundered into it when I was looking for rooms to park all these people in. It's along here."

He led them along a passage and threw open a door.

" Ah, very nice," said Sir Clinton, approvingly, as he entered the room. " He keeps everything very spick-and-span, doesn't he ? Work-bench, nice tidy shelves of reagent-bottles, no litter of old glass on his blow-pipe table, combustion furnace, clean fume-cupboard, even a little lathe. I'm glad he has an orderly mind. That should make things easier for us."

He glanced about the room, pulling open several drawers,

one of which contained a set of neatly-arranged tools. Then he went across and tried the door of a large wall-cupboard.

" Locked ? This looks as if we were getting hotter. Just get a case-opener out of that drawer, Inspector, if you please, and break this open for me."

Camlet did as he was bidden ; and when the door swung open it disclosed an array of bottles of various shapes and sizes, all neatly labelled. Sir Clinton began a systematic search among them, putting one aside at times until he had secured four in all. One of these he picked up and showed to his companions, who read the writing on the label :

$$C_{17}H_{21}O_4N, HBr$$

" I'm no wiser, sir," admitted Camlet, ruefully. " My chemistry goes no further than H_2O or HO_2, if that's the one for water."

To Wendover also the formula conveyed nothing definite, but his mind went back to something Sir Clinton had said to him when describing his visit to Felden's house some time earlier.

" I don't remember the exact figures," he said. " Is it hyoscine, by any chance ? "

" Hyoscine it is, or its hydrobromide, rather," confirmed Sir Clinton. " He's been prudent enough to wash off the original label and put his own one on instead. It would have been risky to leave a hyoscine label on the thing ; and I suppose he thought the formula was safe enough."

" But where could he get a stuff like that ? " queried the inspector. " You can't go into the first druggist's and say : ' Give me a bob's worth of hyoscine,' sir."

" I can't prove where he got it," Sir Clinton admitted. " The main thing is, we've found it in his possession. But I'll hazard a guess. He was the only man who got into Shipman's shop when it went up in flames during one of the raids. I can't think of any other way in which he could have got hold of it without exciting suspicion or leaving a trail. But that's mere speculation. Here's the stuff on his premises. We don't need anything further in Court."

" There's not much of it there, sir," commented the inspector, looking rather doubtfully at the little bottle with its scanty contents.

" One doesn't need much," retorted Sir Clinton. " About the hundred and twentieth part of a grain seems to be as much as is necessary for medicinal purposes. That's about half a milligramme, or a two-thousandth part of this little weight here."

He stepped over to the balance-table, opened the box of weights, and showed a gramme weight to the inspector.

"As you can imagine," the Chief Constable went on, "it takes a fine balance to weigh quantities like that. This one of Felden's can do it, by using the rider that you see astride the beam. I think you'd better impound this balance, Inspector. It'll amuse the jury. They always like to see exhibits. And you'd better learn the technique of weighing with it, so that you can show them exactly what half a milligramme of hyoscine looks like. That'll convince them that only a man who owns a delicate balance could have weighed such minute doses. And very few people have any need for such instruments."

He picked up the second bottle which he had segregated from the contents of the cupboard.

"Now here's another specimen for your jury," he explained. "See the label? $K_4Fe(CN)_6$. That means potassium ferrocyanide. We'll find a use for that, and for this half-pound bottle of oxalic acid also. And now the last one."

He showed the fourth bottle, which contained about a pound of metal filings and was labelled simply: "Ni." Sir Clinton uncorked it and tilted a few of the filings into a test-tube which he took from a rack on the work-bench.

"We'll dissolve this in some acid," he said, suiting the action to the word. "See that brilliant green colour of the solution? You can call it apple-green or emerald-green, whichever you choose. The main point is that it's almost unmistakable. All nickel salts show it."

"Nickel!" ruminated Wendover. "Wasn't there some talk about a trace of nickel in the post-mortem report on Anthony Gainford? Do you mean that he was poisoned with a nickel salt?"

Sir Clinton shook his head.

"Nickel salts aren't particularly poisonous," he explained. "No, it was a bit more subtle than that. The symptoms suggested gas-poisoning, didn't they?"

"They did, sir," the inspector confirmed.

Before he could put the question which was on his lips, one of the constables appeared at the door, holding a large wire rabbit-trap such as Sir Clinton had described.

"We found it in the garage, sir," he reported.

" Good ! " said Sir Clinton. " You can add that to your exhibits, Inspector. And now," he added, turning to the constable, " will you see if you can find Felden's gas-mask, please. I want it also. It's bound to be somewhere about the house . . . By the way, did you notice anything in the garage that looked like a trolley ? Something with wheels on it ? "

" Yes, sir," the constable answered at once. " I did happen to notice it, up at the far end, beyond the motor-van. A board, sir, with four small wheels and a sort of handle to pull it by."

" That's the thing," said Sir Clinton, with a gesture of dismissal. " I'll have a look at it by and by. Meanwhile, get me that gas-mask, please."

When the constable had gone, Sir Clinton turned to the inspector.

" It wouldn't be a bad notion to get Allardyce to bed. He'll be fit to move by this time, but he's probably still muzzy with that dope, and I'm not sure about sending him home. Get him upstairs and let him lie down. If Miss Stanway wants to wait with him, there's no objection. You'll have a constable on guard here for the rest of the night, and the phone's there if anything's needed. Don't bother to take any statement from the doctor until his head's quite clear again. We'll wait here for you until you've got the study clear, and then I'll have a hunt through Felden's papers. They'll be in his desk, I expect."

Camlet went off, and they heard him speaking to Daphne. Then he apparently summoned a constable, and between them they helped the doctor upstairs. Daphne evidently decided to stay with Allardyce, for they heard her voice thanking the inspector as he came downstairs again.

" He's still under the dope, sir," Camlet reported on his return. " Sleepy. Miss Stanway asked me to phone up a doctor, just to be on the safe side. No objection to that, sir ? "

" None whatever," agreed Sir Clinton. " I'll ring up a doctor myself, now, and tell him what's what ; otherwise he might be a bit at sea when he comes to examine Allardyce."

The telephone conversation took a few minutes, and when Sir Clinton came back from the instrument, one of the constables produced Felden's gas-mask which he had discovered. The Chief Constable examined it cursorily.

" I see it has his name on it. All the better. Please take charge of it, Inspector. It'll have to go to an expert first, and then perhaps we can show it to the jury as another exhibit. And now I think we'll take a run over the papers in Felden's desk."

Fortunately, as they found, Felden kept his documents neatly arranged. All his accounts and receipts were docketed and put up in bundles with rubber bands round them. Sir Clinton sat down at the desk, went through the current year's bills and receipts, and after a rapid examination, picked out several papers which he put aside. When he had satisfied himself, he passed these documents to the inspector.

" Keep these, too, please. They all contain evidence that he's been buying ice from time to time, shilling's-worths and sixpenny-worths, usually. I think I've got the lot, but it might be well if you went over the papers here again, just in case I've missed any. And now, if we have a look round that garage, I think that'll finish us for the night. We'll go out by the back door, I think."

In the garage, Felden's little car stood alongside the motor van which the chemist had used in his experiments. It was the van in which Sir Clinton seemed interested.

" A lot of batteries," he commented, opening the door and flashing his torch into the interior. " And a nice little motor screwed to the floor and connected up with them. I suppose that's what he used to drive his air-pump during transits. Yes, here are the clamps for holding it down. Get this photographed by daylight, Inspector, if you please. Then, later on, we can put the pump into place and get more photographs. There's no use leaving anything to the imagination of the jurymen. We'd better show them the van itself, just to be on the safe side. And now let's have a look at this trolley."

It was a crudely-built affair : a mere plank, six feet by three, and fitted with small iron wheels.

" Obviously he'd need something of this sort to shift that box when it had a man in it," Sir Clinton pointed out. " The back door of the house is flush with the ground, so probably he used that, and not the front door where there are steps up. An ingenious fellow, Felden. I wonder if his experiments came to anything. He can leave his results as a legacy to his country. He won't need them himself, when we've done with him."

He glanced about the garage and drew his companions' attention to a charging apparatus clamped to the wall.

" Used for charging his batteries, I suppose. And he

could connect them up to his car dynamo whilst he was running, so as to save too big a drain on them when they were driving his air-pump."

He glanced at his watch

"There's nothing more to be done at present. When Allardyce gets over that dope of his, Inspector, please take his statement. There's no hurry. He won't be able to tell us much, except that Felden got him here under some false pretence or other and then doped his whisky. Probably he won't even remember the box business. They say that hyoscine doesn't deaden pain, but abolishes the memory of a pang almost as soon as it's over. By the way, you'd better get hold of Shipman, the druggist, and warn him that he'll have to give evidence that he had hyoscine in stock at the time of his fire. We must leave no loose ends. . . . And now, I think, Mr. Wendover and I can get back to the Grange. You can ring me up there if anything fresh turns up."

CHAPTER XIX   *That Two-Handed Engine*

"I SEE FELDEN'S TRIAL COMES ON NEXT WEEK," SAID WEN-dover, "That reminds me, Clinton. You've played the mystery-man as usual in this affair, and I never understood what led you to link Felden and Ashmun together to begin with."

The Chief Constable smiled rather sardonically as he answered.

"If I'd told you what I thought at the time, Squire, you'd have been up in arms at once. As a matter of fact, it was a choice between Felden and your young friend Allardyce to start with, on fairly good grounds. But if I'd told you that Allardyce was under suspicion, you'd have been neither to hold nor to bind, you know. So naturally I preferred to keep my own counsel until things cleared up a bit."

"Allardyce?" protested Wendover. "Anyone who knew him could have told you he was out of the question. You ought to have seen for yourself that he's incapable of anything of the sort."

"Ought I?" said Sir Clinton, tolerantly. "Well, I didn't, until I had enough evidence to go on. And this fretfulness of yours seems to suggest that I was wise in keeping my mouth shut at the time."

" What possible evidence was there to make you suspect him ? " demanded Wendover.

" Quite a lot, one way and another ; but you were so blinded by prejudice that you wouldn't see it, Squire. Who was the last man known to have visited Robert Deverell before he died ? Allardyce. Ditto in the case of Pirbright. Who was hard up unexpectedly and in urgent need of money ? Allardyce. Who had easy access to hyoscine ? Allardyce again. And so on. There was quite a lot of evidence, but you wouldn't look at it. I had to ; that's the difference."

" Then where did Felden come in ? " demanded Wendover.

" Look at those stunts that Ashmun used, to impress his gulls. Take that voice that spoke from the card-table, for instance. I spotted it at once as the old talking-crystal. It's used in some microphones nowadays ; but most people have forgotten all about it. Piezo-electricity, they call it. You can do it with a crystal of Rochelle salt. Then the minnow-killing : that was supersonic waves, like the ones that are used nowadays for submarine soundings to get the depth of the sea-bed. The high-frequency ones do kill tadpoles. I remember reading a bit of popular science about it once upon a time. Now it would take a good deal to persuade me that a mission-bred half-caste straight from the Back of Beyond knew enough about affairs of that sort to work them up successfully into his manifestations. Obviously, behind Master Ashmun there was somebody with more than a smattering of science. But Ambledown is not swarming with skilled scientific gentlemen. A doctor *might* be up to scratch. The only other likely bird was Felden, who's known to be a bit of a physicist as well as a chemist. And this scientific accomplice, whoever he was, played a direct part in these Ashmun demonstrations. Ashmun was in the room when the talking-crystal was working ; therefore there must have been a second man on the premises, in another room, talking into the transmitter and telling Mrs. Pinfold all about herself. Simple, isn't it ? "

" And had these two precious villains planned all these murders far in advance ? "

Sir Clinton shook his head decidedly.

" No, I'm sure they didn't. What happened was something like this, as we've worried out after some trouble. Ashmun arrived here, stone-broke, and meaning, I think, to park himself on his long-lost relatives on the strength of his discreditable relationship. The first one he tried was Felden. Our friend Kenneth, knowing the local ropes and knowing especially the silliness of his cousin Agatha and her readiness to swallow any occult bunkum, cooked up a better scheme for Master Jehudi. Initially, the plan was merely to bleed a few gulls with all this stuff about the New Force ; get them to subscribe heavily for experiments, and so forth. A combination of Felden's brains and knowledge with Ashmun's gift of the gab and general impressiveness. Felden had some spare cash, and he set up Ashmun in an establishment of his own. Ashmun pretended not to have any dealings with Felden, and Felden posed as the complete sceptic and sneered at Ashmun in public whenever he got a chance. That was to avoid anyone thinking of the possibility that these manifestations were just a bit of scientific parlour magic, as they might have done if there had been any overt connection between Ashmun and the scientific Felden. At the start, all they had in mind was cheating a few fools out of their money. The idea of murder was a much later development."

" I don't see how you could prove that," objected Wendover.

" Just think, Squire. Murder only came along after the discovery of that vein of stream tin. Felden spotted that when he examined the bomb-crater on the evening when the Viking's hoard was unearthed. But the rabbit-killing was long before that—on January 9th, Allardyce told us, whereas the hoard was dug up on May 12th. Felden must have cursed himself for springing that rabbit-killing on the public, for it connected Ashmun directly with that stunt, and Felden had to use the same method in polishing off Pirbright and Henry Deverell. It was too neat a thing to discard, and he chanced it."

" I don't see my way through it even yet," Wendover confessed.

" Oh, it's well enough known," said Sir Clinton. " Caisson sickness and diver's cramp. I told you it was merely a fresh application of an old principle, Squire. But I'll come to that by-and-by. We've now got the length of the discovery of the tin-stone on the ground affected by old Rodway's will ; and that coincided with the fall of Malaya and an acute world-shortage in tin. In other words, big money for anyone who could profit by inside information which Felden had. But there was one snag in the road. One can't float a company nowadays. The Government doesn't allow that. So the only hope was for Felden to get hold of a capitalist and run the thing as a private show. Where was the capitalist? His cousin Agatha, of course. But she's not very free-handed, as you know. Luckily for Felden, she would swallow anything that Ashmun told her, so long as it was supposed to emanate from occult circles. So that was that, and very convenient, too."

"Very," agreed Wendover, drily. "But why the murders, then?"

"Because if the profits had to be shared out amongst all the Rodway heirs, there wouldn't be much for each; so some of the heirs had to walk the plank. The two Gainfords had personal peculiarities which made them easy victims. The Deverell brothers were business men of sorts and might have been awkward partners; so they had to go. Miss Stanway and her brother wanted money in a hurry and could easily be bought out cheaply. That left Felden and Jehudi, *arcades ambo*, along with the goose with the golden eggs, Agatha Pinfold, whose money they needed. Three people to share the profits instead of nine, which makes a considerable difference."

"So you think Robert Deverell was murdered?"

"There's no need to prove it, since we have enough without," said the Chief Constable, "and it would be difficult to prove. Felden has an alibi for that night's work, for he was on duty. So I suppose they waited for a raid night and then Ashmun went and knocked Deverell on the head, starting the incendiary to cover up the mess if possible. Unexploded incendiaries are not uncommon; we've your young friend Noel's case to prove it; and Felden had plenty of chances of picking up a live bomb in the course of his duty. The real mistake in that affair was the collaring of the crosier and the other things."

"What possessed them to do that?" asked Wendover. "If they'd left the gold alone, no one would have thought of murder."

"They had Pirbright in mind, I suspect," said Sir Clinton. "You remember that we found a filled-in pit up by Cæsar's Camp. Either Felden or Ashmun had been digging there, trying to strike the actual stream tin deposit where it should be richest. Probably Pirbright came on the scene and grew inquisitive. So he had to go. And the gold could be used to suggest that he was Deverell's murderer, by burying it on his premises in such a way as to make its discovery almost a cert."

"Is there really a stream tin deposit up there?" Wendover demanded sceptically.

" There is, quite a valuable one," Sir Clinton assured him. " We've dug down to it just to make sure of things. It's quite near the surface, easily accessible. The three remaining Rodway heirs will do very well out of it. Allardyce won't feel the loss of his Malayan rubber, from all I've seen ; and there's no need for that marriage to be delayed for lack of cash."

" I'm glad of that," said Wendover, heartily. " But go back to the Pirbright case. What happened there ? "

" We're not depending on it, either," explained Sir Clinton, " except to prove that a system runs through the whole business. What happened is plain enough, from what we now know. Allardyce's presence at Pirbright's hut was pure accident, just as it was accidental that he was the last man to see Robert Deverell alive. His tale about going up to pay for these rabbits was quite sound. In fact, he produced a receipt for the money, signed by Pirbright. Pirbright had done him once before in some other matter by ' forgetting ' that he'd been paid for some work he'd done—digging up Allardyce's garden or something of the sort—and Allardyce took a receipt for the rabbit-money just to avoid any further memory-slips. As soon as Allardyce had left, Felden appeared. No doubt he'd watched Allardyce off the premises. One can guess his excuse for paying Pirbright a visit : he'd pretend he wanted to talk about the matter of the digging for the stream tin. I've no doubt that Pirbright either had bled him or meant to bleed him over that business : a little *douceur* to keep his mouth shut about it. Anyhow, Felden turned up with a bottle of whisky—taken from the store in his house and therefore ' Black Swan,' since that was Tony Gainford's favourite tipple—and the two of them settled down to a lubricated chat. But Pirbright drank more than whisky. He got a dose of hyoscine as well, tipped into his cup when he wasn't looking. So there he was, doped and helpless. Felden washed out Pirbright's cup with water and put it on the shelf where we found it, wet. That left no traces of foul play and no sign of a second person having drunk along with Pirbright. After that, leaving Pirbright stupefied, Felden went back to his van and brought up the gold, which he buried where we found it, intending it to be easily discovered so that suspicion of the Deverell affair might fall on Pirbright, whose character wasn't any too good."

" Yes, yes," said Wendover, impatiently. " But what I want to know is how he finished off Pirbright."

" This is where Felden's ingenuity begins to show," said

Sir Clinton. "Pirbright, you see, was Jack-in-the-box Number One, Squire. You laughed at me for laying stress on the matter of the rabbits, I remember. But the symptoms shown in the death of those rabbits were the symptoms we saw for ourselves in Pirbright's case : frightful cramps followed by death. But there was one difference between the two cases."

"Hyoscine in Pirbright's case and none in the rabbits ? "

"Just so. So it occurred to me at once that the hyoscine had nothing directly to do with Pirbright's death. Why use it, then ? The answer stares you in the face. Rabbits can be handled without the least bother ; their struggles amount to nothing. But a rough customer like Pirbright is quite a different affair. Ergo, before Pirbright could be put through the process he had to be doped to make him amenable. That was suggestive. Now hyoscine needs a delicate balance if you want to give only a medicinal dose, which was what Pirbright evidently had absorbed. Who had a delicate balance ? Allardyce for one, in his dispensary ; Felden for another. Further, Ashmun was mixed up in the rabbit affair, though not in the death of Pirbright, where he had a cast-iron alibi. So I began to get a glimmering that a ' two-handed engine ' was at work and that I needn't look for a single criminal at the back of the business. But, as you know, there wasn't a sign of a motive at that stage in the affair. I came up against a blank end, there, and could make neither head nor tail of the case. If I'd only had even an inkling of what lay behind it all, three lives might have been saved."

"I wish I'd told you about the Rodway will long before I did," said Wendover, ruefully.

"You needn't worry over that, Squire. The Rodway will on the face of it wouldn't have helped much. No one could have inferred from it that the Cæsar's Camp ground was of any special value."

"I suppose not," admitted Wendover, gratefully. "But how did Pirbright come by his end ? "

"I didn't guess, at that stage," Sir Clinton confessed frankly. "I didn't believe in friend Ashmun's New Force, but it seemed about the only explanation that would fit the facts, just then. The medicals were as much at sea as I was, thank goodness ! I've got that to comfort myself with. But let's leave that point aside for the moment and go on to the next stage in the plot : the death of that drunkard, Tony Gainford."

" Felden's a clever brute, one of the cleverest I've ever come across in the criminal line ; and in that affair he got tripped up by something which simply could not have been foreseen by him. Hard lines, from his point of view. Look at the case as it appeared on the surface, Squire. The experts found traces of nickel in the body ; but nickel salts are not deadly poisons, and there wasn't anything like enough nickel to account for Gainford's death. Everything pointed to poisoning by carbon monoxide. You remember that the blood spectrum showed that beyond a doubt. And the tap of the gas stove had been turned on, apparently by Gainford in a state of muzziness, when he went up to bed. If that case had stood by itself, it would have passed without the slightest suspicion, I'm sure. But our friends had a bit of ill-luck which was completely outside their calculations. I mean the bomb which fell in Hansler Road at 10.57, after Felden had left the house. It burst the gas main and the electrical cables which fed Felden's supply, and the repair of the main was not complete until 8.15 a.m. next morning. Neither Allardyce nor Miss Stanway noticed any smell of gas escaping when they were upstairs, so the room wasn't filled with gas when Gainford went up to bed. Then came the bomb, and no gas could have reached the tap after that until 8.15 next morning. And yet there was Gainford's blood, loaded up with carbon monoxide."

" I don't understand it," confessed Wendover. " Had Felden led a tube into the room and flooded the place with carbon monoxide, apart from the gas supply ? No, he couldn't have done that. He was on duty all night. Was it Ashmun ? "

" What would be the point of providing a special supply of carbon monoxide when they had a gas tap in the room itself ? " retorted Sir Clinton. " That would have been supererogation. Besides, that doesn't cover the traces of nickel in the body, and it was the nickel that I fastened on, straight away, as being the key to the affair."

" I don't see it," protested Wendover.

" And yet it was you yourself who gave me the clue to the business, Squire," said Sir Clinton in mock reproach. " Don't you remember telling me that in his early days Felden had been employed as a chemist in some nickel-extraction works ? By the time the Gainford case came up, Felden was on my list of suspects. When nickel appeared in connection with Gainford's body, naturally I remembered Felden's technical experience in that line. It didn't immediately suggest much to me, of course. I'm no polymath. I have to look things up when I need them. But at least I do look them up when necessary. So I looked up the Mond process for the refinement of nickel."

" And what did you find ? " demanded Wendover.

" Simply this. If you pass a current of carbon monoxide over metallic nickel at about the temperature of boiling water, the carbon monoxide attacks the nickel and forms a stuff called nickel carbonyl which at that temperature is a gas. If you condense this vapour with a freezing-mixture of ice and salt, you get a liquid, and once you get the liquid it remains liquid at ordinary room temperature, for it boils at 25° C. Now in the human body, this nickel tetracarbonyl breaks up and liberates carbon monoxide, which attacks the blood and gives all the symptoms of ordinary gas poisoning. It's a violent poison, nickel carbonyl. I found that in the early days of modern nickel-extraction they used to have a lot of trouble from that. Workmen got poisoned more or less seriously, simply by breathing traces of escaped carbonyl. Now Felden knew all about this nickel carbonyl and its properties, because he'd been on the staff of one of those factories. That seemed to clear things up a bit in my mind, once I'd hit on the clue. But naturally I didn't hit on it without a good deal of thinking."

" Ah ! Now I see why you wanted to be able to prove that he'd been buying ice," interjected Wendover. " That was his freezing-mixture to condense the carbonyl, I suppose ? "

" Partly that and partly for another affair which came later," Sir Clinton amplified. " But now you can see how the Gainford murder was staged. Felden had his liquid nickel carbonyl ready. When he went upstairs to change into uniform, he tipped some of it into the whisky which was in a tumbler in Tony's room for his ' night-cap.' When Tony got into bed, he swallowed his tot, including the carbonyl ; and that was the end of Tony. Next morning, Felden turned on the gas tap of the stove when he entered the room. By that time the main had been repaired, of course, and the gas was flowing ; so no doubt he thought it looked all right. Evidently he didn't realise that the burst gas main in Hansler Road was the one which fed his house supply. That was too late to remedy, anyhow. But he made other slips as well, in that affair."

Wendover pondered for some moments, and them admitted that these flaws still escaped him.

"For one thing," Sir Clinton pointed out, "he shouldn't have kept that bottle with nickel in it a moment longer, once he'd finished off Tony Gainford. And he should have scrapped the bottle of oxalic acid also. It's used in preparing carbon monoxide."

"You seem to have been reading up the subject," commented Wendover, ironically. "Where did you get all this lore?"

"At the fountain-head," retorted the Chief Constable. "Remember the evening when I called at Felden's house and found him elsewhere? I took the opportunity of reading up nickel carbonyl in his books: Mellor and Roscoe and Schorlemmer. They gave me just what I wanted. And they gave me the preparation of carbon monoxide as well. A child could make it from oxalic acid. And I found plenty of oxalic in his lab. when we searched it."

"Rather like seething a lamb in its mother's milk," said Wendover.

"I shouldn't call Felden a lamb. Black sheep, if you want an ovine comparison. But there was a third slip he made. A matter of his gas mask. But that can stand over till I've dealt with Derek Gainford's case. Before that, I'll take Henry Deverell's death, which came next in order. Actually, it's the case the Crown people have picked as their first charge, because it involves both Felden and Ashmun as principals; and if it fails, there are plenty more charges to fall back upon. So now we come to Jack-in-the-box again. I gave you a straight tip there, Squire: Henry's Law. But you didn't seem to pick it up very smartly. Have you worried it out yet?"

Wendover shook his head.

"No," he admitted frankly. "I still don't know what was at the back of all that box business. Too deep for me, though the results were plain enough."

"Take the facts in order," suggested Sir Clinton. "Deverell drank no alcohol at that bridge-party on the night of his death. Young Max Stanway offered him a drink and I heard him refuse it. When he left the club-house, he was quite normal. I saw him. He wasn't doped in any way. But after death, his stomach contained alcohol and hyoscine. Ashmun admitted that he stood Deverell a whisky and soda when he called to hand in that sketch-map. We can prove that Felden—and therefore Ashmun—had a stock of hyoscine."

"*Prima facie*, any jury would accept that as evidence that Ashmun doped Deverell," said Wendover. "And I suppose that's all you want, in order to prove that Ashmun was an accessory before the fact and can be hanged on the strength of that."

" Shortly after that," continued Sir Clinton, " Deverell was found dying up at Cæsar's Camp. Felden had an alibi of sorts. He had been talking with one of my constables a good distance down the road, just before they found Deverell at the last gasp. No one, apparently, had laid a finger on Deverell. He died in considerable pain, just as the rabbits did, and just as Pirbright did, round about the same spot. Felden had his van, with all his research apparatus in it. Amongst this was what he called his battery box. He invited Inspector Camlet to sit on it while taking down his statement, you remember. We saw that box, later on, at Felden's house. If we'd opened it that night in the van, we'd have found it empty ; but Felden could easily have explained that away by saying that he hadn't needed batteries on that occasion and had left them at home, being charged. I don't pretend that I specially noticed the box at that time, but I did remember seeing it."

" I remember it myself, quite well," admitted Wendover. " It had no glass plate on the front, then. That must have been let in later on."

" Yes, for Miss Stanway's benefit," said the Chief Constable.

" What made you connect it with Deverell's death, then ? " asked Wendover.

" My visit to Felden's library," explained Sir Clinton. " You remember I noticed that he had a copy of J. B. S. Haldane's *Science and Everyday Life* on his shelves ? I'd read that book when it came out, and the sight of it reminded me of a short story I'd once come across. And then I got the key to Deverell's end. Here's the whole thing in a nutshell for you, Squire. Henry's Law, you remember, states that the quantity of a gas dissolved by a liquid depends on the pressure of the gas."

" So Webster says."

" Well, then, call the liquid, blood ; and call the gas, air. When you breathe air into your lungs, a certain amount of oxygen and nitrogen dissolve in your blood at ordinary atmospheric pressure. Suppose you were in a room where the pressure was four atmospheres, your blood would take up four times as much nitrogen and oxygen, wouldn't it ? according to Henry's Law."

" I suppose so," admitted Wendover.

" The extra oxygen does no harm, because your tissues can use it up," continued Sir Clinton. " The extra nitrogen does no harm either, because normally you just breathe in nitrogen and breathe it out again without touching it. So long as you stay in this room, under an air pressure of four atmospheres, your machinery goes on working quite normally. But now, suppose you open the door and come out into the open air. (That was the point in that short story I mentioned.) What happens then? "

" What? " said Wendover cautiously.

" Well, soda water's made by dissolving carbon dioxide in water under a pressure of four atmospheres. There's that pressure in the bottle. But when you unscrew the stopper, the pressure falls suddenly, doesn't it? And under the reduced pressure only a far smaller quantity of gas can stay dissolved in the water. The rest of it can't stay in solution, so it bubbles out at once. Hence the froth when you uncork a soda-water bottle. That's clear? "

" Quite! " said Wendover. " What you're driving at is that if a man were in a room under a pressure of four atmospheres and went from the room straight out into the open air, under a quarter of the pressure, nitrogen would bubble out of his blood just as the soda-water bubbles when you uncork it. That's the point, isn't it? "

" That is the point. If these gas-bubbles form at the man's joints, they cause pains like violent rheumatism—technically called ' the bends.' If they form in the nervous system, you get pain and possibly paralysis. And if bubbles form in the bloodstream, as they're more than likely to do, you get death as a result. The frothy blood gathers in the lungs and can't be forced through the small blood vessels, so the patient struggles for breath, goes black in the face, and dies of suffocation. The only way of saving him is to put him back under the original high pressure, when the bubbles of gas at once dissolve in the blood again and the symptoms cease."

" Ah! Now I see what the box was for," said Wendover. " It was air-tight, and air could be blown into it with that pump. Then, if the air was allowed to escape suddenly, the man in the box suffered all this horrible pain. But you could stop that at any moment by raising the air-pressure in the box again. That's what Felden did when he was putting the screw on Daphne, I suppose. He could torture Allardyce and then bring him back to ease again by pumping more air into the box. A devilish contrivance,

Clinton. But how did you manage to get Allardyce out intact ? "

" If you lower the pressure very gradually, the gas comes out of the blood by degrees, and doesn't form large bubbles. It comes out in minute doses, and gets breathed out via the lungs bit by bit. Take the case of a deep-sea diver. If he goes down to thirty fathoms, the air in his diving-dress is at six atmospheres pressure. Pull him straight up to the surface, and the dissolved gas bubbles out of his blood and he gets ' diver's cramp.' But pull him up slowly, ten feet at a time, with a pause of a few minutes at each stage, and you find that he has worked the excess of dissolved gas out of his blood by degrees without any formation of these dangerous bubbles. They discovered that when they began to work divers at deep levels under water ; and they found the same thing in the case of workmen doing tunnelling in caissons where high air pressure is used. Lower the pressure very gradually, and the man comes to no harm. Lower it all at once, and you may kill him."

" And the doping with hyoscine was to make the man helpless while he was being got into the box ? "

" Obviously. In the case of the rabbits, they could be shoved into the box, whether they liked it or not, so no hyoscine was needed in their case. That rabbit-trap was for catching them, probably up amongst the warrens at Cæsar's Camp. Of course Felden had to catch them himself. They were supposed to be wild rabbits, killed in the open by Ashmun's New Force. If Felden had got Pirbright to catch them, as Allardyce did, Pirbright might have chattered about it and given the show away."

" I see," said Wendover. " The technique was the same in both the Pirbright and Deverell cases. Dope the victim with hyoscine. Then put him in the box and pump in air until his blood was saturated at high pressure. Take him to Cæsar's Camp in the van. Then turn him out of the box with no precautions. And as Deverell took some time to die, Felden was able to drive along the road a bit and have his chat with your constable, so as to establish his alibi. That's it ? "

" That's it," agreed Sir Clinton. " And we have Miss Stanway's evidence to clinch the thing, since she saw the whole process at Felden's house. But with all his cleverness Felden overlooked one factor in his affairs."

" Made a mistake, did he ? " said Wendover, rather puzzled. " What was it ? I don't see it."

" He overlooked one pair of very sharp eyes which were on him continually—Ione Herongate's. You remember that, from the little I saw of them together, I hazarded the opinion that she'd stick at nothing to get hold of Felden. I was right there ; that's a plain fact. She was watching Felden all the time, on the look-out for anything which would give her a hold over him for her own purposes. She started with the advantage of knowing all about old Rodway's will, and she must have had some inkling that these deaths—Robert Deverell, Pirbright, and Tony Gainford's—had something queer about them. I don't suppose she fathomed the details, but I'm sure she guessed that there was something wrong. The deaths themselves didn't worry her ; she was devoured by her desire for Felden and thought of nothing else. She didn't care twopence whether he loved her or not, so long as she got him. Not a very exalted state of mind, of course, but common enough, I suppose. So she watched him, as a cat watches a mouse in the hope that the prey will blunder within springing-range if the cat has patience enough."

" You mean that when she heard he was taking Deverell up to Cæsar's Camp that night, she followed them in her car to spy on Felden, and she saw something that gave her the hold over him which she wanted ? "

" I think she saw enough for her purpose, anyhow," said Sir Clinton.

" Then all you have to do is to call her as a witness, and Felden's number will be up, surely."

" Things aren't always so simple as they seem, Squire. We can't *compel* her to give evidence, and I see no likelihood of her volunteering any."

" You can subpœna her, can't you, and put her in the box whether she likes it or not ? "

Sir Clinton shook his head.

" Not even that," he declared. " But that brings in another facet of the business : her sudden craze for taking rubbings of brasses in churches about the countryside. You'll remember it puzzled me when I heard about it ; it seemed so ' out of character.' But if one thinks hard enough, one often hits on the answer to a problem, and I got to the bottom of that one eventually. She wanted to marry Felden, and she evidently had enough information to force him to agree. Where do most people get married ? In a church, between the regulation hours. But that implies publicity, in the normal way, and Felden, though he might agree to the

214

marriage, stuck out against the publicity for reasons of his own which I'll come to later on. Secrecy was his *sine qua non* in the matter, and Ione Herongate had to fall in with that, whether she liked it or not. Now they had a clerical gentleman to hand, who could be trusted to keep his tongue quiet."

" Ashmun ? "

" Ashmun, of course. As for certificates and registration, Ione Herongate had seen what sort of man the local registrar was, a very stupid and woolly-minded individual who would pay no attention to them and forget about them as soon as they left his office. The church was the only difficulty. Hence this craze for brasses. She could borrow the keys of a convenient church from the vicar, who wouldn't bother to accompany her and wait while she did her rubbings. Felden, Ashmun, and two friends of Felden from London could drop in, and the ceremony would be over in no time, all done absolutely legally and yet no one in the neighbourhood would have the faintest notion of it all. That's what actually happened. As soon as I got on the idea, I went and looked up the archives in the register office, and there were the proofs all in due order. Now, Squire, you see why we can't subpœna the girl. You may accept a wife's evidence if she offers it, but you can't *force* her to testify against her husband."

" So that was why you talked about brasses at the time you arrested her," interjected Wendover. " I couldn't see the point, then."

" *She* did," Sir Clinton pointed out, grimly. " But let's take the case of Derek Gainford now. That was quite up to the Felden standard. You remember these amyl nitrite capsules he used to ease his asthmatic attacks ? Little glass affairs containing the fluid. Felden's an expert glass-blower, like most research chemists. He could easily make a capsule identical with those which Gainford bought at the druggists, and he could wrap it up in a little cloth case taken from a genuine capsule, so that it was indistinguishable from the real Mackay. All he had to do was to take one of Derek's capsules from the box and replace it by his doctored affair. Sooner or later, Derek was bound to use the fatal capsule in one of his attacks. The exchange was easy. You saw yourself how Derek used to leave the box in his overcoat pocket, or in his bedroom."

" But what was in the substitute capsule ? " demanded Wendover. " It smelt all right. I got a touch of headache myself from the amyl nitrite, that night."

" Liquid prussic acid was what Felden put into his special capsule. A few drops of it are enough to kill anyone, let alone an asthmatic like Derek. You can make it from sulphuric acid and potassium ferrocyanide and condense it in a freezing-mixture, since it boils at 25 deg. C. like nickel carbonyl. So Felden needed ice for that experiment also, you see. He couldn't use it alone in the capsule, because it has a marked smell of bitter almonds. But he added amyl nitrite to his charge, and the smell of the nitrite covered the prussic acid odour completely. The real point is that the symptoms of prussic acid poisoning are practically identical with those of a fatal attack of asthma ; and as Derek Gainford had asthma of long standing, no one would ever think of looking further than that for a cause of death. If that had been the only murder in this business, I think Felden would have got away without exciting the least suspicion."

" Do you think you could fasten it on him ? " asked Wendover.

Sir Clinton looked more than a little doubtful.

" We're putting our money on Henry Deverell's case," he said. " But if we were beaten there, we could produce some evidence in the matter of Derek Gainford. We could exhume the body and probably prove the presence of prussic acid in the blood by micro-analysis. Then we know that he had potassium ferrocyanide among his laboratory chemicals, though that in itself wouldn't amount to much, since it's a common laboratory reagent. Then it's on the cards that the kind of glass he used in making his capsule isn't exactly the same as the glass of the rest of the capsules in the box. Glasses do vary slightly in composition. Probably his gas-mask might furnish evidence also."

" I couldn't make out why you laid so much stress on that mask," Wendover confessed. " What's the idea ? "

" Well, he had to prepare both prussic acid and carbon monoxide, you remember, and both are deadly poisons if you inhale them. What's more likely than that he wore his official gas-mask during these experiments. I looked up carbon monoxide in Mellor's book that night I was in Felden's library. Charcoal absorbs twenty times its own volume of the gas, so that though our gas-masks won't stop highly-concentrated carbon monoxide, they ought to offer some protection against traces of it in the air. As Felden's a skilled manipulator, only traces would escape during his preparation of the gas ; but even traces might give one a headache, and there's no use getting a headache if one can help it, is there ? Our respirators stop prussic acid, too, in low concentration, so the same holds good for that also. The two gases would be adsorbed on the charcoal of the mask ; and I'm told that they can be driven out again by gently warming the charcoal. If the gases which came off on warming contained carbon monoxide, it would clinch the nickel carbonyl question, whereas if any prussic acid appeared, it would take some explaining away. So the resources of civilisation are not quite exhausted yet, you see, Squire."

Wendover's mind turned to a fresh aspect of the case.

"One thing I don't understand," he confessed, "and that is why Felden contrived this marriage to Daphne. There seems no point in it."

"I shouldn't care to say that," said Sir Clinton. "There were two sides to that business. First and foremost, from Miss Stanway's evidence, we know something about Felden's state of mind. He's not a very nice type, and his pride was rasped when Miss Stanway broke off her engagement to him. On the surface, he didn't show his feelings, but probably that exacerbated them. His pride had suffered, and some men are apt to brood over wounds to their pride. Felden did, anyhow. He'd grown to hate the girl, bitterly, and if the chance came his way of taking down her pride, he was prepared to seize on it at almost any cost, just to square the account and recover his miserable self-esteem. Her engagement to Allardyce must have been the last straw. Even a decent man would hate to see himself supplanted by someone else. Felden wasn't a forgiving type, so probably it hit him harder than the normal. What a salve to his wounded pride if he could humiliate the girl in the most brutal way possible and also destroy his supplanter so as to prevent her ever getting the happiness she was looking forward to."

"What a beast !" ejaculated Wendover, angrily.

"Besides," Sir Clinton pursued, "he probably believed that he could shut her mouth in Court and prevent her being used as a witness against him. There are only a few charges in which a wife is a competent witness against her husband ; and if the marriage had been a genuine affair, I'm not too sure of the law. Even as it stood, there might have been difficulty in proving that it was a forced marriage ; for he had two witnesses to testify that Miss Stanway . . . she was a willing agent. But . . . board when I found

Herongate. If we fail in everything else, we can certainly have him gaoled for bigamy. But I hope for better things. She can testify freely against him, as things are, and by claiming to prove ' a system,' we can drag in the Allardyce affair, I think. That will put the finishing touch, since it shows the whole Jack-in-the-Box mechanism in operation."

" I can't understand Ione Herongate's rôle in that affair," said Wendover.

"Well, she knew Felden was a murderer, and yet she married him," retorted Sir Clinton. "After that, she could hardly stick at much, could she? And quite likely he did not inform her of all his plans with regard to Miss Stanway. All she'd know would be that Allardyce would be found next morning, dead, up at Cæsar's Camp in the usual way. Having used one murder to get her grip on Felden, she wasn't likely to make a fuss over a second one. She's not an attractive personality, but she certainly has tenacity when it comes to getting what she wants."

" What will happen to her ? " asked Wendover.

" Ask the jury when the time comes. I don't know," said the Chief Constable in a tone which suggested that he did not care, either. " The people I want to make sure of are Felden and Ashmun, and I think we shall manage that, all right."

He paused, then added in a lighter tone :

" Amongst the lot of us, I give first prize for prescience to one fellow."

" Who ? " demanded Wendover.

"The prophetical gentleman whom Tony Gainford described as ' the local Nostradamus.' There's no denying that he was right when he predicted trouble for the finder of that Viking's hoard. Even some people who merely touched it came in for trouble. Curious coincidence. Still, I'm not superstitious over it."

>>> If you've enjoyed this book and would like to discover more great vintage crime and thriller titles, as well as the most exciting crime and thriller authors writing today, visit: >>>

The Murder Room
Where Criminal Minds Meet

themurderroom.com